Falling Under

JASINDA WILDER

FALLING UNDER

ISBN: 978-1-941098-09-7

Cover art by Sarah Hansen of Okay Creations. Cove art © 2014 by Sarah Hansen.

Interior book design by Indie Author Services.

This book is for you, the reader. It's for all of you who have gone with me on this intense, painful, and ultimately rewarding journey. You took Nell and Colt and Jason and Becca into your hearts, and you loved them, as I love them, and you helped make them real.

This book is for all of you who have identified with these characters, with their struggles and with the issues they faced.

Thank you, and I love you.

One: Bluest Blue

Oz

September

I FUCKING HATE BEING THE NEW GUY. It sucks. You'd think I'd be used to it by now, but I'm not. Mom's always moving us—every year or so, a new city, a new school. I wish I knew what she was looking for, who she was running from. Hiding from. Herself, I think. It's like everywhere we go, something spooks her. I've attended a new school every year since seventh grade. St. Louis for seventh grade, Denver for eighth, Biloxi for ninth, Atlantic City for tenth, Rochester, New York, in eleventh grade. Atlanta for my senior year.

So, yeah, I know all about being the new guy. But thankfully, college, especially community college, means everybody is new. Few people know each other, so there aren't roving packs of kids who have all known each other since kindergarten. I can fade into the background here, which is nice. A good change. I approve.

I started taking classes at the community college in Atlanta, and managed to get in a full year and two semesters before Mom decided to uproot us again, bouncing around until we finally settled in Nashville. So I had no choice; I had to transfer. Which means retaking a few classes that didn't transfer, play catch-up. I'm already behind. I'm twenty-one. I should be almost done with my bachelor's, but I'm not even halfway through my associate's. It's bullshit. I told her no more moves until I at least finish my fucking associate's. Give me at *least* that long.

You'd think I'd be out on my own, that I would've just stayed in Atlanta and finished there, and let Mom go wherever the hell she wanted. I thought about it, I really did. I thought about it long and hard. But in the end, I had to go with her. We're all each other have. She struggles just to make ends meet, and that's with me helping out, contributing whatever income I can. She needs me. So…hello, Nashville.

I slump into the back row in my first class, calculus. It's absurdly remedial for me, but I have to take it as a prerequisite for more advanced classes. I wish this was something more advanced than what amounts to high school math. I taught myself this shit in ninth grade. Math is calming for me. It's freakish, I know, but sitting down to work through a bunch of equations quiets the chaos in my head, helps me deal with the constant fluctuation of my moods.

All the other people in this class are the type you'd expect—buttoned-up, backs straight, notebooks out, pencils scribbling. Everything but pocket protectors, most of 'em. Okay, maybe that's a bit of an exaggeration. Most of them are just like me, here to satisfy a prereq. Then there's *her*. Holy hell. She's in the front row, far right side of the room. Sitting facing slightly sideways, so I get a profile view of her strawberry blonde hair and the most electric pair of blue eyes I've ever seen. Jesus. My pulse is pounding, and she's not even looking at me. She seems as bored as I am, too. Slumped back in her chair, twirling a lock of her long-ass hair around a fingernail, chewing gum, elbow on the desk, idly doodling on her notebook, not really paying attention. As if she knows everything Dr. Stuffypants up there is saying. I can't take my eyes off her. I'm mesmerized.

I slide lower in my chair, embarrassed at my own crazy reaction to some girl I don't even know. Everybody knows girls like the bad boys, and I'm thoroughly bad. So I've never had issues getting a girl to hang with me. But I've never had my pulse race and thunder in my ears, never had my palms sweat. Never wanted to stand up, cross the room, and beg for her name, her number, for five fucking minutes alone with her.

I fish my earbuds from my pocket, stick one in my ear, turning away from the room so it's hidden from easy view. Hit "play" and crank up the volume. "Monolith" by Stone Sour fills my ear, and it tunes out the grumbling, droning voice of the teacher. I flip open a tattered Nashville Public Library copy of a book on string theory.

The class passes slowly, and I glance up at the board to keep pace with what they're covering. Nothing I can't do in my sleep, so far. The class ends, eventually, and the students shuffle out, chattering and laughing and glancing at me. The girl with the strawberry blonde hair pauses by my desk.

"It's not polite to stare." She tosses her thick mane of reddish-blonde hair over her shoulder. "What's your name?"

I shrug. "I'm not polite. Name's Oz."

She frowns. "Oz? That's what's on your birth certificate?"

"Does it make a difference?"

"No, but—"

She's interrupted by the professor. "Get moving, you two. I've got another class coming in."

Students are filing in, finding seats early, even though the next class doesn't start for another ten minutes. We both leave the room, and I slip away before she can pester me about my name anymore. She's just a chick, nothing to get worked up about. I make my way to my next class, a fairly generic world history course. Not bad, but boring. As I'm about to go in, I see the girl chatting with a couple of friends. I swerve and beeline over to her. Just to prove to myself that my over-the-top reaction earlier was just a fluke.

"I never got your name." I don't really notice her friends, even though they're both pretty.

Okay, so I *saw* them, but they're just…there. Good-looking enough. But not even in the same galaxy of hotness as this girl. They're eyeing me, but I ignore them completely. I'm fixated on this redhead with the hypnotic blue eyes.

"And I didn't get yours." She lifts an eyebrow.

I roll my eyes. "Name's Oz. I've gone by Oz since the third grade. Not even my mom calls me by the name on my birth certificate."

"Which is what?"

I shake my head in irritation and disbelief. "Why do you care?"

She shrugs. "I'm curious."

"So what's *your* name?"

She shakes her head. "I'll tell you mine when you tell me yours." The way her eyes light up, the brightness of her smile makes something in my chest thump a little too hard.

I walk into class, grinning at her over my shoulder. "Have it your way, then."

I have one more class, an early American literature class. Gag me. Give me Hemingway or Faulkner or any of those guys any day, but this stuffy Puritan crap? No thanks.

On the way out of school, I see her again. She's hugging a big, muscular guy wearing a Vanderbilt Commodores ball cap. He's got dark-tanned skin and close-cropped black hair, and the kind of build that fairly screams "football player." Shit. She's hugging him like she's known him forever, and I feel a stupid thread of jealousy ripple through me. I just met her, don't even know her first name. So what business do I have being jealous? He's obviously here to pick her up, judging by the fact that she's opening the passenger door of his shiny, black, jacked-up Silverado and tossing her backpack in like it's her own car.

I really should just forget I ever met her, take off, and go about my business. Except, jock boy has his monster truck parked by my bike. I act like I don't see them. Zip up my leather jacket, cinch the straps of my backpack, tug my Broncos hat off my head, stuff it into a saddlebag, and pop my helmet onto my head, click the strap beneath my chin. I know she's seen me now, feel her gaze on me as she leans against the truck, chatting with her friend/boyfriend/whoever the hell he is.

I swing my leg over, kick the stand up, twist the key so the engine rumbles to life. It's a 2003 Indian Spirit Roadmaster Cruiser. It's my baby. I bought it with cash my senior year of high school. From the time I was twelve, I mowed lawns, shoveled snow, delivered newspapers, washed dishes, did any kind of odd job I could find, to buy it. Took me almost six years to save up enough for it. It was the only thing I'd ever wanted: my own motorcycle. Mom hated the idea, but after she saw that I was serious about saving every penny, she couldn't say no. She even pitched in a few hundred bucks along the way. Then I'd seen one on the side of the road with a "for sale" sign on it. I passed it every day on the way to my job at the Mexican restaurant. Teasing me. The owner wanted $8,500 for it, and I only had $8,100. So Mom, being Mom, told me she'd help me out, as long as I agreed to always wear my helmet, no matter what the helmet law of the state we were living in. Easy enough.

The rumble of the engine is sexy as hell. The original owner—a real-deal biker in a biker gang—beefed it up, made it loud, made it fast. Put saddlebags on it, and even sold me his own personal helmet, one of those that look like the German helmets from World War One, with a spike on the top. Pretty badass, if I do say so myself. Plus, I found a leather jacket in a pawn shop in Louisville that had a bunch of patches and shit on it, so I looked the part even more. I've put some of my own patches on the jacket, metal band logos and such.

I let the engine rumble, then start rolling the heavy bike backward. I walk it around so my front end is facing the exit to the parking lot, and then gun the engine, creating an ear-splitting roar. I feel her looking at me, feel her wondering if I'm going to say something. I think again about taking off, ending this little flirtation I've got with her.

But then, fuck it, I cast a cocky grin at Blue Eyes. "You coming?" I reach behind me and snag the spare helmet I keep hanging off the back of the seat.

She stares at me, and I can see she wants to. She's curious. I keep my grin easy and arrogant. Inside, my heart is thudding.

"Ky, no," the guy says. She ignores him and moves toward me. He grabs at her arm. "Kylie, I said *no*."

I put the kickstand down. "I wasn't asking you. I was asking her. Let go of her."

He steps toward me, and he seems to swell up as I say, "Or what?"

I don't really want to tangle with this guy. He's big, and he looks quick. It'll hurt, and probably screw my chances with this girl all to hell, but hey, why not. Except…I don't want to fight. I want to go on a ride with her.

I ignore the jock's challenge and glance at her. "Kylie, huh? Suits you." I wink at her. "So. You coming or what, sweetness?"

She glances back at the guy, and then at me. She nods. "Sure. But don't call me sweetness."

"Fair enough."

"Goddammit, Kylie. You don't know this guy. Stay here." Jock reaches for her, but she steps out of his reach, swings her leg over the bike, behind me.

She glares at him. "I'll be fine, Ben." She settles the helmet on her head, unconcerned about her hair getting messy. Which is hot.

"So I drove all the way here to pick you up, and you're just gonna ditch me like this?" He sounds pissed and, honestly, he's got a reason. Not that I care.

I don't wait. As soon as she's on behind me, I kick the bike into gear and gun the engine. We jump forward, and a delighted squeak from behind me has me grinning. Her hands go around my stomach, holding on more tightly. Oh, shit. I can feel her against me. Every inch. Her tits are squished against my chest, and her arms are tight around my waist, and her thighs are wedged by my hips. We rumble out of the parking lot, and then as soon as I hit the asphalt of the main road, I twist the throttle and we rocket away. She's silent after that, but I can feel her excitement. I share it. Riding never gets old, not ever. The wind in my face, the freedom, the road so close under me, the speed. It's addictive. And now, this chick is holding onto me, and it feels even more so. I mean, sure, I've had other girls on the bike with me, but it never felt like this. I've had exactly three conversations with her, each lasting less than a minute, but there's something about her.

I head to a spot I found yesterday, a little cafe not far from the Vanderbilt campus. It's got good coffee, and killer chili cheese fries. I pull into the parking lot, cut off the engine, and hold my hand out. Kylie takes it, and I feel a tingle. Her smile, as I help her swing off the bike, is surprised, as if a guy like me couldn't possibly know anything about manners. Except I've been raised by a single mom, and she expects me to do that shit. For her, and for everyone. I've never had a dad, so she's tried to teach me things she thinks a man should know. Like how to be a gentleman. Kylie hangs the helmet on the handle, and I do the same with my own helmet and my jacket, not bothering to hide my stare as she arches backward to run her fingers through her hair, and then ties it back with a ponytail holder from her wrist. God, she's gorgeous. Willowy, but with lush curves. And Jesus, that hair. On the red side of strawberry blonde, with the milk-white skin to match, a spattering of freckles across her nose. Her eyes meet mine, catching me staring, and I don't look away, don't let an ounce of apology enter my eyes. I was perusing all of her, not just her assets. I'm not going to apologize for looking at a beautiful woman, especially when I wasn't just staring at her tits or something. Which I do get a good look at, because holy hell, are they perfect. She's got this preppy country girl thing going on, girly cowboy boots, skintight faded jeans, a pale pink plaid shirt with slim, rolled-up sleeves, a blingy belt with a wide buckle. The shirt is unbuttoned to show just a hint of cleavage, but it's enough to see that she's got a rack to die for. Big, round, firm, high. Not huge, but probably a soft and tasty handful. I jerk my eyes back to her face, to her breathtaking blue eyes.

She looks me over. I'm tall, over six-four, almost six-five. I'm not an athlete or a workout buff, but I stay in shape, so I'm more lean than anything. Shoulder-length auburn hair pulled back low on my neck. Tanned, swarthy skin, a long hooked nose, brownish-gray eyes. I've got tattoos, an image of a road on my left forearm, two lanes, the double-stripe down the middle and lines on either side. It's done in shades of gray, going from the base of my wrist up to my elbow. I've got some tribal designs on my left bicep, and on my right forearm I have a few lines of lyrics from Metallica's "Wherever I May Roam." The words are inscribed horizontally, done to look like someone had hand-written them there just a moment before, the ink glossy black and almost wet-looking. Pair that with old, faded, ripped blue jeans and scuffed combat boots, and I look every inch a biker.

After our mutual stare-fest is over, I hold the door open, and I'm once again treated to a surprised smile and a stunned "thank you."

We sit down in a corner booth. She orders Coke, and I get coffee and an order of chili cheese fries. "You want something to eat?" I ask her. I grabbed my hat from my saddlebag as I swung off the bike, and I cram it backward onto my head, to cover up my helmet hair.

"What you're getting sounds fine," she says.

"Then we'll share," I say. She just nods, and I decide to get a feel for the lay of the land. "So, that guy, Ben. Your boyfriend?"

"No!" she protests, a little too quickly, I think. She seems to realize it, too, and calms down immediately. "No. We grew up together. Our parents are best friends. We've lived across the street from each other since kindergarten."

"He seemed awful protective of you. A little too much for just friends."

She flicks at her straw with her tongue. It's hot, and distracting. I watch her tongue rather than her face, and I wonder what she can do with that tongue of hers. I almost miss what she's saying. "...always been protective. He looks out for me, that's all."

I stir my coffee, more to get myself to stop watching her tongue and her lips than because it needs stirring. "Looks *at* you, maybe. He wanted to kill me when you got on my bike. I did steal you from him."

Her eyes darken, and she frowns. "Yeah, that's probably not gonna go over well, later."

"I hope I didn't cause you *too* much trouble," I say.

She shrugs. "Nah. He'll just be pissy. Why are we talking about Ben, anyway? Don't you have a pick-up line to use on me?"

I grin. "I already used it, sweetness."

She narrows her eyes at me. "Don't call me that."

"Why not?"

"I don't like it," she says.

"Yes, you do," I say.

She opens her mouth to protest again, but the waitress brings over my fries, which become *our* fries as Kylie reaches out and snags one. She tips her head back and takes a bite, chili and cheese dripping onto her chin. She even eats sexily. It's unreal. The chili on her chin has to be scorching, and she's trying to unwrap the napkin, but can't get the sticky strip of paper undone. I don't even think about it. I just reach out and brush the chili off with my thumb. Dumbass. But...damn, her skin is soft. And then, deliberately, I lick my thumb. Also stupid, and reckless, and bad for everyone involved.

She's fixated on me, as if she can't believe what just happened. I can't, either. I don't know what came over me. I'm not the charm-and-smarm kinda guy. A girl hangs with me, she knows what's up. Mom and I, we're nomads. We don't stay anywhere long. So any relationship I have is, by nature, short-lived. Not gonna waste time on silly mush bullshit, like making a chick think I love her.

So why did I do that, touch her with my thumb that way? Sure, she's hot, but it's not like I'm staying in Nashville for long. A few semesters, finish out the degree. That's it. So…what the hell, Oz?

I got nothin'.

"Where are you from, Oz?" she asks, by way of breaking the awkwardness.

I hate that question. "All over the place."

"Your dad in the military or something?" She says it so innocently, no way of knowing how bitter I am about the topic of fathers.

I shrug, trying to keep the ever-present fury from my voice; it ain't her fault. "No. Just Mom and me. And we just move a lot. Various reasons." *I don't know why,* is the real answer, but I'm not about to say that to this chick.

"You never knew your dad?" She levels a look at me, wiping at her cheek with her napkin. Her eyes are assessing, reading me, piercing me.

I shake my head. It's all she'll get out of me. "You got both your folks?"

She nods. "Yep."

"What do they do?" I'm not just asking to get her off the topic of dads; I'm genuinely interested. Another bad sign.

Her eyes light up, and I envy her that joy. "They're musicians. They're Nell and Colt. They were signed to Columbia for a while, but they're indie now. They have their own record label, and they actually just signed their first new artist."

I'm a little impressed, actually. I know Nell and Colt. I'm a metalhead and will be till the day I die, but I've got a secret soft spot for singer/songwriter music. Thanks to my Mom, mainly. So we have music we can listen to together. She's into hip-hop and pop and country, a bunch of stupid bullshit that I can't stand. I had to find middle ground, so we could listen to music in the car on cross-country moves. Nell and Colt are pretty big in the singer/songwriter world, actually. I call it coffeehouse music, the kinda stuff you hear in little one-off hipster joints where they do art with the latte foam.

"I've heard of 'em," I say. "I like 'em."

Kylie blinks in surprise. "You—you have?" Her gaze flicks to my shirt, which features a skull with a rose growing from it, and a raven perched on the skull.

I wink at her. "I'm full of surprises, sweetness."

She sighs. "Stop winking at me. And stop calling me 'sweetness.'"

"You know that's just gonna make me do it more, right?" I wink at her again, exaggerated. "Sweetness."

She shakes her head, laughing. "Who even winks, anyway? I mean, really? Winking? Isn't that for creepy uncles?"

I laugh. "I'm not a creepy uncle. But maybe you're right."

"I know I'm right. That's why I said it. Duh." She stuffs another cheese fry in her mouth, and again chili smears on the corner of her mouth.

I can't help it. My hand reaches out by itself. My thumb touches her cheek, but her fingers encircle my wrist. Our eyes lock, my gray-brown eyes on her bluest blue, electric, fiery blue.

"Don't," she whispers.

"Why?" I match her volume; I don't know why.

"I don't like it."

"You lie, sweetness. And why are we whispering?" I say it all *sotto voce,* and I know I sound stupid, using lines like that on her, but they just slip out.

I shouldn't be doing this, shouldn't be acting like this chick could ever mean anything to me, or I to her. She's got rich, famous parents. I mean, they're not *famous,* but if you listen to the right kind of music, you've heard of 'em. They've even gotten some country station cross-over airplay. The point is, I'm a nobody drifter, with a nobody drifter mom. And Kylie? She's got roots here in Nashville. Friends, family, the works.

She leans away from me, wipes at her face with a napkin. Slides out of the booth. "I've gotta pee."

I pay the bill while she's gone, and polish off the plate of fries. The girl did a number on them, to my surprise. The chicks I've known wouldn't have gone to town on something like cheese fries, so watching her eat happily and with obvious pleasure was interesting. And hot. Yes, I'm noticing a pattern here. Anything she does is hot. The way she slipped out of the booth, for example. It was graceful, a sleek, elegant motion. No jerking or hopping or awkward movements, just a smooth slide, and then she was off across the cafe with a sway to her ass.

When she came back, I stood up to meet her. "Ready?" I ask.

She glances at the table, at the small pile of ones I left as a tip. "You paid already?"

"Of course."

A third time I get the surprised smile. "You're not what I expected, Oz."

"What'd you expect?"

She shrugs, blushing. "I don't know. You've got the tattoos and long hair and the motorcycle. I thought you'd be…I don't know. You're nice. I misjudged you, so…sorry."

We're outside and standing beside my Indian. I touch her chin with the knuckle of my index finger. "I may have manners, sweetness, but I'm not nice."

"No?"

I shake my head. "Nope. You'll see." I swing on, shift forward to give her room.

Oh, man. The way my zipper tightens as she slides on behind me and wraps her arms around me and crushes her chest to my back, holding on a little too tightly…bad. Not good. Warning signs. She's a good girl with a future. I'm a bad boy with none. Too bad I'm an idiot who never pays attention to warning signs.

She directs me with pointed gestures, and soon we enter a gated community outside Nashville. Huge, *huge* houses. Brick, lots of glass. Wide driveways and three-car garages. Lincolns, Beemers, Mercedes, a few pickups, Rovers, and Hummers. Manicured lawns, everything in place. I'm intimidated. Two-room apartments are all I've ever known. How do you live in places like this? What would that be like? Do you ever get used to such wealth? What's it like to live in one city your entire life? I can't fathom it.

She points at a house on the left side of the street. It's not the biggest on the block, but it's nice. Beautiful. A wide porch in front, a huge deck in back. An open garage door reveals a huge pickup truck with oversize tires, a small, sleek, black BMW, and a classic Triumph motorcycle. The motorcycle was being worked on, judging by the array of tools around it and the grease rag on the seat.

It was being worked on by the holy-shit-he's-huge man standing in the driveway, thick, tattooed arms folded over a hard, muscular chest. I'd heard him sing, even seen YouTube videos of him and Nell performing together, but the man in person is scary as fuck. I don't scare easily, but this guy could do it, if anyone could. I swallow my nerves, call on my reserves of cool. I pull into her driveway, let the bike roll to a stop beside Kylie's dad, kill the engine. I put the stand down and swing off. He's glaring at me. At my leather jacket, the spiked helmet, my long hair. Staring me down. I'd be lying if I said I'm not a little nervous. Not scared, just…nervous. Yeah.

Kylie hops off, hangs the helmet on the back of the bike, and slams into her father for a hug. He does it one-arm, the other hand stuffed into his pocket. "Daddy!" She leans up and kisses his cheek. "You're back!"

He nods. "Yeah, got in this afternoon." He doesn't take his eyes off me while he speaks. "Who's this?"

I step toward him. "Oz Hyde, sir."

"Colt." His grip is crushing, but not with intent, simply because his hands are just that strong. "Oz, huh? What kind of name is Oz?"

"Mine." I meet his gaze levelly. I see where Kylie got her sapphire eyes.

There's something in his expression. Suspicion? Awareness? I'm not sure. He glances at his daughter. "Ben said you'd gone off with some guy."

"'Ben said'?" She says it with a bit of anger. "God, really? Ben is my friend, Daddy, not my boyfriend, not my parent. I don't have to stay with him just because he *says*."

He has nothing to say to this. He looks back at me. "New in town, Oz?"

I nod. "Yes, sir." I can't help but be respectful to Colt. He's dangerous. I can sense it in him. The fighter in me, the survivor in me, recognizes the hardness in him. He's seen some shit, and he may live a cush life now, but he hasn't always. Fists remember.

"Where'd you move from?"

"Atlanta."

He glances at my bike, nodding appreciatively. "Nice bike."

I grin, and nod at his Triumph. "Thanks. I like yours. What year is it?"

"Forty-eight."

"Damn. Sure is sweet."

"Yeah." He blinks at me, assessing, thinking. "Look. My daughter is old enough to choose her own…friends. But listen to me, boy. You take my daughter on a ride, you ride *careful*. Got it? You hurt her, you deal with me."

Kylie blushed, embarrassed, and moved between me and Colt. "Jeez, Dad. Are you gonna get out your shotgun next?"

He doesn't even twitch. "Who needs a shotgun?"

Not him, that's for damn sure.

I meet his gaze steadily. "I got you, sir. She'll be safe."

I see him glance over my shoulder, and I turn to see Kylie's friend Ben approaching with another man who has to be his dad. I recognize his dad, too, but I can't place him. He's a short, muscular man, and he looks like he's in sick shape, especially considering he has a teenaged son. I didn't leave things with Ben on a great note, and I have no desire to rehash the territorial aggression with him, not in front of his dad, and Kylie, and Colt. Talk about outnumbered. Shit. Time for my getaway.

But before I can mount up, they're behind me. Ben's eying me with open hostility, and his dad sees this, glancing from him to me to Kylie. He reaches out and shakes Colt's hand, pulling him in for a man-hug. "Colt! Good to see you. Been back long?"

"Jay. Good to see you, too. No, a few hours."

Suddenly I know who this is: Jason Dorsey, wide receiver for the Tennessee Titans. He played for the Saints for several years at the start of his career, and he was with them for all three of their back-to-back Super Bowl wins. He was a huge part of the reason they were so good, honestly. The QB was nothing astounding, but he could hit Dorsey from anywhere in the field, and once Dorsey had the ball it was a guaranteed TD. He was acquired by the Titans twelve years ago as a free agent, and he's been here ever since, racking up numbers that'll likely get him into the Hall of Fame.

And Ben's his son.

I swallow my nerves. "Mr. Dorsey." I shake his hand. I force myself to be casual, neutral, and pleasant to his son. "Ben."

"Call me Jason." He eyes his son again but says nothing. At least not in front of me.

Ben shakes my hand, but the hostility in his eyes could drill holes into my skull. "Oz." He fairly growls it through it gritted teeth.

I've got to get out of here. Colt is just standing there, a threat merely by his presence. Jason Dorsey is trying to figure out the source of the tension between me and Ben, and Kylie clearly just wants to go inside. I give her a grin. "I'll see you later, Calloway." I give an awkward wave, a nod. "Colt, Jason. Nice to meet you." I don't bother with saying goodbye to Ben.

He and I are going to tangle at some point, and it's going to be a rough one.

Kylie waves at me as I swing onto my bike, letting it roll down the driveway. I wave back and then gun the engine, twist the throttle so my Indian kicks forward. As soon as I'm out of the sub and on the freeway heading home, I open the throttle and let her purr. All the way home I'm thinking of a tall girl with strawberry blonde hair and big round tits and a smile I could kill for.

Fuck. Maybe I'll be the one to suggest we move this time.

Two: Wishes at Night

Colt

KYLIE IS SITTING AT THE ISLAND, sending yet another text to who the hell knows who. I lean against the fridge, slicing cheese off a block and eating it off the knife. She's been quiet this evening, and I think I know why.

"You like him?" I ask, wrapping up the cheese.

She sets the phone down, all too carefully. "Who, Daddy?"

"New guy. Oz. With the bike."

She blushes and looks away. "He's…surprising."

Not a typical answer, and it has me intrigued. "Surprising? What's that mean?"

She shrugs. "Just…not what I was expecting. I kind of judged him by the way he looks, honestly. He has the bike, and the jacket with the patches, and the tattoos, and I guess I thought he'd be—I don't know. Not what he is."

"Which is what?" I don't know exactly why I'm pushing this with her. Except I see something in the kid, something I recognize. And it scares me that she's interested in him.

"Smart. Polite. Easy to talk to." She scratches a smudge on the screen of her phone with a fingernail. "He held the door for me at the café, and he paid the bill without even telling me."

"Wait, the café?"

She bites her lip and shrugs. "We had some fries, that's all. That's not the *point,* Daddy."

"What happened to telling us if you're going somewhere?"

"Sorry. It was a last-minute thing." She glances at me. "And besides, I'm in college now, Daddy. I shouldn't have to check in anymore."

I lift an eyebrow. "You're not in college yet, Kylie. You're taking college classes while still in high school. There's a difference."

"Ugh. You're impossible. You're acting like I'm still a kid. I'm almost eighteen. Trust me a little."

I sigh. "Fine. But at least text Mom or me so we know where you are. That's not checking in—that's just being respectful."

"I will next time. I promise. You're getting off topic, *Dad*."

I let it go. She's a good kid, with a good head on her shoulders. "So he's smart and he's got manners. What's Ben's issue with him? If looks could kill, our boy Ozzy would be long dead."

She shrugs yet again. She needs to learn a new gesture. "I don't know. He didn't want me to go with Oz, I guess."

I can't help but wonder if she knows Ben is head-over-heels for her, and has been since fourth grade. Guess not. Or if she does, she's in denial. "I guess. Just…he's your oldest friend, Ky. Don't make a habit of ditching him for something new and shiny." Not my place to tell her Ben's in love with her. She'll figure it out, or she won't, and I wouldn't be doing her any favors by interfering. As long as no one hurts her, her love life is her business.

Nell may not agree, but what the hell do I know about teenage girls and their social lives? Jack shit, that's what.

Speaking of Nell, here she is, finally emerging from our basement studio. We've been together for over eighteen years, and I swear to God she's even more stunning than the day we met in New York. She beelines for me, tucks up against me. "Baby," she breathes, tilting her face up to mine.

"Hey." I run my thumb over her lips before I kiss them. "Get the track laid down?"

She rolls her eyes. "Yeah, *finally*. It only took about fifteen takes for me to get that one note right. Kept hitting it off-key."

"You? Off-key?" I laugh. "Never."

She shoves at my chest. "Jerk. You know I have trouble with notes that high."

"Then why'd you write the song with that note?"

"It was the best fit." Nell leaves my side to stand behind Kylie and wrap her arms around her. "How's my baby?" she asks with a kiss to the top of Kylie's head.

Kylie huffs and wiggles away from Nell. "God, Mom! You're so *clingy!*" She laughs as she says it, though. "I'm fine. Same old bullshit."

"Language, Kylie Olivia Calloway."

"Sorry, Mom. Usual bullcrap."

"Yeah, usual bullshit, except for our daughter showing up on the back of some guy's motorcycle," I put in, just to watch the drama unfold.

Kylie gives me a horrified look. "Daddy! You traitor!"

I just laugh.

Nell seems torn as to who to lay into first. "Colton. I just got on our daughter's case for her language. You have to set the example." She turns to

Kylie. "And *you,* young lady. Some guy? Motorcycle?" Nell ignores me. "Spill it, Ky."

Kylie glares at me, mouths *I'm gonna kill you.* I just laugh. "It's no big deal. His name is Oz. I don't know much about him, except that he has a motorcycle, he's cute, and he's nice."

I snort. "He may have been nice to you, but I doubt he's nice."

Kylie frowns at me. "He said something similar."

"Smart, well-mannered, and able to hold a conversation do not equal nice," I say. "Take me, for example. I'm a lot of things. Nice is not one of them."

Kylie's frown deepens. "Yes, you are."

I laugh. "I'm your dad, Ky. I'm contractually obligated as your father to be nice to *you.*"

Kylie looks to her mom. "Is he nice?"

Nell snorts. "Nope. To me, usually. To you, always. To everyone else? Depends on how much he likes you."

"You weren't very nice to Oz when he dropped me off," Kylie points out.

I crack my knuckles. "My daughter—my only child—shows up on the back of a motorcycle with some tattooed, long-haired punk. It's sorta my job to scare a little respect into him."

"How old is this Oz?" Nell's voice is calm, but Kylie and I both know she's anything but.

Kylie lifts an eyebrow at her mother. "Mom. Really?"

I watch her gather herself, closing her eyes and taking a deep breath. When she opens her eyes, she's visibly calmer. "How old is he, Kylie?"

Kylie just shrugs. "I dunno. A little older than me."

"You don't know, you mean." Nell sighs. "Just use your judgment, baby girl. Don't do anything stupid. Don't get involved with the wrong crowd, okay?"

Kylie is clearly done with the conversation. She rolls her eyes and walks away. "I got it, Mom." I hear her mumble under her breath, "Everyone seriously needs to chill the fuck out."

I chuckle, knowing her mom would've grounded her for that. I let it go. Once she's gone, I voice a thought that's been nagging at me. "Something about that guy…he looks…familiar. I dunno. I can't place it, though."

Nell doesn't look at me from where she's pulling food out of the fridge to make dinner. "I didn't meet him, so I couldn't say." As she sets a thawed pound of ground beef on the counter she, glances at me, a question in her eyes. "You really thought he seemed okay? You have a hard time denying that girl anything. I don't want to make any hasty judgments, but bad boy stereotypes exist for a reason."

I lift an eyebrow. "Oh, really?"

She waves a messy hand at me. "You're an exception, obviously. And maybe this—Oz, is it?—maybe he is, too. But I don't want to see her get hurt. And what about Ben?"

I lift both shoulders. "I dunno, babe. She'll have to figure him out for herself. The hard way, maybe. You can't learn about love without getting hurt. As for Ben, I'm wondering the same thing. I think maybe she's not seeing the forest for the trees, you know?"

Nell nods. "Yeah, I guess you're right." She finishes mixing the taco seasoning into the beef and tosses it into a frying pan. I wipe the counter off while she browns the meat. "I just wish I could protect her. I don't want her to go through the kind of things you and I did."

"Nothing much we can do about that, I'm afraid."

She sighs. "I know. I know. I just hate it, is all."

"Me, too."

Later that night, in bed basking in the afterglow of a slow and thorough lovemaking, Nell seems lost in thought. Deep, private thoughts. The kind I have to drag out of her.

I turn toward her, pulling my arm from beneath her head, propping my cheek on my palm. "What's bugging you, Nelly-girl?"

She doesn't answer right away. "Sometimes I just…I wish—god, it's stupid."

"Wish what?"

"That we'd had another baby."

I wince, and fall back onto the pillow. "God, Nell. I know. We tried for ten years."

She shrugs, and I see a glint in her eye. "Why, Colt? There were no problems with Kylie's birth. The doctors couldn't find anything. No miscarriages. Except that one, obviously. But…ten years, and just… nothing. Why?"

I want to get up and leave the room, run from this conversation that has come up at random over the years during our entire marriage. "I wish I had an answer for you, baby. It just wasn't meant to be, I guess. That's a shitty answer. A non-answer. But I just don't know. I would've given you another one if I could've."

"We could've adopted."

I groan. "Goddamn it, Nell. We've been through this."

"I know, Colt. I know. " She wipes at her face. "I just…I wish—"

"I wish, too, Nelly. I wanted a son, or another daughter, as much as you did. You know the reasons why we didn't adopt. We didn't have the money, or the time. We were touring with Kylie in a stroller, your mom following us around from city to city. Hiring nannies. And then once we'd settled here, it just wasn't ever…right. I don't know."

"And now it's never gonna happen."

I blow out a long breath, and I can't stay in the bed anymore. "I—we're not—I don't know, Nell. Kylie's graduating this year. Are we really going to talk about bringing another child into our lives *now?*" I step into a pair of shorts. "I love you, Nell. I just don't think I can keep having this conversation."

"Yeah." I hear the bitterness in her voice, and I don't know what to do about it.

I go down to the garage and tinker with the Triumph for an hour or two, because it's what I know. I've spent far too much time in the garage, tinkering, just to get away from a conversation that has no solution. Nell's fine, most of the time. But every once in a while, for no reason I've ever been able to decipher, she just gets this bug up her ass, and there's nothing I can do about it. We tried. I tried. We both got tested; nothing seemed wrong with either of us. But she never conceived again. We talked about adoption, in vitro, surrogacy. None of it was feasible, or possible, or it just seemed wrong for us. Not what we wanted. And every once in a while, without warning, she gets maudlin about it, tears up, asks why. And I don't have the answers. I've never had the answers.

I toss a wrench into the toolbox a little more forcefully than I need to, and go inside. I slam a beer standing on the back porch, watching the lights of Nashville, listening to the rush of cars in the distance, wishing I could find an answer for her, something to close the subject once and for all. And, as always, I've got nothing.

Three: Burn Scars and Shredding Guitars

Oz

I'm alone in the apartment. Mom's working. She's always working. I've got a joint in one hand, my lighter in the other. I'm in my room, the window open to suck out the smoke. I turn up the volume on my iPod dock/alarm clock until "We Stitch These Wounds" by Black Veil Brides drowns out my thoughts, buries my mind beneath guitars and drums and someone else's angst, someone else's anger, someone who gets it.

I let my head thump back against the wall above my bed and look around. There's no bed frame, no headboard. Just the queen mattress and a box spring on the floor. I don't bother with sheets, either. Just a thin blanket over the mattress, and another to cover up if I'm cold. No dresser, either, just a big silver laundry basket with my clean clothes in it, folded, and two black contractor-size garbage bags full of dirty clothes. A bookshelf, filled with novels, mainly sci-fi and fantasy, and several dozen volumes of math texts. Some are textbooks bought for cheap on Amazon, high school and college algebra and physics and calculus. Others are more esoteric, books on quantum physics and string theory and the history of numbers, kabbalah, Sudoku, logic, statistics, books on the relationship between math and chess, and between math and music. The only other thing I own is a battered third-hand Fender Stratocaster, a twenty-year-old amp, and an off-brand pair of over-the-ear headphones.

They are the belongings of a nomad. They'll all fit in the bed of Mom's rusted-out Dodge Ram, and the tiny trailer that she bought in Biloxi. Her room looks about the same, although she has a frame for her bed, and a little nightstand she got at a Salvation Army in Colorado Springs.

I flick the Bic, watch the orange-yellow flame touch the twist of white rice paper. Inhale. Suck deep, and hold it in. It doesn't hit right away. This is kinda shitty weed, but I haven't had a chance to sniff out a good hook-up yet. It'll do, though. It ain't the danks, but it's decent. After another long inhalation, I feel it. Light-headed, slow, floating. Cares are gone.

I watch my hand lift the lighter up. I stare at it. It's my favorite lighter. Red, slim, and translucent, the fluid jiggling low at the bottom. It lights easily, has a good, high flame. It's got an adjuster, so I can turn the flame up if I want. I do that now, slide the little black piece of plastic to the side, all the way. I roll my thumb across the knob, trying to remember why I shouldn't do this. I do it anyway. I light it, the flame almost an inch tall now. Holding my palm facing down, I bring the lighter up, up. I feel the heat. It's a gentle warmth at first. Then, as I move the flame closer to my flesh, it turns to burning. Pain.

Yes.

I suck in another hit, feeling the high whirl through me, tossing me up and away, in the cloud-world of hazy uncaring. The pain grounds me. Brings me down, anchors me so I don't float away. It's just my palm at first, heat baking my skin. I trace the flame along the lines of my palm. Not enough. I run it along my finger, up the pad of my index finger. Now the pain becomes real. It's a true burn. Harsh and furious, deep and aching. The burn sears me, and I relish it. My fingertip reddens. When the heat reaches a threshold I cannot ignore, I let the flame snuff out. I hold my finger up and examine it. It'll blister.

The song fades, and "Home Sweet Hole" by Bring Me the Horizon comes on. I nod in approval.

I like this song. They're a little screamo for my taste overall, but this is a good tune. Another hit, and I blow the smoke out the window, watch it skirl through the screen and get snatched away by the puff of breeze. I'm in the ether now. The joint is almost gone, just a roach. I pinch the cherry between finger and thumb, not even registering the slight twinge of the heat. Opening the lid of the tin Band-Aid box, I toss the roach and the lighter in, on top of the baggie of pot. The box goes into my backpack, way at the bottom of the front pocket, beneath pens and guitar picks and crushed granola bars.

I lie down flat on the bed, close my eyes, and listen to the music, feeling the aching burn of my palm and finger. "Life of Uncertainty" by It Dies Today comes on, and I soak it up, sink into it. Drifting, drifting.

It's a fleeting respite.

When unwelcome clarity starts to penetrate the fog, I slide off the bed, grab my guitar and my amp. Adjust the tuning slightly, flick the volume a little higher, and do some scales to limber up my fingers. My index finger hurts, making it tricky to move from string to string, but it's fine. I'm used to it. The burning is my secret, my release. I smoke pot because it loosens the grip of the anger and the bitterness of my fatherless, nomadic life. The burning is…I don't know what it is. Rage is exhausting, bitterness is exhausting. Burning is a way to feel something else, to alleviate it. To feel something in this life.

"Breaking Out, Breaking Up" by Bullet for My Valentine comes on. I taught myself this song, and I play along. When the song ends, I grab the tiny remote off the floor and click the iPod off. I play one of my own songs. It's an instrumental because I don't sing and sure as hell don't write no goddamn poetry. It's fast and hard, technical. My facility with numbers helps somehow. I can't make any kind of scientific claims about it, but I relate numbers to playing guitar. Each chord is an equation. Each string is a number. I guess I have quick fingers, so that's part of it, but the real playing happens in my head. I see the riffs like strings of equations, one plugged into another and another until there's a whole endless skein of numbers slinging from the six strings.

I lose myself in playing, pressing hard with my burned index finger to keep the pain fresh in my head.

I don't even notice Mom until she reaches down and turns off the amp. I claw the headphones off and glare up at her. "What the fuck, Mom?"

"You were smoking."

I shrug and don't look at her, reach for the "on" switch. "Yeah. So?"

She knows I smoke. She smokes with me sometimes. Only when she's really bad, when whatever it is that's driving her becomes too much. She gets melancholy as hell when she smokes, like she's remembering something.

She grabs my wrists, jerks them up. Shit. I resist, and when she tries to overpower me, I tear my hand from her grip. "Let me see your hands, Oz." She lets go, but kneels in front of me. Concern fills her gray eyes.

I can't look at her for long. I keep my hands flat on my knees. "It's fine. It's nothing. No big deal."

"*Show…me.*" She bites the words out.

I roll my eyes and turn my palms up. She immediately sees the fresh burn on my left hand, the redness on my palm and blister on my finger. "I'm fine, Ma. It's no big deal."

"You burned again. You said you weren't doing that anymore." She sinks back to sit cross-legged on the floor in front of me. She still has her apron on, the server book stuffed inside, fat with cash. She's never been real modest around me, and now is no exception. She works at a nightclub as a cocktail waitress. Which means short skirts, low-cut shirts. I look away at the wall, out the window.

I shrug. "It just happened. I'm fine."

"Burning yourself is not fine, Oz." She pulls the book out of her apron and counts out the cash, stacking it into ones, fives, tens, and twenties.

I watch her count slowly. "Mom, god. I'm fine. For real. It's just a little burn. I'm not...I'm not actively burning again. I swear."

She looks up at me, examines me, the cash now stacked in her hand. "Oz, why do you do it? I don't get it."

I shrug again. "Fuck, Mom. I don't know. You ask me this, and I can't tell you. I would if I knew. I just don't. It just...helps."

Mom tilts her head back and sighs. She pulls a pack of Pall Malls from her apron and hunts for a lighter. Comes up empty. I dig my tin out of my backpack, find the lighter, light her cigarette for her. I take one for myself from her pack, light it, return the lighter to the tin. We smoke in silence, Mom thinking, me trying not to.

Eventually, she breaks it. "Oz, do you hate me?"

I'm shocked. Stunned. "Hate you? What the actual fuck, Mom? Why would you ask me that? Of course not. I love you. You're my mom."

She glances around the bedroom for somewhere to ash. I grab the black plastic ashtray from the foot of my bed and hand it to her. She taps the end of her cigarette against it, staring at the orange cherry. "But I'm not a *good* mom."

"You've done the best you could." It's a meaningless response, and we both know it.

She frowns up at me. "Which means no."

I shake my head. "Jesus, Mom. How am I supposed to answer that fucking question? Huh? 'No, Mom, you've been a shitty parent.' Is that what I'm supposed to say? Or how about 'Well, gee, Mom, it's been great. You're a goddamn miracle worker, raising an ungrateful little shit like me.'"

Her head jerks up, and her eyes are hurt, angry. "Fucking hell, Oz. Really?"

I let out a breath. "Sorry. I just—what am I supposed to say? I don't know. You're the only mom I've ever had, the only *parent* I've ever had. We don't have a typical life. We're not a typical family. But it's what we are, and…that's it, I guess."

She nods, blowing out a thin stream of smoke. "I guess. I'm just sorry I haven't done better for you."

"What's this all about?"

She lifts a shoulder, stabbing the cigarette out. "You, burning again. You shouldn't…that shouldn't happen. But it does. And it's my fault."

I'm not sure what to say her. I wish I could say I didn't blame her, but I do. Shitty, but true. I resist, at great effort, the urge to stab my cigarette out on the back of my hand. Mom watches me, as if knowing what I'm thinking.

Tell me about my father. My lips tingle with the question, but I hold it back. I've asked it a million times, and she refuses to answer. Once she was a little drunk and I asked her about him, thinking the booze would loosen her tongue. Instead, it loosened her hand. She slapped me, hard. She immediately felt horrible and started crying and begging me to forgive her, but she never told me a damn thing. She never hit me before that, or after, but she never told me about my father. The burning is a daddy issue, I think. A shrink would have a field day with me, if I gave enough of a shit to go.

Mom leaves me then, and I let her go. I doubt it's not lost on her that I gave her no reassurances about being a good mom. She's not. It's the truth. She's my mom, though, and she's all I've got.

There's a rhythm to the next couple of months. I find a decent job at a Jiffy Lube, changing oil. It's nothing special, but it's a job. Puts cash in my pocket and helps Mom with the bills.

Kylie and I take to hanging out at the little coffee shop on campus. It's just an easy friendship. I mean, yeah, I'm attracted to her, but I'm not gonna push it.

I kind of feel guilty for hanging around Kylie. She's good, innocent. Clean. Pure. I'm pretty sure she's a virgin. I know she's younger than me by a few years, but I haven't asked how old exactly. She doesn't drink, doesn't smoke, rarely even curses. She's…just *good*. And if she keeps hanging out with me, she'll get tainted. She'll see the scars on my forearms, she'll see the smooth patches of burned skin on my hands. Evidence of my fucked-up mess of a life. I get around my hang-ups by telling myself she can make her own choices as to what she wants, who she wants around her. I make no bones about the fact that I'm a "wrong side of the tracks" kind of guy. It makes me feel a little guilty sometimes, if I think about it too hard, knowing that I like her and I think about kissing her and getting her in bed, and taking her cherry. She's good, and I'm not, and seriously, Ben is the right guy for her. Rich, athletic, from a good family. Nice. He's an actual fucking *nice* guy.

Then, near the middle of November, there's a flyer on the corkboard near the beverage pick-up counter, advertising an open mic night on February tenth. Kylie sees the flyer, stops dead, grabs my arm, shakes it. "An open mic night!" She spins me around to face her, shakes me again. "I've got to do it! It's my chance!"

I'm perplexed. "Chance at what?"

"Perform! I've been writing music, and practicing in my room, but I've been too chicken to do any open mic nights downtown by myself. This is my chance to try performing on a small scale."

I'm even more perplexed. "Kylie. You're the daughter of one of the most popular duos in the world."

She nods. "Well, yeah, duh. I know that. But that's *them*, Oz. I want to do this on my own, without them."

I shrug. "Okay, so do it."

She hesitates. "I'm decent at the piano, but if I'm going to really perform the songs I want to, I'd need a guitarist."

"This is Nashville, Kylie. If I threw a stick, right now, I'd hit at least a dozen guys who can play."

She rolls her eyes. "Well, yeah, duh to that, too. There're guys who can play the guitar, and then there's musicians. I want someone serious. If this goes well, I want to try to eventually get a spot in a bar on Broadway. But for that, I need someone *good*." We've started walking again, and she stops me, a hopeful expression on her face. "You don't play, do you? Tell me you play."

I snort. "Yeah, I play the guitar, but I couldn't play anything you want." I gesture at my Spineshank

T-shirt. "I play this, Kylie. Metal. You want a country boy. That ain't me, sweetness."

She doesn't seem fazed. "Are you any good?"

I shrug. "I guess. I don't know. I don't play for people. I play because it's fun. It's a release. I taught myself. I can't read music or any of that bullshit. I just shred. It's like math. I just do it."

"I want to hear you play."

I shake my head. "Hell, no. I don't play for people. And besides, do you even like metal?"

She makes an *I don't know face.* "I've never listened to it."

"It'll make your nose bleed, babe."

"I want to hear you play. I'll sing for you, you'll play for me. We'll trade music."

I want to tell her no, but I don't. She seems so hopeful. I'll play something hard and wicked, and she'll be disgusted, and that'll be that. The idea of me on a stool in a honky-tonk on Little Broadway, playing a Ron Pope cover is just…comical. Kylie would probably choke if she realized I knew that kind of music.

"Fine. But you won't like it."

"Let me be the judge of that." She smiles up at me, shakes my arm again. It's a habit of hers. I hate it, but I like it. "Okay, so we'll go to my house. My parents have a studio in the basement."

We're in the parking lot, heading toward my bike, having intended to go grab some coffee, but she stops, looking over at the far side of the lot, cursing under her breath. "It's Ben. I told him I didn't need a ride today. Wait here—I'll be right back." She jogs to his truck, leans in the open passenger window, then glances back at me, holds up a finger to indicate *one minute*, and gets in.

I shrug, and continue across the lot to my bike. Minutes pass, and she doesn't return. I keep waiting, watching the truck. Eventually Kylie gets out, starts walking toward me, clearly pissed off. Ben stops her, grabs her arm, and spins her around. I don't like that. I swing off my bike and jog across the lot toward them. I can't help overhearing their fight.

"You don't know him, Ben!" Kylie shouts.

Shit, they're arguing about me.

"I don't have to! I don't trust him!" Ben says this calmly, not shouting, but he punctuates every word with a stab of his finger.

"Tell me why, Ben. Give me a reason. One good reason."

"I just have a bad feeling about him, Ky. I'm trying to protect you. Something about that kid is just… off. Plus, he's older than you. I know he is."

"Yeah? Well, so are you! What difference does it make? I'm not a little girl, Ben! I can take care of myself," Kylie growls, and then whirls around and walks away. "I'm done having this conversation. I can be friends with whoever I want, Benji."

He grabs her arm and pulls her back to him. "He's not safe. And don't call me Benji."

"Let go! He's perfectly safe. You don't have to like him. You don't have to be friends with him. But that doesn't mean I can't."

He doesn't let go, and that's when I step in. "She said let her go, asshole." I drop my backpack on the ground, stepping toward them.

"Oz!" Kylie jerks her arm free and backs away from Ben. "Sorry I'm late, I was just—"

"Defending me. I heard." I want to pull her away from him, but I don't. "Are you okay?"

She frowns in confusion. "I'm fine."

"You don't have to stick up for me, Kylie. If Ben has an issue with me, he can bring it to me." I move past her. "Key words here being '*bring it.*'" I lift my chin, staring him down.

"Yeah? Bring it?" Ben takes a big, aggressive step toward me. "Fine. I don't like you, *Oz*. I don't trust you. I don't want you anywhere near her."

"It's not up to you, is it?" I say. Except, deep down, I kind of agree with him. I'm not safe. I'm not good for her. I'd never say that, obviously. To her, I say,

"Look, I'm going. I don't have the time or patience to argue with this gorilla. You coming?" I deliberately turn my back on Ben, a dare, a challenge, a show of contempt.

I'm spun around and pushed backward, hard. I stumble, catch my footing. I've never understood why guys shove as the challenge to a fight. It's stupid, and lame, and dangerous. As Ben is about to find out. As soon as I catch my footing, I'm lunging forward. I don't fight nice, or fair. My fist slams into his gut, and he doubles over, into me. I step back, cock my fist, and I'm about to let it fly, crush his nose like a goddamn egg. But *she's* there, watching. Crying. Darting in front of me, pushing me backward.

I let my hand fall, and I back away. "Sorry, Kylie. He's right, you know." I back away farther, snag my bag off the ground, and sling it onto my shoulders. "About me, I mean. I'm not safe. Case in point…" I gesture at Ben, who's doubled over, gasping, red-faced.

She stares at Ben, confusion in her eyes. "I'm going with him. Please, just understand. He's my friend, and so are you." Kylie leans in and hugs him. "Are you okay?"

He straightens, steps back away from her. "I'm fine." His eyes bore into me. "You wanna go with him? Fine, then. Go with him. See if I care."

Kylie and I get on my bike. Her arms are warm and strong around my middle, and I can't help but like the way her thighs feel against my hips.

I crane my head to look at her. "Put on the helmet, Kylie."

She twists around, grabs the spare, and stuffs it onto her head, clips it. "Oz, about Ben—"

"He's just looking out for you." I effectively cut off the conversation with the belly-churning roar of the engine.

We don't talk again until we're pulling up into her driveway, which is filled with cars.

"Shoot," Kylie says. "I think the studio is occupied." She gestures at the cars. "This looks like The Harris Mountain Boys. Mom and Dad's new project. Wait here." She's off the bike, tossing me the helmet and jogging into the house.

A few minutes later she comes out. "It's them, and they're recording until late tonight. I told Mom I'm with you. So we're good to go."

"Where are we going?" I ask as she adjusts behind me.

"Your house?"

I blink a few times. "My house? You don't want to go there."

"Why not?"

"Because it's a shithole?"

"I don't care. All we're doing is playing music."

I don't know how to respond to that. It's kind of a non-sequitur. Playing music has nothing to do with the fact that Mom and I live in a not-so-great section of town, and I doubt Kylie's ever spent time anywhere like that. But yet somehow I can't say no to her. I'm pointing the bike across town, weaving through traffic, running yellow lights, dodging onto the shoulder, relishing the way her hands tighten on my stomach and the way her thighs grip me.

The buildings get older, grimier, the streets get dirtier. The cars get rustier. We pass liquor stores and adult video stores, abandoned shop fronts, industrial buildings belching smoke, mechanic garages, apartment complexes. I can sense Kylie's unease with our surroundings, can feel her discomfort, her fear. We pull into my complex, pass the abandoned swing set missing three of the swings, the rusted yellow merry-go-round, the climbing structure tagged with graffiti. The cars are all twenty to thirty years old. A plastic bag whips across the lot in front of us as I pull to a stop outside the entrance to my building.

I don't cut the engine. "Let me take you home, Kylie. You don't belong here."

A trio of black guys with sagging khakis, oversized white T-shirts, and huge hoodies sidle slowly past us on the sidewalk that runs in front of the buildings. Their eyes meet mine, and I don't look away. They seem to recognize that I'm one of them, unlike the chick on the back of my bike, and they keep walking. One of them nods, a kind of acquiescence. When they're gone, Kylie sighs in audible relief.

"Do you know them?" she asks.

I shrug. "Nah."

"Why were they staring at us?"

I don't know how to explain it to her without scaring her. "We're white." I pause, and then continue. "It wasn't a challenge, just…curiosity, I guess. I don't know." I wasn't about to tell her that I didn't dare look away, or show any kind of fear.

She seems to sense that I wasn't telling her everything. "Is it safe here?"

I shrug again. "As long as you're with me." I twist to look at her. "Let's go, Kylie. Let me take you home. We can play another time. At your place."

I feel her stiffen, straighten. "No. It's fine. Let's go in. I want to see where you live."

I sigh. "Okay. But…I warned you. It's a shithole."

With my hand on her back, I push her ahead of me, guiding her through the entryway, which isn't secured. There's a keypad and a series of call buttons, but they haven't worked since before I born, probably.

The door sticks, and I have to jerk it hard to get it open. There's a small foyer, covered in threadbare industrial blue carpet. It smells of old beer and new piss. I nudge Kylie up the four stairs to the landing. A hallway extends to our left, the walls scratched and pockmarked, pale blue doors lining the walls, numbered with tarnished black numerals. A stairway leads up. Five floors, and the elevator is out of order. The steps have no backing, so you can see through them, and they're covered in the same thin blue carpeting that's on the floor.

"Third floor." I gesture up, and she precedes me.

I watch her round ass sway up the stairs, not bothering to pretend I wasn't staring when she glances back at me. I just grin, shrug. She blushes, keeps walking. Maybe even sashays with a bit of exaggeration. Nice.

We reach the third floor, and I curse under my breath when Dion, my pot hook-up, is locking his door. He lives across from us, conveniently enough. He sees me, lifts his chin in greeting.

"Whassup, Oz?" Dion is short, thin, with black skin and a slow, lazy demeanor that hides a dangerous edge. He's cool, but I wouldn't ever want to owe him money. We slap hands, grip palms, and bump opposite shoulders.

"Hey, D." I mentally will him to not say anything, but he doesn't get the message.

He points at his door with a thumb. "I just picked up an 'O.' It's some serious icky-sticky, man. You want an eighter? I'll give it to you for sixty."

I lick my lips. I do want it. I've got cash in my room, and I'm almost out. But I can't buy, not with Kylie here. "Nah, man. I'm good. Hold onto it for me for later."

Dion nods. "A'aight. But I can't promise it'll last long. It's good shit, man."

"Thanks." I unlock my door and usher Kylie in, who's clearly trying to figure out what just went down.

I close the door behind me and lean back against it, waiting for the questions.

"Oz?" She steps into the living room, looking around, then spins to face me. "Do I want to know what that was about?"

I lift an eyebrow. "If you don't know, then no, you don't want to know."

She's frowning. "Is he a…drug dealer?"

I laugh. The way she said that, like she was referring to some mystical creature, like unicorns or griffins. It's funny. "I guess. I mean, he just slings some herb. Eighths and dime-bags. Nothing serious."

She's clearly lost. "Herb? Eighths?"

I shake my head, still laughing. "I thought you didn't want to know?"

Kylie blinks. "No. I don't." She turns away from me and looks around the living room and kitchen.

There's a couch along one wall, picked up from Salvation Army when we first moved here. Mom never takes couches with us. It's easier to just buy one from the Salvation Army when we get to where we're going. There's our TV, a fifty-inch that she got on a rent-to-own program from Rent-A-Center. It's old, but it works. A low oak coffee table with a scratched glass top, a half-full ashtray, a copy of OK!, and an empty Coors can. The kitchen is tiny, of course, with scarred laminate counters, dirty white cabinets, an old fridge, a non-matching microwave and stovetop range. The sink is full of dirty bowls, a pot of leftover Kraft mac and cheese, the remnants of spaghetti. It's embarrassing. I've seen what she comes from. I mean, I didn't go inside, but I can imagine. Clean kitchen, dishes always done. Marble floors. Granite counters. Vast spaces and high-end appliances. The opposite of this, basically.

I point at the sort-of hallway, a six-foot length of hall with a bedroom door on either side and a single bathroom in between. The toilet is dirty, the shower is hard-water stained, and the sink is covered in Mom's stuff: makeup, curling irons, brushes, hair ties, a box of tampons.

"My room is on the right." I lead her there, leaving the door open. More for Kylie's sake than anything else. Mom won't get home before three in the morning, and she wouldn't give a shit even if she did.

It's messy, of course. Clothes cover the floor, heaped in piles of dirty laundry, the clean clothes in a basket. There's an ashtray on the windowsill, and it has cigarette butts in it, as well as a couple of roaches. The room stinks of dirty clothes and smoke. I can't believe I brought her here. Jesus, what was I thinking?

I back away. "This was dumb. I shouldn't've brought you. It's gross in here. Let's just go." I grab her arm gently, and tug.

She moves away from me to sit on the bed, the only place *to* sit. "It's fine, Oz. It's just a bedroom. My room is just as messy."

I snort. "Right."

She laughs. "It *is!* It looks just like this!" She glances at the ashtray. "I mean, it's a little bigger, and it smells better, but…other than that, it's just like this."

I lunge at the ashtray and take it into the kitchen, dump it, and grab the Febreze on my way past the bathroom. I spray liberally, until we're both coughing.

"I think that's good, Oz." She laughs, waving her hand in front her face, and then looks at me with a curious expression. "I didn't know you smoke." I just shrug, and she frowns. "There was more than just cigarettes in there, wasn't there?"

"Don't wanna know, remember?"

Kylie frowns. "Maybe I do. Maybe I'm curious."

I groan and flop on the bed beside her, not too close, not touching. "No fucking way, Kylie. We're not even having this conversation. Be curious with someone else. Ben already hates me."

"Ben's not my keeper."

I don't respond to that. *Maybe he should be* is what I'm thinking, but don't say. I know I should stay away from someone as good and innocent as Kylie, but I'm just asshole enough that I know I won't. It doesn't mean I'm going to go out of my way to actively taint her lightness with my darkness.

Instead of responding, I lean over, grab my guitar, unplug the headphones, and turn the volume on the amp down. I lean back against the wall, feet kicked out to hang over the side of the bed. I glance at Kylie, grin. "Ready?"

She nods. "Let me have it."

I hit a power chord, just to test the volume. Twist the knob a little, hit the chord again, and this time it's just loud enough that I'll probably get some complaints, but not enough to cause any real trouble. Loud enough, essentially, to shock her. I pin my finger to the string, hit it with my pick, then slide my finger down the neck, toward the bridge. An ascending, discordant note fills the air, and when I get halfway to the bridge I send my fingers dancing across the fret board, picking the strings as fast as I can, eliciting a shrieking riff that hits hard and keeps on going. I turn it into a chugging low chord riff, close my eyes, and ascend the bridge, strumming and picking, the whining, wailing notes getting higher and faster with every fret I pass. This is a solo I've been working on for a while, adding notes and chords here and there over the past few weeks, sections of finger work.

With my eyes closed, I can almost see the numbers on my eyelids like silver light, halving and halving again with every note, fractions upon fractions with each shredded, twisted flight of chords. I lose myself in it momentarily. Let the music take over, let it slice through me and push away the knowledge of my impending fight with Ben, my bitterness and my sadness and my loneliness, even my burgeoning and star-crossed attraction to Kylie. For as long as my eyes are closed and my hands work music from my guitar, nothing else matters. I don't even want to burn when I'm playing. It's just for me. I let the solo go, turn to improv, hitting half-notes and staccato power chords, crossing from power metal style solo to metalcore-style crashing and grinding.

Eventually, I remember that Kylie is here with me, and I let a shuddering note hang in the air, open my eyes to see Kylie staring at me. Her expression is unreadable. Horrified? Awed? A little of both, maybe. I'm not sure. I just sit and wait, fiddle with my pick.

"Jesus, Oz!" Kylie breathes. "That was amazing. I had no idea you were so talented!"

I roll my eyes. "I'm not. It's just a hobby."

"A *hobby*?" She shakes her head and leans toward me. "Oz, that was crazy. I've never heard anything like it. You could totally be a professional musician with talent like that."

I'm uncomfortable. I set my guitar on the floor beside the bed and switch the amp off. This seems to have backfired. I dig through the front pocket of my backpack, find my pack of smokes. I ignore the tin that holds my stash, even though I'd like a toke or four right now. I light a cigarette, slide open the window, and stand beside it. Maybe she'll be so grossed out by the fact that I smoke that she'll leave me alone. I mean, I don't want her to leave me completely alone, just to forget this idea that I could ever play some stupid country music for her.

"No way, sweetness. I just do it for fun. For myself. You're the only person who's ever heard me play. Like, not even my mom. I don't know why I played for you, really. My point is, *that's* what I play. Not some twangy country bullshit. I'm not the guy for what you want. Sorry." I blow a long stream of smoke out of my nostrils, and Kylie backs away from the cloud, waving her hand at the smoke.

She moves off the bed, watching me. "Why do you smoke?"

I shrug. "I dunno. I just do. I like it."

"Does it taste good? Or does it make you, like, high? I've never understood why people smoke cigarettes."

I laugh. "Clearly. No one you know smokes, huh?"

"I think my dad used to, but he quit a long time ago. I think he still does, actually, every once in a while when he's in the garage, but never when I'm around." She sniffs the air, and I can tell she's fighting her curiosity. "Let me try." She reaches for my cigarette.

I hold it away from her. "No way. No fucking way, Kylie."

"Why not?"

"Because it's bad. And you're good."

"It's not bad for you?"

I shake my head, not in denial, but in disbelief. "No, it's bad for me. But it doesn't matter if it's bad for me."

She's clearly perplexed by this answer. "What the hell does that mean? Of course it matters. What if you get lung cancer?"

"Then I get lung cancer. The only person who'd even remotely care is Mom."

Hurt registers in Kylie's eyes. "What about me?"

I ignore the pain in her blue eyes and keep pushing. "You'd get over it. You barely know me. This is just shiny-new-thing syndrome going on here for you," I say, gesturing between her and me. I lean toward her, blow smoke right at her. "If you really knew me, you wouldn't be here."

She doesn't back away. Doesn't register my words. She just reaches out, slowly, pinches the cigarette in my hands between her finger and thumb. Takes it from me. I let her. She put the slightly crushed filter to her lips, hesitates. She's nervous. Not sure she wants to do this, knows she shouldn't. But she does. She inhales, a huge hit. Shit. She's probably going to cough so hard she pukes, I'll bet.

Yep. She starts hacking, hands the cigarette back to me, leaning over double and coughing so hard she nearly retches. I grab a handful of her hair and hold it out of the way.

"Breathe in, sweetness. It'll pass in a second. Just try to breathe. You'll be fine." Holy shit, her hair is soft. Like fucking silk slipping between my fingers. She gasps, face pale, eyes watering and panicked. "Breathe in, Kylie. Force the oxygen in."

She opens her mouth and sucks in a deep breath, lets it out with a couple more coughs, and then begins to regain her color. "How—*shit*—how can you do that?"

I shrug. "Everybody does that their first time. I puked the first time I tried to smoke. I did just what you did, took a big ol' hit and sucked it right down. Puked all over the merry-go-round. I, for real, thought I was going to die. Of course, I was ten."

"Ten? You've been smoking since you were *ten?*"

I laugh. "No! That was just when I first tried it. My mom's a smoker, and it was one of hers. That was when she was smoking Reds, and those fuckers are *harsh*. I didn't start actually smoking regularly till I was…fifteen. Sixteen? A few years ago."

"Reds?"

"Marlboro Reds. They're like, almost unfiltered. The smoke is a lot harsher than that." I lift the butt of the cigarette as a gesture, then stab it out. "These are Parliament Lights. They're one of the lightest cigarettes you can buy."

"That was *light?*"

"Yeah, babe. It's like breathing regular old air compared to Reds."

"Ugh. Gross." She shudders. "Okay, enough about cigarettes. Back to music."

"Kylie—"

"No, just listen. Have you ever actually listened to country music? Tried to forget the fact that you think you hate it and really *listened?*"

I shrugged. "No, but—"

"Then just try it." She pulls her phone from the back pocket of her jeans, types in her passcode, and pulls up her music app, scrolls through looking for a specific song. She finds it, I assume, and spots my dock, plugs her phone into it. "Listen. This isn't what I want you to play. I just want to prove something." She hits "play" and I hear what sounds like a music box, a little tinkling sound, and then it's joined by an acoustic guitar.

"What is this?"

She waves me off. "It's 'I'm Still a Guy' by Brad Paisley. It's a funny song. Listen."

I listen. For her, I try to push away my distaste, and really listen. It is a funny song, and against my own will I find myself nodding along. It's soft, it doesn't have the same edge as metal, obviously, but there's something to it that I don't mind. When the lyrics talk about how you can't grip a tackle box with creamy, lotion-y hands, I laugh out loud. "Okay, that wasn't too bad. What else you got?"

She scrolls through her songs again and selects one. "This is 'Goodbye Town' by Lady Antebellum. This is more like what I want to play."

I listen. The harmony is really good, and the melody is catchy. Not too bad, either. I'd never listen to it on my own, but I'm not choking on my own vomit like I'd expected to.

Before I can say anything, she's got another song playing. "You might like this. It's 'Four on the Floor' by Lee Brice."

It's filtered, slightly distorted, and has a rock edge to it. I dig it. "I could get into this. It doesn't sound like country, really."

She nods, and I can tell she's passionate about this. "I think a lot of people who say they hate country are thinking of like, Vince Gill and Randy Travis. Old school, traditional country. All slide guitar and twang. Modern country isn't like that. Not as much. I mean there're still artists like Easton Corbin and Joe Nichols who are closer to that traditional sound, but if you listen to Jason Aldean or Luke Bryan or Lee Brice, it's not like that. It's got a more mainstream sound, more of a rock music undertone. I mean, it's still unmistakably country for the most part, but it's not your preconceived notions of country."

"This is a big deal to you, isn't it?"

"Yes. It is. I like all kinds of music, Oz. I liked what you played. I really did. It was different than what I usually listen to, but if you'll notice" —she rubs at her nose, grinning at me sarcastically— "no nosebleed."

I laugh. "Fair enough. I misjudged you. I apologize."

She frowns and shakes her head. "We're both always misjudging each other." The song ends, and she puts something else on. "I really like this guy. Brantley Gilbert. I think you'll like him, too. This song is 'Hell on Wheels.'"

There's a hard edge to this song, guitar work that I can actually move to, rock-n-roll riffs that touch on my ear for the-harder-the-better music. When the song ends, I nod at her. "Okay, *that* I actually like."

She squeals and claps, literally giddy with happiness. "Yay! I knew I could convert you." She pulls her phone off the dock and points at me. "Your turn. Play me something you listen to."

I think about putting something really hard on, like Spineshank or something, but I don't. I turn on "The Sadness Will Never End" by Bring Me the Horizon. As the slow, melodic intro plays, I tell her the name of the song and the band, and I watch her expression shift to surprise when the guitars and drums hit all at once. Her features turn tight with focus, listening.

The song ends, five minutes of screamo angst-driven glory. I love that song. I cue up another song, a little harder: "In Place of Hope" by Still Remains. She remains focused, listening, dissecting.

When that song ends, she's quiet for a few minutes. I let her sit, let her process. "There's a lot of anger to that. A lot of…bitterness."

"Yeah. That's the point of it."

"Why?"

I shrug. "It…I don't know, I've never tried to explain it before. Um. It's about understanding. Someone else understands how you feel. Understands how anger can be…in your fucking blood. Part of you. How bitterness and rage and sadness can be all-consuming. They get it. They express it. It's commiseration."

She nods. "I can see that."

"And really, that kind of music, it's not as deep as it goes. It's not as hard as it gets. There's more melody and a variety of emotions and sounds and styles to it. You get into stuff like death metal and black metal, it's just…rage. Pure hate made into sound."

She frowns. "Show me."

"Really? Why? It's…"

Kylie's response is almost angry. "Stop thinking you can tell me what I like, or what's not good for me.

That's as bad as Ben trying to tell me who I can hang out with."

"He means well."

She gapes at me. "Why are *you* defending *him?*"

I wish I knew. "I'm not," I say. "It's just true. And fine. If you really want to hear something truly *hard* and dark, then here you go." I scroll through select a song. "This is Amon Amarth. The song's called 'A Beast Am I.' They're actually a lot more melodic than most other death metal bands."

She listens, and her eyes are wide, the edges of her mouth tight. She doesn't like this. The other stuff, it's not as bleak and fury-rife. There's no lightness to this music, nothing redeeming. It's unrepentantly black and edged and bloody.

She's visibly relieved when the song ends. "Jesus, Oz. That's…wow."

I laugh. "Yeah. Told you."

She bobbles her head side to side. "I can see the talent, though. I mean, to play that hard, that fast, for that long? Every song? The amount of sheer energy it must take to play that way is…just staggering."

I'm impressed that she can see past her initial, visceral reaction. "You should see a live show of that kind of music. People leave bloody. For real. Broken bones and shit. It's brutal. But you're right, it takes a sick amount of speed and technical precision to play like that."

She shudders, making a face of disgust. "I'll pass on the live show, thanks. I can imagine."

I laugh. "No, I really don't think you can." I lift up the sleeve of my shirt to show her a thick ridge of scar running along my left bicep. "I got this at a death metal show. It was…shit, I can't even remember who was playing. I was a little…blasted, I guess. Some local band at a dive bar in the back end of Denver. I shouldn't have even been allowed in, 'cause I wasn't even seventeen yet, but security was a little…lax. Anyway, this guy in the pit had spiked bracelets on his wrists, the spikes were wicked sharp and two inches long, and he was flailing around, kicking, thrashing. He must've slashed a dozen people to ribbons, and the band was egging him on. The harder he thrashed, the harder they played. The bouncers had to finally throw him out because he was getting little too psycho even for a death metal show. Well, I got too close, and he caught me on the arm. The spike actually got caught, and I had to kick him away from me to get it loose. It was insane. My mom was *so* pissed. I needed like, thirteen stitches, and we really didn't have the money. She was late on rent because of my ass."

Kylie is justly horrified. "That's…awful." She shakes her head. "I didn't mind the other stuff you played, the first couple of songs. But that's not really my cup of tea."

"I didn't think it would be. I wasn't trying to tell you what to do, or anything. I just really didn't think you'd like it." I pause to formulate a thought. "But then, it's not really music you're supposed to *like*. It's music you *feel*. Experience."

Kylie nods. "Yeah, I can see that. But anyway, about this open mic night."

I sigh. "Really, Kylie? You still want me for that?" I frown. "I'm really not sure I can even play like that. I've never even touched an acoustic guitar. I can't read sheet music or anything like that. I play by ear."

"Just try? Please?"

I really don't want to. Really, really don't. I mean, it's not that I give a flying fuck what people think about me. But then…that's bullshit, because everyone cares what their peers think of them. If you don't care, I mean, *really* don't care, not even deep down where you don't dare look, then there's something truly psychologically wrong with you. Either you're trying to get their approval and trying to fit in and be cool, or you're just one of the crowd, or you're like me, on the outside acting hard and aloof, when inside you wish you knew how to be like them. You don't fit in, and you never will.

Could I do this open mic night? Yeah, probably. I mean, if I can teach myself to shred via YouTube videos and library books and hours of practice, I can probably learn to play some simple acoustic chords, right?

I groan. "Fine. I'll try. But I make no promises."

She does the squeal-and-clap-her-hands thing, and then flings herself across the room to hug me. I'm stiff, frozen. No one hugs me. Mom doesn't hug me. Overnight hook-ups don't hug me. I don't know what to do with a hug. Her arms are around my neck, her body pressed up against mine. Her face is against my chest, and she's up on her toes to reach, 'cause I'm tall and she's maybe five-six. She doesn't let go, but she sinks down on her feet, leans back to look at me, her hands on my shoulders, her eyes accusing.

"You suck at hugs."

I laugh. "I don't get a lot of practice."

"Well, now's your chance. You're supposed to hug me back. Let's try again." She lifts up again, slides her arms around my neck, and pulls at me.

I try, because she wants me to. I let my arms slide around her back, high, just beneath where I'm guessing her bra strap is. Platonic, non-threatening. This girl ain't a hook-up, and I'm not gonna go there with her, not even a little bit. So I hug her. At least, I think that's what I'm doing. I hold on to her, feel her body swell with each breath, ignoring the softness and the way she seems to fit just so, and the fact that I can feel her curves like temptation. It's just a hug. I breathe and hold on to her back, my hands splayed on her shoulder blades.

After what seems like a ridiculously long time for a simple hug, Kylie steps away, nodding seriously. "That was better. We'll get you up to speed in no time."

"Up to speed?"

"Yep. We've got to work on your sub-par hugging skills."

"Work on my…" I trail off.

"Your sub-par hugging skills," she finishes.

I nod. "Okay. If you say so."

She nods with me. "Okay, then. I'll figure out a practice schedule with my parents so we can use their studio. I'll get a list of possible songs together, and we'll pick one together. We've got over a month, so that should be plenty of time to get something ready."

I feel like I've been snowed. "Um. Okay. Nothing stupid, though."

She just laughs. "Trust me, Oz."

Yeah, see, that right there is not really my thing. People say that all the time—*trust me*—like it's so easy. There's one person in the whole world I trust, and that's Mom. And even she doesn't really have my full trust, because she's lying to me and hiding the truth about my father. But other than that, she's always been there for me. I've never starved, never been homeless. Well, except for that two weeks between when one lease ended and another began. We lived out of our truck for those two weeks, but it was okay because it was summer in Mississippi. Mom is my only family, and my only friend, and the one constant in my life.

And Kylie's saying *trust me* like it ain't no thing. I almost laugh out loud.

Maybe Kylie sees something in my expression. "I meant about the song, Oz. Trust me about the song."

I lift an eyebrow. "We'll see, I guess."

Four: Warning Signs
Colt

THE HARRIS MOUNTAIN BOYS ARE *GOOD*. Really good. They're a folk-bluegrass trio: a stand-up bass, a banjo, and a fiddle. Gareth Fink, the banjo player, is incredible. I'm sitting in the booth, watching him pick so fast it's inhuman. Buddy Helms on the bass is a solid presence, head bobbing forward as he thumps the rhythm, fingers slapping and walking across the strings. And then there's Amy Irons on the fiddle. She's a whiz, a whirlwind of frenetic energy. Their name is funny, a kind of thumb-of-the-nose to the established idea of a folk trio, since one of The Harris Mountain Boys is actually a girl, and a gorgeous one at that, but it works for them. Their lyrics are often humorous, tongue-in-cheek, often belying the insane amount of talent the three of them have. I found them busking on Broadway, and asked if they'd like to record a demo in my studio.

I remember busking, sitting on the street with my guitar, playing for the love of playing, sitting on a stool in some dive, no one paying attention. If I'd had a demo, I might've gotten somewhere faster. Which is a moot point, and I'm kinda glad it didn't happen, because I probably wouldn't have run into Nell on the street that day. But I can help these talented kids by letting them record a demo *pro bono*, just because everyone needs a kind gesture once in a while.

And then, once they got the demo down, they saved their bucks and managed to get it pressed into a hundred and fifty discs, which they promptly sold out of after only a handful of gigs. So I had Nell work up a loosely worded contract, basically just saying that if they want to accept a deal with an actual label, they need to let us know beforehand. And voila, Calloway Music LLC had a band signed on. We used our contacts around Nashville and places farther afield to get them a tour of the East Coast and select Southern cities, the bars and coffee shops where Nell and I started out and still play regularly, nearly twenty years later. The Harris Mountain Boys' tour starts in January, right after the New Year, so we've got a couple months to get a full album down for them to tour with.

I hear the door from the basement stairs open into the studio, and I turn to see Kylie enter. She slumps into the chair beside me with the lazy grace of a teenager.

She watches the band play for a few minutes, and then turns to me. "Can I use your studio?"

I shrug. "Sure, when we're done. I wanna cut this last track, and then it's all yours." I turn my attention to the trio beyond the glass. "Good! Let's try it one more time, except Amy and Gareth, you need to actually slow down just a hint." I swivel back to my daughter. "What're you up to?"

She fidgets with a knob on the board. "Practice."

"For what?"

"An open mic night at the college coffee shop."

I nod. "That's cool. Yeah, sure. We're gonna be in here most days until probably around six, so if you can wait until after we're done, you can use the studio for practice." I point at her. "Just make sure you shut everything down when you're done."

She's not done yet, though, I sense. "I was thinking…Oz is going to play the guitar for me. Since I suck. So he'll be practicing with me." She glances at me, nervous. "If that's okay. With you. Please."

I'm a little surprised. "Oz? He plays guitar?"

She nods. "Yeah. He's really, *really* good."

"Huh. I wouldn't have guessed. Judging by the T-shirt he was wearing, I would've thought he'd be more of a hard rock kind of guy."

She shrugs. "He is. But he's going to try to play a few songs for me." She gives me another hesitant glance. "Do you have an acoustic guitar he can borrow?"

I sigh. "I guess. Just…it's not that I don't trust him, but…keep an eye out, okay? This stuff is expensive."

Kylie shoots me a dirty look. "Seriously, Dad? What's he going to do, smuggle the mix board out in his pants? God." She stands up. "I'd think you of all people would be less judge-y."

"I'm not judging him, hon. I'm just saying. You never really know a person." I wonder if I should say something about them being alone down here. I decide to go for it, since I'm a dad and it's my job to be suspicious of guys sniffing around my daughter. "One more thing, Ky. You're down here to play music. That's it, okay? You get me?"

She blushes. "Dad. God. You're so embarrassing. Yes, I get it. We're just friends, okay?"

The blush says she's thought about it being otherwise, but I take her at face value. I rub her back. "I'm just doing my job as your dad."

"I know, I know." She's out the door and up the stairs before I can say anything else.

After another two takes, I'm happy with the cut, and the band packs up and troops upstairs. Nell, Kylie, and Oz are all in the kitchen, munching on hummus and pita. That's a Becca thing. She's got this recipe for hummus that's heavy on the garlic. It's addictive as hell, and she's always bringing over giant Tupperware tubs of it for us, since we eat a metric shit-ton of it. Looks like Oz is chowing down, laughing at something Nell is saying. I watch him from the doorway to the basement. He's a big kid, over six-four, lean and hard, with long auburn hair tied back in a ponytail, hidden under a backward Broncos hat. He's wearing a pretty garish-looking T-shirt, some metal band logo, and a pair of old blue jeans, combat boots. There's a biker jacket hanging over the back of one of the chairs, and it's got all kinds of patches on it. I glance at his forearms, and my stomach seizes a little. He's got scars. Not cut marks, but some kind of scarring. It doesn't look accidental. There are circular marks, rows of them near his elbow. Intentional cigarette burns, maybe? I can't tell from here. There are other marks, too, irregular patches of smooth, shiny skin, the edges twisted and crimped.

Oz notices me, follows my gaze, and immediately tugs the sleeves of a white long-sleeve shirt down to his wrists and shoves his hands in his pockets. His expression doesn't shift, and he doesn't look away, doesn't act guilty, but he covered up nonetheless. My own experience—not to mention Nell's—makes me suspicious. Worried.

The kids from The Harris Mountain Boys have trooped out of the house, and it's the four of us in the kitchen. Should I say something to him? Not yet, I decide. Give him a chance. Maybe it wasn't self-mutilation scars that I saw. I hope not, for Kylie's sake. That shit ain't no joke, and it's not something I want my daughter caught up in. She's gotta make her own choices, and I've got to let her, but I don't have to like it if she gets involved in something so nasty as cutting or burning one's self. I've been there. Nell's been there. It's a fucked-up place to be and, at almost eighteen, my daughter is still impressionable. I don't want that for her.

I can't overreact, though. I know better. I'm not that kind of dad. She's a good kid, and I trust her judgment, but I also know what it's like to be her age. In the end, I let them head down the stairs together, and I keep my worries to myself. At some point, though, I'm going to confront the kid. It'll piss Kylie off, but sometimes as a parent your duty to protect means angering your child. Just the facts.

When they're gone, I notice Nell is staring at the door to the basement with a worried expression on her face. "You saw his arms?" she asks, not looking at me.

I lean on the counter beside her. "Yeah. I saw."

"He's a really nice kid," Nell says. "'Yes, ma'am' and 'no, ma'am' and all that. But those scars. They scare me, Colt."

I sigh. "Shit, don't I know it. Thing is, babe, we're more like that kid than we are like Kylie. We've both got scars we gave ourselves."

Nell's palm skates up and down her forearm, smoothing over the fine white lines engraved on her creamy skin. "Yeah, we do. And that's what scares me. Because we both know the kind of hell it takes to make someone do that." She looks up at me, pleading. "I want to tell her to stay away from him. So bad. I freaked when I saw his arms, Colt. *Freaked*. But I can't tell her that, can I? She won't listen."

"No, we can't, and no, she won't." I wrap an arm around her shoulders and hold her against me. "She's smart, Nell. We have to try to trust her."

"But we can't ignore the warning signs." Nell's hands are rubbing at her scars, almost obsessively. Nell almost never does that anymore, especially around Kylie.

"No, you're right. But listen, babe. Oz having scars doesn't mean he's still doing it, and she sure as hell isn't doing anything like that." I grab her wrists and hold them.

"I know. I just...I don't even want her to *know* what scars like that mean, Colt. I want to protect her from everything we both endured." She turns into me, face against my chest.

"We can't protect her from life, Nell. You know that. She's going to get hurt someday. All we can do is love her, and be there when it happens." Smooth words, easy to say. Not so easy to do.

Five: Acoustic Melodies and Old Pain

Oz

I'M FREAKING OUT, HARDCORE. Like, totally losing my shit. Kylie's house is fucking *dope*. Huge. Nothing is flashy or gaudy, just tastefully, subtly expensive. They've done well for themselves, really well. And they've done it on their own, as indies. It's impressive. And this studio? Jesus. Intensely impressive. All the best equipment, racks of guitars, a piano in one corner, several top-of-the-line recording mics.

And then there's the fact that I'm pretty sure both Nell and Colt saw my burn scars and knew exactly what they were. I don't know what to do with that.

I'm standing in the middle of the recording room, gaping like a fish, frozen in place. Kylie comes up behind me, and I flinch at her touch on my back.

"Oz?" She moves around in front of me. "Are you okay?"

I shake myself out of it. "Yeah. Just...your house is pretty amazing. I've never been in a house this big."

She frowns. "This? This isn't all that big. One of my friends is the daughter of a major label exec. Now, *her* house is massive. Like, I actually got lost once. Wandered around totally lost for literally twenty minutes before I called Lin on my cell phone. She had to, like, get landmarks so she'd know where I was. It was ridiculous."

I can't fathom that. "I don't know why anyone would need a house that big."

Kylie shrugs. "You don't. It's totally unnecessary. Lin actually kind of hates it. She says she gets tired just walking from her bedroom to the kitchen. There's really no point to a house that big." She gestures at the house above us. "This? It's only four thousand square feet. Compared to most of my friends' houses, it's tiny."

I snort. "And my mom and I live in an eight-hundred-square-foot apartment. It'd fit in your kitchen."

She seems chagrined. "Oz, I—"

I push at her arm, gently, teasingly. "Ky, it's fine. It is what it is. We just come from different lives."

"Not that different," Kylie says.

"Yeah, that different. Totally different. Nothing at all alike." I peruse the selection of guitars, admiring all of them. "Which makes me wonder. Why are you going to a community college? Why don't you go to Vanderbilt or wherever, like Ben and your other friends?"

Kylie blushes. "I'm still technically in high school," she mumbles.

"You're *what*?" I demand, turning in place, choking on my own surprise. "How old are you, Kylie?'

"I'm seventeen, almost eighteen," she says. "How old are you?"

Shit. I thought she was at least eighteen. Fuck. Not good. Not good. "I'm twenty-one," I say. "So if you're still technically in high school, how is it you go to the community college?"

She fiddles with the cover of the keyboard. "I tested out of most of my senior classes. I'm in a co-op that lets me attend the community college for college credit. I'll graduate high school with more than twenty college credit-hours."

"Damn," I say, impressed. "So you're wicked smart, huh?"

She shrugs. "I guess."

"When do you turn eighteen?"

"Two months," she mumbles. "Why does it matter?"

It matters because eighteen is on the very edge of acceptable, seeing as I'm twenty-one, but seventeen? Not so much. I don't look twenty-one, which is probably the only reason her parents are even letting me be around her. Because we're not really dating, I suppose. Just hanging out. Friends. Just friends.

I don't know what to say to her, though. "It doesn't, I suppose. I just thought you were older, is all."

She eyes me warily. "You're not going to suddenly vanish on me now, are you? I'll be eighteen soon. Stop worrying about it."

"I'm not worrying about." Lies. I totally am worrying about it. I like her. I want to do dirty things to her. But she's not even eighteen, not even out of high school. Fuck me, I'm an asshole.

"So, let's play," Kylie says, dismissing the topic.

"Okay," I say, and grab a guitar from the rack. Not the nicest one, not the vintage Martin. That one's probably worth more than my entire existence. I take an older one, a classical acoustic Taylor. It's old, but beautiful. Kylie stops playing abruptly, hitting a wrong note.

"No! Not that one. That's Mom's favorite. Pick another one."

There's a Yamaha, mid-grade, basic black. "This one?"

She nods absently, lost in the music-trance. "That's fine." She grins at me. "You should play the Martin."

I make a face of mock-horror. "Are you kidding? Do you even know how much that's worth?"

Kylie frowns. "Obviously. But you're not going to, like, break it, are you?"

I sigh. "Ky. I'm not playing your dad's Martin. Those are worth thousands of dollars *used*, for a standard. *That's* a vintage, in mint condition. Gotta be worth more than a good used car."

"I thought you didn't play acoustic? How do you know the value of Martins, then?"

I growl. "I don't play acoustic. I've looked into it, though. Thought about it. I just haven't been able to afford a new guitar." I find a stool and perch on it, settle the Yamaha across my knee. "This is fine. More my speed."

I try a basic C chord, get used to the spacing on the fret board with a few practice strums. I try a few more chords, just stringing them together without really thinking about the sound, just trying to get accustomed to the different feel of the strings, the different sound. I recall one of Nell and Colt's older songs, try to remember the melody. Try the tune, search for the right chords. Finally, I get it, and I listen to the song in my head and try to make it come out via the guitar strings. I have to close my eyes to focus, and when I finally find the groove, I settle into it. It feels weird, but good to play like this. Slow, soft. Like I'm tapping into some other as-yet untouched portion of my musical soul.

When I finish the song, I open my eyes, and I'm embarrassed to see that Kylie is frozen at the piano, and Nell and Colt themselves are both in the booth, listening.

"Sorry, I—I was just goofing around." I feel like I'm...imposing, or intruding on sacred territory, trying to play and probably murdering Nell and Colt's music in their own home. What the hell was I thinking?

I set the guitar down, but Nell's voice comes from the intercom. "Why are you apologizing? That was amazing!"

I shake my head. "Nah. I was just messing around. I've never played acoustic before. I just—"

"No, for real, that was *good*, Oz." This is Kylie, from the piano. "I've heard Mom and Dad play that live, and you got it just right on the first try. You're seriously talented, Oz."

I shrug, and scrape at a string with the pick. "Thanks, I guess." I'm uncomfortable, embarrassed, and my instinct is to bolt. I want to throw the guitar down and run, fly on my bike back home. I don't. I force myself to stay in place, and to bear up under the scrutiny. I glance at Kylie. "Play something for me."

She strokes the piano keys, thinking. A glance at her parents in the booth reveals her nerves, but she sucks in a deep breath and nods. "Okay. How about… how about this. I've been working on this for a while. It's 'Freedom Hangs Like Heaven' by Iron & Wine."

A few beats of intro, and then she starts singing, and I'm blown away. Just…breathless. Having heard Nell and Colt, I shouldn't be surprised that their daughter inherited their talent, but the scope of how good her voice is totally floors me. It's got a soulful rasp to it, a la Adele, and of course she's just absolutely pitch perfect. I steal a glance at her parents, and I can tell they're both surprised, too, since they sit back and watch, mouths slightly ajar.

The piano hums as the notes fade, and Kylie looks at me for my reaction.

"Holy shit, Kylie. Just…holy shit."

She laughs. "I guess it was okay, huh?"

Colt speaks from the booth. *"Okay?* Kylie, how is it I didn't know you were that good?"

She shrugs. "I practice when you're not here."

"You should let me record you sometime," Colt says.

Kylie shakes her head. "No. Not yet. Maybe once I've gotten a few gigs on my own."

Nell comes around into the recording room. "You want to gig?"

Kylie lifts one shoulder, toying with the piano keys with the other. "Yeah. But I don't want your help. I know you could get me a contract, and get me gigs, and all that. I want to do it on my own. Not because I'm your daughter."

Nell glances at me. "Are you going to gig with her?"

I feel like my throat is clogged. "I. Um. I thought we were just doing the open mic night. I don't know."

Kylie frowns at me. "I told you my plan was to start with open mic night, just to get my feet wet. Now that I've heard you play, I know for a fact we could get a Thursday or Friday night spot somewhere off Broadway."

"Ugh. Kylie, seriously? I don't know." I strum idly at the guitar. "I always saw myself in a metal band, not playing indie folk."

"You can do both. Just do the open mic night with me. Please?"

I pluck my hat from my head and smooth a few wayward strands away from my face, replace the hat. "I guess. I told you I'd do the open mic night with you, so I will. But I'm not sure about the gigs. I've never performed in front of people before. You, and now your parents, are the only people who've ever heard me. And I'm dying here as it is."

Nell pats my arm. "You'll do fine. Just ignore the people. That's what I did when I first started gigging. I was so scared. Ask Colt. He was there for my first gigs. I thought I'd pass out, I was so nervous. But you get used to it. Eventually, it's fun. Although the first moment you step out on the stage? That moment never gets any less exciting, or nerve-wracking."

"Yeah, not sure that helps much, but thanks, Mrs. Calloway."

"My name is Nell." She pats my arm again. "Do the open mic night. See how it feels."

I nod, and then she and Colt disappear up the stairs. I let my inner panic show. "Kylie! Why didn't you tell me they were there? I was butchering *their* music in *their* house."

She just laughs. "You didn't butcher anything. You did great. And I was so surprised by how good you are." She plays a few notes, then glances up at me. "Are you sure you can't sing? Have you ever tried?"

I shake my head. "No. And no way. I'll play for you, but there's no way in hell I'm singing."

She gets up off the piano bench and circles around to stand in front of me. "Come on. Please?

Just try." She puts her hands on my shoulders, pulls me in for a hug. I've gotten better at hugging, she says. Her voice is a whisper in my ear. It's tickling and hot and too much to take. I shrug away and grunt. "Just try. Please? For me?" She's leaning into me, and it's not just a hug. It's too intimate for that.

I let her hang on me, because the only way to move her away is to take her by the waist, and that's entering dangerous waters. Dangerous for her, that is.

"Sing what?" I say, resigned to the fact that I can't seem to ever say no to this girl, even when it ends up with me embarrassing myself.

"Anything. Something you know. I'll sing with you. How about something generic?" She pulls away, but not all the way. Her hands are on my shoulders, held at arm's length. She pops one hip and thinks. "Hmm. How about…god, I don't know. What songs do you know that I'd know?"

Fuck me. She's really pushing this. I don't want to sing. I don't want to go up on stage at all. It's not that I'm scared, I'm just…okay, you know what? I am scared. I'm just like anyone else: afraid of embarrassment and rejection. If she was pushing me to get up there on my own and rip some metal riffs, pretend I'm Joe Satriani or something, maybe. But this? Singing and playing an acoustic guitar like some coffeehouse hipster dick? Yeah, no.

But damn it, look at her, sapphire-blue eyes pleading with me, her hands on my shoulders like it ain't no thing, like her touch isn't making my pulse pound. Like I have a snowball's chance in hell of saying no.

The problem is, I don't know any songs well enough to actually sing—at least, none that she'd know. Except one, and I don't want to sing that one. It's my mom's song. Her favorite song. The one she sings when she's falling down drunk and whatever secret tragedy haunts her is slipping out.

It's the only song I know well enough to sing.

I sigh. "There's one song. 'Come On Get Higher.'"

Squeal-and-clap, giddy, eyes bright. "Matt Nathanson!" Shit, she's gorgeous. "I love that song!"

She has her phone out, and she's scrolling, scrolling, and now it's playing. Tinny, small, distant, playing through her phone's speakers. The guitar comes in, and I'm listening close, trying to track the chords and the rhythm. Easy enough, seems like. Yeah, I could play this song.

I close my eyes, sink in, delve down. I hear my mom's voice. She's got a decent voice, not great, but she can hold a tune. I channel her, because that's the only way I'll get myself to actually sing out loud. I mean, I *do* sing, but it's alone, in my room, the music loud enough to drown my own voice. I try not to hear myself. I just sing along with the song. I hear Kylie, 'cause how could I not? She sounds like a freaking angel over there. I can't help hearing us, though, and goddammit we sound good. Which means I'll have to do this in front of the whole fucking school. I'm not great, but I don't sound like a walrus being throttled, so there's that.

The song ends, and there she is, staring at me like I'm a leprechaun or something. "What?" I demand.

"Just that you're so much more talented than you think you are."

I roll my eyes at her. "I'm not talented, sweetness. I just don't suck totally."

She frowns at that. "You don't suck at all, Oz. At anything. Why are you so down on yourself?"

I groan. "Life? Just leave it at that, okay?"

She sighs. "You know, I'm always underestimating you. You have this habit of surprising me at every turn. You sounded *good,* Oz. For real. I know music, and I know talent, okay? You can play the guitar like nobody's business, and you have a good singing voice. And you and I together? We have *insane* harmony. And that was just us goofing off."

I don't argue with her, since it's pointless. "Why do you need me, again? Your piano skills are sick. You could dominate all on your own."

She shrugs. "No, they're not. I'm decent. I've just been practicing that song for a while, and I still messed up. I hit, like, three wrong notes. I just…I've always wanted to be like Mom and Dad. I love watching them perform together. They have so much fun, and just… I've always wanted to be part of a duet. But all the guys I know only want one thing from me. They'd play and practice with me, and when I don't put out, they ditch me. I've tried, okay? I asked Billy Nicholson to play with me last year, and he was all excited. He's talented, like, for real. But as soon as we were alone in the choir room, he tried to kiss me. And I was like, eeew, because Billy Nichols is a man-whore. He's fucked half the girls at the high school. I'm not that girl, and I said so. I told him all I wanted was to play music together, and he just…ditched me. Just like that." She plucks at a string on the guitar I'm still holding, looking down. "So I tried again with Trey Ulrich. We practiced together for maybe a week, and then he tried to kiss me, too, and the same thing happened. As soon as I made it clear that there'd be no funny business going on, just music, he was all like 'fuck this, then.'"

"Sounds like you know a bunch of horny douche-nozzles, then."

She laughs. "Yeah, you could say that." She gave me a quick glance, and then looked away. "So I kind of gave up after that. Until I met you. We've been hanging out for a while, and I feel like I can trust you."

Bad plan, sweetness. I don't say that, but it runs through my head. Because all this time, she's been within kissing distance, and I've been trying not to stare at her lips, wondering what flavor lip balm she's wearing, and if her lips are as soft as they look. "You shouldn't trust me," I do end up saying. "You shouldn't trust any straight guy."

She frowns, confused. "Why not?"

"Because you're fucking gorgeous, and any guy who spends more than five seconds around you wants you. Guaranteed."

She doesn't back away at the implication. "*Every* guy?"

I nod. "Yep."

"Even you?"

I laugh. "Most definitely me." Our eyes meet, and I hate, for her sake, the gleam of interest I see in her gaze.

"But you haven't tried anything."

I shake my head. "No, I haven't. You're my friend, Kylie. Maybe you've noticed that I don't have a lot of friends in my life, so there's no way I'm going to screw up the one friend I've got in all of Nashville. Plus, you're not even eighteen."

She's thinking hard about that. When she speaks again, it's slow and hesitant. "What if I want—"

I put two fingers over her lips, which is a temptation unlike anything. "No. You don't. You don't know the half of what makes me the way I am."

"I'd like to learn."

"No, Kylie. There's a reason I keep my bullshit to myself, okay? It's not about keeping secrets, or because I'm ashamed. It's because someone like you shouldn't know about the shit I've done. My life ain't pretty, sweetness. I wouldn't be doing you any favors by dragging you through the mud of my messy-ass life. You'd get dirty, and you're way too clean, way too gorgeous, and way too innocent for me to be willing to soil you like that. So no. For your own good, no. We're just friends, and that's all we'll ever be."

She turns on her heel and strides away, shoulders hunched, head down. I'm not sure if she's hurt by my outright rejection, or just angry. Both, maybe. It's for the best, though. I stand up, and place the guitar back on the rack.

"Keep it," she says.

"What?"

"That's my guitar. Keep it. We've got others I can use." She slips through a door leading deeper into the basement, comes back with a basic hard-sided guitar case, sets it on end near my foot. "Here."

I back away. "I'm not taking your guitar."

Her head snaps up, eyes blazing. "Take it, goddammit. It's just a cheap guitar. It's what *friends* do."

"Why?"

She shrugs, a tiny, defeated gesture. "Like I said, friends give each other gifts. That's a gift. It's not charity, because I'm sure that's gonna be your next excuse." Her eyes meet mine, and I see hurt, confusion, sadness. "You're still playing the mic night with me. I signed us up already. So…you need a guitar to practice on."

"What are we playing?" I lay the case on the floor and put the Yamaha in it, snap it closed.

"If you're up for it, I'd like to try a couple of songs I wrote." She's turned away again, her hand on top of the piano, rubbing idly at the polished wood.

"Sure. I'm game."

"Cool. I'll show them to you tomorrow."

"Why not now?"

"Because I'm about to cry, and I want you to leave."

Well, how's that for honesty? I move behind her but don't touch her. "I don't want to hurt you, Kylie."

"You already did."

I groan. "You really don't know what you're asking for, with a guy like me."

"Shouldn't I get to be the judge of that?"

"Yeah, maybe. But I've got a choice, too," I say.

"And you choose to reject me."

My eyes slide closed, and I feel the welling up of pain, guilt, regret. I hate that I've put hurt in this girl's life. I don't see a way around it, though. Her folks saw my scars, and they knew what they are. There's no way in hell they'd let their only child date a hood-rat nobody punk like me. And they'd be right.

"Not reject. Protect."

She spins around, suddenly a lot closer, almost touching, the round tips of her tits a hair's breadth away from my chest, looking up at me. "I think you're just scared."

I nod. "Yeah. For you."

"I'm not scared."

"You should be."

"Why?"

"Because you can do better than me, Kylie. Look across the street, for starters." I gesture in the direction of Ben's house. "Boy's got it bad for you."

She steps toward me, shoves me. "He's my best friend. He's like a brother to me. And that's how he sees me. He's had our entire life to say if he felt otherwise, and he never has."

I shrug. "Maybe he's got his reasons." I rub my face. "Fuck. Look, Kylie. I'm sorry if I've hurt you.

I'm sorry if you don't understand my reasons. But it's all you're gonna get from me."

I'm up the stairs before she can say anything else, trying to be calm and nonchalant as I wave at Colt and Nell, tossing a polite "see ya'll later" at them. Shit, I've got to get out of here. Out of Nashville. Away from the temptation that is Kylie Calloway.

The roar of my motorcycle fills my ears, and I'm ripping around corners, zipping through traffic and running lights and generally driving like an asshole, but I need distance from her. She'd drag my shit out of me, and she'd want to fix me, and she'd say she didn't care. But she would, and she should. I'm nobody's project, and I'm not about to risk the innocence of someone as pure as Kylie. She's a virgin, I can all but guarantee it. The way she looked at me when we were so close, eyes wide and a little scared, like she wanted to get closer and wanted me to kiss her, but was secretly afraid. The way her nostrils flared and her chest swelled with nervous breaths.... god, so seductively innocent.

I'm inside my apartment without any memory of arriving. I slam my door closed and crack my window, toss my backpack to the floor and dig my tin out. Roll a joint with shaky fingers, spilling weed everywhere. Scoop up the spilled green, dump it back in the bag and light the joint. Connect my phone to the dock and blast the hardest, darkest metal I have in my library of music. I don't even know what it is, who it is, it's just grinding and brutal and what I need. Hit after hit, hold it deep, slow exhalations.

I did the right thing. Right?

The doubt is killer. Like a knife, slowly slicing away at the foundation of my certainty, like a rushing flow of water undercutting the riverbank. I lie back and fight the doubts, float on my high.

I hear a faint noise. "No, please..." I sit up, because the voice sounds familiar. It's late evening, maybe seven, and since it's early December, it's dark outside. I pause the music and listen: "NO! Leave me alone! Let go! Please!" Fuck, that's Kylie.

I scramble up and out, the door slamming and shivering, cracking the drywall, tear through the front door and down the steps. I see her in the shadows, pinned against the driver's side door of the BMW. Jesus fuck, she followed me. It's the same three guys we saw when I brought her here last time. One of them has his hands on her, holding her by the arm, leaning into her, mock-thrusting against her, laughing. And now he's pulling at her, dragging her toward the nearest door. The other two are standing back and watching, laughing, egging their buddy on.

I don't even hesitate to think or to plan my attack. I'm lunging across the sidewalk, pivoting on the ball of my left foot and swinging my fist up into his kidney, putting all my weight and force into it. They never even saw me. He stumbles back and I strike again, same spot, three short sharp jabs to his kidney. If nothing else, he'll piss blood later. But I'm not done. Jack him in the jaw, knee to the gut, wrap my palm over the back of his head and slam his face down into my rising knee. He falls back, gagging on blood and teeth.

I feel a blow to my side, grunt, spin, lash out blindly, connect with bone and flesh. Stumble back, find the attacker, half-dodge a punch, catching part of it on my cheek. The skin rips, and I feel blood sluice down, salty and hot on my lips. Another hit to my skull, just above my ear. My head rings, and I see stars. I shake my head, twist to find a target. There he is. My high is gone, replaced by adrenaline and now pain. I kick out, a snap-kick to the knee. He lurches, and I fling myself forward, head-butt him. His nose crunches, and I feel his blood coat my forehead.

Slide-click. "Best step off, mothafucka." Cold metal against my forehead.

"Go, Ky." I don't look at her, but I hear her hyperventilating. *"Go!"* She goes. Good girl. I hear a door slam, then tires squeal, and I hear the smooth roar of the finely tuned German engine, and she's gone.

I turn, glaring hard into cold brown eyes. "Shoot, bitch." It's all bluff. I'm fucking terrified, knees knocking, about to piss myself.

His eyes narrow, and he twists his wrist so the pistol is held on a diagonal. "You wanna die? Huh, white boy? You got a death wish?"

"No. But if you don't shoot me right the fuck now, you're gonna regret it." I'm tensed, ready.

He licks his lips, debating. Hesitating. Hesitation is deadly. I feel the barrel slip, tilt down, and I'm in motion. My hand snaps out, pushing the barrel to the side and down. My fist is flying, connecting with his throat.

I hear the gun go off, and burning pain slices through my leg. It registers as heat and pressure and pain, but it's not enough to stop me. I grab his wrist, twist, wrap his arm under mine and pivot my body so he's bent over and his arm is over-extended. He's moaning and trying to gasp for breath. No fucking mercy here, bitch. I tilt forward and lean down, hard and fast, and his elbow joint cracks. The gun drops from his hand, and I step on it. Throw him forward. He topples, and his face smashes into the ground.

Blood drips from my face, my leg. My fists ache and burn, the skin on my knuckles split.

I don't even register the sound of the approaching engine, or the door opening. I'm limping to stand over the gun owner. "She's *mine.* Got it? Next time you fuck with her, you die."

He can only moan an acknowledgment. I bend and scoop up the gun, eject the clip and the cartridge in the chamber. Shuffle-limp to the dumpster across the parking lot and toss it in. When I turn around, she's there, standing in the open door of her car, staring at me.

"You okay?" I ask, from thirty feet away.

She rushes toward me. "Am *I* okay? You're bleeding. I heard…I heard a gunshot, and I thought you'd…I thought he'd…I thought you were dead."

I hear a groan, and I push Kylie toward the building. "Let's go in. I'm fine."

She grabs my arm and drags me toward the car. "No, you need to see a doctor."

I pull away. "I said I'm fine."

"You were shot. Your leg—"

My leg does hurt, so I glance at it. Didn't go through; it looks like just a graze. I limp toward the door, not waiting for her. "It's not bad. I'm going in. You should go home."

She follows, though, shutting her car off and locking it. It'll be a miracle if it's intact when she leaves, but I can't worry about that. I'm adrenaline-crashing and in pain and shaking with the onset of fear, now that it's over. I slam the front door of my apartment closed, lock it, and lurch awkwardly into the kitchen. Pull a length of paper towel from the roll and press it to my leg. Hiss at the pressure and the pain. I feel dizzy. My head aches. My cheek hurts. That glancing blow hurt worse than I'd thought. I catch a glimpse of myself in the glass of the microwave; my face is a mask of blood. Kylie is pressed against the wall near the fridge, shaking, staring at me, horrified and terrified and about to collapse.

I gesture at the hand towel hanging off the handle of the oven. "Hand me that." She does, and I replace the now-sodden paper towel with the cotton one, tossing the blood-soaked wad into the sink. "Kylie, relax. I'm fine. I've been hurt worse. This is no big deal."

She shakes her head. "There were—there were three of them. They shot you. They could've killed you. Because of me." She shudders, wraps her arms around herself. "You're a bloody mess. You're hurt."

"C'mere." I hold out my arm, and she rushes to me. Judging by the twinge of pain in my side when she slams into me, I've got a bruised rib. I ignore it, breathe through it, and hold her against me. "It was worth it, as long as you're okay. They didn't hurt you, did they?"

She shakes her head. "No. Just scared me. They... he was telling me what he wanted to—to do to me. It was so awful. And he was going to. I couldn't get away. And I knew he was going to—"

"But he didn't." I rub her back. "Breathe, sweetness. Just breathe. Everything's fine now."

She pulls away. "Um, no. You're hurt."

I wipe my forearm along my chin, smearing the dripping blood away to keep it off her. "Cuts to the head or face bleed a lot. It's just a split cheek. For real, I'll be fine. Like I said, I've had worse."

She tugs me by the hand, and I follow her reluctantly, limping behind her. She leads me to the couch, helps me sit. Brings back a few dampened squares of paper towel and wipes gingerly at my face, folding the paper towel over and over until it's a pink-red wet wad. This goes on for several minutes, until the bleeding finally stops. She touches my cheek, and then my forehead, which I realize belatedly stings, too.

"You've got two cuts." She touches near each of them. "Here, and here. They don't look deep, though."

"Like I said, I'm fine." I'm dizzy, though, and reeling. Aching, hurting. Shit, it hurts.

Kylie leans over me and oh-so-gently pries at the edges of the cut to my thigh. "This is pretty bad. It needs stitches."

"Not happening."

She looks up at me, confused. "Why not?"

"Don't have the money, don't want the attention. It'll heal." I point at the bathroom. "There's a roll of bandages and some Neosporin in the medicine cabinet. Can you grab it for me?" She nods and gets up, and it's not until she's back that I realize I can't bandage it with my jeans on. I struggle to my feet. "Need to change into shorts. I'll be right back."

"Oz, you should go the ER. I'll pay for it."

"The fuck you will." I shouldn't be so harsh, but I'm in pain and frustrated and confused. Why'd she come here? This complicates things. She's gonna feel like she owes me something now.

"Then let me help you. Please. You can barely walk." She's behind me, following my slow progress to my room. I can barely move my leg for the deep throbbing ache that seems to originate in the bones of my thigh.

I make it, and fall back onto my bed. "What, you're gonna take my pants off me?"

She blushes, but enters, sinks to her knees by my feet. "Yes." She's tugging on the laces of my boots, slipping them off my feet.

Resistance is futile. Shut up, yes, I did just make a *Star Trek* joke. But seriously, I don't know how to stop her, because it hurts and I've never had anyone take care of me. Mom's not the cuddly, huggy, baby-me type of mom. She's more my friend than anything else. So this is new, and I don't know how to deal with it, especially because pushing Kylie away earlier today was seriously fucking painfully difficult, the diametric opposite of what I wanted. I let her take off my shoes, and my socks. The sock on my wounded leg is sopping wet with my blood, and she makes a face as she peels it off me. She looks around for somewhere to put it.

"Garbage in the kitchen," I tell her.

She leaves, and I fumble with the button and zipper of my jeans, fight to get them off, but shitfuck-damn it hurts so bad, the edges of the denim stick to my skin and to the open wound, the blood clotting now. I've only got my jeans halfway off before she comes back.

"Goddamn it, Oz. You stubborn asshole."

"Finally got something figured out," I say, relinquishing my pride and letting her finish tugging the jeans off my legs.

I'm wearing boxers, thank god. I do sometimes go commando, if it's been awhile since I've done any laundry.

My side aches, throbs. The rib is definitely bruised at the least, possibly cracked. That was a good hard hit he got in. And my head, god, my head is throbbing from the head butt, on top of the two punches I took. Public service announcement for you, kids: Head-butting someone hurts *you,* too. Don't be fooled by the movies.

"Holy fuck, Oz, this is *really* bad. Please, please let me take you to the hospital." She's near tears, and looking pale, like she might puke.

I sit forward and give my leg a good look. It *is* pretty deep. Not to the bone, but it's a pretty harsh gash on the outside of my thigh. It'll heal on its own. I know this from experience. Not from a gunshot wound, but from similar injuries. I shake my head. "It looks worse than it is, Kylie. It's just a cut. Gimme the gauze."

She swallows and blinks, presses her lips together, hands me the roll of gauze, the Neosporin, a bottle of peroxide, medical tape, a pair of scissors. I realize the Neosporin probably won't do much good, so I set that aside. I take the towel I used to sop up the blood and hold it beneath my leg.

"Dump the peroxide on that bitch," I say to her. "A whole bunch."

She blanches. "Won't that hurt?"

"Like a motherfucker. But it's better than getting an infection. Do it quick." I grit my teeth and watch. She twists the little white cap off the brown bottle, glances at me. I nod, and she pours peroxide over the wound. I can't help a groan from escaping. "F-ffffuck that hurts. Goddamn." I suck in a deep breath for courage. "All right, do it again."

She's near tears still, but she does it. And fuck me running, the raw agony is nearly unbearable. The wound bubbles crazily, and I dab at it with the corner of the towel.

"Once more."

I can't watch this time. I stare at Kylie instead, at the fall of her reddish-blonde hair draped in loose waves across one shoulder, her downcast electric eyes intent on my legs. Her T-shirt is tight and gray, her boobs round mountains that I want to explore with my hands and my mouth and my eyes. That thought doesn't help, especially since I'm only in my boxers, and if I pop a woody, she'll know. I go back to looking at her hair. Thick, lustrous, copper. Waves and waves, with a slight curling twist at the ends.

"You're staring at me." She caps the peroxide, and then looks at me.

I shrug. "Yeah."

"I thought we were just friends."

I cut a long ribbon of gauze, fold it over a few times, and then place it against the wound. "Wrap it." I watch as she winds the gauze around my leg, passing the roll from hand to hand. "We are."

"Then why are you staring at me like you could eat me?" She snips the bandage and tapes it in place, then sinks back to sit cross-legged.

"Because what's right and what I want are not necessarily the same thing." I point at a pair of loose cut-off khakis. "Can I have those?" She tosses me the frayed shorts and I slip them on, wiggling them past my hips.

Kylie's frowning at my answer. "What about what I want?"

I button the khakis and draw the zipper up, then wiggle backward and reach into my bag for my cigarettes and lighter. "Same answer applies." I light up and take a deep drag, closing my eyes as the bliss of a nicotine rush hits me. "What you want and what's best for you are not the same thing. You just saw why. My life isn't safe. *I'm* not safe."

She crawls on the bed and sits next to me, watches me smoke. Her fingers slide against my palm, and she takes the filter from me, puts it to her lips, takes a small draw, holds in her mouth, and then inhales. She coughs a little, but not as bad as the first time. I watch her eyes dilate, and her head thumps against the wall as the dizziness of the rush hits her.

"Oh, shit. Wow. Now I see." She blinks, hands the cigarette back.

I chuckle. "Yeah. No more for you, though."

"Is it always like that?" She reaches for it, and I keep it out of her reach. "Come on, I want to try it again. Please?"

God, I'm gonna get her hooked. But, like a dick, I hand it to her anyway. "No. Once you're used to it, you only get that feeling if it's been, like, twelve hours or more since your last smoke." I take it back and drag on it. "If you get addicted, there'll be a lineup for who gets to kick my ass."

"No, if I get addicted, it'll be my fault, not yours." She sees the open Band-Aid tin on the floor beside my bed and snags it, looks in. Pulls out the baggie, opens it, sniffs. "This is pot?"

I nod. "Yeah. That's pot."

"Are you gonna smoke it?"

"Not in front of you."

She puts the bag back in the tin and sets it between us. "Why not?"

"Because that's just one more reason why you and I being more than friends can't happen. Drugs have no place in your life."

"But they do yours?"

I sigh. "Yes, they do. If I amount to anything, it'll be as part of a band. That's it. I'll be playing dive bars and shitty clubs, and I'll get high in the alleys and do lines in the bathrooms, and eventually I'll OD and that'll be that." I glance at her. "Is that the life you want?"

She runs her hand through her hair. "No. But you can be more than that, Oz. You could, if you wanted to. Your talent with math? You could do a lot of things with that. And you're a good enough musician that you could be a hell of a lot more than some asshole druggie snorting coke in dive bar bathrooms. You should want more for yourself than that, Oz. I want more for you than that."

I shrug. "Yeah, well, I don't." Lies. That's a dirty fucking lie. I do want more. Maybe not picket fences and a dog with a floppy ear and two little kids snotting on my jeans, but something better.

She rolls toward me, and her eyes are close, her breath on my cheek, her hand on my chest. "You don't believe that. I can hear the lie in your voice, and I can see it in your eyes."

I closed my eyes. "Maybe so. Doesn't change the facts."

"Yes, it does. There are no facts, not about your future. You make your future. You're talented. You're good-looking. You can do a lot of things, if you believe in yourself."

I snort. "What is this, a 'The More You Know' commercial?"

"Yes, and I'm Sandra Bullock, so you know it's gotta be true."

I can't help but laugh. "You're *way* hotter than Sandra Bullock." I pause for effect, and to consider whether I'll regret saying this. "And Sandra Bullock is *hot*."

"She's older than our parents!" She laughs.

"So she's hot for an older lady. And it's parent, *singular* for me." I say it without thinking; it just slips out.

This sobers up the conversation real fucking fast. "You've never known your dad?"

I shake my head side to side. "Nope. Never even seen a picture. Don't know a single goddamn thing about the man."

Kylie is bursting with questions, I can tell. "Your mom won't tell you anything?"

I shrug. "No. It's…a sore subject for her. She gets pissed off if I bring it up. He's gone, and that's all I need to know." I sigh. "I think I'm named after him, but I'm not a hundred percent on that."

"You're named after him, huh? What was his name?"

I laugh. "Nice try, sweetness. Still not telling you my real name."

"Damn it. I thought that'd work." She's on her side, head propped on her hand, looking up at me from way too close. "Why won't you tell?"

"Because my name belongs to him. And I don't know a single goddamn thing about him. So I need—I decided in third grade that if I'm gonna be myself, with no help from his ass, then I might as well have my own name. So I chose Oz."

"Why Oz?"

I shrug. "It's a…derivative. And it fit. Also, I'd just seen *The Wizard of Oz* for the first time, and thought the wizard was cool. I mean, he wasn't supposed to be, but he projected this huge image of himself when inside, in reality, he was totally different. And that's how I felt, like to survive in the world I had to be totally different from the way I felt inside, different from who I wanted to be. I mean, I grew up rough, Ky. I did. What just happened? Not unusual. I'm a fighter, okay? I've been to juvie. I had to fight every day when I was in juvie. I had to fight at school, and I had to fight on the playground, and I had to fight in the neighborhoods where we lived. When kids have something to prove, shit gets rough. And in the 'hood, everybody's got something to prove. But inside, I hated fighting. I just wanted to be left alone. I wanted to know who my dad was, where I came from. Why my mom was alone. Why we were alone. Why we moved so much."

"You've moved a lot?"

I nod. "Yeah, you could say that. Like, every year or so, for most of my life. The longest I've lived in any one city or state was in Dallas, from the time I was like eleven until junior high. Just before seventh grade Mom moved us from Dallas to St. Louis. It was every year, year and a half before Dallas, and the same after St. Louis. A new school, new apartment, new city, new friends. Then, eventually, I stopped bothering with the whole friends thing, since I'd just leave 'em after a few months. Now, I just bide my time till the next move. Keep to myself, do my own thing…shit, I don't know why I'm telling you all this. I've always been lost. Like I'm just shuffling around the world, just me and my mom, and I know there's a whole tragic story Mom won't tell me. I'm not really anybody, you know? You *know* who you are, where you come from. You're Nell and Colt's daughter. You're a musician. You know your parents, each of them. I mean, yeah, for sure they have stories and secrets you don't know, but they're both *there*. You don't even know what a huge thing that is. Mom is…shut off. I don't know how to explain it. She's…present in my life, and she's raised me to the best of her ability, and I'm thankful I've got her. But there's a part of her that's…gone. From me, at least. I've asked her about it, but she just gets mad." I have to stop for a minute and grit my teeth and try to get past the renewed throbbing in my leg and my side.

Kylie lays on her back, staring up at the ceiling. "God, Oz. There's so much I want to know, so much I want to say. I don't even know where to start."

"Nothing to say. It is what is." My teeth are clenched against the pain, which is blazing with sudden intensity.

"You said you were in juvie?" She asks this hesitantly, not looking at me.

I shrug. "Yeah. Tenth grade. New Jersey."

"What for? I mean, what happened that you ended up there?"

I sigh. "Nothing too exciting. I got jumped by some assholes after school one day. Got the shit stomped out of me. So I got even. Of course, I might've gotten a little *too* even. Hunted all four of them down, one by one, and hospitalized 'em. Apparently, revenge isn't an excuse for aggravated assault and battery."

"Hos-hospitalized them?"

"Yeah, sweetness. Bash a kid in the back of the head with a brick, he needs more than a couple stitches."

"God, Oz."

I laugh, but it's a bitter sound. "Yeah. Maybe you're starting to see why I said I'm no good for you. They deserved it, sure. They'd been picking on me for weeks. Knocking me around, slugging me in the hallways, and then I get in trouble when I retaliate. See, they were the cool kids. The ones with both parents. Mommies on the PTO and daddies on the school board. Established members of the community, that kind of horseshit. And I was just the new guy from the shitty end of town."

"They were bullying you, but you got sent to juvie? I mean, what happened to them after they jumped you?"

I laughed again. "Nothing, sweetness. Not a damned thing. I dragged my sorry carcass home and skipped school the next day."

"You didn't tell anyone?"

"Fuck no. Wouldn't have done any good, and even if they would've gotten in trouble, they'd've just gotten suspended for a few days. No point."

"You said you've been hurt worse than this. Was that what you were talking about?"

"God, the questions. No, Kylie. That was a couple busted ribs and a black eye. Cuts and bruises. Nothing I hadn't dealt with a dozen times before." I hate telling her this. I hate the pity I see in her face. "The one other time I've been really, truly hurt, like not just beat up, but *hurt*...it was junior year. First week of school. There was this kid, Greg Makowski. Big, I mean *huge*. Stupid as the day is long, but just massive. A bully, of course. What you gotta understand is, when you're in juvie, the new guy is nothing but fresh meat. You get jumped soon as they close the door behind you. Especially the juvie I was in. Well, I learned real quick that to fend off the beatings, I had to make a point. Prove I wasn't someone to fuck with. So I chose the biggest, nastiest kid on the block and kicked his teeth in. Nobody messed with me after that, unless they were new and wanted to try to prove that same point on me. Well, this kid, at the school last year. I started a fight with him. Won, too. Only, he had buddies. A *lot* of them. Big ones. They cornered me on a cul-de-sac. A high wall with the freeway on the other side, empty lots on either side. Nowhere to go. Must've been eight of 'em. Broke four ribs and my wrist, fractured my cheekbone, broke my nose, loosened a few teeth. Nearly choked on my own blood. Spent over a week in the hospital, and couldn't move for another two weeks after that. Mom had to sell her car and pawn some jewelry to pay even part of the bill. Still owe, like, five grand on it, as a matter of fact.

Mom worked back-to-back double shifts every day for almost a month to get enough money to buy another car so she didn't have to walk three miles to work, one way. Almost got evicted, too. But we made it, and after I was released from the hospital, we moved again and I transferred schools." I shift to try and ease the ache in my ribs, but only succeed in causing more pain. "So that's the sordid story. Glad you asked, huh?"

Kylie is silent, and I look over at her. She's *crying*.

I roll over toward her and force myself to sit up. "Hey. What's wrong?"

She sniffs, wipes at her eyes. "What's wrong? God, Oz. Just…god. You've been through so much. And you say it all like it's no big deal."

"But why are *you* crying?" I honestly don't get it. "I don't need your pity, Kylie."

She sits up, eyes blazing. "It's not pity, Oz! It's called fucking compassion! There *are* people in this world capable of *caring* about you. Not everybody is going to beat you up and betray you and abandon you."

"Yeah, well, that's been my experience. So forgive me if I'm a little jaded, okay?" I can't take it anymore.

I open my tin and thumb a nugget of weed into my little glass pipe. I don't typically like smoking from a bowl, but I'm too impatient to roll right now. I flick the Bic, and the pot crackles, glows orange, and the smoke fills my lungs.

I hate myself for doing this in front of Kylie.

I hold the smoke in until my lungs protest, and then lie down, blow it out, toward the ceiling. Kylie is watching me intently.

"No. Don't even ask." I take another huge toke, and then set the pipe and lighter on my chest.

"I wasn't gonna ask. It smells funny." She glances at my bedroom door, which is open. "Won't your mom smell it?"

"She knows." I'm high now, and my eyes are heavy and the pain is distant. "She lost her fucking mind the first time she caught me smoking pot. Like, total meltdown. Hysterical. We fought about it for weeks. I wouldn't stop, and she kept grounding me and shit, but I just ignored her. I kept going out whenever I felt like it, because what was she going to do, nail my door shut? Wrestle me into my room? Ground me again? Finally, she just gave up. Said if I wanted to destroy myself with drugs, go ahead. Sometimes, when she's really upset, she'll smoke with me. And when she does, I can tell she's remembering….him."

I've got the lighter in my hand, and I flick it to life. Flick the Bic. Flick the Bic. The flame is short and yellow, wavering and bright and hot and inviting. It's not something I even think about—I'm just drawn to the flame, like a moth. My hand descends, palm an inch above the fire. It's just hot at first. Heat on my skin. Nice. Easy and slow and warm. Then hotter. Feel it. It's better than thinking about how Mom won't tell me the truth, and that's not something I can endure anymore. She's got the secrets, the answers, but she won't share them. And I get angry, hurt, filled with rage. Did he abandon us? Was he a criminal? Was he killed? Was he just a slacker douchebag who bolted as soon as he found out he'd knocked her up? Was he a good man who wanted to be a father and Mom's the one running? Is that why we've moved so often? Is she running from him? Or is she looking for him? Following him? I don't know, and I'll never know. I think sometimes that my desire to burn myself is an attempt to burn the need to know out of my body. Trying to sear the questions from me. But that's stupid. All I know is, the flame calls to me. I need it, and when it's got me in its thrall, I can't pull away.

The heat grows, turns to pain as I lift the lighter closer to my hand. I watch as the flame touches my skin, turns to searing agony.

"*Oz!*" Kylie smacks the lighter from my hand, shrieking, "WHAT THE FUCK!"

I'm startled to awareness, and I clench my hand into a fist, feeling the pain in my hand take over from my ribs and leg. It's better. Familiar.

She grabs my hand and turns the palm face up, examines it. "You burned the shit out of your hand, Oz. What the hell was that?"

I tug my hand away, but she doesn't let go. "It's no big deal, Kylie. For real."

And then she sees. Hand. Forearm. Fingers. "Oz?" Her voice is so small and hesitant, and hurt. Like each patch of shiny, burnt skin causes her pain. Her fingers drift out and touch each burned spot on my forearm. I close my eyes and let her touch. She understands now that these scars aren't accidental. "*Why?*"

I jerk my arm away, fumble for the lighter, and take another toke. "You say that in the exact same tone of voice that Mom does. So I'll tell you what I tell her. I don't know. It just helps. I can't explain it to her, so I can't explain it to you. I can't even explain it to myself."

"This *is* a big deal." She's still tracing the contours of each scar, on my forearms, on my hands. On my fingers. God, the tenderness in the way she touches me is…fucking unbearable. "I don't know how to deal with this."

I make myself look at her. "Kylie. Eyes on mine, babe." Her blue, blue gaze locks on me. Her tears well, unshed. I give her a sad smile. "Now you get it? Why you and me won't work? You don't get it. You don't get me. You could've been *raped,* just by visiting my apartment complex. You watched me fucking brutalize your attackers. I'm..." I swallow hard, force the reality out. "I'm *tainting* you, Kylie. Making you dirty just by association. It wasn't about you not being good enough. It's not...it's not even about *me* not being good enough. It's about my world and my life and why I am not compatible with yours, with who you are. Who you could be. Compatible isn't the right word. I'm fucked up. I've got a shitload of issues. This burning thing? It's not going away any time soon. I try not to burn. Mainly because it makes Mom lose her shit, and she's got enough to deal with. But like today? Just now? I wasn't even thinking about it. It just happened. And it *should not* have happened in front of you. I've let so much of my dark and dirty world taint you, and I hate myself for that."

Kylie doesn't answer for a very long time, and I let her have the silence, have the time to process, to think. She just stares at me, at my hands and arms, at my face, at the bed, at the pipe and lighter lying on my chest. I stuff the pipe and lighter into the tin, toss the tin into my backpack, shift to a sitting position. Kylie is sitting on her shins, hands on her thighs, head down, blinking away tears. I don't know why she's crying. No clue. Because I'm fucked up? Because of what happened earlier? She was assaulted, threatened with rape, and witness to a hell of a fight. She has every right to feel traumatized, to be in a bit of shock. But that's not it, I don't think. It's about me.

And I don't want her to cry for me.

I lift her chin with my fingers, and she closes her eyes, turns her head away. A single tear trickles down her cheek. I brush it away. I can't help it. I feel like my touch is far too rough, but I try to be gentle.

"Don't cry, sweetness. Please?"

"I can't help it. I want to make everything better for you. I know I can't fix you, that's not what I mean. I just…I want…I want to be able to help. To—I don't know, not take away your pain, but…help you deal with it somehow. I don't know, Oz. I'm so mixed up. And you keep saying how you don't want to taint me, but I don't feel like you are. I want to be a part of…of your life. Even if it's messy and dark and dirty and—and violent." She looks up at me. "I was so scared, but then you appeared out of nowhere, and I knew I was safe. But then I was scared for you. But you—you won. And it was scary, but I know…I know *I* don't have to afraid of you."

I don't know how to react. Do I tell her she shouldn't want to help me? That she can't? It's a nice feeling, knowing she cares. I mean, I know Mom cares, but she *has* to. Kylie doesn't. My head is spinning with crazy thoughts, my heart is pounding with emotions I don't understand and can't sort out and don't know what to do with, and my body hurts, and I'm high, and Kylie is so beautiful and so tender and sweet and kind and good, too good for me. And I should keep pushing her away, but fucking goddammit, I don't want to, and I'm not sure I can.

Then she reaches out, and I'm frozen. She sweeps my hat off my head. I feel strangely naked without my hat. I always wear the hat. As if that wasn't overwhelming enough, she reaches for the black elastic band tying my hair back. Not even my mom sees me with my hair down, except rarely. But yet, for reasons I can't decipher, I let her tug the band down, and off. I have to hold perfectly still, or I'll bolt. My hair hangs just below my shoulders, thick and auburn, just like Mom's. Kylie runs her fingers through it, gingerly and hesitantly, hands sliding past my ears and fluffing it away from my neck.

"Oz, I'm not scared of you. I'm not afraid of your life. Of getting dirty. So quit trying to protect me and let me make my own choices. Let me—"

I kiss her. Cut her off, my lips brushing hers and eating her words, my hand cupping her cheek. She shifts forward on her knees, closer to me, leans into me. I'm doing this consciously. I have control over my actions. I'm kissing her because I want to, because I've wanted to kiss her since the first moment I saw her. So I kiss her, and I try to make it good. Her hands slip through my hair and rest on my shoulders, and then curl around the back of my head, and one of her palms goes flat on my cheek, and now she's almost in my lap, so close to me, leaning into me.

God…*god,* she tastes good. Faintly of cigarette smoke, and of something citrus. Sprite, maybe. And cherry lip balm. Her mouth is warm, and her lips are soft and damp and hungry. I tease the seam of her lips and she opens for me, and now her tongue slides into my mouth, taking over, searching, aggressive. She's eager for this. She wants this. It feels right, like it means something. It's not empty, not just a precursor to sex. It's an exchange, an admission. It's foreign to me, to feel this connected to another person. I don't feel connected to my mom, and there's never been anyone else. Just girls slumming it with me for a couple of hours. Kylie? Fuck, she's kissing me like she could kiss me forever, like there's never been anything in the whole world, in her whole life, so perfect as this kiss.

Our lips part, and she's gazing into my eyes from an inch away, searching me. My hands don't leave her face, her hair. I've tangled one fist in her long strawberry blonde locks, the other still cupping her face with a tenderness and a gentleness I've never showed to another human being in all my life.

"Oz." She says my name, maybe just to say it. I don't know. But then she brushes the corner of my mouth with her thumb, and my heart clenches, stops. "Don't tell me that didn't feel the same for you. Like it—"

"Meant something real?" I owe her the truth, at least.

"Yes!" she exclaims, a soft excited breath. She slides one thigh over mine, facing me, straddling me. "Like it meant something real. That's *exactly* how it felt."

"That your first kiss?"

She shakes her head. "No. I've kissed a couple guys. I mean, I kissed them back. Not…those two guys I told you about, the ones who kissed me. These were guys I kissed because I wanted to. But…it never felt like this. It was okay, but not…so intense."

I allow myself the liberty of skating my palms over her back, down to her hips and back up. She shivers at my touch. "For what it's worth, I've never had a kiss like that, either. Like you said, it was intense."

"Why 'for what it's worth'?"

I roll my eyes and shrug. "I dunno."

"You *mean* something to me, Oz. Everything about you means something to me. You make a difference to me."

"Why?" I toy with a lock of her hair, spinning the ends in my fingers. "I don't get it."

"You're different." She sits on my legs, reaches out to put her palms on my chest, smoothing and touching. "So different. And I like that. There's… something real about you. Everyone else I know seems like they're…putting on a show."

I blink at that. "I'm just me."

She smiles at me. "Exactly. And that's special. To me at least."

Her T-shirt has hiked up a bit in the back, and when my hands make a circuit from shoulders to spine to lower back, I feel her warm, soft skin. It's like a compulsion then, to slip my fingers under the cotton and find more flesh, just her back, the knobs of her spine, brushing the lower edge of her bra strap. No more, neither lower nor higher. I'm careful, hesitant. But temptation is a powerful thing, and I have to fight it, for her sake. I tear my hands away, curl my fingers into fists to keep from devouring her flesh with my palms and fingertips and lips. I've never felt such need before, never had to fight it so hard, never denied myself the luxury of touching if the girl was willing.

This girl? She's different, and deserves better.

But Kylie has different ideas. "I liked that. It felt nice." She arches her back. "Do it again."

"I shouldn't."

"Why not?"

I sigh, close my eyes so her hot hungry eyes don't see so deep into me. "I shouldn't, because I don't want to stop at just…touching your back. Won't want to, won't be able to."

"So don't."

"You don't mean that."

She curls her fingers into my hair, leans in. "I'm a virgin, Oz."

I laugh. "Yeah, sweetness. I know. And that's why."

"I've had opportunity. Choices. I decided not to. I waited." She shifts forward, her hips closer to mine. "Just because I waited didn't mean I didn't want to. I *did* want to. I *do* want to. I've wanted to for a long time. But I wanted it to be with the right guy. To mean something. I know it's not always, like, true love the first time. I'm not naive. And I know…I know it'll hurt. And I know it will probably be different than I'm imagining. But I want it. And Oz?" She leans in and kisses me, so hot and so hard and so hungry, clutching me to her and crushing our bodies together, kissing me with such frenzy and such desperate abandon that I feel myself going hard, and I know she feels that, too. "I want it with you."

Six: Performances and Gestures and Ghosts

Colt

The open mic night is kind of dumb. I mean, most of the kids just aren't talented. It feels like bad karaoke, only no one is drunk. There are a few people, aside from Kylie and Oz, who have a modicum of talent. One kid did a pretty decent cover of Jack Johnson, and the rest is just blah. Shitty covers of crappy songs. So, by the time Oz and Kylie go on, near the very end, I'm antsy, irritated, and ready to go home. The coffee shop is packed, the tables and chairs pushed back to make a small circle of space to one side of the counter where the baristas continue to make drinks, slamming the espresso wand, steaming milk, making the blender whir.

The second-to-last act finishes butchering U2, and Kylie and Oz take their place in the center of the open area. Oz is holding Kylie's black Yamaha by the neck, and a beat-up black and tan Stratocaster is slung by the strap behind his back. There's a tiny black upright piano that someone shoved into the corner, and Kylie slides onto the bench.

I've heard them practicing in the basement over the last couple of weeks, and I have a feeling they're about to slay it.

Kylie pulls the mic stand over to the piano, adjusts the arm so she can sing and play at the same time. Oz, meanwhile, drags a stool and a mic stand and sits near Kylie, partially facing her and partially facing the audience. He leaves his electric guitar hanging at his back and settles the acoustic on his knee, does some unplugged strumming and tuning.

Kylie glances at Oz, offers him a shaky smile, and takes a deep breath. Oz just nods at her as he plugs in, and the corner of his mouth quirks up, and this tiny excuse for a smile seems to reassure my nervous-looking daughter. "Hey, guys," Kylie says. "I'm Kylie Calloway, and this is Oz Hyde. I hope you'll like what we've got for you. We're actually going to do two songs for you guys. As long as you don't boo us off-stage first."

She nods at Oz, who sucks in a deep breath, and then starts playing. It's a slow, lilting melody, rolling like deep ocean waves. After a few beats, Kylie joins him on the piano, playing the same melody but with piano embellishments sliding above and below and weaving through Oz's bass line. The crowd has gone silent, realizing they're about to hear something good. Even the coffee shop employees have stopped working to listen. You can sense it, smell it, feel it. You can see it in the way Oz plays the acoustic guitar with easy skill, hear it in the rising beauty of Kylie's piano.

And then Kylie starts singing:

"Watching this unfold, watching hours become moments
Become weeks become days,
It's all a game, all a trick, hopeless despite my intents.
I'm watching you close and I'm lost in your maze
I can't find my way, don't have a map of your terrain.
I'm trying and I'm diving in, but I'm caught up in your pain,
I'm lost and I'm looking for you, but your secrets are a stain,
They leave a shadow on the clarity of what I feel.
Your secrets and the hidden scars

Are holes in your skin, but light shines through, bright as stars."

Her piano goes muted, quiet, and Oz's melody continues, dark and deep and slow. Then he sings, and I'm blown away. His voice isn't…good, but it's rough and mesmerizing, something raw and fascinating.

"You wish you knew me,
You wish you could see me,
Maybe you think a few kind words will free me.
But darling, they won't.
Darling, they won't.
Your eyes betray your fear,
You come close to me, draw near,
Afraid, maybe curious, maybe thinking you can save me.
But darling, you can't.
Darling, you can't.
Your world and mine,
They're a million miles apart,
And baby, maybe you think you can bridge the gap,
But darling, you can't.
Darling, you can't."

Oz lets the melody play out once more, and then strums three harsh, muted chords, a waiting beat, one-two-three, and then with a sudden crescendo, they're playing together, full volume, their melodies intersecting and weaving and complementing. Together, then, they sing, each singing their own chorus, overlapping and competing and harmonizing:

"I want to know you—"

"Baby, you don't—"

"There's no darkness too dark, no scars too deep—"

"You can't save me, darling you can't, darling you can't—"

"I'm not afraid of you, I'm strong enough, if only you'd let me try—"

"Darling, I can't, darling, I can't—"

"Let me love you, let me love you, let me let me let me love you—"

"I can't, I can't, I can't, darling I can't, Darling you can't—"

"Let me—"

"Darling, I can't—"

"Let me please—"

"Darling, I can't—"

This goes on, a musical argument, sung back and forth and back and forth, their voices rising in volume and intensity until they're both shouting, pleading, singing exactly in unison, but singing different words. It's an incredible performance. There's an element of folk-style simplicity to the song, the way the notes themselves and the chords and the sequences aren't complicated, but they're haunting and compelling.

They end abruptly, mid-chorus, his guitar striking a muted chord.

There's a fraught moment of tense silence, and then the audience loses it, howling and screaming, shocked and awed.

They don't silence the screams and applause, they merely wait, and then Kylie gives Oz a nod. Oz unplugs the Yamaha and sets it on the floor by his foot, and then swings the Fender around, plugs it in. Slides off the stool, adjusts the strap to a more comfortable position, turns it on, and then touches the strings. I haven't heard him play electric, and I'm curious. The way he strokes the strings at the fret board before he starts playing, the way he seems to fall inward, makes me think he'll be pretty good.

He hits a chord, a low, discordant thrum, and he nods, jerks a thumb up. The guy at the little mix board recognizes this signal, turns a knob, and the thrum become a roar. Kylie is sitting at the piano, just watching. Oz renews the chord, and it fills the room, and he's nodding as if to a beat no one else can hear. Then we're all struck, assaulted, battered by a sudden frenzy of notes, all played up high on the neck, near the bridge, and it's a kind of sustained hailstorm, relentless and chaotic, but there's a rhythm to it, or there's a rhythm falling out of it, the way the notes slow and lower, becoming a melody. It's as if he's dragging a melody by main force out of the chaos, and then Kylie's piano joins the frenetic mass of sound, which somehow becomes tune, becomes melody, becomes something unexpectedly lovely. She's playing fast, all tapped high notes, mirroring his flying fingers. I don't think any of us can believe what we're hearing. Oz is a magician, an artist. He's lost, subsumed within the music. Kylie? She's lost, too, but as much in *him* as she is the music.

Then Kylie sings, and it's…perfect. And I again cannot believe how talented my daughter is, the beauty in her lyrics and the purity of her voice.

"Flaws are the fabric of a soul,
And yours are deep,
Twisted thick into the damask of who you are
But I see past the flaws.
I'm not blind, I'm not blind, I'm not blind.
It may not be love,
It may be love,
It may be something else,
Maybe something in between love and not
I don't know, and I wouldn't be writing these

words if I did,
I wouldn't be lost and drifting and scribbling at three in the morning,
If I did.
So your flaws, the tangled web of secrets and sins and scars,
They're you, you, you,
And I see you,
I see you
I see you.
You hide behind the hard and impenetrable flesh of your scars,
You hide behind the things that make you human,
And that's all I want,
The human, the inside and the outside, and the good and the bad,
It's all I want,
The everything,
The ugly and beautiful and the gray in between
All mixed up like a slush and a slurry of pieces.
I don't miss the way you look at me,
The disbelief that I could see through the mask you wear,
The truth you wield like a disguise,
The weapons of your fists and the ink of your tattoos,

They're you, you, you,
But not the whole, not the entirety, not the everything,
And don't you know,
Don't you see,
Can't you understand that all I want
Is only the everything,
Only the everything,
Only the everything
That is you."

While she sings, Oz is playing with the kind of desperation and fervor that tells me he feels the words, hears every single one, and he's playing to sustain his disbelief. I'm watching him play and watching him deny. It's an intimate moment between them, and I'm stunned by the bravery it takes to play something so revealing on stage, to sing so openly and, for Oz, to play along knowing the words are about him, for him, to him.

Kylie's voice fades, and Oz's guitar fades, and only Kylie's piano remains, a repeating melody, something short and high, communicating wistfulness and longing.

The applause is deafening. There's a huge crowd standing everywhere there is a space; people drawn from the hallways have come by to listen. When the noise doesn't immediately die away, Kylie speaks into the mic, grinning. "Ya'll wanna hear Oz play a solo?" There's a chorus of agreement, and Kylie's grin grows brighter. "Yeah, me too. Oz, what do you say? How about that piece you played for me the other night?"

This is a community college open mic night that has somehow become a concert.

Oz looks frozen, stunned, and uncomfortable. He stares at Kylie, who just gives him a nod and a smile. Oz lets out a nervous breath, and then sits on the stool, closes his eyes, strums the strings almost idly, thinking, falling under and into the zone.

If I was shocked before, I'm doubly so now. The guitar solo he plays needs no accompaniment. It sings for itself, plays its own backbeat. It goes on and on, and you just can't breathe for the intensity of it, the way it spans the register of notes, high and low, wailing and shredding, low and slow, passionate and angry. He's deep into it, the guitar on his thigh, held at a slight diagonal. His eyes are closed, his face a mask, not making any of the expressions you so often see in guitarists. He's blank, except for a slight furrowing of his brow, and a tightness in his jaw. As if every emotion he has is being pushed and poured into the guitar.

Finally, he walks his fingers from the top of the fret board to the bottom, all the way down the neck, and when he reaches the highest note, he holds it, lets it hum and squeal and moan, sends it to wavering, echoing, becoming somehow mournful.

Slowly, he lets the note fade, and lets silence swell.

The silence becomes a single clap, then two, then thunderous applause. I'm with them, amazed.

They were the last act, and the MC, a young guy with thick glasses and a scraggly goatee, thanks everyone for showing up, and then that's it. People who were only there for the open mic night leave in ones and twos, and the rest go back to studying and sipping coffee. I order lattes for Nell and me while we wait for Oz and Kylie to pack up.

They find us at our table, and I stand up to hug Kylie "I'm so proud of you, babe!" I say. "That was incredible."

She blushes. "Thanks, Dad. I was so nervous I thought I'd puke."

"You'd never have known."

Nell joins the hug. "For real, sweetie, you're amazing. That was one of the best performances I've ever seen. And I don't mean that just because I'm your mother."

I look up at Oz. "You're a talented kid, Oz. There's maybe thirty people that can play at your caliber. No joke."

He nods and gives me an oddly shy half smile. "Thanks, Colt." He gestures at Kylie, who's hugging friends and chattering excitedly. "She's the real talent, though. She wrote all the music. Except for my electric guitar part, I mean. All the acoustic music, she wrote. All the lyrics, the arrangements, everything. It was all her. And she was the only reason I got up there at all."

"They encored you, pal. At an open mic night. *You.*" I can't help trying to emphasize this to him, trying to build him up. I see something in him, and it both scares me and makes me want to help him, the way no one did for me.

"Yeah. I might let her talk me into doing a couple more gigs. That was pretty fun. Scary as fuck, but fun." He winces. "Sorry, shouldn't swear, I guess."

I laugh. "I'm not gonna bite your head off for dropping an F-bomb, Oz. Nell might, but I won't."

We chat for few more minutes, and then she and Oz are walking, hand in hand, toward the exit.

I have so many questions about him, about them. About whether my daughter is safe, whether her heart is safe with him, whether I should ask if they're sleeping together. If I even want to know. What I'm supposed to do if they are. Should I try and stop them if they are? As they walk away, Oz turns and nods at me, a gesture of thanks. I nod back, and I don't miss the fact that he scratches at his left forearm.

It's a move eerily similar to the one Nell makes, rubbing at her scars. When she was actively cutting, she'd scratch almost manically, frantically. Even now, almost twenty years later, she'll rub at her forearms and wrists if she's really upset, or if something reminds her of those days, those feelings.

Seeing that gesture in Oz, in the guy my daughter is interested in? It scares the fuck out of me. What frightens me even more is the fact that I don't know what the hell to do about it.

Seven: Heaven Breaks Through

Oz

"OH, MY GOD, OZ!" Kylie shrieks as soon as we're outside. "That was a*mazing!*"

I set our gear down by the trunk of the car and then pick up Kylie by the waist, spinning her around. "We totally fucking killed it, didn't we?"

"We did. We totally did." Kylie leans against me as I let her slide down to her feet. "I knew we would. But holy shit, does that feel good. I *love* performing. I want to do it all the time. We've *got* to get a gig, Oz!"

"We will, sweetness. I've got no doubts."

"I did, but not anymore." She lets out a long, happy sigh.

I open the trunk of Kylie's car. It's her mom's, really, but they let Kylie drive it most of the time, unless both Colt and Nell have to go somewhere separately. As we put away our guitars—or *my* guitars, as Kylie keeps insisting I keep the acoustic—I ask a question that's been nagging at me since we met. "Why don't you have your own car, Kylie?"

She slides in behind the wheel and starts the engine, which comes to life with a smooth purr. "It was a deal my parents and I made when I turned sixteen. They said I had two choices. They'd buy me something then, when I turned sixteen, but it would be, for all intents and purposes, a piece of shit. Older, used, and cheap. And most of my allowance would go to paying for gas and insurance. Or, alternatively, I could choose to wait to have my own car when I graduate. The payoff there was I'd keep all my allowance as spending money, I'd drive my mom's car, which is pretty fucking sweet, I have to say, and they'd help me buy a car when I graduate. The closer to a four-point-oh GPA I get, the more they'll spend on the car, especially if I don't get any tickets or get in any accidents. I chose the second option, obviously. I've been putting a third of my monthly allowance into a savings account, so I'll have money to put toward whatever I end up buying. It's a good deal. There's rarely a time when I can't take the car, and in those circumstances, either Dad'll take me where I need to go, or someone else comes to get me."

I'm impressed. "I don't think most people would've gone for the delayed gratification."

She just shrugs. "No, probably not, but when Mom and Dad said they'd spend at most five thousand dollars on my car, I did some online research as to what five grand can buy, and decided I'd rather wait."

She's taking us toward downtown Nashville, but I don't know her exact destination. I decide to let it be a surprise.

"Five grand can buy a really nice car, Ky." It comes out kind of judgmental.

She doesn't miss it. "Yeah, well, maybe so. But… look. I'm privileged, okay? I know it. All my friends drive nice cars. Their parents bought them basically whatever they wanted, no conditions. That friend I told you about, the one whose house I got lost in? She drives a Mercedes-Benz. A G-class. It costs more than a lot people's houses. And she's already wrecked it once. My point is, yeah, I know I'm used to certain level of…luxury. It's what I know. My parents are trying to instill a sense of values in me, and that's a good thing. I mean, sometimes I get a little irritated, like, they could afford to buy me my own BMW if they wanted to, but it would be *their* car. Not mine. I haven't earned it. They've worked for what they have. I guess even the fact that I understand why my parents won't buy me a fancy car makes me weird, for a teenager."

"I think it's awesome," I tell her. "For real. Most people don't appreciate shit. Like, the house they live in, the car they drive. They don't understand how much they have. You do, and that's…it's amazing."

She glances at me. "Honestly, Oz, I didn't really appreciate it very much until I met you."

I laugh, and it's not a little bitter. "Until you saw how I live, huh?" She doesn't answer right away, and I know I've gotten it right. "Hey, like you said, it's all I've ever known. It's not like I went from rich to poor, like I know what I'm missing by not living like you and Ben and your pals do. I've always been dirt poor."

"Are you, like, resentful?"

I have to think about that. "I don't know. Resentful? No. Mom's busted her ass to provide what we do have. We've always had to scrape to make ends meet. I've been working since I was fourteen to have my own money. And now I stay with her and help out with rent and whatever. It's why I'm still living with her. She works herself ragged, Kylie. It's a vicious cycle she's stuck in. She never went to college that I know of, and because she had me, she couldn't. She had to keep working to take care of me. She just kept working and couldn't ever seem to scrape together the time or money to go to college or anything. So she's been a cocktail waitress her whole life. For me. So am I resentful? No. I'm glad to have had what little we did. But do I wish we had more? Yeah. Do I wish for better for her and for myself? Yeah, obviously. I've seen how hard Mom's worked just to keep food in the house and a roof over our heads, and I want more than just the bare necessities, more than just paycheck to paycheck."

The conversation shifts to other topics as Kylie parks in a lot just off the main strip of downtown Nashville. I pay for parking, and she takes my hand. She leads me to Broadway, where the bars and the lights and the shops are, the famous stretch of Nashville. It's a busy night, despite the chill in the winter air. Couples stroll hand in hand, families, groups of guys and clusters of girls, everyone laughing and going from bar to bar and shop to shop. She's taking me somewhere specific, I realize, and I go along with her. She finds the door she's looking for, and I start to balk.

"No, Kylie. Hell no."

She grins at me. "Come on, Oz. Please? Just look?" She doesn't bother to wait for my response, just drags me by the hand into the boot and hat shop.

The door is rickety, and an old-fashioned bell sounds as we open it. The floor is covered in old wood planks that squeak and dip as we walk over them, almost as if we might put our foot through a board at any moment. It smells of leather, and the walls are lined with a dizzying array of cowboy boots. There's a line of benches running through the middle of the store, with piles of boxes between the benches, single boots displayed on top. There are cowboy hats, fedoras, huge belt buckles, a glass case displaying spurs and string ties and expensive gold-and-silver belt buckles. I have never in my life felt more out of place. I'm wearing my beat-up combat boots, a pair of baggy black jeans, a black November's Doom T-shirt with a gray long-sleeved shirt beneath it. My hair is bound at the back of my neck, and for once I'm not wearing my hat, at Kylie's insistence. I look every inch the metal kid, and I'm getting looks of confusion from the guy behind the counter, an older man with an actual handlebar mustache and an enormous white cowboy hat, tight jeans, and a flannel shirt tucked behind a thick leather belt and shiny oval buckle.

"Kylie, what are we doing here?" I ask, trying to inch away toward the door.

She just laughs. "Oh, don't be a sissy, Oz. We're buying you a pair of cowboy boots."

I snort. "The fuck we are. For one thing, I don't have the money for boots, and for another thing, hell, no. I'm not wearing cowboy boots. What about me says I would ever wear something like *that?*" I point at a pair of boots. They're black with orange and red flames, gaudy and dizzyingly bright. "Or those?" These are silver, actual snakeskin, with metal scroll-work at the toe and heel.

Kylie just waves at me. "Of course you wouldn't wear those. We've got to find something that suits you."

"Um, newsflash, sweetness: you ain't gonna find it here." I stuff my hands in my pockets and stop in place, refusing to follow her farther into the store.

She keeps going, perusing the selection. At the far end of the store, she seems to find something, and hustles back to me, a box in hand. "Sit." She pushes me backward until a bench hits my knees, and I sit automatically. "Shoes off."

I cross my arms over my chest. "No."

She lifts an eyebrow. "Okay, be stubborn. But you know you can't say no to me."

"No. No. No." I fake a glare. "See?"

"Doesn't mean you're going to *really* say no. Now, boots off, or I'll take 'em off you for you."

"What am I, three?"

She lifts both shoulders. "Well, yeah. You are sort of acting like a three-year-old about this." I just stare at her, and she huffs in irritation. "Just look at them, would you?" She opens the box and hands me a boot.

It is pretty cool, actually. It's more of a biker boot, square-toed, black, with a strap of black leather running over the top and around the heel, buckled at either side with chunky silver.

"Goddamn it, Kylie." I glance at the small white price tag sticker with the ***$300*** scrawled on it. "No way. No way I can afford those. They're not bad, but no."

Kylie kneels in front of me, grabs my foot, and reaches for the laces. "Who said I was letting you buy them?" She tugs my combat boot off, and for some reason, I let her. "Oz, please. Just try the boots on."

I sigh. "Fine. But you're not paying for them."

"Yes, I am. We fucking killed it, Oz. I'm proud of you."

I stop with my foot partway into the boot. "You're proud of me?" I'm not sure whether I'm pissed off at the implication of condescension, or pleased. A little of both.

Kylie glances up at me; my mixed reaction must show on my face, because she says, "Not like…god, that sounds condescending, doesn't it? I'm just…I'm happy you did it. I had fun. And I know you were as nervous as me, and you did it anyway."

I stomp my foot into the boot, and then the other foot, and I hate the fact that they're the most comfortable boots I've ever worn. "I get what you mean. And thanks."

"How do they feel?"

I lift an eyebrow. "Expensive. Really fucking expensive."

"But good, right?"

I sigh. "Yeah. Comfortable as hell. But you're not—" I'm cut off by Kylie taking the box up to the counter and whipping out her debit card before I can blink twice.

I watch helplessly as she signs away three hundred dollars and then returns to me, shoves my old battered boots into the box, and grins at me.

"Am too," she says, with a shit-eating grin.

"Kylie—"

She takes me by the hand, and I let her lead me out of the store. The boots are really, *really* comfortable, and they look badass. When we're on the street, she shoves me against the wall between the store and a bar, and presses into me. "Just say thank you, Oz. It's a gift. It's me repaying you for giving *me* the best night of my life. Performing? With you? It was magical. It's not charity, it's not because you can't afford it. It's because I want to see you in a pair of badass biker boots. It's because I want to. Because I can. It's a thank-you. And it's a 'please, please will you gig with me again?' bribe."

I can't help but let my hands wrap around her back, resting just above her hips. "Kylie." I let my forehead touch hers. "Fuck, you're impossible."

She smiles at me, her lips nearing mine. "I know. It's a talent."

"One of many." I kiss her, and even on a crowded city street, I feel my resolve wavering.

I've refused to sleep with her thus far. I want to, and she wants to, but…I just won't. She's waited. She's still a few weeks from her eighteenth birthday, and she's a virgin. I'm…not. Decidedly not. Very much not. She thinks she wants her first time to be with me, but she deserves more. She deserves romance. Love. And I'm not sure I can give her that. I like her. I appreciate who she is. Her talents. Her beauty. Her innocence. And it's for all those reasons that I keep pushing her away, keep telling her no, keep ripping myself away from her when all I want to do is bury myself in her, kiss her and never stop, strip her naked and leave her limp and breathless and ruined for anyone else but me.

But I can't. I'm not that guy. Not for her.

Yet she perseveres, refuses to take no for an answer, thinks she can outwait me. Seduce me. And fuck, she just might be right.

The kiss ends, and she's staring up at me, breathless, flushed, panting slightly. Each deep breath swells her amazing, enormous tits in her pale purple sweater, teasing me, tantalizing and tempting me. It's a low-cut sweater, fitted to hug her figure, scooped deep in the front to offer me a mouth-watering expanse of cleavage.

"Oz. Take me to your apartment. *Please*." Her voice is a whisper, a plea.

"No."

She pouts. "Why not? What's wrong with me?"

I groan. "Jesus fuck, Ky. We've been over this a thousand times."

She slides her arms up around my neck, breathes in my ear. I can't take it, can't handle it. The heat of her breath and the scent of her skin are intoxicating, making me forget why I'm no good for her. "You say *I'm* impossible, but you're the idiot who's refusing to take what's offered. What belongs to him."

"It doesn't belong—*you* don't belong to me. It's not—god. Why are we always talking about this?"

"Because I want you." She nips at my earlobe. "And you're frustrating me. Making me mad."

"Good. Get mad. Storm off. Walk away. I'm just doing what's best for you."

She pushes away from me, genuinely pissed now. I follow her, and she ignores me. We near an alley, and she stops abruptly and shoves me into it, a nearly violent move. I stumble, catch my footing, and then she's on me, attacking me, arms like soft silken serpents around my neck, her legs leaving the ground and wrapping around my legs, and I'm hard as a rock in my jeans and holding her by the ass, feeling in my hands the supple muscle barely contained by her tight jeans, feeling her lips on mine, and I'm drunk with her. I can't help it. I'm not a saint. Not a good person. That's my point. I'm not nice and not good, and she's all over me, and I can't resist such a determined assault on my resolve.

I hold her and press her back against the wall, kiss her back and pin her with my hips and let my palms soar over her ass and her hips and her thighs, and I'm breathing her in, sucking her breath into my lungs and devouring her tongue and sampling the wild innocence, the hunger of a virgin who has tasted sin. I'm the poison she thinks she wants, and I'm trying to summon the goodness to save her from me, from herself.

I break away, let her slide to the ground. She's shaking, barely able to stand up, and I'm weak in the knees, too, but I step away from her.

"How dare you tell me what's best for me?" She's furious; the kiss was an angry one. She puts her fingers to her lips, as if to feel the imprint of my mouth on hers. "You make your own decisions in life, Oz. You're your own person. No one tells you what to do. Well, what if I want that same freedom? I've always done what my parents want. What I know is good and safe and right. I've been a good girl because I love them and want them to be proud of me. And yeah, that's still true. But you want to know something? I didn't stay a virgin for *them*. I didn't save my virginity for *their* sake. I waited for my *own* reasons. I've waited for the right guy for *me*. Because I've heard stories and watched my friends pair off and get laid. Some of them regret it, some don't. Some felt pressured, some didn't. And I knew I wanted to choose my own time, with someone I cared about. Someone who cared about me. It doesn't have to be *love*. I'm young. I'll be eighteen in two weeks. I have my whole life to find the kind of love Mom and Dad have, or their friends, Jason and Becca, have. I don't expect that of you. If you feel that way about me, I would—I would be so happy. So happy. Because I think you're amazing, and I could see us having that together. I really could, Oz. But it doesn't have to be that. Not yet, or not ever. I know you have your own plans. I know you're gonna leave Nashville eventually, and I won't ever try to keep you here, no matter what.

But I still want my first time to be with you. That's what I want. And you know something?" She wraps her arms around her middle and stares at me from three feet away. People pass by on the sidewalk just beyond us, and cars rush by honking their horns, and from everywhere there's the sound of music playing, a cacophony of competing bands. "I think you're scared. Of me. I think you're telling yourself you're protecting me from yourself, but in reality, you're just scared because I make you feel things you don't understand."

"Kylie—"

"NO! I'm not done." She steps forward, eyes so hot and blazing that I can't look away. She's hypnotic when she's mad. "You and I? It may end badly. I may get hurt. But guess what? I don't care! I've never had my heart broken. Maybe I'm fine with risking it, because it's better than being afraid and going through life bored. I have friends. I have Ben. I have my parents. But none of them have ever challenged me to feel new things. I've never had to risk anything. I've never risked being hurt. I'm going into this with you, *knowing* you're bad for me, according to you. Yeah, Oz, I get it, you're a bad boy. You're a drifter. You kick ass and take names and ride a hog. You're all those stereotypes. Got it. I'm not trying to change you. I just want a piece of you."

I lean back against the wall behind me, wondering what the hell I'm supposed to say. I'm a stereotype? That bugs me a little.

The fact remains, though, that I don't want to hurt her. She doesn't know about heartbreak, or she wouldn't be talking about it so casually.

"All right, you know what?" I take a step toward her. "I don't want to talk about this here. You want to talk about this? Then let's go. Take us to my place."

She doesn't speak, just whirls on her heel and storms back to the car. I follow her, watching her ass move in her jeans and watching the tense set to her shoulders, and wondering what the hell I'm going to say when we get there, because I have no idea. She's right. So right. It should be her choice. And I am afraid.

The ride to my apartment is silent. The radio is off, and Kylie is chewing on the inside of her cheek, mad and tense and I don't even know what else. I'm confused, and nervous, and trying to figure out what I think, and what I really want, and what I'm afraid of, and why she makes me feel things I've never felt before, and what to do about it.

I keep her close to me as we go in, and I lock my bedroom door and sit down, dig a cigarette out and light it, and wait for Kylie to clear a space on my bed, shoving dirty jeans and T-shirts aside. It's a mess in here, but she doesn't seem to care.

I blow a smoke ring, and then bat my hand through it. "Ky, look. You're right about a lot of things. About me. About how I'm scared of what you make me feel. Yeah, I am. Maybe I'm being a fucking sissy about this, but…it's more than that. Being scared of how much and how intensely I feel for you. I've never been as close to anyone as I am to you. And it's more than that. You want some truth? I'll give it to you." This is going to be cruel. "I'm not a virgin, okay? I think you know that. My first time was in ninth grade. Biloxi, Mississippi. A Cuban girl named Nina. She was two years older than me, and she was…experienced. She wanted me, so she made sure I wanted her back. It wasn't hard. We got blazed, and she kissed me, and started touching me, and that was that. She was my first, but she wasn't my last. And since then sex, for me, is just….a girl who knows what's up. We smoke a joint or two, we bang, and go our separate ways. Nothing else."

Kylie blanches. "A girl who knows what's up, huh?" She sounds bitter, hurt. "What's that mean?"

"That it ain't gonna be more than what it is. That I ain't gonna stick around or talk about feelings. No complications. Just a quick fuck."

She flinches at my words, keeps her eyes cast down. "So sex has never meant anything to you?"

"Nope."

"Have you ever…been in love?"

I laugh. "Yeah, actually. Once. Senior year of high school in Atlanta. Amy Peretti. Upper-middle-class white girl, not popular, not a loner. Pretty, but not gorgeous. But she was…nice. Really nice. We were chemistry lab partners, and we ended up hanging out here and there. Never sat with her for lunch or hung out with her friends, but she'd talk to me in the hallways. We met at the mall once. Just walked around and talked. She was the first person who ever…saw me for me, I guess. Saw past the fact that I was the new guy, saw past the fact that I was always in detention and getting suspended for fighting and all that. I liked her. By the end of the year, I was convinced I was in love with her. Started making excuses to see her. Finally got up the nerve to ask her out on a date. Had fucking roses and shit." I swallow hard, trying to tell the story without reliving it. "I got her alone in the hall after school, by my locker. Handed her the roses, and asked her if she'd go out with me. She just stared at me, surprised, panicked, even. I can hear her, remember every word. "Oh, god, Oz. I'm sorry. I thought you understood that we're just friends. You're nicer than most people realize, but…no, I couldn't ever date you. Sorry.' And then she walked away, and that was that. It was two weeks before the end of the year. I skipped the rest. Had to take summer classes, but there was no way I could go back and see her. It hurt, Kylie. The look in her eyes. The surprise. The pity. Like…how could someone like me ever even *think* I'd be good enough for someone like her? The worst part was…she wasn't mean about it. She didn't laugh or make fun of me, and I don't think she ever told anyone I'd asked her out. But she just…seemed so surprised that I'd even think of it. Like it was obvious all we'd ever be was friends. She gave the roses back." I laugh again, bitterly, angrily. "Thirty bucks, wasted. I gave 'em to the secretary in the main office."

Kylie takes my cigarette from me, which I've held without smoking while I talked, so the ash is long and dangling. She holds it over the ashtray, taps the filter gently, and we both watch the quarter-inch of gray ash topple down and lose shape. "That's…shitty. And sad." She puts the filter to her lips and inhales, and I hate the fact that she doesn't cough as she pulls the smoke into her lungs, holds it briefly, and blows it out through her nose. She doesn't smoke without me, and never smokes a whole one, just a hit or two, but it's enough. I haven't touched pot when I'm around her since that one time, and I'm determined to keep to that. "Oz, I'm not her. I'm not like her."

I shake my head and take the cigarette from her. "I know, sweetness. That's not what it's about."

"Then what is it?" She pivots on her ass and crosses her legs to sit Indian-style facing me. "I really don't understand. I mean, do you really think you're not good enough for me?"

I sigh. "God, you make it sound like I have self-esteem issues. I don't. I know who I am, and I'm good with it." I gesture at my room. "This is my life, Kylie. It's probably all I'll ever have. Shitty apartments in the shitty, ghetto end of town. I can't give you…anything. Not for a long time, if ever. I mean, let's say I am as talented as y'all seem to think, and I manage to get a record deal or something. It would be years and years of work to get there, to get noticed. And in the meantime, my life would be beans and rice and Ramen noodles and one-room shitholes in neighborhoods that sound like war zones. Maybe I will amount to something in my life. I do want more than this, Kylie. I do. But I can't give you more than this. And I'm not a stupid kid, okay? I know just…being hot for each other, even being in love isn't enough to take care of someone. It won't pay the bills. It won't provide food and rent, much less the kind of life you're used to, the kind of life you deserve." I squeeze my eyes shut and feel the cherry on the cigarette nearing my fingertips. I welcome the burgeoning heat. "So, no, Ky. It's not about me not being good enough. It's about you. You being worth more."

My skin is being singed by the cigarette, and I let it happen. It doesn't count as burning, because I'm not doing it intentionally. It's just a side benefit of not caring if I get a little burnt.

"Goddamn it, Oz." I feel the cigarette being taken away. I don't open my eyes, but I can feel her gaze on me. So blue, so hot, so conflicted and angry and needy. "My worth isn't for you to determine. My future isn't for you to decide. I don't care about any of that. What if I told you I'd be willing to live in one-room shitholes? That I'd learn to live in neighborhoods that sound like war zones and eat Ramen and Kraft mac and cheese and whatever. That I'd be willing to live that way if it meant I could be with you. What if I said all that would be worth it? Does it sound fun? No. Do I *want* that? No, not really. But I *do* want you."

I feel her hand on my thigh. I wince at the twinge of the still-healing wound, and then I feel the mattress dip as she leans forward, slides one leg over mine. Feel her straddle me. The slight ache of her weight on my thigh isn't enough to make me move her off me. Her palms cup my cheeks, and I hate how much I cherish the feel of her tender touch, how right it feels. I hate it, because it makes it so much harder to pretend I don't desperately want her. Need her. Yearn for her. That I wouldn't give everything to have her in my life, every day, every way. That I wouldn't tell her all my secrets, and show her all my scars, and share all my sins and shadows. She already knows more about me than anyone. She's seen me burn myself, and seen me smoke pot and seen me break bones. The only secret she doesn't know is how desperately I need to know who my father was, and what happened to him and if I'm like him, if he was a good person or a fuck-up or a thug or a loser or a rich yuppie or just an average guy. Why he left me. Why he couldn't stick around long enough for me to know him. Why he couldn't be my father and why Mom is so fucked up about him. No one knows how deeply into my psyche and into my soul that need is tangled.

She's sitting on me, holding my face. Waiting. I open my eyes, and I'm seared by the vulnerability in her bluebluebue eyes. She's begging me and pleading with me, silently, and with razor-sharp precision. Her knees are at my hips, her thighs strong and tight in her skinny jeans. Her breathing is harsh and ragged, her hands trembling on my skin. Her hair is a fall of sunset-copper rivulets and loose spirals, and her skin is pale as porcelain and dotted with freckles across her nose and on her cleavage, and I want to kiss each freckle, count each one across every inch of her flesh. I suddenly understand how sex can mean something. Before it just felt good. It's given me a bit of distraction from my life and my pain and poverty and questions. The girls have been hot and willing, but our time together has always been momentary, fleeting. Despite being naked, there's never been vulnerability. We both knew we'd never see each other again, and so any imperfections could be ignored, any flaws could be glossed over. I'd be gone within the hour, or she was. With Kylie, it wouldn't be that. It *couldn't* be that. We've exchanged too many truths. Seen too much of each other's soft and easily damaged inner selves. I've shown her who I am, beneath the metal shirts and the tattoos and the cursing and violence.

She's seen that I'm just a guy, nothing special.

Yet here she is, wanting me, and refusing to let me protect her from me. Acting like I *am* something special.

Kylie's eyes burn into mine, and my mind and heart and soul are all giving in, telling me that she's right. Who am I to decide what's best for her, what's wrong for her? If she wants me, wants who I am, why should I deny her myself? I lick my lips and prepare to say this, but she beats me to it.

"Oz, I've thrown myself at you. I want you. I care about you. I feel things for you that are powerful and confusing and scary, and I'm not holding them back. I'm here, and I'm telling you I want you for you, for who you are, *as* you are. But I can't keep getting rejected. So I'll put myself out there one more time." Her eyes are scared, her breathing coming in long, deep swells. Her hands shake, and her eyes waver as they search me. "Don't deny me again, Oz. Don't tell me I'm not old enough, or that you're not good enough. Because…if you don't want me, then I'll go. If you're too scared to be with me, to be with me *for real,* no matter what anyone thinks, I'll leave you alone. I can't just be friends with you anymore. I want too much more than that. So tell me what you want, Oz."

She takes her hands off of my face, sits back so she's on her haunches and my legs. Shakes her hair back, out of the way. I'm frozen, speechless, mesmerized. Her beauty is too much for me. Sculpted features and fiery hair to match her personality and skin, fair and perfect and soft, a body to kill for, to die for. Talent to rule the world, passionate, and here with me. With *me. Wanting* me. God, she's demanding all of me. And I don't know how to deny her.

I'm going to hurt her, someday, somehow. I know it. And yet I can't seem to refuse her.

She wipes her hands on her thighs, and then crosses her arms around her middle. Grasps the hem of her sweater. "Tell me to leave, Oz. Tell me you don't want this. Tell me again you don't deserve this." Then, slowly, she lifts her sweater, revealing a sliver of white skin and the round dip of her navel. God, my heart is pounding at that tiny glimpse of flesh. "Stop me, Oz. If you're not in this with me for real, stop me. I'm not going to give this to you if you're not all the way in with me. But I want you. And I believe you want me. You're scared of yourself, but I'm not. So this is your last chance, Oz. Grab my hands and stop me, because if you don't, you're mine. And I'm yours, and whatever else happens, we'll have something beautiful and perfect, and it'll mean something, for as long as it lasts."

My ability to speak is shattered, ruined. She's drawing her sweater off slowly. It's just beneath her bra now, her ribs showing with each deep breath. I can't speak, but I can't deny her. I can't tell her to stop. I can't send her away. Because I *do* feel things. And, yeah, I'm scared of myself. I'm scared that I'll never get out of shitty apartments, that I'll be like Mom, living paycheck to paycheck, never aspiring to anything, traveling a thousand miles and never going anywhere. I'm scared I'll do something stupid and end up in jail, or dead. Grow up living in a dozen different ghettos, you learn to fear that. You watch the ambulances show up and cop cars skid to a stop and watch guys disappear into the system, or into the morgue, and you wonder if that's gonna be you. And I don't want that. Not for me, and sure as shit not for Kylie. Can I be more? Maybe. Hopefully.

But now, none of that matters. All that matters is the girl sitting on my lap, straddling me, lifting her sweater up slowly in a deliberate striptease, daring me to reject her yet again, knowing I can't.

My throat is dry, shut tight. My heart is a double-kick drum in my chest, and my hands are curling around her thighs, sliding up to her waist, to the pale skin. Her eyes widen, and her nostrils flare and the fear in her eyes ratchets to something approaching panic, but she doesn't stop. My palms slide over her skin and up, thumbs tracing her ribs and the hint of black underwire.

"Oz?" Now she's stopped, the sweater lodged on her chest, at the threshold of following through or covering up. "What do you want?"

I have to speak. She deserves to hear it. "You." It's whispered, rasped, but she hears it.

Her arms lift, her back straightens, and now the pale purple sweater is up and off and her hair is streaming through the opening, falling to sway against her back. I'm blinking, barely breathing. My hands skate up her sides, roam around to trace her spine. Her head is bowed, her eyes closed, her nerves taking over. She's trembling. She needs reassurance.

"You're beautiful, Kylie." The words barely make it past my lips, but she hunches her shoulders as they pelt her. "So beautiful. The kind of gorgeous that needs words we don't have."

She forces her eyes open, and I can see unshed tears glistening. "I'm scared, Oz. Now that I'm here, with my shirt off, I'm scared."

"Then put your shirt back on, sweetness. There's no rush. I'm not going anywhere."

She sniffs, shakes her head, and wipes beneath her eyes with her two middle fingers. "No. I'm not scared because I'm topless. I'm scared because…what if we do this, and it's not what I think it is? What if you're just…playing me? What if you get what you want from me, and then you leave? What if…what if…so many what-ifs, Oz. I don't believe any of them, but they're still there, and they're scaring me."

"If I was going to take what I wanted from you and leave, I would've done it a long time ago."

"I know," she says. "I believe you. It's just…all these things are in my head suddenly, now that being with you is on the verge of becoming a reality."

"What else is in your head?"

She lifts one shoulder, a tiny, unsure shrug. "So much. What if I'm no good? What if I don't know what to do? What if I'm too scared to go through with it? What if you don't like it with me? I've never done any of this before, and you have. With girls who knew what they were doing. I don't. They probably weren't so scared they're shaking, but I am."

"If you're that scared, Kylie, then let's wait. Just… wait." *Wait till you're eighteen,* I think, but don't say it.

"No. I don't want to. I'm scared of disappointing you, that's all."

I have to laugh at that. "Jesus, Kylie. You couldn't. And…what we're doing? It's not like anything I've ever done before. I care about you, and I want to be everything you think I am. And I want…if we're going to do this, then I want it to be everything you've hoped it could be, and I'm not sure how to give you that. So…I'm just as nervous as you."

"How are you nervous? You know what comes next."

I shake my head. "No, I don't. Caring about you, caring how you feel, that's new for me. I've always been…selfish. And so was whoever I was with. It was just…taking. I want to…to give something to you. Give everything to you." I blink hard and suck in the truth with a deep breath. "I don't have much to give, but what I do have, I want to give to you."

This brings a smile to her lips and to her eyes. "That's all I need, Oz." She reaches forward and tugs the hem of my shirt up. "That, and to see more of you."

"I could probably manage that much." I lift my arms, and my shirt flies across the room.

Her eyes rake over me, as if she can't get enough of what she sees. I know the feeling. I let my hands slide up her spine, hover over the strap of her bra. I hesitate there, questioning with my expression. Her chin lifts, the corner of her mouth curls up in a smile, and she takes the button of my jeans in her fingers, flicks it open, and then pinches the tab of my zipper between thumb and forefinger. She waits then, and I know this game. I pull the ends of her bra strap together, feel the clasps loosen, and she pulls the zipper down. I feel my cock going rigid, pressing up against the elastic of my boxers. Her eyes lock on the fabric of my boxers, visibly tented. I swallow hard, and free the first eyelet on her bra. Tug, free the second. Meet her eyes, and let the third and final clasp fall open. The strap hangs at her sides, dangles from her shoulders, and I reach up, brush it off and down her arms. She lets it fall, sets it aside. I can tell she's fighting the instinct to cross her arms over her chest, but she doesn't. My cock goes from rock-hard to painfully hard.

It's hard to swallow, hard to breathe. So beautiful, so perfect. Round and high and firm, big, Jesus, so big. Dark pink areolae, thick nipples, begging to be touched. I can't help but reach up and gingerly, reverently, cup one of her breasts, drag my thumb across her nipple and feel the way she twitches as the pad of my thumb brushes her sensitive skin. She blinks hard, bites her lip, and then arches her back. Pushing into my touch. Wanting more. I'm leaning against the wall, a pillow scrunched behind my back, and she's sitting on me, tall and nervous and the sexiest thing I've ever seen. I run my hand over her diaphragm, the "V" between thumb and forefinger sliding under the heavy weight of one of her boobs. I lift it, holding the soft perfect globe in my hand, kneading, pinching her nipple gently.

"God, Oz. I really like that." She's barely breathing, eyes closed, lip caught between her teeth.

"Not as much as I do, I can guarantee you that," I say.

I lean forward, totally giving in now, and I vow to make her feel so good, so free, so perfect, that she'll never forget this night as long as she lives, that she'll never forget how good I made her feel. I don't care if I get nothing out of it, if she goes limp and falls asleep, sated, before she touches me. My lips touch the upper swell of her cleavage, and then I press a series of small, hot kisses to her warm satin flesh. Her hand rests on my shoulder, and her nails dig gently into the muscle as my lips near the peak of her breast. She's not breathing at all now, and my tongue slides and slips around the circumference of her areola. I can't make myself wait any longer. I suck her nipple into my mouth and groan at the taste of her, and she's gasping, clawing at me.

"Shit, Oz. Holy shit."

I move to the other tit and give it the same attention, hot wet kisses down the slope, tongue flicking out, and draw her erect, diamond-hard nipple into my mouth and taste her perfection.

She abruptly remembers that she too has hands, and that I'm still mostly clothed. Her fingers fumble at my belly, finding the partly open fly, and she lowers the zipper the rest of the way. I struggle with my boots, toe them off, and then she's pulling down on my pants while trying to keep upright with her tits in my face. She wants to be everywhere at once. I do, too. I want to strip her jeans off and see the rest of her, caress the marvelous glory that is her ass. But I'm not there yet. I'm still paying homage to the perfection of her tits, kissing and holding and fondling and lifting and running my tongue all over her flesh.

Somehow we get my jeans down around my hips and I'm kicking them off, and Kylie is moaning softly, gripping my thighs and staring up at me, sliding her palm across my belly and inching lower. This is going so fast, and I want to slow it down, I want to enjoy her, I want to make her feel everything, give her every ounce of pleasure I can, for as long as I can.

"Kylie…god, you taste so good." I whisper this to the space between her tits, cupping both of them. "I could spend hours here, just kissing your tits."

"I wouldn't complain."

"But there's more. I want to see more of you. Kiss more of you." I lean into her, wrap my arms around her and twist, taking her to the mattress. "I want to kiss you everywhere and never, ever stop." I don't know this me; I don't know who this is saying such things.

It's the kind of thing she deserves to hear, the kind of thing I'd never thought I'd hear myself say, but yet my lips let the words tumble out, and I wonder who I'm becoming, here in this room with Kylie. I like him, this guy she brings out of me. I like the tenderness her sweet naked skin elicits in me. I've never been like this, never felt such intense emotions. Emotions I don't want to burn away.

Now she's spread out beneath me, her hair a fiery halo on my pillow, her eyes twin azure novae blazing and burning and piercing me with such innocent trust and not-so-innocent hunger and oh-so-seductive desire. I open the button of her jeans, keeping my eyes on her, watching for any slightest sign of demurral or refusal. There is none. Only willingness to help. She lifts her hips and lets me pull the skin-tight denim past her thighs, and her tongue runs over her lips, her eyes going wider than ever as her jeans join the pile of clothing beside my bed. God, she's beyond perfect. Black panties to match her bra, a tiny scrap of lace and silk.

"God, Kylie. How am I supposed to breathe when you're so beautiful?" I run my hands down her sides and over her hips, the generous curves so soft beneath my palms.

"Don't have—don't have to breathe," she gasps. "I'll breathe for us both."

She clutches at my neck and pulls me down, and our mouths slam together, teeth clashing and tongues tangling, and her hands carve over my taut shoulders and down my back and I'm gone, lost, abandoned to the way she touches me, the way no one has ever touched me before. Her palms arc over my hard hips, and now she's catching at the waistband of my boxers with hooked fingers. I choke on my own nerves, on my own desire to feel her touch me all over. Our breath is lost, drowned, halted. I pull away from the kiss and see her open eyes slipping down my chest, looking up at me briefly, then raking back down. She watches her fingers run around the elastic to stop an inch on either side of my navel. Her knuckles are against my skin, and I'm throbbing, aching. Her eyes meet mine again and I nod, knowing she's asking, as I did. Her teeth catch her lower lip, bite down so the plump flesh turns white. I'm frozen in place, a statue, waiting for her. She takes a deep breath, and her chest swells. I feel the elastic move, and she's pulling my boxers away from my waist, tugging them down. My heart pounds, and I'm truly nervous, afraid for this in a way I wasn't my first time.

Shitshitshit. I'm exposed now, hard and thick and throbbing and aching and bare to her sight. I watch her eyes go round, flick up to mine and back down. I don't move, don't breathe. I want to know what she's thinking, but words are completely impossible.

My boxers are around my knees, so I lift up and kick them away, totally naked now. Never has nudity been so vulnerable. She sees the real me, all the way down into my soul, and I feel like all my flaws are on display. But her expression is one of wonder and surprise and a little hint of nerves.

"Holy shit." She looks into my eyes, and I see that she's unsure what to say. "I—you're beautiful, Oz." She blushes, and her eyes go back down to my cock. "Really beautiful."

"Say anything, Kylie. Say everything. Embarrassing, crazy, weird, say it all." I know there's more inside her, things she's not sure she should say.

"It's bigger than I expected. I mean, I've seen pictures, and…videos. But you…here, *real*…it's different." Her eyes flick up to mine. "I'm going to touch you."

"Okay."

I'm on my hands and knees above her, and I watch her hand splay against the trail of hair at my navel, follow it down, and then she's grasping me in her fist, her eyes wide and her lips parted slightly. Her hand is small and soft and pale against my skin, and she's just holding me, her eyes going from my face to my cock. Then her fist slides down, and back up, and I'm the one shaking, trembling.

"God, Kylie. You don't know how good that feels."

She smiles at me. "I like the way you feel. Soft, but hard. Your skin is…hot. And *you're* hot. All over."

I have to remember to breathe. "You'd better stop, or this'll be over all too soon."

She just grins. "I wouldn't care. I could just touch you. Feel you touch me. Kiss me. Hold me."

But I'm not quite ready to embarrass myself that way, so I pull away, out of her grip, and grit my teeth, clamping down with all my strength. And then I lower my face to her flesh, kiss her ribs, down her side, to the elastic of her panties. Curl my fingers in the waistband and kiss her navel below it, going farther. She's panting, making little sounds in her throat, and I want those tiny noises, want to hear them louder, so I peel her panties down around her hips, baring the upper swell of her cleft. As I touch her, she reaches out and takes my ponytail in her hand, slides the band off and shakes my hair loose. I feel even more naked with my hair down, for some reason. She runs her fingers through my hair, and again I'm rocked senseless by the gentle power of her touch. I nudge my face into her hand, kiss her palm, and then return my attention to her body. Her underwear is partly off, so I draw it down past her thighs, and she squeezes her legs together, eyes closing, nerves rampant in every tense line and curve of her body.

"Hey." I let my hands roam up her torso to cup her breasts, and then up farther to brush her cheeks. "It's okay. We can stop, if you—"

She shakes her head. "No! No. I've just…I'm just nervous."

"Me, too," I tell her.

She opens her eyes. Looks at me, swallows. "Take them off."

I pull back and tug the black fabric past her knees, past her feet, and toss them aside. She blinks twice, hard, takes a deep breath, and forces her legs to relax. "You're beautiful everywhere, Kylie."

I put my hands on her thighs, just above her knees. Slide my palms forward, over the smooth curves of her thighs, nearing the apex, where she's as lovely and perfect as everywhere else. Pale skin, taut and tight, plump lips damp with the moisture of desire, slight haze of curls, the same color as the hair on her head. She's watching me, her hands curled into fists by her hips, clutching the sheet. I caress her thighs again, and then let my touch roam over her navel, down, down. She tenses, but her thighs remain apart, granting me access, letting me look and letting me touch. She wants this, I can see it in her eyes, but she's nervous. I let my middle finger slide down her cleft, and she inhales sharply.

"Oh, god, Oz. Do that again." Her eyelids flutter, lock on me. "Touch me again."

I drag my middle finger down her crease again, feeling the slick wet essence coat my finger. I lie down beside her, on her left, so she's between me and the wall. She's gazing at me, reaches for my face and meets me for a kiss. As our tongues flick and slide, I dip my finger into her, eat her gasp of surprise and pleasure. My cock is brushing her hip, and she reaches between us, takes me in her hand, caresses me, and now it's my turn to sigh and groan as her palm rolls over the tip, making me judder and push into her touch. I wet my finger in her juices and then slide the tip of my middle finger up to her clit and stroke around it, over it. She writhes as I do this, gasps into my mouth, and her grip on my cock tightens. I groan, and she loosens her fist. A circle, slow and deliberate, and then I slide my finger into her channel and explore her inner walls, bring my touch back to her clit, and circle again. This time, her hips lift in rhythm with the circular slide of my finger. Again, a little faster, and again, and now her mouth falls open away from mine and she's moaning, lifting and writhing.

"Oz…Oz…god, that feels so good. It feels like… like I'm gonna—oh, shit, yes, just like that—like I could just go crazy. Blow up. Come apart." She's mumbling, rambling, and it's so hot.

"Keep talking, Kylie. Tell me what you want. Tell me what you like."

She runs a hand up her ribs and clutches her breast, fingers clawed into the supple flesh. "Kiss me here again."

I lean over her and flick her nipple with my tongue, then gently saw my teeth across it. She gasps, arches, and I suckle her into my mouth. My finger is moving inside her, dipping and circling, keeping her hips writhing, slowing and speeding, and she's gasping, groaning. But she's not going over the edge, and there's one more thing I want her to feel, one more way to make her go crazy and lose all control.

I kiss her ribs, her side, her hip, beneath her navel.

"Oz? What—what are you doing?" She sounds almost panicked.

"Remember when I said I'd kiss you everywhere?"

"Yeah?" she breathes.

"*Every*where." I kiss the inside of her thigh, breathe out on her pale flesh, and then kiss the hot wet flesh of her cleft, and she whimpers.

"God, Oz. There? Oh, god." Her hands curl into my hair, and I know she's completely and totally sold to this, eager for everything and anything when she brushes my hair out of my face and holds it out of the way.

I lick between her lips, tasting her essence, and then lick again, stiffening my tongue to slide in, a slow penetration. Kylie groans, a low, protracted sound, and her fists tighten in my hair. I lick up her opening again and again, and each time she gasps or groans or whimpers. Then, with just the very tip of my tongue, I swirl around her clit, and she shudders violently. So close, so close. I reach up with one hand and explore her breast, find her nipple and roll it between my fingers, and now she's shaking all over, her stomach tensed and her breathing ragged.

"I can't—I can't take it, Oz, it's too much! I feel like I'm going to explode. *Fuck,* Oz! Don't stop. Please…"

I glance up, and she's got one hand in her own hair, pulling as she arches, and the other is cupping the back of my head, keeping me buried between her legs, as if I'd ever stop. I lick and circle, pinch and twist, and she's bucking into me, moaning, and I feel her entire body shuddering, and yes, now, now, I feel her entire body lift off the bed and she's shrieking loud through gritted teeth. Jesus fuck, she's sexy when she comes. She lights up. Glows. And god, does she taste good. She shivers and judders with every swipe of my tongue, and finally she pushes me away, pulls me up, and I lie beside her, watching her tremble, her hair mussed and tangled across her face.

I brush a lock aside and smile down at her. "Hi."

She blinks up at me, and her mouth falls open, her eyes searching me. "What—what did you just do to me? And can you do it every single moment of every day for the rest of my life?"

I feel intensely, powerfully, all-consumingly proud of how thoroughly flushed and limp and shocked she is. I'm possessive, needy. I'm in so deep now. So far gone. "I made you come, sweetness. And yes, I sure can."

I'm surprised at my own words. Stunned might be more accurate. Did I really just say I'd spend every moment of our lives making her come? 'Cause that implies a lifetime spent together. There's a whole hell of a lot subtly implied in that promise.

Her hooded eyes rove from my face, down to my chest, and farther down to my painfully rigid cock. "I want to make you feel that way." She rolls toward me, her hair falling around her face, and pushes on my shoulder. "I swear I saw the stars, Oz. It felt like you broke open my soul and let heaven into my body."

"You should put that in a song," I say.

"I will." She kisses my shoulder, presses her body flush against the length of mine, sends her palm skating down my chest to my stomach, slides her hand flat against my skin beneath my cock. "Later."

She wraps her hand around my erection, and lazily slides her fist up my length, twists at the tip, and plunges back down. I hiss through my teeth, watching her hand on me. We're both watching her touch me, and the expression on her face is one of excited disbelief, like she can't believe she's really here, really doing this, with me. I know the feeling. I'm kind of lost in the wonder of it all, too. But then all that fades away as her slowly, gently sliding hand on my cock brings me to groaning, arching splendor. Nothing has ever felt so good as this. Just her hand, her fingers and her palm, rising and falling, twisting and sliding and gripping, her soft skin on mine, her lips touching my shoulder and smiling a tiny, private smile as I start to buck up into her touch.

"Kylie, you better stop, or I'm gonna lose it."

"So?"

"Oh, god, Kylie. Shit, the way you touch me… it's—it's fucking magic." I lick my lips and try to push away the impending release. "So, I thought we were gonna—oh god, oh god—" I can't make any more sense, can't control the ache in my balls and the need to move and the need to let go.

"I'm not in a hurry, Oz. I want this. I want to watch you come. All this is new territory for me, and

I'm enjoying this, touching you like this." She's mumbling this, almost absently, more focused on me, on her fingers wrapped around my aching cock.

I'm boiling, my balls are heavy and tight and full, my eyes won't stay open and my breathing is ragged and my body is arching off the bed, my hips thrusting helplessly. She's touching me slowly, exploring. Her goal isn't to make me come, it's to merely touch me, to learn the way my cock feels in her hand, to learn the way I react. It's beautiful torture. Kylie cups the head in her palm, squeezes gently, and then slides her fist down my length. I'm so close, so close.

And then I feel her hair drifting on my chest, feel her face on my stomach. "I feel like I want to kiss you there, like you did to me. I want to taste you."

I should stop her. "Ky—you don't…don't have to do that, just 'cause I did."

She doesn't answer, and I feel her lips kiss the tip of my cock, and I'm holding back, tensed, every muscle iron-hard, teeth grinding together. I feel her tongue touch me, feel her lips wrap around the head, just above the groove, the tip of her tongue sliding along the tiny opening, tasting the leaking pre-come. I can't hold back much longer, and I don't want to come in her mouth. But this feels…beyond amazing. Everything she does, every touch, every kiss of her lips takes me further and further into bliss. I don't want it to ever stop, not ever. I'm shaking, muscles trembling as I strive to hold still and keep the release at bay. She's holding me by the root, her mouth hot and wet around the head of my cock, and she's kissing, tasting, licking, as if I'm some kind of treat, licking and sucking and sliding her lips all over me as if I'm ice cream.

"I can't—*fuck*—I can't hold it anymore, Ky." I growl it, the words grating and rasping in my throat and my teeth. "I'm about to come, Ky."

Her mouth leaves me, and the selfish part of me wants it back, wants to explode in the warm wetness of her mouth. But I won't. Not yet, not until she's ready for that, and I know she's not. This is more about her exploring, discovering. I feel my spine arch off the mattress, my hands fisted in the sheets at my sides, fighting to keep it back, hold it back. Her soft small warm hands both wrap around my cock and slide up and plunge down, slowly and gently, and I want it faster and harder but she doesn't give me that—she continues the slow and lazy drifting from root to tip, and it's driving me wild, making me crazy. Her cheek nestles against my hipbone, and I feel her breath on me, and she's watching me writhe and struggle, and now she strokes me in a rhythm, down against my up-thrust, both fists around me, faster now. I force my eyes open, and goddamn is she gorgeous, strawberry blonde, almost red hair vivid against my dark skin and the white sheet, and her wildly blue eyes are locked on my cock in her hands, watching for the moment when I explode.

"Kylie!" It's the only sound I can make as I feel the volcanic detonation unleash.

Heat in my balls, my cock tightening and her hands gripping me and stroking me and her face against my leg, and her hair and her eyes and I'm gone, gone, everything is a hot wash of lightning bliss, and her hands never stop, hot and soft, and I watch her through hooded heavy eyes as she watches me come harder than I've ever come in my life.

I feel the stream of come hit my belly and still she's touching me, and I'm groaning and sighing, and now another blast of release shoots from me, and a final, smaller gush, and then I'm only able to flutter my hips into her touch, never wanting this moment to end.

She moves back up to lie beside me. Her eyes search mine. "Oh…my…*god,* Oz." She covers her face with her hands and burrows into the hollow of my neck, giggling. "That was awesome!"

"I can't—I can't move, Ky. I can't feel my toes. Holy fucking shit. You killed me." I curl my arm around her and hold her close.

"It felt good?" She seems uncertain.

"Good?" I pull her hands down. "Babe, did you see what you did to me? That was…incredible."

She smiles. "Good. I'm glad. I wanted to make you feel as good you made me feel. And…I liked watching you. I liked knowing I was making you feel that way, like…I was…in charge." She blushes, embarrassed. "God, that sounds so stupid."

I laugh. "No, sweetness. It doesn't. Not at all. You *were* in charge. You had total control over me."

"Really?"

I nod. "Absolutely."

She's thinking. "Yeah, I can see that. That's how I felt, when you were—with your mouth. Down there."

I grin. "Oh, come on, Ky. You can do better than that. Don't be shy. Not with me. Not after what we just did together."

"What?" She's bashful, playing innocent.

"Say something dirty. Tell me what I was doing to you. Use the dirtiest words you can think of."

She chews on her lower lip, eyes flicking back and forth on mine. "What is it you want to hear, Oz? You want to hear me say something nasty?"

I nod. "Yeah. It'll be hot."

She shakes her head. "You go first, then. I'm embarrassed."

I snort. "Embarrassed? You just had your hands all over my cock, Kylie. You sucked my cock. You made me come all over myself. I've never done that before, you know, just…lost control."

She blushes, but her eyes go to the come on my stomach. "I love your cock, Oz." She giggles, and then goes serious. "I do, for real. I love the way it feels in my hands. I even like the way it tastes and feels in my mouth. Is that weird?"

I shrug. "Nothing's weird. It is what it is. Everyone's different. I like the way you taste, too, babe. I love the way your pussy tastes."

She blushes even harder and buries her face in my neck. "God, Oz, I'm blushing so hard I'm gonna burst into flames in a second." She peeks up at me, looking at me through her shielded hands. "You really do?"

I nod. "Yeah, I do. A lot."

"What's it taste like?"

I frown. "I don't know how to describe it. Kind of…musky? A little sweet, a little sour. I don't know. That's not right." I slide my finger down to her cleft and swipe through her nether lips, finding her wet again. I drag my finger through her lips again, deeper, letting her essence slick my index finger. Then, with her eyes wide and nervous on mine, I put my finger into my mouth. "Mmmm. Yeah. Tasty. Can't explain the way it tastes, though."

"Oh, my god, Oz. You're so crazy." She blinks at me, grinning.

I slide my finger into her again, and this time I bring it to her lips. "Taste it. Taste yourself."

She locks her eyes on me, and then, with only a slight hesitation, opens her mouth and closes her lips around my finger. Jesus, I feel my cock twitch and tighten at the way she slides her mouth off my finger, erotic, teasing, tempting. Her eyes widen as she tastes herself, and then a smile curves her lips. She puts two fingers to my belly, smearing through the pool of my come, and before I can react, she tastes me on her fingers.

"Mmm. You taste good, too." She licks her lips, and then glances down at my cock. "How long until you can come again?"

I shrug. "Not too long. Sooner, if you touch me."

She laughs. "In that case…"

"Wait a second, though. Let me clean up." I grab a dirty shirt off the floor, but Kylie takes it from me.

"Let me do it." She smiles at me, gentle, hesitant, and sweet.

She wipes at my stomach, folds the fabric and wipes again, once more, and then I'm clean and the shirt is across the room in a ball. And she's touching me, thumb and two fingers holding my still-flaccid cock. But at her touch, I feel myself respond, feel the tightening deep inside. I watch her touch me, and my hands are on her skin, moving over her shoulders, brushing her hair away and sliding down her arm. I cup one of her boobs, touch the nipple and feel it go hard under the pad of my thumb. She grins at me, and strokes my hardening member. We're silent, touching each other, feeling no hurry. I just want to memorize the feel of her skin, her soft pale skin. I want to touch and kiss every inch of her. She looks at me, and I lean in and our lips meet, and now we're truly lost, the kiss flying us up and away. Her hand tightens on my cock, which is nearly fully erect, and my hands are palming her ribs and her tits and cupping her hip, tilting her toward me to finally get a handful of her ass. And oh, god, her ass is so perfect. Firm, full, supple, a wonderland I could never get enough of.

She breaks the kiss and nuzzles my chest. "God, Oz. I seriously love the way you touch me."

I should be afraid of how easily we're both tossing around the word "love," but I'm not. Why, I don't dare examine. But I'm not.

"Kylie, have I mentioned yet how much I love your ass?" I pull her toward me, move out of the way so she rolls to her stomach. I kiss her spine and take a long time to look at her gloriously round ass. I palm it in both hands, knead, grip, caress. "Like, for real."

She sighs. "Really? It's not too big?"

I can't help but laugh. "God, no. Just like your tits. Big and round and perfect, and so fucking gloriously gorgeous I can't even stand it. Every single time we hang out together, it's an ongoing effort to not stare at your ass."

She hides in the crook of her arm. "You aren't very successful at not staring, Oz, I hate to tell you." She glances at me through a tangle of hair. "I've caught you staring so many times, and you know what? I don't mind it. I like it. I like knowing you can't stop looking at me."

"And now that I've seen you naked, seen every perfect inch of you, I'll never be able to stop looking. Or touching."

"You don't have to." She shifts to her side, her hair a messy curtain across her face. "You can touch me whenever you want. You can do what you want. I trust you, Oz."

I brush the hair from her eyes. "Are you sure that's wise?"

She frowns. "Of course. You'd never hurt me."

"Not on purpose."

She puts her hand on my back and pulls me toward her, down to her. "No, not on purpose. And here's the thing, Oz: I know you'll hurt me someday, somehow. That doesn't scare me. Everyone gets hurt. But I'm strong, Oz. I can take it. As long as you're honest and real and you don't flake out on me, or run from me without telling me, nothing can keep me away. Just…just don't ever lie to me. And don't leave me. If you have to go, if for some reason you decide you've had enough of us, or of me, just tell me. Promise me that? It's the only promise I'll ever ask you to make me."

This is serious suddenly. Can I promise her that?

Fuck yeah.

"I promise. No lies. I won't run. I swear."

Her eyes go soft and deep and tender, and full of something that could be the seeds of love. "Does this make us officially a couple?"

"Do you want us to be?"

She nods. "Yes. Do you?"

I have to consider that. Eventually, I nod. "Yeah, I do. And you should know, Kylie. I've never had a girlfriend before. Not anything real, or serious."

This makes her inordinately happy. "I'm your first real girlfriend?"

"First real friend. First real girlfriend. You're my first real anything, sweetness." I sweep the back of my knuckles across her cheekbone. "You're the only real thing in my whole life."

"God, Oz." She seems on the verge of crying, but she doesn't. Instead, she pulls me down for a kiss, pulls me over her so I'm kneeling between her legs. "I want to…be with you. I want to have sex with you. Make love with you. I don't know what to call it, but that's what I want. Right now."

A bolt of reality hits me. "Shit, Kylie. I don't—I don't have any condoms. And you're not on birth control, are you?"

She shakes her head. "No."

I rest my head between her breasts. "We have to wait, then. I can't—I *won't* take any chances with that." And maybe this will be a bit of salvation, holding off on at least full-on sex with her until she's eighteen.

She touches my cheek. "That's okay, Oz. I'm glad you thought of it, because I didn't. All I was thinking of was how good you make me feel."

"After school tomorrow. We'll buy some. And… if you're for real about being with me, you might want to think about getting on birth control. I hate to sound like I'm telling you what to do, and I know it's, like, killing the mood or whatever but—I just want to be careful." I fall to my back beside Kylie.

She takes a moment to collect herself, then rolls to her side. "No, you're right. Will you go with me? To get me on birth control?"

I nod. "Yeah. Of course."

She touches my chest, her hand roaming across my pecs and down to my stomach. "We can do other things, though, right?" She touches one finger to the tip of my rigid cock.

I grin at her. "Yeah, sweetness. We can do anything you want."

"Anything?" she asks. I nod. "Then will you… god, I'm gonna die. Will you do that thing? With your mouth?"

"Say it, and I will."

She bites her lip. "Lick my pussy, Oz. Please?"

I growl, turned on to epic proportions by her erotic words. "Fuck me, Kylie. That's hot. Say it again."

She takes my face in her hands and pushes me downward, sighing as I settle between her thighs. "I want you to make me come with your mouth. I want you to lick my pussy until I explode."

"Then what?" I swipe her opening with my tongue.

"Then?" she gasps as I flick her clit. "Then I'm gonna suck your cock, and I'm going to make you come in my mouth. And I'm going to swallow every drop."

"Holy shit…" I have to remember to breathe. "God, Kylie. You talking like that makes me crazy."

There's no room for words then, no breath, no time. I'm eating her out, driving her wild with my mouth, slipping a finger inside her and feeling her writhe. Her pussy is hot and damp and ready for me, her motions jagged and desperate as I bring her to the brink of orgasm, slow to back her away, and then push her over the edge with two fingers inside her and my tongue circling her clit. She comes around me, her thighs clenching my head and her juices flowing thick and slick and wet. Barely a moment after she's come, Kylie has me on my back and she's got my cock in her mouth and she's working me with her hands, and I'm lost to her control, in thrall to her touch. I give in completely, don't hold back. She takes her time, stroking and licking and sucking and I'm crazy, wild, arching and groaning, and she's loving every second of it, glancing up at me every now and then, joy and pride and excitement on her face as she watches my helpless reactions.

I gasp a warning as I feel my release approaching, and she takes my thick, aching cock in both hands and wraps her lips around my head and sucks with vacuum force, and I explode violently. She's surprised, but she takes it all, her fists plunging on me, her mouth and throat working.

She fumbles for the blanket, tugs it over us, nestles into my shoulder, and murmurs something inaudible. We're floating, drifting. Sleepy, sated, happy.

This moment, here with Kylie Calloway, it's the single best moment of my life.

Eight: Lost Chances and Hard Choices

Colt

IT'S WELL PAST MIDNIGHT, and Kylie isn't home. The open mic night ended hours ago, and I'm fighting the urge to worry, to get angry. She doesn't have a set curfew, since there's never been a need. She's a responsible kid usually. My brain is whirling, worrying me with possible scenarios. They got in an accident. They're off doing drugs. They're having sex. Not knowing what she's doing is making me crazy, and not knowing what I'm supposed to do when she gets back is making me crazier. Should I just trust her? Should I interrogate her? Demand the truth? Ground her? Forbid her from seeing him?

I know none of those will work. She's about to turn eighteen. We've always tried to give Kylie as much freedom as we could, and she's always been responsible. She's never had a serious boyfriend, and she's only been on a few dates. And now this Oz character shows up out of the blue, and she's suddenly with him all the time. And he's everything a father worries about for his daughter. He's me, in so many ways, and I wouldn't have wanted to be the father of the girls I dated as a young man. I was reckless, wild, irresponsible. I lived alone, answered to no one, followed no rules. It wasn't until Nell and I got together that I started giving a fuck about anything.

But I can't keep her from him. He's given me no reason to distrust him, and I of all people know better than to judge him on the fact that he has tattoos and a piercing and rides a motorcycle, or that he comes from a rough background, that he's clearly seen violence, that his fists have drawn blood. I recognize my own kind in him, and that scares the shit out of me. But I'm here, a father, a successful musician and now producer, a husband for the last nineteen years.

I have to give him the benefit of the doubt. But I don't have to like it.

And I don't.

I'm in the driveway, indulging in a rare cigarette. I gave them up years ago, but every once in a while I have one. When I'm super stressed, or after especially intense sex with Nell. She knows I smoke every once in a while, and she's fine with it, as long as I don't make it a habit. I glance across the street at Jason and Becca's house, and I see the glow of a cell phone on the front porch, lighting up Ben's face.

As I notice him, he shoots to his feet, stalks with angry, stomping steps down the driveway, running his hand through his close-cropped hair. He's agitated, pissed off. I cross the street, tossing the butt into a drain.

"Hey, Ben. What's up?" I stop a few feet from him, and I can see he's beyond pissed, frantic, raging.

"You know where Kylie is?" He grates the question through gritted teeth.

I hesitate. "Um. She's…not home." I'm pretty sure I know what's eating him, and I'm not sure I should get in the middle of it.

"Yeah, I know. But do you know *where* she is?"

I clear my throat, blink, hunt for a good answer.

"She's with *him,* isn't she?"

I can't lie to him. "Yeah. She is."

"*Fuck*. I knew it." He rubs his face with both hands, tilts his head back, spins in place, and groans. "I don't get it. What the fuck does she see in that tool?"

"Ben, I'm not sure this is a conversation I can have with you." I wish I knew what to say, how to bring him down from this angry place. But I don't.

"She won't answer my texts. Won't answer my calls. She didn't even so much as say hello to me at the show tonight. She hasn't spent one fucking second with me since that…that cocksucker showed up." He's raging. "Eighteen years we've been best friends. Then just like that, *poof,* I'm fucking chopped liver—"

"Ben, listen—" I start, but he's not paying attention, he's venting, pacing and nearly shouting.

"She should be *mine*. I've been…waiting until she graduated. I've been saving and planning. It was always supposed to be me and her. She was never interested in anyone else, because she's *mine*. *My* best friend. *My* girl. Not his. And now…now she's as good as gone. She's with *him*. She's probably *fucking* him right now—"

"BEN!" I shout, shaking his shoulder. He finally seems to realize who he's talking to. "That's my daughter, kid."

"Shit…" His eyes widen, and he backs away. "Sorry, sir. I just—shit." He turns away, fists clenched behind his head.

"Ben." I bark his name, a little harsher than I intended to.

He halts in place and turns around. "Colt, Mr. Calloway, I'm sorry, I didn't mean—"

"Have you told *her* any of this?" I really like this kid. He has all the best qualities of both Jason and

Becca. He's athletic, smart, caring, and—usually—fairly even-keeled. I've never, ever seen him this agitated about anything. I feel like I have to help him somehow. "If she doesn't know what you're thinking, what you've—how you feel—how is she supposed to do anything about it? I'm not saying it'd change anything, 'cause it might not. But it can't hurt to at least talk to her."

"You're right. God…dammit, you're right." He scrubs his hand through his hair again, his posture and mannerisms so much like Jason's it's scary. "Look, Colt, I'm sorry I blew up like that. I had no right to say any of that, especially to you, sir. So—I'm—I'm sorry."

I slap him on the back. "It's all right, kid. Women can fuck with our heads, man. I get it." I squeeze the back of his neck, a little harder than strictly necessary. "Just—don't talk about my daughter like that ever again, huh?"

He winces, ducks away from me. "Yes, sir. I won't. I swear."

I let him go, and I watch him go inside. This is shaping up to get messy, and I don't envy Ben his position. I've seen the way Kylie looks at Oz, and I don't think any amount of talking is going to change her mind. Unless, of course, Oz does something stupid. I honestly don't know what to think.

It's not until Ben's in his house and I'm trudging up the stairs to my room that the realization hits me like a sledgehammer. I've only seen the two boys in the same place once, but now that my brain's going, I'm realizing that there's something similar about them. Not their personalities, but physically. Something… something I can't put my finger on, but there's a nagging sense of the familiar about Oz, and somehow that includes Ben. The thought doesn't make any sense, but it strikes me as true nonetheless.

Nell is sitting up in bed, the blankets pulled up around her chest, reading an old paperback novel, a well-worn book she's read at least a dozen times. "I heard shouting. Was that Ben?" She glances at me, setting the book face down on her lap, then looks at the clock on her bedside table. "And it's past midnight. Where's our daughter?"

"I'm not sure where she is. With Oz, I'm guessing." I shed all my clothes except my boxers and climb onto the bed beside her. "And yeah, that was Ben. He's all sorts of worked up."

"About what?"

"Kylie. And Oz. Or, more specifically, the two of them being together."

"He feels left out?" Nell slips a bookmark into her page and sets the book on the nightstand, turning toward me.

I shake my head. "No, more that he feels like Oz stole her from him. He just put it…more colorfully."

"Oh." Nell's eyes widen. "Oh, boy. He likes her?"

"I think it's more than that. It sounded to me like he's had feelings for her for a long time, he just never told her. And now it's looking like she's with Oz, for all intents and purposes, and he feels like he's lost out." I grimace. "God, Nelly. What's our girl gonna do? I told him to talk to her, and I'm not sure I should've."

Nell nods. "Yeah. She's goo-goo eyes for Oz." She sighs. "This isn't going to go well for anyone."

"No. That's my thinking." I reach for her, and she shifts toward me. "What do we do?"

She shrugs the blanket away, and I realize she's been waiting for me, naked beneath the sheets. "What can we do? She's not a little girl anymore. She's graduating in a couple of months, Colt. Going to college. I think we have to let her deal with this on her own."

"Someone's gonna get hurt."

"Yeah. We can't protect her from everything."

"I know."

"It sucks, though." I roll to my back, and Nell moves above me, reaches between us, guides me to her entrance. I hiss through my teeth as she impales herself on me. "God, Nell." I caress her ribs, her breasts, her hips, her thighs, kiss every inch of skin I can reach.

She plants her palms on my chest and kisses me, moving slowly. The kiss ends, but our lips only barely part, and we exchange breath and whispers and sighs as we move together, and then she's groaning, moaning, our foreheads touching.

"Colt..." She starts to lose her rhythm and moves with increasing desperation. "Oh, god...oh, god...oh, my *god,* Colt..."

"*Fuck*...Nell..."

We come apart at the same moment, collapse together. Nearly twenty years, and she makes me come as hard as the first time we slept together in that New York City apartment. Harder, if anything. I've learned every nuance of her body, learned every one of her secret desires, learned how to bring her to the cusp within moments, learned every curve and how to elicit every sigh and grunt and curse, and it never gets any less intense. The longer we're together, the better it gets. I think it can't get any better and then, every single time, it does.

She falls asleep on top of me, her head cradled on my chest, our bodies slick and sticky and messy, and I don't even care. Eventually, I roll with her, and she twists so I can spoon her and we sleep.

It's past one in the morning, and I've been sleeping with one eye open. So when I hear the garage door, I slip quickly out of bed, tug on some shorts and a tank top. Before I can get downstairs to meet her, I hear her voice, and Ben's.

"Dammit, Ben, I'm tired. I want to go inside. I'm probably in major trouble, and I don't have the energy for this conversation right now." She's on the other side of the door leading from the house to the garage.

My hand is on the knob, just like hers probably is. I debate giving her privacy for about six seconds, but then I remember that my job as her father is to be there for her, no matter what, and do the best for her. I have a feeling she'll need me on this side of the door in just a few minutes. So I lean against the doorjamb and listen.

"Just answer me, Kylie," Ben demands.

"What, Ben? What do you want to know?" She sounds tired, and wary.

"Were you with *him?*"

"Yes, Ben. I was. I was with Oz." The doorknob twists. "Is that it?"

"No. That's not it." He's angry, and I know from experience that's the quickest way to get Kylie to clam up. "What were you doing with him?"

"That's none of your business, Ben."

"The fuck it isn't!" He sounds a little closer. "You're—you're my best friend, and he's—who is he? Some fuck-up new guy. I know for a fact he does drugs. He smokes cigarettes. I smell smoke on you, Ky. What were you doing?"

"I don't owe you any fucking explanations, *Ben!*" She lets go of the knob and her voice sounds farther away, as if she's moving toward him.

"YES! YOU DO!" Ben is loud, and so, so angry. *This wasn't what I had in mind, Ben,* I want to say to him.

"Why?" She asks this quietly, far too calmly. She's got that deadly quiet kind of anger, just like me. "Why do I owe you explanations of what I do, and with whom? Tell me, Ben. You're my friend. Not my father. Not my mother. Not my boyfriend."

"You should be. It should be me." He sounds deflated, defeated.

"I—what?" She's confused now.

"It should have been me. With you. It was always supposed to be me. But it's him, and I don't fucking get it."

"Where is this coming from, Ben? We've never been anything but friends. You've…you've never given me the slightest hint that you were interested in me as more than a friend. If it was always supposed to be you, then why didn't you ever say anything?" Her voice is small, wounded, and fraught with tragic despair.

"I—because I thought—you—*fuck*. Because I thought I had time. I wanted to wait until you graduated, till you were eighteen. You've never been even remotely interested in anyone else. Not in our whole lives. And we're…we've always been together. Sure, we didn't kiss or whatever, but you're—you've always been *mine*. I thought when you graduated we'd spend the summer together. Go on a road trip. I had—I had it all planned out. We'd head west, and see where the road took us. We'd be friends, at first, like always, and I'd—and in time you'd see how perfect we are for each other." Ben lets out a long, groaning sigh. "And then *he* came along and…fucked it all up."

"Oh…hell. Benji—why didn't you ever say anything? Why? A year ago? Even six months ago? I'm not saying I would've—that anything would've happened for sure, but if you'd said something *then*…there may have been a chance." She groans, and then her voice raises to a shout. "And *why* is everyone so fucking concerned about me being eighteen? Is there some magic in being eighteen versus seventeen? I'm not going to suddenly change in the next two weeks. FUCK!"

"Don't call me Benji. I'm not your Benji." His voice hardens. "Have you had sex with him?"

"*That*" —she hisses the word, venomous— "is none of your business."

"You have." It's not a question. It's an accusation.

"I'm done talking about this." I hear her footsteps nearing the door, and the knob twists.

"I've been in love with you since I was fourteen, Ky. I've been waiting for the right time for *six years.*"

The knob snaps back into place. "God*damm*it, Ben." She sighs. "You waited too long."

"He'll wreck your life. You're choosing him over me, and I promise you, a loser pothead like him will only break your heart."

"That's my choice, Ben." She sniffs, and I hear the hurt in her voice.

"Yeah, well, excuse me for thinking it's the wrong one."

"Is there anything else you'd like to say? If you're gonna call me a whore, now's the time."

"You're not. You're just...misguided. And you know what? I'll always love you." I can almost hear him gearing up for one last attempt. "I'll wait. You'll get tired of his bullshit, and you'll come back to me. And I'll be there."

"I'm not sure if that's sweet or crazy. I'm not coming back to you. I was never yours. You had your chance and you waited too long. You were—my best and oldest and truest friend, Ben. And I—I probably shouldn't say this, but I'm going to. There were times when I wished you would just stop being my friend and kiss me. I thought you were going to, a couple times, but you never did, so I figured I'd been imagining it. I didn't want to ruin what we had. I thought there was no way you'd ever be in love with me. You never showed it. And you've dated all those girls... Lindsay, Alissa, Grace. What was her name, the redhead? Breanna. Oh, yeah, and Hattie. Who has that name, anyway? Hattie? I don't know what you saw in her. She's a lunatic. If you were so in love with me, what was all that about?"

"I thought...if you saw me with other girls, you'd get jealous. And I was...I felt like I'd been waiting for so long, and maybe I was just holding on to how I *used* to feel. So I thought if I dated other girls it'd clarify things. And it did. It showed me I only wanted you. Those girls, they were fun, and cool. But they weren't you. And yeah, Hattie was a bit...weird. That's why it only lasted two weeks."

"Did you have sex with any of them, Ben?" Her voice now is sharp and accusing.

The silence is deafening.

"You *did!*" She's shrill with disbelief. "Yeah, Ben. Really in love with me. Waiting for me, huh? You want to know the truth? No, I haven't slept with Oz yet. But I'm going to. We care about each other. I've waited my entire life for the right time, the right guy. It just possibly could've been you. But now…? No. And not just because I'm with Oz. All this? Everything you just told me? Acting like 'oh, I'm so in love with you,' and then oh, wait, just kidding, 'look at all the girls I've fucked.'"

"That's not fair! I didn't sleep with all of them, only—"

"I DON'T WANT TO KNOW!" She shouts him down. "I don't care. It's your business. We're friends, Ben. That's all we were, all we are, and all we'll ever be."

"There's no chance?"

"No. None."

"Fine. Fuck you, too, then." I hear his footsteps moving away.

"Ben! That's not—fucking *hell*." A long silence extends, and I imagine her watching him walk away. "Goodbye, Ben."

A few seconds later, the door opens and she steps in, closing the door behind her. Her head is down, and I can tell she's crying. She doesn't see me leaning against the counter until she's about to run into me.

She shrieks and drops her keys. "Oh, my god, Dad! You scared the shit out of me!" She picks up her keys, blinking, trying to act like she wasn't crying. "Why are you here in the kitchen by yourself? At…1 a.m.? Shit, it's 1 a.m. I'm in trouble, aren't I?"

"I was waiting for you."

She seems to realize where I'm standing, and glances at the door. "How much of that did you hear?"

"Pretty much all of it."

"You can't just eavesdrop on my private conversations." She wipes at her eyes with her finger.

"Yes, I can. It's my job as your father to know what's going on in your life." I take her by the shoulders and pull her to me. "I'm sorry about Ben, sweetheart."

"Did you know how he felt about me?" Her voice is muffled by my shirt.

"Not until recently. Not until Oz showed up, and he started acting weird."

"You didn't say anything."

"Should I have? Would it have changed anything? And would you really have thanked me for butting into your life like that? I don't think so."

She sniffs. "Yeah, you're probably right." She pulls away and sets her keys on the counter, turns to rummage in the fridge for a can of Sprite. "If you heard the whole thing, you probably heard what I said about—about me and Oz."

"Yeah, I heard that, too."

She sips, waits. When she realizes I'm not saying anything, she lets out a muffled belch and frowns at me. "And?"

"Well, shit, Kylie. What am I supposed to say? You're turning eighteen in less than a month. It's going to happen at some point. And I'm glad you've waited this long. I don't really know how to handle this, Kylie. I don't. Just being honest. This is one of those moments I don't think any father is equipped or prepared to deal with. You're not a grown-up yet, but you're close. And I know all too well what would happen if I grounded you forever, or tried to keep you from seeing him. I don't like it. You're my little girl. My only child. And I want you to stay innocent forever. But you won't, and I can't pretend you will. So what do I do? I wish I knew. If I just let you go on with this relationship with Oz, does that make me a bad parent for ignoring what I know for a fact is going on?" I rub my eyes. "And I'm conflicted about Oz. I don't want you to get hurt and, unfortunately, Ben could be right. I mean, anyone can hurt you, and if you're in a relationship, you *will* get hurt at some point, somehow. But Oz…there're warning signs, Kylie. He's…I'm not saying he's bad news, or that he's a bad person. But—"

"I know, Dad. But there's more to him than everyone seems to see."

"I know that, Kylie. Like you said, I of all people should know that." I let out a long breath. I don't want to bring this up, but I have to. "Have you seen his forearms?"

She closes her eyes and doesn't answer for a long time. The pain I see in her eyes tells me more than her words can. "Yes. I have."

"Do you know how he got those scars?"

"Yes. I do."

This is tricky. "Is it an…ongoing thing?"

She shakes her head. "I don't think so."

"But you don't know for sure."

She drinks from the can and then sets it on the counter, rotating it so the logo spins and spins and spins. "For one hundred percent sure? No. But…we talked about it."

"Kylie, listen." I have to be circumspect about this, careful. "People who…do things to hurt themselves. It's a warning sign of something deeper going on with them. And there's nothing anybody can do to help or to fix that person unless they're ready to be fixed or to be helped."

"This is about Mom, isn't it?"

"It's about Oz, Kylie."

"I've seen Mom's scars, Dad. I know what they are."

"I know, hon. That's from a long, long time ago. She went through a very hard time, and—look, that's her story to tell you, not mine. But, yeah, I know this because of what your mom went through. And I don't want to see you go through…that. Being on the other side of that. Self-mutilation is a big deal. If it's a problem for him, he needs to get help. Help you can't give. I'm sorry, it's just the facts."

Kylie's gaze is sharp, knowing. "You know about it, too, don't you? From your own experience."

I sigh, and find myself unwittingly rubbing at my chest, where my own scars lie, hidden by tattoos. "Yeah, I do. I've been on both sides."

Her eyes latch onto my hand, and I drop it. She looks back up at me. "So you…you understand why he'd have the—the compulsion to do that to himself."

I groan. "Yeah. I do." I don't want to delve into my own history. Especially not with my daughter. She really doesn't need to know about the darkness and the skeletons that haunt my past. "If you're hurting inside, if you've been through something really, really painful, sometimes you just want to feel something else. Anything else. Even if you know it's wrong—that you're hurting yourself. The people in your life who care about you can find it very tough to get through to you. If the pain inside is big enough and bad enough, you don't care. You just need an escape, a sense of relief. No matter how fleeting it is. Same with getting high, or wasted all the time. And that lifestyle? It's bad, Kylie. I don't want you anywhere near that. It's dark, and it's dangerous, and it can suck you under so fast. So fast."

"He's not like that."

"No?"

She ducks her head. "You don't know him, Daddy. You don't know what he's been through."

"I'm not judging him, Kylie. I swear I'm not. I may not know the specifics, but I understand him better than you could ever imagine." I move closer to her, kiss the top of her head. "But you're my daughter, and *you're* my priority. And you getting dragged through the hell someone like Oz has the capacity for, even unwittingly, without meaning to? I can't stand that. I know I have to let you live your own life, and make your own mistakes and all that, but there's got to be a limit."

"So…now what?"

"You're a smart, responsible girl, Kylie. I trust you. I trust your judgment. You've never given me any reason not to. So I'm going to give you your freedom in this, as much as part of me screams otherwise. Just be careful. With him. Around him. Don't get sucked in. Don't let him continue to hurt himself. And if he can't stop, the only thing you might be able to do is to step away and tell him you can't be with him if he keeps doing it, that you care too much to watch him destroy himself that way. It feels like betrayal, but it's not."

She nods. "That makes sense. I don't think it'll be a problem."

I narrow my eyes. "As for cigarettes—which I do smell on you—and pot, and drinking…don't be stupid, Kylie. Just don't. None of that is worth it. Thinking you'll only do it when you're around him is only lying to yourself. And I *will* be watching for that. If I catch you smoking, drunk, or high, you'll be in trouble. I expect better from you. This is your one warning." I pause to let that sink in. "As for sex—"

"Got it covered, Dad. Not having that talk with you." She won't look at me, toying with the pop-tab on her can of Sprite.

"I'm going to say it anyway. I don't like it, it makes me uncomfortable, but I'm going to say it anyway. My instinct is to forbid you, to crack down and all that. But unfortunately, I know better. It wouldn't stop you. So all I'll say is be careful. Be safe. If he's been with anyone else, he needs to be tested before anything happens between you two." She starts to protest, and I talk over her. "Shut up and listen, Kylie. This is awkward for me, too. But If I can't stop you, I have to make sure you're safe. You told Ben you haven't…been with…Oz yet. So take precautions *before*.

Be safe in more than one way, okay?" I take a deep breath and force blunt honesty from myself. "That means birth control *and* condoms. God, I hate having to have this conversation. Not just one or the other, but both. No excuses, no exceptions. I do *not* want to be a grandfather for a *very* long time. Got it?"

She nods, still not looking at me. "Yeah. I got it."

I touch her chin. "Kylie. Look at me." She does, and I let her see all my fear, all my worry. "I love you, Kylie. Please, *please*…just be safe. Be careful. Not just with your body, but with your heart and soul. And trust me when I say, if Oz does anything to hurt you, he'll answer to me."

She lifts her head, her eyes fierce. "No, Dad. He won't. If I get hurt, it'll be my own fault. I'm going into this with him knowing he's…different. He's not—I don't know…*tame*. But neither are you, Dad. Are you? And you're what I know. You've been my example in life. You're not tame, or safe in some ways. And you may not be *nice,* but you're good. And so is he."

I nod. "I get it. And I respect that. But my prerogative as your father is to break the face of anyone who fucks with you. And I will, whether you like it or not. So if our boy Oz prefers to have his face in one piece, he'll treat you like the precious thing you are."

Her face softens. "He does, Daddy. He really does."

I hug her. "Good." Another kiss to the top of her head. "And try to get in before one next time, huh?"

She just nods, and I leave her to go upstairs. Nell is standing at the top of the stairs, wrapped in a robe, staring off into space. She follows me into our room, and I close the door.

"She's all grown up," Nell says.

"I know."

"When did that happen?"

I shrug, shake my head. "I don't know. We blinked, I guess."

She gives me tender smile. "You're a good daddy, Colt."

I sigh. "Am I doing the right thing? Letting her go through with this thing with Oz? It doesn't feel like it. But mentally, I don't think I have any other choice."

She sheds the robe and climbs back into bed, naked. "I think you're right. I'd rather know what she's doing, even if I don't necessarily like it, than forbid her and have her sneaking out."

"Or worse, running away." I'm thinking of myself, seventeen and alone in New York. So young, too young to fend for myself. It's why I swore, when Kylie was young, that I wouldn't make the same mistakes my parents did. But am I making different ones that are just as bad? I worry that there's no way to know, and no way to avoid making mistakes as a parent.

I shed my shirt and climb in beside Nell, feel her warmth against me and her hair tickling my cheek.

No matter how good your kid is, sometimes life has a way of bringing shit to them that no one can foresee or protect against. If that happens to Kylie, I'll just have to be there to help her get through it.

Nine: Germinating Seeds
Oz

KYLIE ASKED ME TO GET TESTED, so I did, and came back clean. I sat in the waiting room of her doctor's office while she got birth control, and then we went together to buy protection. It felt odd, and strangely comforting, to do all that together. As if we were making decisions together, not merely thinking about the moment but looking at the future. As if we're planning for a future together. The idea gives me hope.

She's eighteen now. I spent her birthday at her parents' house, eating cake, hanging out, laughing, having fun. All the things I've never done on my own birthdays. I gave her a book of sheet music of some of the popular country songs. She loved it.

So now she's eighteen, we're both tested and protected, and there's nothing left but the right moment. I'm thinking she deserves better for our first time together—to be somewhere other than in my nasty room on my mattress on the floor. I've never been into romantic gestures, but I want to do something. The only problem is, romantic gestures cost money I don't really have.

All that happened a few days ago, and it's been tense and difficult since then. The doctor was very clear that we couldn't do anything until the pills had had time to get into her system, and waiting, waiting, waiting has been so hard, so impossible. We have to pull ourselves back from the edge, pull our heated fiery need back, reel in the messy drowning kisses before we get carried away and lose ourselves in each other and forget why we have to wait. We try to distract ourselves with studying for tests and finishing assignments, but it's hard. We get lost in a delirious fervor, lose ourselves in the silence of my room, kisses stolen in her car, on my bike in a parking lot far from anywhere. A week of hungry looks, and ravenous hands, and roaming trembling bodies.

To distract ourselves, we study together, and we play music. We write songs, we learn covers, we learn how to play together, how to read each other musically, what we can do well and what we can't. She's teaching me to read music, which is easier than I thought it would be. And now, now finally we're clear to do what we want.

We're in her car, cruising through Friday late afternoon traffic, heading downtown. Kylie has a list of honky-tonks and bars she wants us to audition at. We've spent the last few days practicing some original tunes and a few covers. The first place is a dark sports bar off the strip. Kylie arranged the audition last week, so the manager is expecting us. He shakes our hands, introduces himself as Dan, and points at the stage. It's a one-step-up platform in the corner of the bar, our backs to the windows facing the street. There's a battered, scratched tan upright piano on one wall, and a couple of stools, mic stands. Kylie and I have no gear except my guitars and amp, so I haul my amp in and set it up, plug in my electric guitar, and settle on the stool while Kylie tinkers on the piano keys, testing its sound and tuning.

"That piano's kind of a piece of shit," Dan says. He's a guy in his late thirties with a high-and-tight haircut, a muscular build, and a goatee. "Needs tuning. But it'll work for an audition, I guess. Ready when ya'll are."

Kylie nods at me and I dig deep, nodding my head to count out the beat, and then I'm into the opening of the second song we did for the talent show. It's a pretty killer intro solo, and when Kylie comes in with the piano and starts singing, it turns into something hypnotic. The manager is impressed, I can tell. We finish that song, and then I switch electric for acoustic, and Kylie brushes her hands across the keys as if to sweep away dust on the black and white, as if to brush away the old song to make way for the new. It's a gesture of hers that I've noticed. It's cute. I hit a muted chord three times, counting out the beat, and then Kylie comes in, playing a stripped-down version of Ed Sheeran's "Kiss Me." I'm the most nervous about this song. Our version of it relies most heavily on our harmony. I can play the guitar part easy enough, and Kylie's piano is the real backbone of it musically, but hitting the right notes together at the right time…it's hard, and I'm not super confident in my own singing. I quickly realized that when Kylie had claimed to be "decent" on the piano, she meant crazy fucking good. She does suck at guitar, though. She wasn't exaggerating about that.

We get through the song okay, although I messed up the words in one spot.

"That was good. Real good," Dan says. "I mean, that song in particular may not be right for the crowd we get, but ya'll can jam, that's for sure. Got anything a little more…country?"

I nod. "Yeah. How about 'Cannery River' by Green River Ordinance?"

We get a nod, and I switch guitars again. This was the trickiest song to arrange for a duet. Neither of us plays the fiddle, but I figured out a way to emulate one with my electric guitar taking the melody originally written for the violin. Kylie did the rest with a complex piece of piano composition. It sounds good, I think, but it's up to this guy, not us.

We dive in, and I'm playing long, mournful, wailing notes, and Kylie is bent over her piano, fingers flying. The vocals are almost all me, which scares the fuck out of me. I feel my voice go shaky midway through, nerves threatening to screw me up. I close my eyes and focus on the guitar, focus on the words, suck it up and keep going.

We get a couple claps out of Dan. "That was fucking fantastic. You guys are in." He points at me, grinning. "You almost lost it there for a second, didn't you, pal?"

I nod. "Yeah, almost."

He slaps his thigh and stands up from the bar stool. "Well, you pulled it off. Give me more of that, and some originals. How about three weeks from now? Thursday the twenty-first, 8 p.m. I can't let you play past like nine-thirty unless you're twenty-one.

So give me a good performance, and we'll see how it goes." He squints at Kylie. "You look familiar. What'd you say your name was?"

"Kylie."

"Kylie what?"

She obviously doesn't want to reveal her last name, but she does. "Calloway."

"Calloway. Shit, you're Nell and Colt's daughter, aren't you?"

She sighs. "Yeah. But—"

Dan talks over her. "You were in before I knew that, so don't think I'm hiring you because of that. Does he know you're trying to gig?"

She shrugs. "Yeah."

Dan nods. "Good. I'll call Colt and talk to him. If he's okay with it, I might let you play a bit later, in the busier bar hours. I'm not really supposed to, but since you're Colt's kid, I might let it slide."

"I don't want any special favors just because—"

Dan cuts in again. "Look, kid. This is a tough-as-fuck business. Getting any gigs at all is hard. If I were you, I'd take whatever leg up you can get. I respect that you want to do this on your own, but an in is an in. And believe me when I say that you'll only make it so far on your parents' name anyway. They can get you in to clubs and bars, but they can't make the crowd like you. The crowd don't give two shits who your folks are. All they want is good music to drink to."

Kylie sighs, and nods. "That makes sense."

Dan shrugs. "All right, then. See you on the twenty-first." He hands Kylie a business card. "Give this to your dad."

I pack up my guitars, and lug them and the amp outside and into Kylie's car. We get in and Kylie starts the engine, then turns to me. "HOLY SHIT!" She grabs my arms and shakes me. "We've got our first gig, Oz!"

I smile at her. "We did it, sweetness."

"Now we just have to actually play the gig!" Kylie pulls out into traffic and heads toward her house.

We talk about what covers we're going to do, and discuss writing some more original material. By the time we get to her house, we're both excited about possibilities and have the first stanza of a new song planned out. Our excitement is doused when we see Ben in his driveway getting into his truck at the same time as we're getting out. Kylie is obviously upset at the mere sight of him, and I feel it. For his part, Ben is staring at me with what looks like open hatred. It's a little shocking, and unexpected.

He slams his door shut, squeals his tires as he backs out, and floors it, roaring at a reckless speed down the residential street. His front door opens, and his mother comes out, stands on the front porch staring after him.

I glance at Kylie. "What's the deal there?"

She sighs. "A lot." She shakes her head and looks up at me. "He's being pissy."

"Kylie."

"We got into a fight the night I left your place late—after our first open mic. He was waiting up for me."

"He's jealous?"

"Yeah. Apparently you were right. He said he's been in love with me since he was fourteen."

I groan. "Shit. I told you." I walk away from her, worry shooting through me.

She follows after me. "Oz, it's fine."

I spin in place. "Fine? How is it fine? He's your best friend. I never wanted to come between that."

"He had our whole lives to say something to me. He never did. Not once. He never let on how he was feeling." She looks down the street where his truck disappeared, as if she could see him wherever he is now. "I wanted him to, you know. A long time ago. Ninth grade, tenth grade. He's awesome, you know? Hot, cool, fun, athletic, popular. Everything a girl could ever want, and I thought he and I could have some kind of fairy tale ending together, so I waited and waited for him to suddenly profess his undying love and whatever, but he never did, and I didn't want to risk ruining our friendship. And then last year he suddenly started dating all these girls, and I gave up. And then this year you show up, and everything happens between us, and now suddenly he tells me how he feels when it's too late."

I'm torn. He's everything she said he is, and I'm not blind enough to miss that. He has every reason to hate me. Part of me, the part that knows I'm wrong for Kylie, tells me to push her to him. But the selfish part of me won't let that happen.

Kylie clearly knows me all too well, because she turns to me. "Don't even think about it, Oz. He had his chance. I'm with you."

I laugh. "I didn't say anything."

She narrows her eyes at me. "But you were thinking it."

I nod. "Yeah."

"Well, don't. Just don't." She pulls me toward her front door, lets herself in, shouting for Colt. "Daddy! Where are you?"

He comes up from the basement. "What's up, buttercup?"

She bounds over to him and wraps her arms around his middle. "We got a gig!"

He hugs her back. "Awesome! Where at?"

She hands him the card. "This place. The manager's name is Dan. He said he would let us play later if you were okay with it. He said it'd be hard to get gigs during prime time since I'm underage."

Colt nods. "Yeah, he's right about that, at least when it comes to the Music Row bars and clubs. But there are a lot open mic nights ya'll could do. It's a good way to build a name for yourselves. The whole open mic night crowd of singer-songwriters is a small world, at least when it comes to real talent."

He claps me on the back, his other arm around Kylie. "Good job, you two." He glances at Kylie. "You mind if Mom and I come to watch you and Oz play?"

She shakes her head. "No, that's fine."

"When is it?"

"Thursday the twenty-first."

"Cool. We'll be there." He heads back to the basement, and Kylie and I go up to her room.

She leaves her door open as I sit at her desk and she sits on her bed. We spend the next few hours alternating between studying for a calculus exam and working on a new song.

We're interrupted around seven-thirty by Nell. "Dinner's ready." She looks at me. "Are you staying?"

Kylie answers for me. "Yes. He is."

I laugh. "I guess I am."

A few minutes later, I'm sitting at the round table just off the kitchen. Kylie is on one side of me, Nell on the other, Colt across from me. There's a huge bowl of rotini and meat sauce, garlic bread, and salad. I wait and watch as they pass each item around, and take a helping when it comes to me. This is…odd. I've never had an actual sit-down dinner like this before. It's always just Mom and I, and the rare nights we're both home at dinnertime, we eat whatever's quick, sitting on the couch watching TV. I don't know what to do. Should I wait for everyone else to eat? Do they pray first? They don't strike me as religious or spiritual people, but I have this idea—a dumb one, I'm sure—that nice unified suburban families like this always pray before they eat. Do I close my eyes? Are there rules or manners I'm supposed to know about? I didn't wash my hands. I'm still wearing my hat. Should I take it off? A thousand things run through my head. I'm not eating, just watching Kylie and her family as they dig in without fanfare, chattering amiably, asking each other questions about their day, sharing stories, all of it around mouthfuls of food.

Nell notices I'm not eating. "Is it okay, Oz? You're not eating."

I blink. "No, it's—it's good. It smells good."

Colt comes to my rescue. "It's just dinner, Oz. Relax. Eat."

Kylie sets her slice of garlic bread down and looks at me. "You okay?"

I laugh, uncomfortable, and take bite of rotini. "It's good. Really good. Thanks for having me." I hope she'll let it go.

She does, for now at least, and I slowly relax a little. I answer a few questions, innocuous ones about where I've lived, which cities I've liked and which I haven't, my favorite bands. Colt and I get into a discussion about motorcycles, and it's during this conversation that I notice Kylie's eyes on me, watching me, happy, curious, eager. Like she's happier than I could ever imagine that I'm here in her home, talking to her dad.

It's weird for me. I never thought any girl would ever want to bring me home to meet her parents, but here I am, eating pasta and talking about Triumphs with Colt Calloway. And it feels okay.

When dinner is over, I help clear the table, and Kylie and I load the dishwasher together. That, too, feels strangely and wonderfully domestic.

Colt catches my eye, gestures for me to follow him. "I'm stealing your boyfriend, Kylie. We're gonna go look at the bike."

"Be nice," Kylie says, a note of warning in her voice.

I don't know what to expect, but I follow him out into the garage. He opens the garage door, throws the cover off his Triumph. I squat and examine the engine. I hear him rummaging in a drawer, and then I hear the distinctive *scrape-click* of a lighter, and smell cigarette smoke. He holds out a pack of Camels, and I take one, light it.

A few moments pass, and then he leans back against the workbench. "You get my daughter hooked on these, I'll kick your ass." He lifts the cigarette.

"That's what I told her. I don't let her smoke, and I try not to smoke around her."

He nods. "Good." He narrows his eyes at me. "Listen, I'm not gonna give some big speech to you, or try to scare you. I don't need to, I don't think."

I shake my head. "No, sir, you don't."

"There are a few things I do need to address, though. One, those scars on your arms. Is that going to be a problem?"

I turn my forearm so the underside is facing up and stare at the scars. "No, sir." I swallow hard. "I'm not gonna lie—it used to be a pretty big problem. And sometimes I do still get the urge. But I don't burn anymore. I'm not saying your daughter was the reason I stopped, because she's not. She helps, though. I don't want to be that guy. She's…she deserves better than that."

"Fucking right she does." Colt's eyes are all-knowing. "You quit burning on your own? Or did you see someone?"

I debate what to say. In the end, I go for the truth. "I spent two months in a psychiatric hospital a while back. Just before I graduated high school. Burning myself was becoming…a habit. It got pretty bad. Things were really shitty. I was always in trouble at school. Um. There were these kids, bullies. No one stopped them, and no one even tried. They ran the school. I wouldn't put up with their bullshit, to the point that I almost got expelled for beating the shit out of a couple of them. It just kept getting worse. It wasn't physical bullying. It was…psychological. It was a very socially and economically segregated school, and I didn't fit in with any of the groups. I was failing all my classes, my mom was riding my ass, the principal was about to expel me, and I just—there was no good answer. That was when I really started burning. My mom noticed. Freaked out. I kept doing it, and by the time the year was over, Mom was seriously on the verge of a nervous breakdown about it. So she took me to a shrink. I wouldn't talk, wouldn't cooperate."

I hesitate, not wanting to share the next part. "The burning got bad. Really bad. Mom couldn't handle it, thought I'd, like, try to kill myself. So she had me involuntarily committed to a psych hospital. At first, I treated it like I did everything else. Uncooperative, all that. But then I realized that maybe they could help me out with the urge to burn. See, I never wanted to. It was this…compulsion. I couldn't stop it. My hands would do it without the rest of me agreeing. I don't know if that makes any sense to you, but that's how it was. I hated the hospital, but they did help me understand a bit."

"Did you think about suicide?"

I shake my head. "No, sir. It wasn't about wanting to die or end my life. It was just…the burning pushed away the other things I was feeling, things I didn't know how to deal with."

"What about hard drugs?"

I shake my head again. "No way. Seen that shit kill people. No."

Colt sighs. "Word is you still smoke pot."

"'Word is'?" I lift an eyebrow. "Whose word?"

"Ben."

I grimace. "Ben. He hates me."

"I know. But answer the question. Do you?"

I nod. "Sometimes. Not often." My heart is hammering.

"Has Kylie?"

"Not with me."

"Quit that shit, Oz. It's not doing you any favors. I've been there, and that's the only reason I'm this calm about it. I don't want it around my daughter. If I catch even a whiff of that shit on my daughter, bad things will happen." He points at me with his cigarette. "My daughter likes you. You and I have a lot in common, Oz, and that scares me. But I turned out okay, so I'm taking a chance on you, letting you around Kylie."

I nod. "I hear you. And thank you."

"Yeah, well, I'd rather know you and know where my daughter is when she's with you than have her running off to elope with you or some bullshit because I tried to keep you apart." He says this with a trace of bitterness.

"I want good things for Kylie, sir. I know you and Nell are important to her, and there's no way I'd try to take her away from ya'll like that."

"Good." He eyes me speculatively. "You got any experience working on engines?"

I bobble my head back and forth. "A little. I'd like to learn."

Colt digs through a small box on the workbench, comes up with a business card. "This is a buddy of mine. He needs an extra hand in his garage. Go see him tomorrow. I'll tell him to expect you. He'll pay you good if you work hard."

I take the card. "That's legit, Colt. Thanks."

"You can do better than changing oil." He jerks his head at the house. "Go on. She's waiting." I head toward the door, and he calls me back. "Oz? One last thing. You knock up my baby girl, you and I are gonna have problems. Very serious problems."

I freeze with my hand on the knob. "That won't happen, sir. You have my word."

"Better not."

Kylie is waiting for me, and as soon as I come in from the garage, she's dragging me back out to her car. I wave at her mom and thank her for the dinner, and then Kylie and I are flying out of her sub, toward my apartment.

"What did my dad say?" Kylie asks.

I shrug. "Wanted to make sure the burning wasn't an issue. Wanted to know about what Ben said about me smoking pot. Wanted to make sure I don't get you pregnant."

"What Ben said?" Kylie seems confused.

"Apparently Ben told him I smoke pot. I don't know."

Kylie frowns, and then her expression clears. "Oh. Dad overheard my argument with Ben the other night. Ben said he knows for a fact that you smoke pot. That must be what he's talking about."

"Well, all things considered, I think it went well."

She glances at me. "What'd you tell him about the burning?"

"The truth. It used to be a problem. I told him about the whole psych hospital thing."

"The *what?*"

Shit. I forgot I hadn't told her about that little detail. So I go back and give her the same rundown I did Colt.

She takes my hand and squeezes. "That's awful, Oz. Why do people have to pick on you?"

"I don't know. I'm different. I think it's partly the schools Mom put me in. She was always trying to make sure I went to the best school in the city. She'd find a place to live that would let me go to the better school. I appreciate the idea, and the safer schools, and whatever, but I'd have fit in better at the shitty schools. No one would've paid me any attention there, not like they do where she always had me going. I didn't fit in. I never have."

We arrive at my apartment, and I hustle her inside, into my room. She makes herself at home, kicking aside a pile of dirty clothes and sitting on my bed. I watch her, and decide to broach the subject that's been nagging at me all day.

"Kylie, I've been thinking."

She laughs. "Uh-oh."

"No, nothing bad. I just hate the fact that this shithole apartment is the only place we have to be alone. I just wish I had somewhere nicer we could go to be together. For our first time together, I mean."

She frowns at me. "I couldn't care less *where* we are, Oz. As long as we're together, I don't care. This is your room. Your space. And…some of my best memories are here in this room. Getting to know you." She grins at me, blushing. "Kissing you. Touching you. All the things we did together. That happened here. I don't need the Ritz-Carlton, or a million-dollar penthouse. I don't need you to be anyone or anything other than who you are." She extends her hands to me.

I move to sit beside her on the bed, but she grabs my wrists and jerks me toward her. She lies down, pulling me, and I fall forward, laughing, land on top of her.

"There. Now I'm somewhere nice." She grins up at me.

"Fuck, Kylie. You're too much. Way too awesome for a guy like me." I plant my fists beside her shoulders, taking my weight off her. "But I'll take it."

"That's right. You will." She runs her palm up my cheek, sweeping my hat off and tossing it aside, tugging my hair out of its ponytail. "I liked seeing you in my home, talking with my parents. I like having you in my life."

"Me, too. It was a little strange at first, but I liked it."

She tilts her head to one side with a confused expression. "What was? Dinner? What was that about, anyway?"

I shrug. "I've just never had dinner like that. At a table, a whole family all together. It was just weird. I wasn't sure what I was supposed to do."

She laughs. "What you were supposed to do? It's just dinner. You eat!"

I snort. "Yeah, I got that part. But it's a little nerve-wracking, okay? A formal family dinner with your girlfriend's parents is a big deal."

"Oh." She's serious now. "I didn't think about it like that."

"It's fine. I had a good time."

"And now we're here," she says, slipping her fingers under my shirt to roam my back.

"Now we're here."

Her fingernails skim up my spine, pushing my shirt with it, and then she's tugging it off and sliding her palms down my sides, cups my ass and pulls me closer.

"You should get me naked," she whispers. "There's no reason for us to stop this time."

"I awoke a greedy little monster in you, didn't I?"

She's wearing a white button-down shirt and a knee-length gray cotton skirt. I lean back on my knees and unbutton the top of her shirt, and then the second button.

She rests her hands above her head, her eyes locked on me. "You sure did, baby. A very hungry monster. Ravenous. Insatiable."

I pop the rest of the buttons open, and suck in a breath. She's wearing a skimpy red push-up bra. I'm instantly hard, and her eyes go to my crotch. "It's a front clasp," she breathes.

I keep my eyes on hers as I unhook her bra, and then she's leaning up toward me, letting her shirt and bra fall away off her arms and shoulders. Jesus, those tits. So fucking amazing. I graze my palms over them, feel her nipples harden under my touch, cup their weight. She sighs, a breathy moan of delight, and then she's opening my pants, pushing me backward and jerking my jeans down. I'm fumbling desperately at the stretchy waistband of her skirt, pulling it haphazardly down around her hips, one side sticking at her waist, the other rolled down to show a scrap of red thong strap. She kneels between my legs and lets me shove the elastic down, and she's kicking the cotton away, and she's there above me, red-blonde hair a curtain around her face, her vivid blue eyes hot and eager on mine. She's almost naked, clad only in the thong, a tiny bit of red silk matching her bra. I run my hands down her back and over her ass, and the feel of her taut, plush-soft, and perfect backside in my hands makes my cock go harder, achingly rigid, bursting full of need to feel her on me, soft around me, touching, licking, kissing, sucking, fucking, loving. I growl as I dig clawed fingers into the muscle of her ass, clutching and pulling her closer to me. I rip the thong down, tugging the little string out from between her ass cheeks, strip it off, and I can smell her desire, smell the need-juices seeping from her pussy.

She's not idle as I'm doing this — she's pulling at my boxers, getting the elastic stuck on the head of my engorged cock, tugging them away and down and off, and we're naked together, free together, breathing in the silence, breathing each other's breath and feeling skin against skin, eyes on eyes, electric blue on gray-almost-brown.

We meet in an instinctual frantic kiss, arms sliding serpentine on heated flesh, hands grasping at curves and muscle and searching for everything, needing everything. My fingers find her slick hot cleft and delve in, drag a moan and sigh from her sweet lips as they move on mine, and her hand slides between us and finds my cock and caresses it and squeezes it, and we're panting, panting.

"I can't—I can't wait anymore, Oz. Please?" Kylie's face, inches from mine, is pleading.

She grabs her purse from the floor, keeping as much of her body against mine as possible while she finds the little gray box of condoms and opens it, pulls the string of foil squares out, rips one free. Tears it open, examines it. Figures out which way it rolls, and sits up to straddle me.

I'm still, letting her do this. Watching her beauty, breathless at the fantasy of this happening, the implausibly incredible truth of this gorgeous, perfect, girl, this woman, naked with me, wanting me, needing me, allowing me to touch her and kiss her. It shouldn't be me, but it is. I'm just a hood rat, a metal kid, a pot-smoking fighter, the kid who's been to juvie and psych wards, who's been suspended more times than I could ever count, expelled once, beaten up countless times, shot, nearly stabbed once, left for dead in a parking lot, fatherless, friendless, homeless, rootless. How could I possibly deserve to have this glorious pale-skinned fire-haired, lightning-eyed beauty, this goddess? But here she is, in my room, with me, wrapping her tender eager little white fingers around my aching cock and sliding the condom on, rolling it down, so gently erotic that I don't dare breathe or move or feel or un-clench my muscles. And she's watching me, perhaps seeing all the thoughts in my head, seeing me for me the way she always has.

"Oz?" she whispers. "Are you here?"

I slide my hands up her thighs and grasp her waist. "Yeah, babe. I am. I'm just marveling."

"At what?" She's sitting up on my thighs, balanced easily, her heavy tits not quite covered by the copper fall of her hair, her thighs opened enough to show me her pussy, to show me how wet she is for me.

"You." I swallow hard, blink, emotional in a way I'm not sure how to deal with or express. "Just fucking amazed that you're here with me. That I get to have you, get to do this with you. You've waited so long for the right guy, the right time, and for reasons I just cannot fucking fathom, you pick me. Messed-up, fucked-up me. You…you're perfect, Kylie. So perfect. Every inch of your body is perfect. Your soul is…so beautiful. Your mind, your heart, your personality — you just glow like a sun in the darkness, Kylie. You light up the blackness that has been my life, and I don't know how to ever be the kind of man you need and deserve, but I want to try. For you, for me, and for us. For the possibility of us." I'm letting all this come out of me, honesty, truth, things I'm not all that acquainted with. "Goddamn, listen to me, going on like some emotional sissy."

Kylie is crying. Fuck, I've messed this up before it can begin. "Oz. Jesus, Oz." She leans down, and her big soft boobs squish against my chest, and her mouth trembles against mine. Her hair falls to either side of our faces, and I feel her tears, the hammering of her heart, the shaking of her hands as they clutch my face. "I don't even know what to say to all that. Except, you already are what I want, what I need, what I deserve. And I'm not perfect, but the fact that you think so makes me so happy. Because I think you're perfect, too, messed up, fucked up, beautiful, tough, strong, sweet, and sexy."

She rolls off me, pulls at me. I move above her, slip my hips between her knees, and she hugs me with her thighs, holds my shoulders and looks up at me, expectant, waiting, begging without words.

"Kylie, this is what you want? With me? Now? You're sure?" I have to ask, have to make sure.

She laughs. "Yes, Oz. So sure. So ready. Please, please. I'm aching. My insides ache. My—my pussy is on fire. I need you. Touch me. Make me come."

Shit. How am I supposed to resist that? I can't, and I don't have to. I touch her with my two middle fingers, and find her wet and tight. Slip my fingers inside her, caress her, stroke her, spread her essence over her clit and pinch that little erect nub of nerves and rub and stroke it until she's gasping and moving beneath me, moaning. I circle, swipe, circle. Delve deep, touch her deep inside, curl my fingers to find that spot that makes her writhe and growl in her throat, circle her clit until she's bucking, and watching her come apart makes me harder than ever, makes my cock ache to be inside her.

"Oz…oh, fuck, Oz." Her eyes fly open, and she drives her hips upward, spine arcing, breasts heaving as she comes to my touch.

"Ready?" I nudge against her opening.

She nods, breathless, a jerky bob of her head, and she reaches between us, grips my cock and nestles the head between the wet lips of her pussy. "Yeah, baby. I'm ready. So ready."

I gently, slowly slide into her, and I can barely hold on, barely hold back, because every notion of good or pleasant or perfect is blasted into nothing by the feel of her slick, tight heat. I can't breathe, can barely support my own weight. I feel resistance inside her, and know that this is the part that will hurt her. She feels it, her face tight, brows drawn.

I still. "Okay?"

She nods. "Yeah. Just...give me a second."

"Does it hurt?"

She nods. "Yeah. It does. Not bad, but it does."

I'm shaking all over, need desperately to move, but I don't, can't, won't. "Tell me what you need, what you want."

She grips me by the shoulders, her fingers claws in my skin. "Just—do it. Push through it." I take a deep breath and hesitate, then touch my forehead to hers, and push deep. I feel the skin of resistance break, and she gasps sharply. "Oh, *shit*. That hurt."

"I'm sorry, Ky, so sorry—" I hate the pain on her face, but even as I watch, stilled inside her, I see her expression shifting.

She shakes her head, and the fingers of her left hand press over my lips to silence me. "Don't apologize. It doesn't hurt anymore. It's okay. I'm okay."

Her eyes widen, and I can't help but shift my hips a little, seeking relief from the burgeoning pressure inside me, seeking relief for the aching need of my throbbing cock. She feels so good, and I need to move, but I won't until she's ready. Yet I can't help the little wiggle of my hips, and she gasps.

"Oh. *Oohh*, do that again, Oz." Her voice is shaky, but with equal parts awe and pleasure. As slowly and gingerly as I possibly can, I pull back, and her grip on my shoulders moves to my waist, then to my ass, one hand on each of my ass cheeks, and when I hesitate, she pulls at me ever so slightly. "Ohhhhmygod. That feels so good, Oz. Again, again, baby."

I love that she calls me baby. It makes the ridiculous, emotional part of me go all sappy. I draw back and slide deep, all in one motion this time, and she gasps, and now she's pulling at my ass to get me to move, move, and her back is arching off the bed.

"God*damn*, Kylie. You feel so, *so* good." I whisper this to her, press my lips to her ear and huff the words low and mumbled to her. "I love the way you feel. You're so tight."

"Oz, oh, *fuck*, Oz, I didn't know, I didn't know…" Her voice is thick and emotional with awe and bliss and other things I can't sort out. "I didn't know it would be like this. I feel…so full. Filled with you. I didn't know. And I'm so glad I waited. So glad it's you."

Our eyes meet, and she's crying, slow fat tears sliding sideways toward her ears. I put my weight on one hand and brush the tears away. I know, somehow, that they're good tears. Her arms wrap around my neck and pull me close in an embrace, and we're moving together, her hips lifting to meet mine now, and there's only Kylie, only her body and mine merging.

There's never been anyone or anything before this. Whatever I may have felt or done before this is irrelevant, something totally unrelated to what I'm experiencing now. Those other meaningless moments were a single candle flame flickering weakly in the corner of an empty room. This…this, it's—it's a sun. Kylie, her breath in my ear and her arms around me and her lips whispering my name in pleading awe and her legs curling around my waist to hold me deep and close, it's not just a sun, it's a galaxy, a whole universe of numberless stars scintillating with matchless glory.

"Oh, Oz. Oz. My Oz." She writhes against me, breathing only to whisper my name.

"Yes, Kylie. Yours." So true. I am hers. I've never belonged anywhere, to anyone. Now I do.

I feel her tightening around my cock, and I feel myself losing control, slipping over the edge. The motion of her hips becomes frantic, slamming against mine. Our hipbones crash and clash, and her arm clutches my neck with fierce strength, and I'm holding myself above her with one fist, the other hand tangled into hers. Our fingers grip each other, and I hear myself grunting, groaning, gasping.

"Oh, god, oh, god," she's panting, "ohgodohgodohgodohOz, oh, fuck, Oz. Don't stop, dontstopdontstop."

I laugh. "Why the hell would I stop?"

She laughs with me. "I don't know, but please don't. I'm gonna come so hard, so fucking hard."

"Me, too, sweetness. Right now. God, I'm coming right now, Kylie."

"Yes, yes!" Her fingernails gouge down my back, dig into my ass, and her hips slam, slam, slam against mine, and she's shrieking a wordless wail.

Together, then, we come. It's nuclear explosion, every cell in my body lighting up and striking nova-hot, and I can't stop myself from crashing into her again and again, but she welcomes my hard thrusts with frantic slamming strokes of her own, and the only sound coming from her lips is my name, over and over and over again, chanting as we finally slow and go limp.

I slump onto her for a moment, unable to hold my weight any longer. Her arms slide around my shoulders and her hands circle soothingly on my back and neck. Her lips touch my ear, and she's gasping for breath, her heels hooked around the back of my knees. I move to get up, but she holds me in place. "No, don't move. I love this. I love your weight on me."

"I'm crushing you."

She wraps her arms and legs tighter around me. "Good. Crush me."

"You're crazy." I laugh.

She nods against me. "Yep."

We stay like that for a time I have no need to measure. Eventually, I roll off her and pull out of her, duck into the bathroom to wrap up and throw away the condom. When I come back, Kylie is sprawled on her stomach on my bed, the sheet low over her ass, her hair a tangle on my pillow. I open the window a crack and light a cigarette, smoke it slowly and watch Kylie sleep in my bed. I'm drowsy, too. I crush out the cigarette and slide down and lie beside her, my back pressed against the wall, giving her space, not wanting to disturb her. She murmurs something inaudible. Her eyes crack open and she sees me, shifts toward me. I pull her head onto my chest, tug the sheet over us. Another first for both of us. I sleep with her, holding her, and I sleep better than I ever have in my life.

"Shit!" Kylie's panicked curse wakes me.

I sit up. "What's wrong, sweetness?"

"It's almost one in the morning, Oz. I should go home."

"What time are you supposed to be back?"

She shrugs. "I don't have a set time."

"Then how about you just send your dad a text to check in?"

She taps at her phone, and I read the text over her shoulder: **hanging out with Oz still. Just checking in.**

A few seconds later, her dad's response comes through: **Thanks for checking in. Be home by two. ILU**

K. Thx and ILU too. She sends the text, puts the phone away, and scoots off the bed.

We both see the splotch of blood on the sheets at the same time, and neither of us knows quite how to react. I meet Kylie's eyes. "Are you okay?"

She nods. "Yeah. A little…sore, I guess. But really, really good. Sorry about your sheets?" She says it like a question.

I shrug. "No big deal. They're just sheets. I'll take care of it."

"Good. I have to pee." She stands up, still naked, and I simply cannot take my eyes off her. "Will your mom be home anytime soon? Should I put on clothes to go to the bathroom?"

I wave my hand. "Nah. She's never home before two or three. You're good."

While Kylie is in the bathroom, I strip the sheets off the bed and wad them into a ball. I take them out into the kitchen and stuff them into the kitchen trash, which I then tie up and set by the front door. I put the single set of clean sheets on my bed and sit, thinking how strange it is that I have absolutely zero desire to get high right now. Always before, with the random girls in my past, we'd smoke before and after, to numb the sense of vulnerability. It's easier to pretend it doesn't mean anything, to act as if the casual, one-time-only nature of our liaisons was normal when we're blazed out of our skulls. With Kylie, I'm sober. I'm totally me, totally aware of how significant what we just shared was. I relish the significance, admit that having it be so real, so meaningful and deeply potent, makes it infinitely better. It's not the same act at all. Not even close.

My door opens, and Kylie enters, closing the door behind her, and then just stands there, weight on one leg, a shy smile on her lips, eyes bright and happy. She stares at me, just looks until I'm unnerved.

"What?" I ask.

She shrugs. "Nothing. Just looking at you. You're gorgeous, you know. Like this especially. Naked, with your hair down. All for me."

Finally she closes the distance between us, sits on the bed. I notice she's brushed her hair, and I smell soap. "Me? No. But thanks, babe. You're the gorgeous one."

"Hey, if I say you're gorgeous, then you are. To me. You don't have to think so for it to be true to me."

She laughs. "This is kind of a backward conversation, isn't it?"

I shrug. "Yeah, kind of, I guess. Does it turn you off that I'm not all…alpha and confident and all that?"

She shakes her head. "No, it doesn't. But the thing is, you are, when you're not thinking about it. You just don't know how to take a compliment. When you're being yourself, you are confident. You know exactly who you are, and you don't make any excuses or apologies for that. That's hot. It's part of what drew me to you. You were so different, and you just don't give a fuck. I love that about you. You just need to accept that I think you're a beautiful person, inside and out. You have flaws, sure. You've had a rough life, and the fact that you're so sweet with me despite how hard you've had it is just incredible."

"Well, thank you."

She shrugs. "It's just the truth." A slow grin crosses her lips. "I still have an hour before I have to be home. Whatever are we going to do to fill that time?"

I play along. "Hmmm. I have no idea. We could watch TV? Play Scrabble?"

She laughs, a light, delightful tinkle. "Sounds boring. I think you should lie down and let me see how long it takes to get you hard again."

I shift down onto my back, and she sits astride me. "I like this game," I say, and then my eyes slide shut as her fingers find me, stroke me. "I'm pretty sure it won't take too long."

She feathers her fingers over my length, and then rolls the tip between her fingers. Already I feel the blood rushing south, filling me. "Not long at all, it looks like." Kylie murmurs. "What if I did this?" She lowers her mouth to my cock, licks me, flicks me with her tongue, and then resumes using her hands when I start to grow. "God, Oz. I love this so much. Watching you get hard, touching you and knowing I make you react that way. It makes me feel…powerful."

"You make my cock hard just by being you," I tell her.

She strokes me, long slow lazy slides of her hand along my now fully erect length. "I think you're ready now."

I nod. "I think so, too. Tell me what you want, sweetness."

She opens a condom and rolls it onto me. "Uh-uh. How about I just…show you?"

I groan. "God, I love how you do that, put it on me." I hold her hips as she settles over me. "Do whatever you want, baby."

"I plan to."

Oh, man, I'm so deeply enthralled by her, captivated by the way she's taking over, taking what she wants, the way she's so eager and passionate and ready for everything with me.

She's got my cock in her hand, the other planted on the mattress by my face to support her weight. She's straddling my hips, her ass in the air, and she's lining my cock up to her entrance. Her eyes narrow and her mouth falls open, and she doesn't hesitate one single second. She slides me into her tight wet heat, gasping with an open mouth as I fill her.

"Oz…shit, you're just…just *so…fucking…big.* It doesn't seem possible that your cock could fit inside me." She sinks down so our hips meet, and I'm deep, so deep. "But it does, and it's so perfect. Like you were made to fit inside me like this."

Her spine bows outward and her head descends to press a kiss to my throat, and my hands are roaming her body, sliding over her hips, up her sides, cupping her boobs and caressing her face, and all this while she's just impaled on me, not moving, both of us reveling in how we puzzle-fit together, how insanely beautiful this is, her above me, kissing all over me, as if her mouth can't get enough of my skin, and I'm kissing her the same way, all over, everywhere my lips can reach to sip my fill of her milk-pale skin, silk-soft skin, fire-hot flesh.

Nipples between my teeth, tits in my hands, hips between my fingers, eyes like hottest fire, like lightning, like electricity, like the ocean, her breath in ragged puffs, and now she leans onto me, head on my chest, spine bowing out, drawing my cock so I'm almost slipping out, and I'm trembling with the need to glide in hard and deep, but I don't—I let her guide us, let her taste the ache of emptiness. She groans and drives me up into her. Rises up on her shins, balancing, and her tits sway heavily as she weaves her fingers into her hair, eyes closed, back arched, head tilted back.

"Ready?" She breathes the question.

"So ready." I hold her hips and stare at her, filling my eyes and my soul and my memory with this vision of her seductive, erotic beauty.

She grinds on me, a roll of her hips, bites her lower lip, and grinds again. Lifts up, sinks down. Moans my name. Lift, sink, moan. A rhythm then, slow, savoring the out-stroke and the emptiness and the glide as I fill her, and then the deep, grinding fullness, each motion deliberate. Faster then, lifting strokes, her thick, strong thighs rippling as she rises up, her fucking glorious tits bouncing, swaying, and I'm meeting her, matching her, driving up as she sinks down.

"Lick my tits, Oz." She looks down at me, never slowing our rhythm. "Suck on my nipples."

I lift up and she leans down, and I take her left nipple into my mouth, suckle it, nip it, bite gently, lick, kiss the areola and the impossibly soft skin around it. She moans, holds my head to her chest. I shift to suck on her right nipple, bite it just a little too hard and she shrieks, but a smile is on her face when I glance up at her, so I know I didn't hurt her.

She's rolling on me now, riding me in a hard, fast rhythm, leaning back and balancing, riding, grinding, taking everything she wants from me and giving me what I need so badly in doing so. It's all of us, an us that's fused, two beings merged and made one. I've heard the lines about how sex is a man and woman becoming one, and I never got it, scoffed, made fun of it, but *god,* do I get it now. This is so, so intense, almost frightening how intense. How much I feel every particle of her soul within me, how I know she's consuming all that I am and that I have absolutely no wish to take myself back. I've never belonged, never fit, never been a part of anything. Now I do, now I'm part of an "us" with Kylie, and I'm totally abandoned to it.

I watch her come. It's honestly the most beautiful thing I've ever seen. She doesn't quite scream, but the sounds she makes are loud and breathy and desperate, and her hips are rolling violently on mine, grinding with my cock deep inside her, and she's clawing at her own body, as if there is a fountain of fire inside her and she's got to get it out any way she can. Her hands lift her own tits, crush them as she whimpers and moans, riding me wildly, and I can only match her thrust for thrust, and I feel my own release pouring through me. I grip her hips and jerk her down onto me, drive up into her, and the groans coming from me are her name, chanted the way she did mine last time.

Her eyes are open and watching me, and I can't take my gaze from her, even though as I come my instinct is to close my eyes. I keep them open and let her see into me as I release. Our hips meet in slow clashing stuttering grinding, and then we go still and she collapses on top of me, panting. Her weight on me is nothing at all, and I hold her, smoothing her hair back and scratching her back and caressing her ass.

"That was even better than the first time," she mumbles. "I can't wait to see how good it is next time."

"Me, neither."

"Can I just sleep here?" She burrows into me, and I hold her tight.

"Yeah, babe." I feel myself slipping out of her, and grimace. "Let me just get rid of this." I pull out, and she shifts forward so I can pull the condom off, tie a messy, clumsy, but effective knot it in and stuff in the crack between the bed and the wall to throw away later.

"I don't wanna ever move. I wanna stay here forever, just like this," she murmurs into my ear.

"Me, too."

Silence stretches between us, comfortable and easy. I feel her slipping into sleep, and I know I have to stay awake to make sure she's home on time. It's hard, though. She's a warm, comforting weight on me, her hair tickling me, her breath on my neck, her hands affectionate and tender in my hair, curled by my face. Nothing has ever been this perfect. Nothing.

I pull the flat sheet up to partially cover us, and feel myself getting drowsy. I try to stay awake, but it's futile.

I'm woken by the front door opening and closing, the sounds of Mom coming home early, setting her things down, lighting a cigarette. I glance at the clock: 1:39. Shit, Kylie has to go.

I hear my door open, and Mom squeaks in surprise when she sees the naked girl asleep on top of me. "Close the door, Mom." I say it calmly, although I'm anything but.

Kylie jerks awake at the sound of my voice, twists to look, and I feel her go tense. "Shit."

She rolls off me and tugs the sheet over herself. "Mrs. Hyde—" But Mom is closing the door, and we're alone again. "Oh, my god, Oz. She saw us. I'm so embarrassed!"

"It's okay, babe. It's fine. It's not a big deal." I brush a lock of hair away from her eyes. "It was good timing. though. It's getting late."

Kylie glances at the clock. "Dammit, I do have to go."

I groan. "Yeah. I don't want you to, though."

"Me, neither."

I stand up and hold my hands out to her, help her stand. We both dress, and then we leave the sanctuary of my room.

Mom is sitting on the couch, smoking a cigarette and drinking a beer, the TV tuned to some reality show rerun, a bunch of rich bitches yelling at each other. She glances at us as we emerge, and the air in the room gets very, very awkward. "Hi. Um. Oz. Who's—who's this?"

"Mom, this is my girlfriend, Kylie Calloway."

"Hi. Um. How's it going?" Kylie clearly doesn't know what to say, how to act, whether we should address what just happened.

I decide to tackle it head on. "Look, Mom, about just now—"

Mom holds up her hand to stop me. "Oz, you're an adult. We don't need to talk about it. I'll knock from now on, and you keep your door closed."

"Thanks, Mom."

"You are being…safe…right?" Mom says through a cloud of smoke.

"Yes, Mom. Promise. Now we're not talking about this anymore." I put my hand to Kylie's back, nudging her toward the door.

"'Bye, Mrs. Hyde," Kylie says.

"Call me Kate. See ya later, sweetie."

I walk Kylie to her car, make sure she gets in, and lean through the open window. "Lock your doors, and go through the red lights if there's anyone nearby."

"Oz." She runs her hand through my hair. "I wish I could stay. I wish we could just…never have to do this. Never have to say goodbye."

"I know. Me, too."

She makes a face, scrunching her eyebrows and pursing her lips. "Your mom took that better than I expected."

"Well, we're basically just roommates at this point. I only moved here with her and live with her to help her out with rent and bills. I live my life, and she lives hers."

"So she's really just...your friend?" Kylie asks.

I don't answer for a long time. "Do we have to talk about this now?"

Kylie shrugs. "No. I'm just curious."

"I guess you could say we're friends. But there's a lot she's always refused to tell me. I know absolutely zip about my father, and she won't ever tell me shit. I know I've mentioned this. I don't know much about her, either. And I sure as shit don't tell her about my life. So...friends? To me, friends share things. Tell each other shit, whatever. Mom and I don't do that. So are we friends? I don't know. I've never really had any friends, so I'm not sure I'm the best judge of what a friend really is. She's my mother, and my only family. She's the only constant I've ever had in my life. In her own way, she's reliable. She's kept a roof over my head, food in my belly, clothes on my back. She didn't, like, abuse me, and there was never a constant train of boyfriends. I don't know if she's ever had a boyfriend, actually. If she has, I haven't known about it." I realize this as I'm saying it, and I'm not sure what to think or feel about it all. "So she always...fulfilled her responsibilities as my mother. She made sure I went to school, packed my lunches, kissed me if I got hurt as a little kid. But...are we *close*? I don't think I could say we are. Not like you are with your folks. I think Mom and I are…just two people thrown together by fate."

Kylie shakes her head. "That's kind of sad, Oz."

I shrug, going for a nonchalance I don't entirely feel. "Maybe it is. I don't know. It is what it is."

Kylie frowns. "I hate that phrase. It's an excuse to accept something that isn't always acceptable."

"What am I supposed to do about it, Ky? I can't change Mom. I can't change the past. Sometimes you really do just have to accept the unacceptable." The bitterness in my own voice, the jaded apathy…it disgusts even me.

She tugs on my hair, which is still loose around my shoulders. "I wasn't—I was just talking about that phrase. Not about you or your life, Oz."

I sigh. "I know. Talking about Mom makes me a little crazy sometimes." I lean in through the window, and she tilts her chin up to meet my lips. "Go. Be safe."

"I'll text you when I'm home."

I nod and step back, watch her twist in her seat to look behind her as she backs out, then go back inside to my room, marveling at my life, what it's become. For the first time, I'm starting to see something like potential. Like life isn't something to just *get through,* but something that could be…enjoyable.

The hope germinating in my chest scares me, because it's such a fragile little shoot, tender and green and new, and the slightest breeze could kill it. And the many bones in my darkened closet ache from the impending storm.

Ten: Tension in Your Gut
Colt

SOMETIMES, YOUR GUT IS TENSE. For months, or weeks, it'll be just this ache, this emptiness, this sense of something *coming*. I hate that feeling. It's like knowing you've forgotten something, but not knowing what. Like that moment, that split second when you look in your rearview mirror and you see the car behind you coming way too fast, and you're stopped at a light and you know there ain't dick you can do to stop the crash.

It's not Nell. Nell is fine. She's herself, doing what she does. It's not us. We're great. We're in love. We fuck each other senseless several times every week, and we never get tired of it. It's not me, I'm just...

me. I tinker with my Triumph, which is almost done. I work with The Harris Mountain Boys, getting their album cut so we can really get this tour going.

So then…what is it?

Kylie, Oz, and Ben. It's the only thing that makes any sense. I know Kylie and Ben had that shitty argument in my garage, and I haven't spoken to Ben since. He goes to classes, football conditioning, works out. But he's just drifting, I think. I see him on the front porch, and I get the sense that he's fuming, stewing. Brewing and brooding. And I know better than anyone that brooding doesn't do shit.

Kylie is giddy. She comes back from seeing Oz and she's glowing. She really likes that guy, and he seems to be doing good things for her. So…good for him. Good for them. I like seeing my daughter happy.

She's in the basement every spare moment, practicing like mad for their gig, bringing Oz over for jam sessions that last into the night. Then she goes home with him and doesn't return till late. I'm not an idiot, of course, but what's a guy to do? She's graduating in a few months. She'll be off to college somewhere soon, and that'll the be the end of me having any kind of day-to-day influence on her. At least right now I know when she comes and goes and who she's with, and I can sniff her clothes when she passes me, smell her breath and watch her eyes and listen for the slur in her speech. And, so far, no warning signs.

Just her, happy with Oz.

And Ben, brooding.

And the feeling like something is coming. I don't know what it is, and I don't know when it will happen.

But, worst of all…I don't think there'll be anything I can do about it.

Eleven: Falling Under

Oz

It's Thursday, seven fifty-eight. The bar is buzzing, humming. Busy. Not insane, but a lot of people in varying stages of intoxication. All of them, it seems, are eyeing Kylie and me with idle curiosity. Nell and Colt are sitting at a little round table a dozen paces from the low stage, sipping on draft beer and chatting quietly as they wait for Kylie and me to start.

We've plugged in, tuned up, arranged sheets of music, gone over our set list, checked that our mics work and all that necessary pre-show bullshit. Now it's time to start performing. This isn't an open mic night. They're just strangers with no vested interest in Kylie or me or our music. We're about to play for money like real professional musicians.

Shit, I'm gonna puke.

Except I can't. I take a deep breath, flip my pick between my fingers, and lean in to my mic. "Hey, everybody. How are ya'll doing?" I look out at the crowd and a few people glance our way, there's a couple random claps, and a whole hell of a lot people just ignoring me. "Okay, cool. So I'm Oz, and this is Kylie. But you don't really give a shit, do you? Not yet, at least. So let's just jam, huh?"

I tap my index and middle fingers against the guitar just beneath the bridge in a quick three count, glancing at Kylie sitting at the piano adjacent to me, turned partially toward me and partially toward the crowd. She grins at me, and on three we're into a cover of "Down" by Jason Walker. The crowd digs it, digs the groove we give it. By the time we finish the song, the audience is starting to pay attention, realizing we don't suck horribly. We do a few current country songs, stripped down and rearranged a bit for our style. They're really into us then, shouting out suggestions, whistling, heads bobbing. Kylie and I are both pumped, grinning crazily at each other. This is fun, exciting, exhilarating. I feel alive, as if electricity is running through my veins, as if my entire being is humming, as if I'm sucking the life and the energy and the excitement rising from the crowd into my soul. There are no nerves, no fear, no inhibitions, only confidence. We dive without pausing into one of our original songs, the first piece we played at the talent show. The crowd isn't quite sure what to make of it at first, but by the end they're howling wildly.

We let the notes fade, and I shift on the stool, clear my throat, and lean into the mic. "Yeah, so that last song we just did was one we wrote ourselves. We hope you liked it. We've got a couple other originals we're gonna do for you. First, though, this next one is a really cool song by a band called Snow Patrol. This is 'Set Fire to the Third Bar.'"

There are a bunch of whistles and scattered applause as I name the band and the song. I let Kylie splurge on a set of effects pedals for me, and I've been spending the last week playing with those, finally discovering how to get the perfect distortion effect for this song.

We shift from that into a few more stock country songs, boring but the kind of thing the crowd can really get into, songs they know and can sing along to, slosh their beers to. Finally, it's time for a break, and Kylie and I slip out into the alley behind the kitchen. As soon as the door closes behind us, Kylie is jumping up and down, squealing and clapping.

"They love us, Oz!" She flings herself into my arms and buries her face in my neck, kicking her feet as I lift her off the ground. "Can you believe it? They really like us! I think we have a real shot at this."

I let her down to the ground, and my hands slide against her back, hold her flush to me. "It's crazy, but I love it. I never thought this would be me, but I really love performing."

She lifts up on her toes and wraps her arms around my neck. "I never doubted you, Oz. You're so talented it's insane."

I can't help but kiss her. "It was all you, Kylie. You believed in me, pushed me. I would never have discovered that I was even any good at this if it wasn't for you."

She smiles, her lips curving against mine. "I'll take the credit for that. But the talent is all you."

The smile and the laughter become heat, become a kiss, become her hands against the back of my neck, pulling me closer, keeping me locked against her, as if I'd ever willingly pull away. The door to the bar opens, and we break apart, only our hands remaining in contact.

"You guys are back on in five," Colt says, lifting an eyebrow.

"Gotcha," I say.

He reaches out a hand and I take it, shake it. "You two are seriously fucking killing it. I'm proud of you."

It should sound condescending—I should be irritated or pissed at the way he says that, but I'm not. I'm giddy, I'm all sappy and happy-clappy at his praise. Coming from an industry pro like Colt Calloway, it's huge.

"Thanks, Daddy. And thanks for coming. Having you here makes it that much better." Kylie goes in for a hug, and Colt smiles tenderly at his daughter.

"Wouldn't miss it for the world, Ky." He kisses the top of her head, and then nudges her toward the door. "Ya'll better get back in there. You've got fans waiting. And I think I saw Andersen Mayer from RCA out there, just by the way."

"Way to make me nervous all over again, Dad, thanks." Kylie smacks Colt's shoulder.

"Nah, he's cool. He knows talent when he sees it."

Kylie's eyes narrow. "Did you tip him off?"

Colt gives his best impression of innocence. "Tip him off? No."

"Dad."

He sighs and waves a hand. "For real, I didn't. I was talking to him and just mentioned, in passing, that I was going to watch my daughter play her first gig tonight. That was it, I swear. He came on his own."

Kylie groans. "That counts as tipping him off. You knew he'd show up."

"I didn't *know*. I just hoped." He takes Kylie by the shoulders. "Listen, Ky. Andy won't even talk to you after the show if he doesn't see potential in you, and that'll have nothing to do with me. He wouldn't sign someone, not even my own daughter, unless he thought they'd sell records. He owes me nothing, so me hinting that you'd be here, hoping he'd come, that was just…stacking the odds in your favor a tiny bit. The rest is up to you. I know you want this to be on your own talent, without using me and Mom, but you can't fault for me for wanting to at least *help,* just a little."

Kylie kisses him on the cheek. "I know, Daddy. And thank you."

He nods, and pushes her toward the door. "Now get. Go play your ass off." I follow a few steps behind Kylie, but stop when I feel Colt's hand on my bicep. "Hey, one quick thing. She's happy with you. So… good job. You're a good guy, Oz."

I feel emotion squeezing my throat. "Thanks, Colt. That means a lot." I suck in a deep breath and push the emotions down. "Gotta go play. I'll see you after."

The rest of the gig goes even better than the first part. There's an older man sitting at Nell and Colt's table. He's slim, trim, wearing a pair of faded dark-wash jeans and a white button-down, black belt, and black boots. Silver hair swept back, glittering, sharp dark eyes, thin mouth. He's focused on us, on me. Watching my hands as I play, I can tell he's thinking, considering, listening carefully to each note. This has to be Andersen Mayer, the record label guy. What is he, an executive? Talent scout? I don't know. I know jack shit about the music industry, the way it works behind the scenes. I try to push him out of my mind and focus on playing, on singing, on my breathing, on not straining my vocal chords. Nell sat in during a few of the practice sessions in Kylie's basement, and she gave me some pointers on how to improve my singing. After I started using her advice, I heard an immediate difference in the sound of my voice. The breathing especially made things a shitload better. Knowing when to draw breath, how to let it out with the notes, it all made a huge difference. So instead of wondering what Andy Mayer thought, I focused on my breathing. On each chord, each shift of my fingers.

We did two more original songs, and we closed with "She Is Love" by Parachute. We stripped that song down to a very basic series of chords, making our harmony the focal point of the piece. We'd practiced this song a hundred times, I think, knowing it was probably our best cover, and I couldn't help glancing at the man sitting with the Calloways, watching his eyes and the toe of his boot tapping, the nod of approval, the way he leaned in to whisper to Colt, his eyes on Kylie and me.

When we say goodnight to the audience and unplug is when the nerves really hit, when the disbelief that we really pulled this off slams into me. I mean, shit. I learned enough material for a two-and-a-half-hour set in less than a month. I messed up a couple of times, missed a word, skipped a line, but nothing major. Which, to my thinking, is pretty amazing, considering I'd never even thought about actually performing before the talent show. I mean, sure, I'd daydream about being in a metal band or something, but it was just daydreaming, idle thoughts that I never tried to turn into reality.

We don't have much gear to pack up, so it doesn't take us long. I'm stacking the guitar cases into Mom's pickup, which I borrowed for this gig, when I feel a hand on my shoulder. I turn around to see the guy from the label standing behind me. Kylie is leaning against the truck, facing away, tapping at her phone. I nudge her as I shake his hand.

"Oz Hyde," I tell him.

"Andersen Mayer, RCA records." His grip is firm, but not crushing, and his smile is easy. "I have to say I was very impressed by your performance today, you two. Miss Calloway, you are every bit as talented as your parents, which isn't surprising. But you, Mr. Hyde. I have to admit, when I first saw you, your appearance threw me off, led me to expect a…different kind of sound. You're far more talented than I'd initially expected."

Kind of a backhanded compliment, but I only shrugged. "Appearances can be deceiving. I'm glad you liked our music, Mr. Mayer."

"Do ya'll have any other original material you didn't play today? Your covers were excellent, of course, but your original songs were fascinating. They almost defy genre, but with the right producer in the booth, I think we could tweak your sound enough to appeal to both the mainstream rock crowd and the edgier country people." Andersen seems excited. "In fact, I think I have a producer in mind, actually. He's kinda new to the game, but he's done some really amazing work. Would you be interested in a meeting?"

Kylie and I exchange glances. "We'd love to," Kylie answered for us. "I'd have to talk to my mom and dad first, but—"

"Of course, of course. I know you'll want their help navigating the sometimes treacherous waters of the music business." He fishes a business card from a metal case in his back pocket. "Call me first thing in the morning. I've got to go over my schedule with my assistant, but I'd like to set up a meeting with ya'll sometime in the next week or so. I'll get ahold of Jerry and see when he can hook up with us."

"Sounds good," I say, and we both shake Andersen's hand.

He's gone then, striding down the street with his phone in hand, already dialing a number. When he's out of earshot, Kylie turns to me, eyes wide as saucers, giddy excitement shivering through her. She's about to hyperventilate, I'm pretty sure.

"Holy *shit,* Oz! Holyshitholyshitholyshit! That was Andersen Mayer. We've got an interview with Andersen Mayer. And Jerry? I wonder if he's talking about Jerry Gross? Dad would know, but if it is, that would be huge, too."

"Why?"

I can tell Kylie's brain is going a million miles a second. "He's the producer behind some of the best music to come out of Nashville over the last three years. He did Brent Howell's new album, which was edgy as hell. A lot like Eric Church's harder stuff, 'The Outsiders' and whatever."

"You really know a lot about this business, huh?" I ask, impressed.

She shrugs. "Well, yeah. I've grown up listening to my parents talk. They're indie, on their own label, but they know everyone in this town, and I've paid attention. Music is…all I know, really. It's what I've wanted to do since the first time I watched Mom and Dad perform live. I was six, and I sat in a little chair just off-stage, and I was just…in awe. I knew then that I would be just like them."

"And now you're on your way."

She grins at me. "*We're* on our way." She leans up and kisses me. "Come on. Let's go celebrate!"

We get our cash from Dan, say goodbye to Nell and Colt—after updating them on the quick conversation with Andersen—and head out. We go, of course, to my place, but after carting the gear into my room, Kylie pulls me back outside.

"I don't want to stay in. Not yet. I'm too excited. Take me for a ride on your bike! Please?"

"Where do you want to go?" I ask.

She shrugs, smiles. "I don't care. We don't have to go anywhere. Just ride."

"Sounds good to me."

So we ride. I bought Kylie a leather jacket to wear while we rode, and she's got it on now. The engine roars in our ears, the road flies under the tires, and Kylie's arms wrap tight and low around my waist.

Her cheek rests against my shoulder, her breasts squish against my back, and all is perfect. It's a warm spring night, clear, the moon high and a few bright stars shining through the city-glow. I head out of the city, away from the suburbs and away from the city lights. We ride until the night turns black and dark and thick, finding a two-lane highway cutting through rolling fields.

I turn off the highway, onto a narrow dirt road beside a fenced-in pasture. A stand of trees lines the pasture on one side, and a single orange light glows over the road, suspended from a power line. I let the bike slow to a stop beneath the light, at the edge of the road, kick out the stand, and slip off my helmet, hang it from the handlebar. Kylie does the same, leaning over me to hang the strap. She doesn't back away but lifts up on the footrest to press her nose into my neck, her breath hot on my skin, her hands sneaking up under my shirt to graze my stomach and chest.

Crickets sing, and a bullfrog croaks from somewhere in the distance. An owl hoots, eerie and haunting. Out here, far from the city lights, the stars are a diamond veil across the black sky, the crescent moon pale.

Kylie stands on the footrest, swings her leg around to sit on the gas tank, facing me. Straddling me. Kissing me. Hands on my cheeks, breathing my breath, eager for me. Needing me. I brush my thumb across her cheekbone, deepen the kiss, and search for the hem of her shirt. Find it, slide my palm up her back.

"I want you, Oz," she whispers in my ear.

"On the bike?"

"Why not?"

"Well, we'll just have to be careful of the pipes. They're hot as fuck still."

Kylie slides off the bike, shrugs out of her jacket, stands facing me, peels off her forest-green long-sleeve T-shirt, slips out of her bra. Unbuttons her tight black jeans, kicks off her flats. Hangs her clothes on the handle of my bike, stands before me in nothing but a pair of black-and-white lacy panties. She turns around, showing me how the panties are cut high across the cheeks of her ass. Bends at the waist, teasing me with the round perfection of her ass, sliding off her underwear. Straightens, turns, approaches me. Stuffs the scrap of lace into my hip pocket. Pushes my jacket off. Unbuckles my belt. Lowers the zipper. Opens the button. Pulls my cock out of my boxers, slides her fist around me.

"This is so fucking hot, Oz." She puts her feet on the tops of my boots, swings astride the bike. "Being naked outside like this, with you? On your bike? God, I could come just from how exciting this is. It feels naughty."

"It is naughty. We could get caught."

"That just makes it even more fun." She lifts my shirt up and off, pushes at my open pants to free more of my cock.

I lift up and wiggle my jeans under my ass. Lift her by the hips, lean in to suck her hardened nipple into my mouth. She moans, lets her head hang back on her shoulders, writhing into my mouth, moving her wet slit against my aching cock.

Just before I slide into her, I pause and groan. "We don't have a condom. I didn't bring any. They're in my bag at home."

Kylie grips my shoulders with clawing fingers, lifts higher, and impales herself on me. "It's fine. I'm on the pill. I can't wait. I need this, Oz. You don't even know how bad I need this."

I bite the round of her shoulder, growling. "Fuck, Kylie. I think I do. I need it just as bad. I just don't want to make any mistakes."

She sinks down so we're flush. "Nothing about us could ever be a mistake. Nothing. Oh, god, oh, god. Yeah, Oz, just like that."

I push up with my hips, grinding into her. She's riding me hard, rolling her pussy onto me, deep and fast. No finesse, no gentility, just my mouth on her tits and her hands gouging reddened claw marks in my skin, her moans loud and unbridled, our bodies merging. There's nothing between us, just my flesh and hers, her wet slick heat clinging to my cock, her embrace around me, her tits bouncing beautifully with our motion. This, us bare to each other, there's never been anything better, no intimacy more profound than this.

I hold onto her ass, slip my fingers into the crease, clutching the firm hot globes and lifting her, letting her fall. She moves, groans, rests her forehead against mine, pushing down on my shoulders to lift up. By accident, my middle finger slides in a little too far, touches her tight little asshole. I feel her muscles clench, her body freeze, her breath cut in, sharp and surprised.

"Oz...oh, god, Oz. What are you doing?" She pulls away enough to meet my eyes.

I start to move my hands. "I'm sorry, babe, I didn't mean to—"

She sinks down, pinioning my hands between her ass and my thighs. "Wait...just—it just took me by surprise." She lifts up, eyes on me. "Try it, Oz. Just—just a little."

"Wait, what? You want me to..."

"Just touch me there. Just a little bit." She's breathless. I hesitate, and then wiggle my middle finger. Just a tiny, slight pressure. She tenses, shifts up, and then arches her back, and I feel her relax. I apply gentle pressure, and tight warmth pinches the tip of my finger. "Yeah—oh—oh, yeah. Oh, *fuck*, Oz. I—I like that. I like it, just like that."

She lifts up, sinks down, and my hand stays flush against her ass cheek, and she moans, writhes on me. Her moans become shrieks, and her grinding on me becomes frantic. I can only move with her, keep us balanced, let her do the work. I can't even breathe, can't even believe she's doing this, letting me touch her like this, and how much she likes it. She's rolling hard and fast, wild, screaming. The quiet is sliced by her voice, by mine now grunting and growling and cursing and murmuring her name, and I feel the tight heat around my finger pinch, release, pinch, release, pulsating, and then she's lifting and sinking with manic, rhythmless frenzy.

The stars themselves brighten above me, and the moon fills out, and the earth rumbles, and I come apart inside her as she screams with deafening volume, and the tip my finger is almost crushed by the way her body clenches around me, and we're moving, moving…the sky shatters and the planets wobble in their orbits.

Kylie rests her mouth against my shoulder, gasping. "Oh, my fucking god, Oz. I came so hard it literally hurt. I can't—it's hard to breathe. I can't move. Oh, god. You just killed me, baby."

The starlight coats her pale skin silver, and I can only marvel, wonder, hold her and hope she never stops wanting me. Words tumble in my head. Emotions whirl, collide. A thought hammers in my head, demanding release. But the fear of what it means, of saying it, of meaning it, it's almost too much.

"Say something, Oz." Kylie sits back. "I feel you thinking." Her blueblue eyes pierce me, demanding my truth.

I hesitate, suck in oxygen and wish it was courage. "I love you, Kylie."

Holy shit, I said it.

She's stunned silent. Her eyes fill, waver. A tear falls. She swallows hard. "You—you do?"

I laugh. "Yeah, I do. I have for a while, I think. I'm just now realizing how much."

"And how much is that?" She's unabashedly weeping, smiling, clinging to me.

I blink and swallow. "A fucking lot. Like, so much it scares me. Like…if you ever—if we didn't—shit. Just…it's scary. I've never needed anyone. But now I need you, and it's makes me feel so—weak. Vulnerable. Like you own a piece of me, and you could just crush it, if you wanted."

She clutches me, presses our bodies together, my softening cock starting to slip out of her. "I won't, Oz. I swear to you, I promise you on my life, on my soul, on everything I am. I'll never…never hurt you, never leave you." She pulls away so I can see the truth in her eyes. "I love you, too, Oz. I'll never want anything or anyone but you. Not ever. I never will."

"Me, neither, sweetness." I hold her tight. "Me, neither."

After a moment, Kylie starts to wiggle, and she slides gingerly off the bike, wincing. "I'm…a little messy now."

I lean back and dig a spare T-shirt out of the saddlebags. It's old, and not in the best shape, but it's clean. I hand it to her, and I watch her clean herself, folding the shirt and then handing it back to me. I stuff it back into the saddlebags, and watch her dress.

When we're both dressed, we lie on the grass at the side of the road, staring up at the stars, talking. We talk about performing, about songs to cover, about possibly getting a record deal this quickly. We talk about all this, and everything is "we" and "us." We're planning a future together. Going on tour, possibly. All sorts of possibilities, and the future we plan is bright and perfect and hopeful.

Sometime past one in the morning, we decide to head back. We stop once for gas, and for a quick bite at McDonald's. I'm a little tired, so I get a large Coke, and drink it all. We're back on the road again, and I'm only now realizing how far we really went. We must have driven a good two, two and a half hours outside of Nashville. It's a longer drive home than it felt on the way out, but it was all worth it. Kylie holds me tightly, rubbing my chest and stomach, nuzzling against me.

Then it happens so fast. So fucking fast. I'm on the freeway, passing beneath an overpass, approaching an on-ramp. A semi rumbles beside me, blocking my path to the left. He's seen me, I know that much, but it's not him I'm suddenly worried about. It's the sleek red Corvette roaring onto the freeway from the on-ramp. He *doesn't* see me. My heart is hammering suddenly. I brake hard, but it's not enough. He's in my space, I'm caught in his blind spot, he's not even looking. I can see him texting with one hand, the detail burning into my panicked brain. I can see the glow of the screen on his face, a hint of red and black leather seat, a profile of a face, the instrument panel, one hand on the wheel, the other holding his phone, not paying attention, not seeing me. Not seeing us. Kylie's gripping me with clawed fingers, and I know she's starting to realize the danger now. The semi doesn't move, not realizing the problem.

Seconds split and fracture, splintering into moments, into individual pumps of my heart. Breathe—breathe—breathe. *What do I do?* Gun it? Try to squeeze past them both? Not enough room. I'm trying not to panic, but I am. I hit the brakes, praying with all my non-believing heart that I can hold it steady. The semi roars past, and the Corvette slips ahead of me. I'm in the clear, I think. I sigh in relief. It'll be okay. It'll be okay.

Only, another semi is behind me, loud and huge, horn blaring, tires squealing, groaning as it tries to slip to the left of me, but there's a car there and he can't, and I'm already braking, close to losing it. I have no choice but to swerve away, onto the shoulder. My heart is about to vomit out of my throat, adrenaline crashing like thunder, fear slamming like tribal drums.

Kylie is screaming. My back tire is skipping, sliding, bouncing. I'm losing it. I'm gonna lose it. I'm gonna put it down. Thank god I'd brought the bike down to less than forty, but it's going to be bad. I remember the training from the class: go limp. Don't tense. But Kylie. Kylie. Shitfuckgoddammit, no, Kylie…

I feel the back tire going out from beneath us. The bike is sliding sideways. I let it drop, let it go, let it slide away sideways. No time for anything else, no choice, nothing but this happening in slow tragic awful motion, entirely too fast to stop.

fuckohfuckohfuck

Moments shred, and then time stops.

I feel the ground hit, force myself to stay limp, loose. I'm on my ass, sliding, and the bike is skidding away, and I feel Kylie, hear her screaming. Momentum starts to roll me. As I twist, I see Kylie. Instinct rather than choice causes me to grab her. Crush her to my chest as hard as I can. Cradle my arms around her body, tense them like bars around her fragile form.

I'm rolling. Pain. Fracturing time. Tumbling rolling spinning sliding. A bounce, and my grip on Kylie is broken. I watch her flip and twist away from me, and then my own sight is ground-sky-ground-sky and agony is lancing through me, and finally I stop, on my face.

I can't breathe, can't move, but I have to get to her.

Someone is screaming: "KYLIE! *KYLIE!*" It's me—I'm screaming. Hoarse, raw, desperate.

"Oz…" I hear her, barely audible, breathless. But I hear her.

I crawl. I can't get my legs to work, and my arms won't cooperate, either. All is pain. Something hot and sharp is slicing at my elbow, my upper arm. My knees. But I have to get to her. I crawl anyway and refuse to look at my body, refuse to acknowledge the damage. Grit is bitter in my mouth. I spit, taste blood, salty and tangy and slippery and warm. I'm gasping, and sand and dirt spray away from my mouth and nose, settle on my tongue and in my nostrils. Scrabble on the asphalt, feel fingernails ripping, tearing, toes pushing and knees sliding. A foot. Two. Four.

There she is. Thank god I made her put on her leather jacket. It's a thin thing, expensive, soft leather, but it protected her skin. Her jeans are shredded and red, but she's writhing, and I don't think her legs are broken. "Kylie…Kylie. I'm—I'm here." I reach her, blink, blink against the sweat. Or maybe it's blood in my eyes. I don't know. She's gasping, dragging in shuddering breaths. "Kylie. Breathe. Please, breathe."

She's got the helmet on still, a full-coverage cheap black helmet. I fumble at it, and she helps me tug it off. Her hands are bleeding, knuckles red and scraped and raw. "Oz?" The helmet rolls away, crunching in the road grit on the shoulder. Sweat pastes her hair to her face. Her eyes frantic, searching, seize on mine. "Oz?"

I reach out, brush at her hair, lying on my stomach, one elbow braced beneath me. My fingers, as they touch her face, are dripping blood, the nails ripped off. "Where are you hurt, Kylie? Talk to me, talk to me, baby."

"You—you're bleeding."

"I don't care. I'm fine." I rake my eyes over her body, hunting for breaks, blood. "Are you okay? Are you injured?"

"I can't—can't catch my—my breath." She's opening her mouth, sucking in short, desperate breaths. "Chest, hurts. Ribs."

"Don't move, okay? Just try to breathe, little breaths." I flop onto my back, groaning as the impact sends spears of agony through me. I dig in my hip pocket for my phone. It comes out in pieces, smashed. "You—you have your phone?"

"Jack—jacket…ins—inside pocket." She's shaking, blinking, fighting for breath, and I don't fucking know what to do.

I unzip her coat, gingerly. Find the phone in the inside pocket, intact. Lift her shirt, see bruises already forming on her ribs, something looking out of place. Broken, maybe. Jesus fuck. *Don't let her lungs be punctured. Please. Please. Let her be okay.* I don't even know who I'm pleading with, but the thoughts ramble through my head, unstoppable. It all falls apart into *pleasepleaseplease.*

I dial 911.

"Nine-one-one what's your emergency?" A calm male voice, neutral.

"Motorcycle accident. On I-40." I peer behind me, and I can just barely make out the exit number. I tell her.

"Is anyone hurt?"

"Yeah. My girlfriend. I think—I think she broke her ribs. I don't know. She's having trouble breathing."

"And you, sir? Are you okay?"

"I don't—I don't know. I don't fucking care. Just get someone here. Help her. Please. Help us."

"Units are en route to your location, sir. Can you tell me your name?"

"Oz. My name is Oz."

"Oz what?"

"Oz Hyde."

I glance at Kylie, who is still taking short gasps for breath, her eyes hunting for me. I drop the phone, reach for her hand, squeeze. I hear a tinny voice calling my name. I fumble the phone back to my ear.

"Sir? Sir, are you there? Oz?"

"I'm—I'm here."

The man asks me a series of questions, and I answer them all, but I'm only really paying attention to Kylie, to watching her face, her blue-tinged lips, her chest shifting shallowly with each tiny panting breath. Our eyes never leave each other, and her hand squeezes mine, weakly.

"Kylie? Keep squeezing my hand. I'm here. You'll be okay. We'll be okay." I blink, and this time the salty wetness sliding down my face is tears, not blood. I don't care. I have no thoughts but that Kylie makes it through this okay.

I hear sirens in the distance, getting closer. Lights flash, tires skid and crunch, doors open, voices speak in calm tones, I see blue uniform-clad bodies crouching beside Kylie, shining a flashlight in her eyes, probing at her ribs, fitting an oxygen mask to her face. A young, clean-shaven, acne-scarred face fills my vision, calm brown eyes. "Sir? You're Oz?"

I nod. "Yeah. Kylie…is she—is she okay? Will she be okay?"

He shines a light in my eyes. "Yes, sir. She'll be okay, I promise."

I twist to watch them load Kylie onto a stretcher, lift her into the ambulance. Now, finally, I can feel my own pain. And suddenly, whiteness and heat and pain shoot through me, as if it was waiting in the wings, waiting until I knew Kylie was okay, taken care of. And now it's blazing through me, and I'm dizzy, can't see, can't breathe, can't move, blinking, gasping, see stars, and they're replaced by a roof, lights, walls, the interior of an ambulance. Something hard touches my nose, around my mouth, and I feel cool oxygen filling me, and I can almost see, almost breathe. Hands do things to me. Touch me, cut away my pants. My shirt. I've still got Kylie's phone clutched in my hand.

There is a sense of motion. I need Kylie. Need to see her. Need to talk to her, need to know she's okay. I need to call her parents, tell them I almost got her killed, that I got her hurt, that I couldn't protect her, couldn't keep her safe.

I replay what happened in my head. I can see each individual second of the accident, remember what I did, and think about what I could have done differently. Nothing. That's what. Nothing. I couldn't have done anything differently. But…if she hadn't been on that bike with me, this wouldn't have happened.

Guilt and fear and pain all twist together, form a shredding ball of barbed wire in my chest, and I'm barely cognizant as the ambulance interior is replaced briefly by the entrance of a hospital, and then the white walls of a hallway. I don't know what's happening, or what's wrong with me, and I don't care. All I know is Kylie is hurt, and I have to find her.

I see a face above me, female, older, care-lined eyes, sharp and gray and intelligent. "Kylie? Where is she?"

"She's being attended to, Mr. Hyde. Please, be still. Let us take care of you."

"I need…I need to see her. I need to know she's okay. Will she be okay?" I'm begging, fighting to get off the bed, but hands hold me down. "Just tell me she'll be okay."

"Miss Calloway will be okay. She's alive, and she's getting the best care we can give. We'll let you see her as soon as we can. You have to let us take care of you, Mr. Hyde."

But I can't calm down. Panic and desperation ripple through me, force me to move, to thrash, and I'm being held down; I feel a poke in my arm, and then darkness swallows me.

I wake up, and my arm is in a cast, resting on my chest. I've got bandages on my other arm, hands, on my legs. My forehead feels tight, burns. The pain is a vise, clenching all of me in an unrelenting grip. I try to breathe, and look around. I see Mom, asleep in a chair, her long legs stretched out, head lolling on her shoulder. She's snoring gently, a light, feminine rasp. I can see the circles under her eyes from her, the worry on her face even as she sleeps.

My mouth is dry, tight, and my throat burns. My eyes are scratchy. I shift and twist on the bed, find the call button and press it. Within minutes a nurse appears, a small, compact woman with brown hair tied back in a bun.

"Mr. Hyde. How are you feeling?" Her voice is a low murmur.

"Like hell. It hurts. I'm thirsty."

"I'll get you something for the pain and some water." She starts to turn away.

I grab her arm. "Kylie. I need—I need to see Kylie."

"Let me get you something for the pain, and then I'll see about bringing you to see her."

I know better than to argue. My best bet is to cooperate and let them bring me to her. I slump back in the bed, blinking against the pain, watching Mom sleep.

What feels like an hour passes, and then the nurse returns, and I see her name tag hanging from a clamp attached to the pocket of her scrubs shirt. *Marie King, RN, LPN.* Her picture looks nothing like her, but such pictures rarely do. She hands me a small paper cup with two large white pills in it, and a cup of water. I swallow the pills, drink all of the water, and set it aside, shift higher in the bed.

"Your girlfriend just woke up as well. I'll bring you to her." Marie moves across the room and unfolds a wheelchair, brings it to me. "Now, don't try to be a tough guy. Let me help you, okay?" She smiles at me, and I slide my legs over the side of the bed, let her put her shoulder underneath my arm.

She's a hell of a lot stronger than her small frame would suggest, lifting me almost without my help off the bed, to my feet, and then keeping me balanced as I twist and lower myself into the chair. Any thoughts of walking myself to Kylie's room vanish with that brief effort. Everything hurts. I'm sweating and out of breath. My chest aches and my ribs seem tight, sending rocketing lances of pain through me as I move. The pills are working, though, and I'm feeling less of the pain. I'm lighter, and a little dizzy. It's nice.

Mom wakes up, stretches, yawns, and then sees me. "OZ!" She lurches to her feet, falls to her knees beside my wheelchair. "God, baby, I—I was so worried."

I let her hug me, and I hug her back, and it's the first time in at least ten years that a hug between us isn't awkward. "I'm okay, Mom."

"What *happened,* Oz?" She's brushing my hair away from my face. It's loose around my shoulders, and I hate it.

I pull it back with one hand, grimacing as that motion shoots pain through me, harsh despite the medicine. "I got cut off on the I-40. This asshole in a Corvette. He didn't even look as he got on the freeway. He was fucking texting. Never even saw me. A semi was on the other side, so I couldn't avoid him, and there was another semi behind me. Hit the shoulder, tire went out from beneath me. I couldn't—there wasn't anything else I could do but put it down." I blink against the tightness in my throat as I recall the accident.

Flashes of memory hit me like lightning. The driver of the Corvette, face lit by the glow of his phone. The semi behind me, so close, blaring its horn and trying to swerve. I don't even know if anyone stopped to help, to see if we were okay. I don't remember seeing anyone, but my memory is hazy. All I remember is pain, and Kylie bleeding and trying to breathe, and my bike in the distance, tire spinning.

I blink again, and try to shake the images away.

Fuck.

"I couldn't do anything, Mom. It was an accident. I didn't…I didn't mean for it to happen. I tried to stop it, tried to keep her safe." My throat hurts, burns, and my eyes are hot and heavy.

Mom's arms go around me. "I know, sweetie. It was an accident. I know. I'm just glad you're both okay."

"I need to see her." I glance up at the nurse, Marie. "I need to see her, please."

"Of course." Marie moves behind me, pushes me through the door and down the hallway, around several corners.

Mom trails a step behind and to my left, sneakers squeaking on the floor. The hallway echoes with the distorted voice of someone paging someone else. Other nurses pass by going the opposite way, emerge from doors, charts in hand, converse behind desks, tap at keyboards.

Then we're pushing through a doorway, into a dimly lit room identical to mine. A bed, a chair, a monitor turned off, no leads connected. Kylie is sitting up in bed, talking to Colt, who sits in the chair, drawn close to her bed. They both glance at me, and Colt straightens from leaning toward Kylie, stands up, moves toward me.

I'm scared. I wish I could stand up, but I'm dizzy and lightheaded, and it still hurts. "Colt…Mr. Calloway." I glance past him at Kylie, and all I want is to go to her.

But Colt is standing in front of me, looming over me. His blue eyes, so much like Kylie's, are tight, narrow, concerned. "Oz. You okay?"

I shrug. "Yeah. I will be." I blink up at him. "I—I'm sorry. I'm so—so sorry. It happened so fast. So fucking fast. I tried, but there was nothing—nothing I could—"

A heavy hand touches my shoulder, rests there. "I know, Oz. It was an accident. Kylie told me what happened. You did everything you could. No one blames you." He squeezed my shoulder and let go. "You're both alive, and that's all that matters."

I blame me, I don't say.

"Oz." Kylie's voice breaks through the tense silence. "Come over here, Oz." She glances at her dad, the nurse, Mom. "Can we have a few minutes?"

Marie rolls me as close to Kylie's bed as I can get, and then they all leave, closing the door.

I reach out with my free hand and take hers. "Kylie. God, baby. I'm so sorry. I should never have—I almost got you killed." I look at her, and my eyes burn again. "I'm so sorry, Kylie. So sorry."

She reaches out with both hands, puts her fingers over my lips. "It wasn't your fault, Oz. It wasn't your fault. You did everything you could." She swallowed hard. "It was so scary, Oz. You were—there was blood everywhere. I thought you were going to die. I thought—I thought you were going to bleed to death. There was just so much fucking blood, and—and I couldn't breathe—" She stops, blinks, wipes at her eyes. "But you're okay, and I'm okay. We're okay, right? Everything's okay."

I try so fucking hard to keep my eyes clear, but the pain-relieving medication does something to me, and although it doesn't hurt as much anymore, the thickness and the heat in my throat, the burning, the residual fear in her lovely azure eyes and the way she's tense and stiff and clearly in pain…it conspires against me, and I just can't stop the tear from sliding down my face. Fucking crying like a sissy, but I can't help it, and Kylie's hand wipes across my face.

"No, Oz. You can't do that. It's all okay." She blinks and wipes my face again, runs her thumb across my lips. "Accidents happen, and we're okay."

"Yeah, we're okay." I breathe hard, shove it down, stop it, blink hard and blink hard and blink hard, squeeze my eyes shut, swallow the lump, breathe deep and steady myself. "I was just so scared I'd gotten you killed. They took you, and I didn't know what happened to you."

"I've got two broken ribs, and a couple more are bruised. Some cuts and scratches. A few stitches on my left leg. I'll be fine in a few weeks." She looks me over, and worry fills her eyes. "That chair—you're not—you're not…Oz…please tell me you're not—" She can't even say it.

I shake my head and move both of my legs for her, wiggle my toes. "No, no. I'm fine. I'm just…it hurts, and I had some drugs for the pain, which is making me a little lightheaded. I'm fine."

Marie comes in right then. "You both need to rest."

"One more minute," I say, and Marie nods, closes the door. I lean in, kiss Kylie on the lips. It's soft and slow and sweet, and I want to get lost in her kiss, but I can't.

She hisses and has to straighten. "Holy shit…*ow*. God, it hurts." She tries to shift, trying to get more comfortable. "I'm not gonna lie, Oz. It fucking hurts *so* bad. Every breath, every little motion. It all hurts."

"I'm so sorry, Ky. If I could take it from you, hurt for you, I would."

She smiles at me, faint, tired, tight. "I know, Oz. I know." She takes my hand and tangles our fingers together. Her eyes meet mine, burn bright and sincere. "I love you."

That sound, her voice speaking those words to me, it erases everything else. I lean in, rest my cheek gently against her arm. "I love you, too, Kylie. So much."

We're silent, just sitting together. Eventually, Marie, Colt, and Mom come in, and I'm taken to my room and I fall asleep, dream of the accident, and of the glorious heaven that came before, her whispered *I love you* and her skin in the moonlight and then the Corvette is there, phone-lit face, too close, crashing impossibly through the darkness where we clung together on my bike, everything blurring, merging, nothing right, nothing the same.

I wake up sweating, and pain is a wracking spear in my gut. My arm aches, and I realize I don't even know if it's broken.

The next day, we both go home.

We both miss some school. Weeks pass slowly, during which we both heal, moving around stiffly. My arm is broken, and it'll be a long while before the cast comes off. Other than that, I'm fine. My ribs are bruised, but they heal quickly, and the various cuts and deep scrapes on my legs, and the stitches on my head heal as well. Kylie and I just hang out, doing nothing much. Watch TV, do homework together. Anything kinky is off-limits for Kylie until her ribs heal. For the first week, she can't move, can barely breathe.

I never got the chance to take up Colt on his offer to check out his friend's garage, which sucks. That would've been a good job. But I'm not in any shape to work on cars yet. It takes nearly a month, and we're both back to almost normal. My arm is still in a sling, but the cast will come off soon. I'm sitting with Kylie on her front porch, watching a show on Netflix on her laptop, watching night fall around us. We're holding hands, the laptop on both of our laps as we rock gently on the two-person rocking chair. It's become our favorite spot lately, since there's not much else for us to do but sit around.

My gut clenches when I see a black Silverado pull into the driveway across the street. Kylie tenses, too. She hasn't mentioned Ben in a long time, but I have a feeling there was some kind of discussion between them after the accident.

He sees us, and I move the laptop over to Kylie, stand up. Ben is coming this way, hands fisted at his sides.

"Oz." His voice is calm, but sharp.

"Ben." I extend my hand to him, hoping this can be a civil conversation.

I hear the laptop close behind me, and then the chair squeak as she stands up. Her footsteps shuffle. She still has a hard time moving around, her ribs still causing her some pain. Ben's eyes narrow and go hard as he watches her move to stand beside me.

No one speaks for a long time, but Ben's eyes betray a roiling maelstrom of emotion.

"Got something to say, Ben?" I ask. "Then say it."

"Yeah, in fact. I do have something to say." He seems to swell, anger puffing him up. "You almost got her killed, *Hyde*. You and your stupid motorcycle. She can still barely walk. What's going to be next? It'll be something else. I know it. You're a fucking hazard, Hyde. I knew from day one that you'd get her hurt. And you did."

"I'm fine, Ben—" Kylie starts.

Ben talks right over her, ignores her. "You know those ribs almost punctured her lungs? It was a matter of fucking *centimeters,* dude. It could've been her heart. Killed her in seconds. And it would have been *your* fault. Because you just have to try to be so goddamn cool, on your stupid fucking motorcycle."

"You're being an asshole, Ben. It was an accident. It wasn't his fault." Kylie pushes between us, stares him down. "Go home."

"No, Ky. Yeah, it may have been an accident, but that's just the start of it. What's gonna happen with you two? You're gonna go off and, what? Do your little music thing? Play at being musicians? You're gonna drag her around with you on the back of your bike, and eventually you're gonna get her killed."

"Stop it, Ben! You're being ridiculous. It was an accident. And what we do is none of your business."

She frowns up at him, shakes her head. "What's happening to you, Ben? Who are you? And what's this really about?"

Ben spins away, turns back, raking his hand over his head. "What's this about?" He jabs a finger in my direction, and I force myself not to react. "It's about this fucking *asshole*. He's all wrong for you, Kylie. He always was, and he always will be. He's nobody, from nowhere. He'll never be good enough for you! And you're just so fucking blind that you can't see how wrong he is!"

"That's my choice, Ben!" Her voice is raised in a shout, and she pushes at him. The effort is too much, and she stumbles forward, hands on her knees, groaning, sucking in air.

"Fuck off, Ben. You're upsetting her." I step in front of him, blocking his access to her.

"Get out of my way, *Oz*. You don't fucking deserve her, and you know it." His voice is hard as iron, hard as steel, sharp as razors.

"Yeah, you know what? You're right. I don't." I step closer. "I never have and I never will. But guess what? She chose *me*, pal. Not you. You had your chance. You blew it. And now you're jealous. I get it. She's incredible, and I'd be jealous, too. But don't cause problems where there don't need to be any." I make sure he has nowhere to go but through me.

"Get out of my way, Oz." He pushes toward her, tries to go around me, toward Kylie, who is holding a hand to her ribs, gasping for breath, eyes wet, fearful, and she's trying to reach for us.

I stay between him and her. "No. Go home. She asked you to go home. So just fucking go. Leave us alone." I step closer, so I'm nearly touching him.

"Get out of my face."

"Oz…Ben…please…don't—" Kylie gasps.

"I *said*…get *out*. Of. My. Face." Ben bites each word, fists clenched, chest swelling, eyes going manic.

I shrug my arm out of the sling. Ignore the pain. "Walk away, Ben." I swallow my pride and try it nicely. "Please. Just go."

"Or what?" He smirks at me. "Gonna sucker-punch me again?"

I growl. "*You* started that, Ben. Just like you're starting this."

"And I'm finishing it." He shoves me. "Fuck. Off. Get out of here. You don't belong here."

I stumble backward, and habit takes over. Instinct. Fight reflexes kick in. I rocket forward, swinging my good fist. I connect, hard. Ben's head rocks back, and I hear Kylie screaming, pleading for us to stop. It's too late, though. Ben is coming for me. I dodge out of the way, and his fist misses. I pivot, step away, and he follows, swinging again. His face is a rictus of rage, and his fist is huge, coming hard and fast, and it hits me square in the nose, knocks me backward. Pain explodes in my face, blood splatters, and he's still coming, and Kylie is stumbling for me, crying, pleading. I see the terror in her eyes, and I step backward, hold up my hands.

"Ben, hold on—" I don't want to fight him, don't want this pain in her eyes.

But it's too late. Too late. I see him coming, and I try to move, try to block, but I can't. He's too fast, and I'm off-balance. My foot hits the curb, and I stumble backward, out into the street. Headlights bathe me in yellow, a horn blares in my ear. I'm on one foot, on the ball of my foot, spinning, windmilling for balance, but I know this is happening. I see the grille, a Land Rover. I see the emblem, the green and silver, and then I feel my leg shatter, feel the hood sliding under my side and my back, and then my skull impacts the glass of the windshield, and I only have a split second to feel the all-consuming pain, and then darkness rises up within me like a flood. I hear screaming, voices. I'm almost under, fighting to stay above the black cold waters of silence, and I see Kylie, her face above me, tears streaming, her lips move.

Ben is behind her, and why is he crying? He's not hurt, but he's bawling, shaking his head, backing away. I blink, blink, but the darkness won't clear from my eyes, and I focus again on Kylie.

I love you. I love you. Am I saying it? I don't even know. I'm trying. Are the words coming out? Does she know? Can she hear?

Darkness. Cold. Weightlessness. Is that a light coming for me? Is that what they mean when they talk about the light at the end of the tunnel? I don't want it. Stay away from the light.

I cling to the image of Kylie's face. Picture her pale skin lit silver by the moonlight, her eyes the blue of the Caribbean, her lips moving as she tells me she loves me, the impossible beauty of her face and the impossible beauty of the fact that she loves me.

I struggle to hold on to her, onto the warmth, onto reality, onto life.

"Don't go…please, Oz…stay with me…stay with me…" Her voice is broken, so sweet, and I want to reassure her.

"…love…you…" I think that's my voice, but is it really out loud? Is that tattered shred of sound my voice?

I can't fight the blackness anymore. Cold implacable hands drag me under.

"No!" Kylie, pleading. *"NO!"*

I'm falling under.

Silence.

Twelve: Fallout

Colt

Oh, fuck no. I watched it happen, and I watch his chest struggle up and down, and Kylie is screaming and Nell is pulling at her and I'm silent. I see Jason and Becca, our neighbors. The driver of the Land Rover, puking into the grass. Ben, sobbing like a baby, *I didn't mean it, didn't mean to, I'm sorry* tumbling from his mouth. Jason is holding him by the shoulders. Becca is on the phone with 911. They said not to move him, help is on the way.

I kneel beside Kylie, watching Oz as his breathing goes shallow and reedy, and I watch the blood seeping from beneath his skull.

Without warning, Kylie is lunging across the street, screaming viciously now, not in pain but in hate, in rage. I catch her just before she reaches Ben, catch her swinging arms, clenched trembling fists before they hit him.

"YOU KILLED HIM!" she's shrieking, "You *fucking* killed him, you bastard! I hate you *IhateyouIhateyou!*"

Ben lurches to his feet, throwing his father off. "I didn't mean to..." He stumbles toward her, eyes red, grief and guilt ravaging his features. "I'm sorry, I'm sorry, I didn't—"

"I told you *months* ago I'd chosen him, but you couldn't accept it!" She's struggling in my arms, but I can't let go, won't let go. "I chose *him!* I love *him!* You were my best friend, Ben." She's abruptly limp. "You were my best friend. How could you do this to me? How could do it to me?" And now she's limp.

I lift her in my arms. "He's not dead, baby. He's not dead. He'll be okay. He's just unconscious. Stay with me, sweetheart." I'm murmuring in her ear. "Stay with me, baby. Look at Oz, okay? See his chest moving? He's alive, okay? There's the ambulance—they'll fix him. They'll fix him."

She struggles out of my arms, to her feet, watching everything with sudden manic energy, pacing, as the EMS guys do their grisly work, blue-gloved hands turning red, their voices calm but urgent.

"Will he—will he live?" she asks, her voice cutting through the noise.

One of them looks at her. His eyes are reassuring, calm. "We got here in time, I think. He's got a good chance."

A good chance. It's not much, but it's something. Better than dead.

Kylie follows them as they lift him inside the ambulance, and no one dares stop her as she climbs in and sits to one side, trying to touch his hand while staying out of their way. The doors close and the sirens go on and the ambulance wails away. Nell has the truck running, and we're following close behind.

The next several hours pass in a sludge-slow blur. He's in surgery for nine hours, and Kylie eventually falls into a fitful sleep in the waiting room, stretched across two chairs with her head on Nell's lap. We sit in silence, watching the news on mute, Brian Williams' face moving without sound, images flashing, meaningless nonsense that doesn't penetrate anyone's awareness.

Kate Hyde is in the room as well, sitting across from us, eyes red-rimmed, a Kleenex clutched in her fist. She stares listlessly.

Sometime in the small hours of dawn, a green-gowned surgeon approaches, a face-mask tugged down past his chin, a green cap on his head, rubbing hand-sanitizer on his hands. He glances around the room, pale, pale blue eyes searching. He's a middle-aged man, a little older than I am, I think, thick-shouldered and fit.

Kylie senses something, wakes up, sees the surgeon. Lurches to her feet. "Is he okay?"

"He's a fighter," the surgeon says. "He suffered an extreme trauma to his head, but he stayed with us."

"Will he—will he be okay?" Kate asks. "When he wakes up?"

The surgeon bobbles his head from side to side. "There's never any way to tell one hundred percent until he wakes up. I think he has an excellent chance of making a full recovery with no lasting side effects, but I can't make any promises just yet. We've done everything we can do for now." He sighs. "He'll have a long road ahead of him when he wakes up. The head trauma was the biggest worry, but he has other equally significant injuries. He broke his femur in three places, and re-fractured his arm. Those will take time to heal, of course, but it's the head injury that we have to keep the closest eye on right now."

"When can we see him?" Kylie wants to know.

"He's unconscious at the moment. It's not a coma, though, just natural post-op sleep. You can probably see him in a few hours. Sometime later today, I'd say. Ya'll have been here for a long time, so why don't you head home and catch some sleep?"

Kylie shook her head. "No…no. I need to see him. Can't I just—just *see* him?"

The surgeon shook his head. "I'm sorry, but I really feel it's in his best interests to remain undisturbed for the time being." His expression softens. "You won't do him any good if you're in a state of exhaustion. You need to rest. I can tell you from experience, the sleep you get in a waiting room in a hospital is no kind of rest at all. Go home. Sleep. Come back this evening, and you'll be able to see him, hopefully speak to him."

I wrap my arm around Kylie's shoulders. "Come on, Ky. He's right. We're all exhausted. We know he's okay now. He'll be okay. Let's get you home? Just for a few hours."

Kylie nods, and then slips out of my hold, reaches for Kate. "He's all right, Kate. He'll be fine." Kylie and Kate embrace, and I can see Kate visibly shuddering and trying to hold it together.

"He really loves you, you know. I wasn't sure he'd ever find that." Kate pulls away, holds Kylie by the shoulders. "I'm so glad he did. You've really brought him to life, Kylie, and I can't ever thank you enough for that."

"He's amazing," Kylie says.

"Yeah, he is. No thanks to me." Kate squeezes her eyes shut and turns away.

"Hey, hey." Kylie shakes Kate's arm. "No. You've always been there for him. You gave him…so much. Everything. And he knows it. He's told me as much."

"He—he did?"

Kylie nods. "He loves you, Kate. For real. Don't ever doubt that."

Kate smiles. "Thanks, Kylie." She shakes her head, wipes her eyes. "Sorry. Sorry. I'm just so emotional. Go home, get some rest. We'll all come back later and see him." She gives Kylie one last hug, and then she's gone.

As Kate shuffles down the hallway toward the elevators, Jason and Becca return from the cafeteria, Styrofoam cups of coffee in hand, Ben trailing behind them, looking subdued and miserable. Becca halts in the doorway, staring after Kate.

"Who—who was that?" Becca asks. It wasn't quite a stutter, more of a stumble, but it spoke volumes about how unnerved Becca is. She turns to Kylie. "Who was that?"

"That?" Kylie is visibly confused. "That was Oz's mom. Why?"

Becca doesn't answer right away. "Nothing. She just…she looked familiar. Must have been my imagination." She shakes her head, dismissing the thought. "I just thought for a second—oh, never mind. How is Oz?"

"Oz is out of surgery. He's asleep now, but they said he should be fine." Kylie hiccups, and her effort to sound strong crumbles. "He broke his leg and re-broke his arm. And his head—he…they say he *shouldn't* have any—any lasting damage. But they won't know till he wakes up."

Becca gathers Kylie to her. "He'll be okay, honey. You'll see."

Kylie nods, and pulls away. "Yeah, I know. He's tough."

We all head home, and Kylie is asleep on her feet by the time we get inside. I follow her upstairs, tuck her in to her bed the way I used to, when she was a little girl.

"Daddy?" Her voice is tiny, sleep-slow.

"Yeah, babe."

"I'm so mad at Ben. I'm so mad it scares me." She sniffles. "Don't let him—if he comes here looking for me, don't let him in. I can't see him. Not yet. Maybe not ever."

I sigh. "Oh, honey. It was an accident. A stupid accident that should never have happened. It wasn't his fault, honey. He didn't mean for it to happen."

"He was picking a fight!" Kylie is furious, but too tired to really express it. "Oz had a broken arm, and he was trying to be rational about it. But Ben was just… just spoiling for a fight. I *told* him I was with Oz. I *told* him, Daddy. Months ago. But he couldn't accept it."

"He's been your friend your whole life, Kylie. Try to see it from his point of view, just for a second. He's been in love with you for a long, long time. Then, suddenly, you're with someone else, and he's frustrated."

"He never told me. Never let on. How was I supposed to know?" She rolls to her back and lets her eyes close. "If he'd told me, before I met Oz…maybe there could've been something. But…he just got so crazy, so jealous. It's so unlike him, too. He said such horrible things to Oz, Daddy. It wasn't *my* Ben saying it. It was like…like he was somebody else. It was so scary."

"I'm not excusing his behavior, Kylie. I'm not. I'm just saying…give him time."

"I'll try."

"That's all I'm saying." I pat her shoulder. "Sleep. We'll go back there together later."

She didn't answer, because she was already asleep.

Thirteen: Revelations

Oz

WAKING UP FUCKING SUCKS. Especially that initial stage, where you're just starting to become aware that you're waking up, and you don't want to. You want to sink back down. You want to stay under. You want to stay where it's warm and safe and where life can't touch you.

But you can't. You're dragged upward, fumbling toward the inevitability of waking.

Waking up in agony? Even worse.

Slowly, torturously, I come to awareness. I've felt pain before. I've endured all sorts of horrible shit. But this? It's the worst thing I've ever felt. A thousand, thousand points of pain, little stabbing sparks of agony all throughout my body, centered on my head and my leg and my arm, spreading out like a spider web.

I hear a monitor beeping. I'm in a goddamn hospital again. Fuck.

I didn't die. I distinctly remember realizing I was dying. But apparently not.

I blink, find the ceiling above me, the walls, the monitors with their wires all leading to me. A cannula in my nose. I feel heavy. My leg is wrapped in a cast from waist to toe. My arm is in a hard cast again. And my head, fuck, my head aches like someone is pounding on it with a sledgehammer.

My door opens and Kylie's barging in, rushing for me, and her expression is shell-shocked, haunted. "Oz." She says it strangely. "Hi, baby."

I feel lost. Something is going on. She's acting weird. "Hi, sweetness." I hold out my one good hand for her. "Come here."

She sits on the edge of my bed. Touches her forehead to mine. "You're awake. You're—you're alive." She hiccups, sobs. "I—I thought you were dead. You—you were barely breathing. I thought I'd lost you. *Again.*"

"I'm okay, Ky. I mean, I'm all kinds of fucked up, but I'll be okay." She nods, but doesn't say anything. "What is it, Kylie? Something's wrong."

"The front desk...they wouldn't tell me your room number."

"What? Why?"

"Be—because I didn't know your real name."

"Oh. Shit."

She sniffles, makes an odd sound that I can't decipher. "Yeah. I asked for you. For Oz. I just wanted to see my boyfriend. I was a little crazy, and they just wouldn't—they wouldn't tell me where you were. 'His name is Oz Hyde,' I said. You want to know what they said? What they told me?"

"What?" I almost don't want to know. It's just a name. I don't see why it matters, but she's acting so strange.

"They told me your name. Your whole, real name." A pause, a deep breath. "Benjamin Aziz Hyde." She pronounces it slowly, each syllable succinct and clear.

"Yeah. So?"

My door opens then, and Ben comes in. As he approaches me, hands in his pockets, his eyes... they're...god, I've never seen such torture in a person's eyes before.

"Ben. What—what the fuck are you doing here?" I demand.

He just stares at me for a moment, and then he squeezes his eyes shut as if to hold back strong emotions. "I'm sorry…Oz. I'm so sorry. I should…I should never have…acted the way I did."

I blink. He's the last person I ever expected to see walk through that door, and I certainly never expected an apology from him. "I'm not sure what you want to me say here, man."

"Nothing. You don't have to say anything. I was…I was way out of line, and I'm sorry. That's all I wanted to say." He draws a deep breath, and lets it out. Looks at Kylie.

"I think Kylie's the one you should be apologizing to, not me." The pain on his face makes it impossible to hate him. "It was an accident, Ben. A fight's a fight, but getting hit by a car like I did, it could've been either of us."

He just nods, and it seems like he wants to say something else, but can't get it out.

An awkward silence ensues.

Finally, I can't take it anymore. I look at Kylie. "What is so important about my name?"

"Your name is Benjamin. So's his."

I shake my head. "So? It's a fairly common name. It's just a coincidence."

She leans forward. "But you two—you almost look alike. I mean, both of you have almost the same color of skin, like, exactly the same shade. Your noses, they're almost identical, too. And your eyes… Oz, yours have more gray in them, but your eyes are almost the same, too. It's eerie. I've noticed it before, but…having the same first name? It's too weird to be a coincidence."

"So what? We're…like, long-lost brothers or something?"

Kylie shakes her head. "I don't know. It's just bizarre."

Ben paces away, across the room. "No way we're fucking brothers. There's no fucking way in hell my parents would keep a secret like that from me. And besides that, I know for a fact my parents have never been with anyone but each other. It's impossible. It is weird, though." He growls and heads toward the door. "I need some air."

He leaves, and Kylie fits her feet onto the bed, lies beside me, and nuzzles into me. "It's crazy, but it doesn't even matter." She carefully rests her hand on my chest, avoiding my injured arm and leg. "I love you. You're alive. That's all I care about right now."

"I love you, too." I twist my head to kiss her temple, and she turns her face to meet my lips. It's a quick, shallow kiss. I break it first. "But for real…what the hell is going on? I don't—I don't get it."

Kylie sighs. "I talked to your mom. She's on the way, too." She kisses my jaw.

I lift my good arm so she can rest her head in the nook. We let silence wash over us, except for the beeping of the monitors and the occasional squawk of the PA. I almost fall back asleep, but then I hear footsteps approaching, and my door opens. Mom comes in, followed by Ben. Kylie doesn't move from my side, but I know she's awake and watching, waiting.

Mom leans over me and kisses my forehead. I don't remember the last time Mom kissed me. "Oz, baby. I'm so glad you're awake. How do you feel?"

"Hurt. Confused. Fucked up." I glance at Ben, then back at Mom. "Where did you get my name?" I demand.

She pales. "What? Why are you asking now?" She backs away, shaking her head. "I'm not—we're not discussing that now. We'll talk about it when you're feeling better."

"We'll talk about it *right the FUCK now!*" I shout. Kylie flinches, but doesn't otherwise move or speak.

"Hold up, Oz. Wait till my folks are here," Ben says.

Mom is staring at Ben as if she's seeing a ghost. "Who—who are you?"

"Ben Dorsey." He shakes her hand, his expression impassive. It's as if he's shoved all emotions down, deep into a locked closet of his soul.

"Ben Dorsey," Mom repeats. "You look—you look like—"

She doesn't finish, though, because the door opens one more time, and Jason comes through, Becca right behind her. Jason steps aside, and Becca moves forward, past him, toward me. She sees Mom standing at the side of my bed, on the opposite side of Kylie.

"No..." Becca breathes. "It's not...it's not possible." She stumbles, pale, hand over her mouth. "Kate?" She leans into Jason, staring at Mom in shock and old pain.

Mom sags backward against the wall, clutches the railing of my bed as if she's about to faint. "Becca. My god."

I look from Mom to Becca. "Wait...you know each other?" My fists clench. "What the hell is going on? Somebody start giving me some goddamn answers."

Kylie puts her hand to my cheek. "Oz...baby, it's okay. We're all here. We'll talk it through. I'm here. It's okay."

I take a deep breath. "Mom. How do you know Becca Dorsey?"

Mom closes her eyes, steps away from the bed, stumbles a few feet, and then collapses to her knees.

Her shoulders shake, and I hate that I can't get out of this bed to help her. "Oz. Baby…I know you've got a lot of questions."

"A lot of questions?" I say this with so much bitterness my voice breaks. "I've gone my whole life with nothing *but* fucking questions, Mom."

Becca steps forward. Touches Mom's shoulder, sinks to her knees beside her. "Kate. I can't believe it's really you. I've spent so many years wondering what happened to you. You just disappeared, and I—I was never able to find you." She sounds almost angry, and a lot sad, and lost in the past. "I looked. For years, I looked."

"You did?" Mom's voice is disbelieving.

"Of course I did!" Becca shuts her eyes, breathing shakily. "I told you, I *t-told* you we'd be there for you. We'd help you. But you just…vanished."

"It was too hard. I was scared." Mom's voice is distant, small. "I couldn't handle it, being so close to—to everything that reminded me of him."

Him? I wanted to ask who, but I knew. I stayed silent and let it all come out.

"You think—you think it wasn't hard for *me*? He was my *brother*, Kate. You were…you were c-c-carrying…his-his *child*." Becca's eyes turn to me. "My *nephew*."

The world spins around me. "What?" I try for breath. "What's going on?"

Mom seems stuck, sitting on the hospital room floor, head hanging. Becca glances at her, sucks in a deep breath, and I can see her visibly counting, calming herself. She stands up, moves to my side.

"Your father was ... my brother. His name was Benjamin Aziz de Rosa." Her voice wavers. "I named my son after him, and so did Kate, it seems."

I can't breathe, but a million whirling skirling questions batter at my brain, flutter just this side of my lips. One slips out. "What...what happened to him? Where is he?"

"Your mom never told you anything about him?" Becca asks.

I can only shake my head.

"I *couldn't!*" Mom shouts, hysterical, manic, suddenly sobbing. "It was too—too hard! He—he—*oh, god*...I couldn't. I just couldn't. I'm sorry, Oz. I just couldn't. It was too hard. It's still too hard."

Becca blinks hard twice, breathing deep. "My brother was very troubled, Oz. He struggled with bipolar disorder his whole life. He got into drugs. When he met Kate, your mother...he seemed to get a little better. But it—it wasn't enough, I guess. He wouldn't take his meds...b-b-be—bec—because..."

She trails off, struggling. She pauses for a moment, breathing deeply. "God, I haven't stuttered like this in years. He wouldn't take his meds. He said they made him feel…empty. Half-dead. Like he was in a cloud. Not himself. He hated them. The drugs just made it all worse, I think. Your mother loved him, and he loved her. But…it wasn't enough. He had…so much darkness in him. So much self-doubt."

She pauses again, and clearly, this next part is hellishly difficult to say. I don't dare interrupt. Mom has her face in her hands, sobbing quietly.

Becca continues. "It was all too much. My brother committed suicide. It was April ninth. He hung himself. I found him." She stops then, and I see the tears in her eyes. She starts again. "Your mother had just found out she was pregnant."

I don't even know what to say. "So…he couldn't handle the fact that he was going to be a father? So he just…offed himself?"

Becca flinches at my coarse words. "I don't know. There's no way to really know what he was thinking."

"He—he was scared. He thought he'd ruined my life. His life." Mom, for the first time in my life, was offering answers. "That's what he thought. He was scared he'd pass his sickness on to you. That's how he saw it, his bipolarism. A sickness. A disease. I just…I just thought he was different. Just Ben. But he—he suffered a lot, so much, just to try to function. And when I told him I was pregnant, he just couldn't handle it. He felt guilty. He thought—I think because he struggled so hard just to take care of himself, he'd only fuck up a kid that much worse, but he couldn't run away from me. I think—I think he didn't feel like he had any other way out."

I look at Ben. "So Ben's my cousin." It's a rhetorical question, and no one answers. I look at Mom. "Why, Mom? Why did you never say anything? Why did you keep this secret from me for my whole fucking life? Why? All I wanted was to know…even his goddamn name! One single thing about him."

Mom sucks in a shuddering breath. "It hurt too much. I loved your father. I loved Ben. So much. I wanted…I just wanted him to be happy. I didn't care if he was bipolar. I'd take him any way I could get him. As long as he wasn't doing drugs, he was okay. To me, at least. He'd have his ups and downs, and they were rough, yeah, but it was manageable. And then he—he killed himself. It—it broke me. I've never been okay. I haven't been okay since…since he died. I just couldn't handle it. You're so much like him, Oz. So much. It scares me, and reminds me, and it's—so hard sometimes." She looks up at me, eyes wet, tears flowing freely down her face. "I'm sorry, Oz. I'm so sorry. You deserved the truth, but I just couldn't—couldn't face it. When you were young and asking about him, how do you tell a six-year-old that his father hung himself? And then the older you got, the more it was just easier to pretend like I was protecting you from the awfulness of the truth. It was easier to let you think he'd run off, or abandoned us. Because the truth that he killed himself rather than even *try*...to me, was so much worse. More than twenty years have passed since Ben killed himself, and I'm still—still so *mad* at him. And I miss him. I loved him, Oz. I loved him so much. And I would have done anything for him. But it wasn't enough. I wasn't enough."

I'm near tears. Again. I'm sick to fucking death of all this bullshit drama making me emotional. But it all makes sense. It answers so much. "So...am I like him? Am I bipolar?" I've heard of bipolar disorder, of course, but I don't really know much about it.

Mom shakes her head. "No, honey. I've watched you like a hawk for your whole life, and you've never showed any signs of it. I've made a god-awful mess of your life, so if you have any—any emotional issues, they're my fault. But I don't think you're bipolar."

A nurse comes in, a stout, middle-aged black woman with gray streaks in her curly dark hair. Her tag announces her name to be Shawna. "All right, ya'll. My patient needs to sleep. I've let you disturb him long enough. Now shoo. Let the boy rest." She's friendly and polite, but firm, hustling everyone out. Except Kylie, who remains where she is, nestled against me.

I say goodbye to everyone, hugging Mom, and then they're gone, trooping out silently.

Shawna shuts the door and then stops in the middle of the room, staring at Kylie and me. "A'ight, honey. If you *promise* me you'll let Benjamin sleep, I'll let you stay here for a few minutes."

"Oz. My name is Oz." I mumble it, more out of habit.

"I promise," Kylie says to Shawna, then turns to me. "So you're still going by Oz?"

I shrug, a weak lift of one shoulder. "It's who I am. It's the name I chose for myself a long, long time ago. I'm not Ben, or Benjamin. I'm Oz."

Shawna is checking leads, the monitor, fiddling with various things. "You need something for the pain, sweetie?"

So much has been raging in my head and my heart that I've almost forgotten about the pain. "Yeah. It's starting to catch up to me." It's not a lie. Aches ripple through me. My head pounds, and a thousand pinpricks hit my arm and leg.

She bustles out of the room, and as soon as she's gone, Kylie lifts up, cradles my face in her soft, trembling hands, and kisses me, hard and deep and desperate. She kisses me with the frantic need of someone who thought she'd lost her one true love. I kiss her back, holding on to the back of her shirt with my good hand.

"God, Oz. I thought I'd lost you. Again. It hurt so bad. I was so afraid. I couldn't live if I lost you. I can't lose you again. Please, Oz. Promise me, *promise* me you'll never leave me. Thinking you were dead, not knowing if you'd be okay, if you'd wake up, it was just...*hell*. It was hell. I love you, so, so, so much. Don't ever leave me. Promise me, Oz. Promise me."

I wrap my arm around her neck and hold her face against mine. We're both trembling, shaking, and she's crying, and yet a-fucking-gain I'm trying not to. "I promise you, baby. I promise. I'm yours, Kylie. I'm not going anywhere. Ssshh. I'm okay. I'm okay." Rhythmic reassurances flow from me, nonsensical and repetitive, and she eventually stills, breathes in.

"How did I fall in love with you so hard and so fast?" Kylie pulls away to look into my eyes. "It's crazy. I don't get it sometimes. I don't know how it happened. It's not just the sex, it's...you."

I can only shake my head. "I don't know, Ky. I wonder the same thing." I sink farther back into the pillows and let my eyes slide shut. "I remember everything. I remember knowing I was dying. And my last thought was you. That I loved you. That I didn't want you to be sad for me. I remember how cold I felt. Seeing a…a light. And not wanting to go to it. I don't fucking know. Maybe I was…imagining it, but that's what I remember. Seeing a light and knowing it meant death. Dying. Giving up. Leaving you. And I couldn't. I wanted to hold on, to come back. I fought it, Kylie. I fought so hard, but I…I couldn't fight it. It pulled me under. Waking up was a surprise."

"Thank you."

I have to think about that one. "For what?"

"For fighting. For coming back to me."

I can't summon the energy to respond. I just try to squeeze her, so she knows I heard her. The door opens, and I hear soft footfalls nearing me. I force my eyes open, let Shawna help me take the pills, and then I fall under the spell of sleep, holding tight to Kylie.

A week in the hospital. Tests, scans, more tests, more scans. All making sure the blunt force trauma to my skull didn't scramble my brains. It didn't, it seems. Finally I can go home. Mom drives me, with Kylie sitting in the back seat of the pickup. She spent nearly every waking moment with me, as much time as she could. She'd come after school, before school, during lunch hour. She'd skip classes. Talk her way back to see me after hours. Slip into my bed with me, lie there with me and talk to me, hold me, kiss me when no one was looking.

Going home means a wheelchair, since I'm now a fucking invalid. Thank fuck the elevator in our apartment got fixed. The cast on my leg goes from above my hip to my toes, keeping me totally immobilized from the waist down. With my re-broken arm, I can't use a crutch, and probably couldn't with the size of my cast anyway. So I've got be pushed around everywhere. Helped from bed to chair and back. I'll need help to go to the bathroom. To take a shower. Everything.

It sucks.

But as the days pass, Kylie stays with me, basically living with me now. She's made arrangements to do most of her schoolwork here, so she almost never leaves my side. I make her go out every once in a while. I make her go see her friends. But she does everything for me. It was insanely awkward at first, but eventually Kylie and I both have become used to her being my nurse.

One of the most annoying things about the whole accident and surgery was that they had to shave the back of my head, just above the hairline. I still have my hair, but it looks weird if I keep it tied up, so it's down all the time and gets in my eyes. Kylie showed me how to just tie back the front so it doesn't get in my eyes, but then I look like some stupid elf or something. Whatever. Nothing to be done about it yet.

Ben came over once, on a Saturday afternoon, a few weeks after I got home from the hospital. It was supremely awkward, incredibly tense. Neither of us knew what to say, and being family doesn't erase the conflict between us.

I've got family. An aunt and uncle. A cousin. A cousin with the same name as me is weird. I mean, I don't go by my first name, but it's still weird. Having family is weird. I don't know what to do with it. Am I supposed to just forget the way Ben acted, simply because he's my cousin? What is a cousin, really, anyway? I mean, are we supposed to be friends now? Is it like having an almost-brother? I don't know. Seems silly if you're not me, but I just don't know what to do with family. I've never had any. But when Ben came over we just sat, talked. Listened to music. Turns out Ben likes similar music to me—hard rock and heavy metal—so we have something to talk about at least.

His eyes still watch Kylie a little too closely, a little too sharply. Follows her every movement. Checks her out. I mean, she's gorgeous, so what guy wouldn't check her out? But I don't know how to deal with it. It makes me crazy. She's mine. But can I stop him from looking, from watching? I know he still wants her. He's still in love with her. You don't just get over something like that all of a sudden. So what do I do? Let it go and hope he moves on eventually? I don't know. I don't have any answers, and I'm hesitant to bring it up to Kylie. He's her best friend still. They've known each other their entire lives. I feel like maybe I need to leave it up to her. Let him look if he wants. Let him hold onto his feelings for her in secret if he wants. She's with me, and that's not changing.

I'm not sure what the future holds. Being injured, for both of us, has put an indefinite hold on our musical ambitions, which Andersen says he understands, and the offer will be there when we're ready. Does that mean I'm staying here in Nashville? Possibly. I mean, for once, I have a reason to stay. A family to hold me in one place. Mom and Becca have been spending time together, which is good. She comes home with red eyes, as if she's been crying, but for the first time she's open to my questions, and I have a lot of them. She's talking to Becca about my father, I think. Remembering who he was, and she tells me stories. Good ones, and bad ones, too. She tells me about his mood swings, his cycles. How he'd get depressed more easily and for longer in the fall and winter, and be more manic in the summer and spring. He'd have mini-cycles, swings within swings. Manic days during winter depressions and vice-versa. She tells me how sweet he could be, how talented he could be, if he wanted. I get my music from him, apparently, which is something not even Aunt Becca knew. My dad—I still have a hard time deciding how to think about him: Dad? My father? Ben? I don't even know—but I always harbored a desire to be a musician. He taught himself guitar, wrote songs. Never went anywhere with it, never believed in himself enough to try. My capacity for math is from Mom. She'd thought about going to college for physics, but life got in the way. She never went, never had the money, and then she met my dad and had me, and it never happened.

We got a bill in the mail for my two hospital stays. Mom's never put us on Medicaid, never had health insurance. Mom sat at the kitchen table, hand over her mouth, staring at the paper. I tried talking to her, but she ignored me, just stared at that astronomical six-digit number, shaking.

And then, a week later, I find her with her cell phone in her hand, sobbing, sitting on the kitchen floor.

"Mom? What's wrong?" I hobble over to her, dragging my now significantly smaller walking cast along behind me.

She lets me help her up, sets her phone on the counter. Kylie is gone for the moment, handing in our assignments to the school. Mom sucks in a deep breath. "The hospital bill. It's paid. Someone paid it. All of it."

I felt the world spinning around me. "What? Who?"

Mom shook her head. "They wouldn't tell me. But…who else could've, or would've, but Jason and Becca?"

I wobble in a circle, move toward the door. "Come on. We've gotta go talk to them."

Mom drives us to the Dorseys' house, and I send Kylie a text to meet us there. Becca is on her front porch, sipping iced tea, waiting for us, Kylie sitting next to her, laughing and holding a sweating glass of tea. I make my way slowly up the driveway and up the two shallow steps to the porch, lean back against the wall beside Kylie. Mom stands on the sidewalk at the bottom of the steps, staring up at Becca with emotions shining in her eyes.

No one speaks for a long time.

"Let's get one thing straight," Becca says. "There will be no talk of not accepting charity, or paying us back. You are family. Oz is my nephew, the only one I'll ever have. So just say 'thank you' and be done."

Mom sniffs, wipes at her eyes, head bowed. "'Thank you' can't even begin to express it, Becca. Not even close."

"Kate. You're *family*. There's nothing we wouldn't do for you." Becca descends the steps, takes Mom by the shoulders, looks up into her eyes. "You should never have run, Kate. I could've…we could've been like sisters, all this time. I would've helped you with Oz."

"I was so scared. Of everything. I didn't know what to do. I've never had family. I ran away from home at fourteen." Mom turns away, arms folded across her middle, staring into the blue afternoon sky, her voice distant. "My parents were…well…not parents. I don't think there's a living person on this earth who knows any of this. They beat me. My father…did things. Bad things. To me. To my sister. I ran away on my fourteenth birthday. I stole a hundred and fifty dollars from the coffee can on top of the fridge and took the first bus out of there. Ended up in a homeless shelter in Kansas City. I got a job in a Chinese food restaurant, washing dishes. Soap, water, a sponge, and a sink. They let me sleep in the kitchen at night. I used the sink to take sponge baths. I saved my money for two months, and then I took a bus out of Kansas City. I—I never stayed anywhere for more than a couple months after that. At least not until I met Ben. I was always afraid my father would catch me. He was an evil man. I know he looked for me. He told me once, when I was twelve, that if I ever told anyone what he did to me and Kaylee he'd hurt us. He said we'd never get away from him. Kaylee was four years older than me. She ran away when I was eleven."

Shock, surprise…there are no accurate words for how blown away I am by Mom's revelations. I didn't know this. I had no idea. Not a single clue. "What—what happened to your sister?"

Mom shrugs. "I don't know. She's probably out there somewhere, if she's still alive. Teenage runaways…well, they don't often make it. They end up on drugs, prostitution. Sex slaves. I saw it happen. It almost happened to me. I got…taken, once. In Fisk, Missouri. Just snatched off the street in broad daylight. I waited until they were getting me out of the van, pretended to be unconscious. Then I started kicking, biting, punching. Managed to get away, hid in a dumpster until the next morning. So…Kaylee? I don't know. I always thought about trying to look for her, but…" Mom shrugs. "I never did. Never could. I've Googled her name a few times, but nothing ever came up." She turns to glance at me. "That's why we moved so much, Oz. It's what I knew. I lived in

Michigan longer than I ever lived anywhere, and that was because of Ben. I thought I'd found a home, a family. Someone to love me. Someone to care. Four years. That's the longest I've ever stayed in any one place in my life, that and Dallas. It's just habit now. No reason to stay, so why bother?"

"Holy shit, Mom."

She twists her torso around to smile at me. "It's old news, honey. I'm just sorry you had to be born to someone like me. You deserved a better life, and I just couldn't give it to you." She shifts her gaze to Becca. "I didn't know how to trust you. I wanted to, but...I've never trusted anyone. I never even told Ben about how I grew up."

"Well, maybe it's time to try," Becca says. "Stay here in Nashville. Put down some roots."

Mom laughs, a slightly bitter sound. "People always say that. 'Put down roots.' I don't even know what that's supposed to mean."

Becca moves to stand beside Mom. "It means... let us be your family. Come over for lunch. Have drinks with me. Don't run off. Just...stay here."

Mom doesn't answer for a long, long time. When she does, her voice is hesitant. "Family. You really want to be my family?"

Becca laughs, pulls Mom in for a hug. "We already are, Kate."

"Oh." Mom glances up at me. "Oz?"

I lean toward Kylie, who wraps her arm around my waist. "I'm not going anywhere. I've got at least one reason to stay here."

Becca turns to me, frowning. "Only one?"

"At *least* one, I said. And…I like the idea of family, too, honestly."

Six weeks later, and I'm out of my casts, back to normal. And I'm nervous as hell. I'm sitting in a barber's chair, an apron around my shoulders. A pretty, friendly woman has her fingers in my hair, waiting for me to give her the signal to start. I stare at my reflection in the mirror, staring at my long auburn hair. It hasn't been cut since before junior high. I let Mom trim the ends once, two years ago.

Kylie doesn't know I'm doing this. She thinks I'm looking at effects pedals. Which, I did. I even bought a new one. I've got a new job, working for Andersen Mayer at his office. I'm his assistant's assistant. I also work at the garage, with Colt's friend. It's a good job, pays well, and I'm learning some useful skills. It's good to be busy, to be done with college. I know an associate's degree doesn't do shit, but it's a degree I earned, on my own. I might go for my bachelor's, might not. Kylie graduated high school with crazy honors, obviously, and is thinking about where she wants to go after she finishes her degree at NSCC.

Kylie and I are still planning on pursuing music, but we feel like we shouldn't rush it. Let it happen in its own time. In the meantime, I'm working a lot, playing guitar and learning new songs, even messing around with writing my own. I haven't burned in months, and I haven't smoked pot since before the accident. I don't even have any. Kylie watched me throw it away, watched me give my pipe and papers to Dion.

"You have beautiful hair, Oz," the stylist says to me. "Maybe you'd think about donating it?"

"Donating it?" I ask.

"Yeah. Locks of Love is a charity that takes hair like yours after it's cut and turns it into a wig."

I shrug. "Sure. Sounds good."

She smiles. "Cool." Her fingers run through my hair once more. "So. Ready?"

I take a deep breath and let it out. "Yeah. Let her rip."

I watch as the scissors snip through my hair, watch as a huge hank of hair flutters to the floor. Holy shit. My head feels so light all of a sudden. She's not done, though. She cuts and cuts and cuts, until I'm sure I must be bald. I've got my eyes closed, refusing to look until it's over.

Finally, after trimming the hairline at my neck and above my ears with a pair of clippers, she steps back, blows my skin clean with a hair dryer. Styles it with some kind of paste. Fiddles, blow-dries, twists, plays. Finally she unsnaps the sheet and turns me around.

"So what do you think, Oz?" Even she sounds nervous.

I open my eyes, and I'm honestly stunned. It's *short*. Like, there's nothing at all on the sides, buzzed close to the scalp. There's a messy ruff on the top of my head, artfully mussed, dark, spiky. Holy shit, I fucking love it. I run my hands past my ears, down the back of my neck, up the back of my head, feeling the soft bristles under my palm.

"It feels like my head is ten pounds lighter." I turn my head from one side to another, pluck at a strand of hair, play with it. "It's amazing. I feel like a different person."

"You had a *lot* of hair." She sounds almost wistful. "You had a gorgeous head of hair. I mean, it was thick and you had, like, no split ends or anything. But you look amazing, I have to say. You do look totally different." She tilts her head, touches my shoulder. "Now you just need a less…icky shirt."

I've got a metal shirt on, of course. I don't think I own anything else. This one has a spray of blood that turns into a flock of birds, and the name of the band written in barbed wire–style font. It's pretty graphic, I guess.

"Yeah, maybe you're right. If I'm gonna look clean-cut, I might as well go all the way, huh?"

"Exactly. There's a resale store a few doors down that has some nice stuff. You should take a look." She leads me up to the counter and cashes me out.

I thank her, leave her a tip, and step out into the late spring warmth. I check out the resale shop and find a short-sleeve button shirt, plaid and preppy and ugly as fuck, but it fits and doesn't look half bad on me. Especially after I find a pair of faded, well-worn blue jeans, just tight enough. Add a plain tan leather belt, and a pair of Doc Martens, and I look like someone totally other than the metalhead punk who left my apartment this morning. I toss my old clothes onto the passenger seat of my truck and let the engine idle as I send Kylie a text.

Yeah, my bike was pretty much totaled, so I used the insurance money to buy an old black F-150. Colt helped me fix it up, replacing and souping up the engine, beefing up the exhaust, switching out the tranny. The truck is almost as old as I am, but it's smooth and powerful and rumbles like a beast.

Meet me at the park, I text Kylie. **I have a surprise for you.**

I head out, and a few minutes later, my phone chimes. I wait till I'm at a red light and then read the message. **Sure thing. C U then.**

It drives me nuts when Kylie uses text-speak, so of course she does it just to fuck with me.

I find a spot for my truck in the parking lot and shuffle out across the overgrown soccer field, an old quilt under one arm. We found this park a few weeks ago. It's hidden at the back of a subdivision. There's a few swings, an old merry-go-round, some benches and a play structure and some splintery picnic tables gouged with initials and swear words. No one ever comes here, so we like to lie in the field and talk, write songs, kiss. A bit more than kiss, late at night, sometimes.

I spread out the blanket and lie back on it, drowsing in the warm sunlight until I hear the quiet purr of Kylie's car. I hear her door close, listen as her footsteps get closer. I tilt my head to one side, see her legs approaching. I stand up, face her.

"Holy—holy *shit,* Oz!" She covers her mouth with her hand, hiding a stunned grin. "You look—holy shit! Is that even you?"

I scrub my hand through my hair, still amazed at the way it feels. "You like it?"

She moves closer, brushes her palm over the close-cropped hair at the back of my head, giggling.

"Like it? I *love* it. I mean, I loved the way you looked before, but this…you look so fucking hot I can't stand it." She steps back and takes in my outfit. "Even your clothes? God, Oz, what got into you?"

I shrug. "I dunno. It just felt like it was time for a change. I got the haircut, and then figured I might as well do it right, you know? So here I am. I feel weird, though. I can't get over the way my head feels."

She laughs and runs her hand across my neck. "I bet. I got my hair cut really short once. It was in junior high, I think. I got, like, six inches cut off, and it felt like my head was going to float away."

I nod. "That's pretty much it."

"You didn't do this for me, did you? Like, you didn't feel like I wanted you to—to change for me, did you?"

I frown. "No, not at all. It's not about changing myself. I'm still me. I just don't need the metal shirts and black jeans and long hair to be me. I'm me regardless of my appearance."

"So wise, yet so young," Kylie teases.

"Hey, kid, I'm older than you."

"Not by much."

"Still older."

She smirks at me, then slips her hand up under the hem of my shirt, touches the skin on my back. "Why are we still standing up?"

We sink to the blanket together, and she leans back on her elbows. Her lips part in expectation, her eyes closing as I lean in for a kiss. She's wearing a loose white button-down blouse and a pair of skin-tight blue jeans, and I rest my hand on her hip, touch her lips with mine, taste her vanilla lip balm, smell soap and lilac something and faint perfume. Her hand slides up my back, clutching the back of my head. The kiss deepens, and I can't help but free the top button of her blouse, and then the second. In moments, both of our shirts are open, her hands roaming my side and my palms cupping her tits.

We lose ourselves in the kiss, in the exchange of heat and passion, and though we won't let it go any further than kissing, it's intense and overwhelming.

She pulls away, bites at my lower lip. "God, if we don't stop now I'm going to jump you right here, in broad daylight."

"That would be bad....right?"

"Yeah. I mean, I do hear kids." She smiles at me. "Let's go home."

"Home?" I ask. "Where's home, for us?"

"For now? Wherever we can be alone. Wherever you are is home."

Fourteen: Creekside Wisdom

Colt

I'M TINKERING WITH THE TRIUMPH, putting the finishing touches on it. It just needs some fine-tuning on the brakes, some polish all over, and then she's done. I'm already planning my next project. I want to try something a little different. I've got my eye on a 1935 Studebaker President Eight. It's little more than the shell, but I know a guy who can get me parts for Studebakers.

I catch a glance of Ben across the street, hand-washing his truck. He's scrubbing hard with the round yellow sponge, a little too hard, I think. He's turning his head every once in a while and glaring in this direction, and the pain and anger in his eyes is rife and hot. I realize Oz and Kylie are sitting on our porch, watching Netflix.

Man, Ben's got it bad. I thought maybe after the accident he'd back off a bit, but it doesn't seem as if he has. Months have passed, and he's still pining away. Still hoping, maybe, watching and waiting. I sigh, and sit back on my heels. This has got to end. I know Jason's talked to him about it, but what kid Ben's age ever wants to hear what his dad has to say? Especially about matters of the heart.

As I watch, Ben throws the sponge down onto the ground, splattering soapy water everywhere. I can almost hear him cursing as he grabs the hose and sprays his truck. I put my tools back in the box and make my way over to Ben. I glance back, and I see that Oz and Kylie are doing that almost-kissing-while-they-whisper thing, prompting Ben's tantrum.

I stop at the bottom step of the porch. "Hey, you two. I got no problem with any of this," I say, gesturing at them. "And I know you can't tiptoe around Ben's feelings all the time, but don't be cruel about it, huh? Just...at least *try* to be a little considerate."

Kylie sighs. "Ugh. You're right. I hate it, but you're right. I just...I hate this whole situation with him, Daddy. I don't know what to do. It's like he's not even trying to move on." She stares across the street, meeting Ben's gaze. "I'll go talk to him."

"What are you gonna say?" Oz asks.

Kylie shrugs as she stands up. "I don't know. Something. Anything."

I wave her down. "I don't think there's anything you *can* say, Ky. I'll talk to him. Might be nothing I say will make any difference either, but…it's worth a shot."

I duck inside the house, let Nell know where I'm going, grab my keys, and head across the street. Ben is drying his truck with a rag, and I wait until he's done. He ignores me until he's dried the last quarter-panel.

"Yeah?" He tosses the rag into the now-empty bucket, along with the sponge, and then sets the bucket in the garage.

"Come on," I say. "You and me gotta talk, kid." I head back across the street, not waiting to see if he's following. He will, if he knows what's good for him.

I climb into the driver's side of my truck, close the door, start the engine, and wait. After a minute, Ben slides in, closing the door with a slam. I back out, and it doesn't escape my notice that he stares at Kylie and Oz as long as he can, until they're out of sight, at which point he continues to stare out the window, chin in his hand, brows furrowed, visibly brooding. The radio stays off, and I'm silent. I pull into the parking lot of a convenience store.

"Sit tight," I say, and head inside.

I buy a six-pack, and hit the road again. I head out of the suburbs, into the countryside. Find a back road and burn up the dirt. Follow the twists and turns until we come to one of my favorite spots. It's little more than a grassy knoll overlooking a creek, but it's secluded and beautiful and quiet. There's a fallen tree by the bank of the creek, perfect for sitting on and watching the water flow. I grab the six-pack from the back seat, step out of the truck, and make my way to the tree.

Ben follows, and I take a seat on the trunk, twist the tops off two beers and hand him one.

I take a long swallow, and then glance at him. "Got anything you wanna say before I start talking?"

Ben take a sip, shakes his head. "Nope."

I shrug. "All right. Well, I expect you to *listen,* Ben. Not just hear me, but actively listen. Okay?" He nods. "You're trying to dig a hole in the sand, Ben. You're never going to get anywhere doing what you're doing."

Ben frowns. "What the fuck is that supposed to mean?"

"It means you're waiting for something that'll probably never happen." I pause, drink, and start again. "Look. Let's forget the fact that we're talking about my daughter for a minute, okay? I'm just Colt, and you're Ben. You're my best friend's kid. You're like a son to me, Ben. I've watched you grow up. I've watched you grow into a hell of a good athlete, and a good man."

"But?" Ben prompts.

"But you gotta let her go, kid."

"I can't. I've tried. *Fuck,* have I tried. I work out like a fucking lunatic. Condition, practice, study. Stay away as much as possible. Try not to think about her. But...it's fucking hopeless, Colt. I can't get her out of my head. I can't—I can't stop hoping and wishing and praying that she'll change her mind. I dream about her. I have this recurring dream that she's waiting for me after practice one day, and she tells me how wrong she was, that she made the wrong choice and she wants me. That she loves me back. It's torture. I wake up just before she kisses me, just before her lips touch mine, and I realize it was all a dream, and...I just want to rip my fucking heart out. Except she's already done that."

The pain in his voice makes my heart ache for him. I finish my beer and toy with the bottle, slowly peeling the label off and sticking the shreds down the neck. "She didn't mean to, Ben."

"No. I know that. But is that really supposed to make me feel better?" His voice takes on a mocking tone. "'Oh, well, see Ben, the girl you've loved your whole life didn't *mean* to rip your heart out and shit in the hole, so it's fine. Just forget about her.'"

I sigh. "No, you're right. I suppose that isn't any consolation. But here's a shitty fact of life, Ben: sometimes you get your heart stomped on, and there's just no consolation. Sometimes you get hurt, and there's nothing that will make you feel better. No way to mitigate the pain, no way to change the facts. You just hurt. It fucking sucks." I crack another beer, hand it to Ben, and one for myself. "Tell me the truth. You love her? You really love her?"

"Yeah. I do."

"What does that mean, for you?"

He doesn't answer right away. He swirls the amber liquid in the bottle, staring down at it, thinking. "It means I want to be around her all the time. I want to talk to her. It means I want a physical relationship with her. It means I think she's talented and beautiful and amazing. My life isn't the same without her in it. I miss her."

I nod. "Sounds about right. Except…that ain't love. That's your *feelings*. How *you* feel. What do you want for *her*? You ever hear that old John Mayer song, 'Love Is a Verb'?" He shakes his head. "Look it up some time. But do you hear what that means? Love isn't just something you feel, Ben. I hate to sound like I'm Confucius or Yoda or some shit, but it's just the plain facts. You like who Kylie is, and you want her. Okay, that's all good and well, but so what? What are you going to *do* about it? Not to put too fine a point on it, or sound harsh, but you waited too long. Your reasons for waiting were admirable and respectable, and exactly what I would expect from a guy like you. But you lost your chance. Kylie's in love with someone else, and I don't see that changing. And even if, let's say her and Oz don't work out. Are you really gonna just wait around for that possibility? And if that were to happen, is that really how you'd want to get the girl? With her heart broken? On the rebound of pain? I know the feeling of rejection is fucking harsh, Ben. I do. Trust me on that shit. But having your heart broken when a relationship breaks down and ends, that's even worse. You know what you had, and it was taken from you. It's better to have loved and lost than never loved at all. Isn't that how the quote goes?"

Ben shakes his head, swallowing the mouthful of beer he'd just taken. "Almost." He takes a deep breath and then lifts his head, staring at the sky. "'I hold it true, whate'er befall; I feel it when I sorrow most; 'tis better to have loved and lost, than never to have loved at all.' That's 'In Memoriam A.H.H.' by Tennyson."

I'm impressed. "Damn, Ben. You can quote poetry?"

He shrugs, laughing. "Yeah. I like poetry. I get it from Mom, I think."

I nod. "Pretty badass." I pause to sip. "Well, see, sometimes I think that phrase is just complete horse-shit. Losing love fucking blows and, yeah, you may have the memory of the time you had with that person, but you also have the absolute agony of having lost them. I'm not sure it's an even trade."

"Yeah, I wouldn't know." Ben's voice is thick with bitterness.

I ignore that and keep going. "Getting back to my original point. Love is something you *do*. It's active. You show it. If I relied on my feelings for Nell all the time, we'd have broken up a long time ago. We've gotten in some really bad arguments over the years. The kind where we're both spitting mad at each other, can't even look at each other. My *feelings* of love in those situations aren't worth shit, because all I feel is wronged and pissed off and ready to walk away. But you know what keeps me from doing anything stupid? The *choice* to practice love." I jab my finger into his arm as I emphasize the word. "The decision to ignore my feelings and focus on the fact that, even though I don't *feel* the happy, fun, exciting emotions in that situation, I do love Nell and would do anything for her. Including apologizing for something I don't agree that I did was wrong, or let her win an argument simply to get the peace back. Now, she'd get mad about what I just said, that I 'let' her win. And I don't mean that in any kind of condescending sense, Ben. I just mean, fuck, whether I'm right or not, whether she's right or not—diffuse the fight and apologize, or do whatever it takes to get back to where the feelings will do some good. And, in your case, you love Kylie, but what are you gonna do about it? Are you going to keep moping around, glaring at her, staring at her, getting mad when you see her and Oz together? Or are you going to make a choice to do what's best for her?"

"Which means what?" Ben finishes his beer and sets the empty bottle into the empty square of the six-pack box. I do the same, and let him take a third.

I leave the last beer where it is, and try to find the right words for Ben. "You have to decide if you love her enough to let her go."

"I'm *trying* to let her go, Colt! I don't fucking know *how!*"

"No, Ben. You're trying to *get over* her. Not the same thing."

He gets up, stalks over to the creek, silent, thinking. "Whatever it takes to show her love, huh?"

I nod, even though he's not looking at me. "Yep. Whatever it takes."

"Walk away, you mean?"

"If that's what it takes. No one wants you to…I dunno…*go* anywhere, but if the only way to move on and let her go, to let her have her own happiness, is to walk away from the situation, then so be it. And, honestly, sometimes, the only way past the hurt, the only way to really move on, is to put time and distance between you and the situation." I stand up and move to stand beside him, clap him on the shoulder. "My daughter does care for you. She doesn't want to cause you pain. She wants you to be happy. You were her best friend for a very long time, and she's sad that she's lost that. She's said as much."

Ben just nods, and I can tell he's lost in thought. I walk away, lean against my truck, and watch a flock of starlings whorl in the distance.

"This sucks," Ben says.

"Yeah."

"Like, the only way I can think of to really truly walk away from the situation is just…leave Nashville. There's nowhere here I can go that's far enough away from her, from *them*. But where do I go?"

"Sometimes, Ben, there is no *where*. There's just *go*."

Ben laughs. "*Now* you sound like Yoda."

"Trying, I am."

He laughs again, and then lets out a long breath, rubbing the back of his head. "Thanks, Colt."

I shrug. "What's the point of getting old and going through a bunch of shit if you can't pass on some wisdom every once in a while?"

We talk for a few more minutes, and then head back home. He's quiet the whole way, but the silence is different. Less morose, less angry. When we're back and parking in my garage, Ben thanks me again and heads across to his house. He doesn't look back to see if Kylie and Oz are still on the porch, which I think is an improvement.

Nell meets me in the kitchen. "What'd you say to him?" She leans in for a kiss, then hangs on to my neck, standing on her tiptoes.

"I told him love was a verb, and that he had to let her go, if he really loved her."

"John Mayer. Good choice."

I laugh at the fact that she knew exactly which song I'd reference. "Yeah. The allusion was lost on him, but hey, it was worth a try."

She goes flat on her feet and rests her head against my chest. "Do you think he'll listen?"

I nod. "Yeah, I think he will."

"Good." She kisses my jaw. "I'm glad you talked to him. Someone needed to."

"Where'd Oz and Kylie go off to?"

"Back over to his apartment."

I frown. "I wish he lived in a safer neighborhood."

"Me, too. But our choices are to let them move in together, which I know they're already discussing, or let the situation stand as it is. I'm not comfortable with them spending time behind closed doors here."

"Me, neither."

Nell shrugs. "I have a feeling Oz is going to be getting his own apartment soon. Hopefully it'll be a safer one."

"Yeah, and Kylie will end up there as often as we let her." I sigh. "Rock and a hard place."

"Also known as 'parenting,'" Nell quips.

I laugh. "Very true."

She smiles up at me. "But, since the house is empty…" She slides her hands up under my shirt, and I grin down at her and let her peel my shirt off.

"Now *this* is a benefit to having an empty house," I say.

Epilogue: There's Only Go
Ben

I HAND IN MY TEST PAPER AND LEAVE the lecture hall, step out into the sunlight, blinking as I slide my sunglasses on. That was my last final for the semester. Possibly my last final at Vanderbilt. I don't know for sure. I don't know anything for sure.

Well, that's not entirely true. I know my heart is still cracking and crumbling under the weight of what I have to do. I know my truck is packed. Three duffel bags, five thousand dollars in cash and twice that in my bank account. A full tank of gas. No destination. No road map. I'm heading west, I know that much.

Except first I have three stops to make. First, my house. Give Mom a hug, tell her goodbye and not to worry. Then over to the stadium and say bye to Dad. They both know I'm leaving, and why. They weren't real thrilled, obviously, but I convinced them this is what I have to do. I've promised to call every chance I get. Last stop? The recording studio downtown where Oz and Kylie are cutting tracks. Colt told me they were there. I have to say goodbye. I can't just vanish on her.

I find a parking spot, walk a couple of blocks to the studio. I charm and flirt and smile my way past the receptionist and back to the booth where they're playing. I step into the booth, say hi to the producer. Jerry, I think his name is. He holds up a hand for silence, so I bide my time. He punches a button, and the booth is filled with music, Kylie's voice, Oz's. Jerry slides the headphones down to rest on his neck.

A few more chords, and the song ends. Kylie and Oz haven't seen me yet.

Then they do. Kylie's eyes narrow. I wait, and I know she knows I want to talk to her.

"Let's cut one more, Jerry," Kylie says, never taking her eyes off me.

"Okay. What'cha got?" Jerry asks.

"I just wrote this one," Kylie says. "I'm calling it 'Not Your Me.'"

She shifts on the piano bench, touches the keys. Oz glances at me, then away to Kylie. He seems surprised, too, as if this wasn't planned. When she sings, she stares at me, eyes sad, unblinking. Her voice is thick with emotion, lovely and surprising and perfect, just like her:

"A lifetime of you and me
A lifetime of here we are
Day in day out of just be
Of talking free
Of easy and slow
But there have always been
Moments of what if
Moments of does he doesn't he
Can we, could we, should we
Dismiss it, ignore it, pretend
I never had those thoughts
Put the wishes to an end
Live and breathe and move
Find a brand-new groove
Keep going and just be
You and me
Day in day out
You and me
Day in day out
And then like a flash flood
Like a sudden slide of mud
I'm in love with someone else

And you and me aren't you and me
You're you
And I'm someone else
You're not you
And I'm still me
And who are we
Who are we
Where's the we
We used to be
Discover does he doesn't he
Has always been does he
Only I never knew
And the moments are too few
Too late
The time is gone
Long ago and long
And my heart is full of someone else
But you're still you
I'm still me
There's just no longer any we
Because your heart is full of me
But I'm not that me
Your me
I'm his me
And you want what can't ever be
But you still look at me

As if all the we and all the what if and all the as if and all the used to be
Could ever add up to
A new you and me
And I don't want this guilt
I don't want this guilt
I don't want you to wish
Don't want you to keep hoping
Keep holding on and holding out
I want you to find your own someone else
Your own brand-new you and me
Your own fresh lifetime of here we are now
Day in day out
Of talking free
Easy and slow
I wish you could know
How much I miss you
How much I miss
The way we used to be
But god can't you see
I'm no longer that girl
I'm not your me
I'm not your me."

I don't deny the slicing ache in my heart. I accept it. It's old news at this point. I let her see into me, let her see my hurt and my resignation.

Jerry glances at me, pushes a button, and gestures at me.

"Can I please have just five minutes alone with you, Kylie?" I ask.

She nods, slides off the piano bench. She stops by Oz, whispers in his ear, kisses him quickly. He nods, glances at me. I think he knows. I hope he does. I'm doing this for him, too. The guilt over having almost gotten him killed makes this all that much worse.

Kylie steps out of the recording booth, and I follow her outside, into the sunlight. We stand in an alley, dumpsters to either side of us. I put my back to a wall, wait for Kylie to quit pacing and face me.

"Ben, I don't even know—"

"You don't have to say anything," I cut in over her. "Just listen. I've loved you for a long, long time. No, please, Kylie, just listen. You're with Oz. I lost my chance. I get that. I hate it. It hurts. It fucking cuts me apart every single moment of every single day, is what it does." I don't bother to hide my emotions. "It makes me crazy. It should be you and me, not you and him. But I can't change that. I know that. I really do. And…if I really do love you, then I wouldn't want to change that. I'm just weak enough that I still *do* want you for myself, even though I know, I can fucking *see* that you're happy with Oz. So good for you. Be happy."

"Ben—" Her voice breaks.

"No, I'm not done." I force myself to stay absolutely still, barely even breathing. If I don't keep going, I'm liable to do something stupid, like try to kiss her to change her mind. "I'm not done. I do want you to be happy. I want you stay happy. And if—*fuck*—if Oz gives you that, then so be it. I'll accept that because I have no choice. But I can't just pretend it's fine for me. It's not. It hurts to see you with him. It makes me angry and crazy and jealous, and I don't know how to stop that. How to change that in me. I can't. I've fucking tried. For months, I've tried. It's not that I keep hoping you'll change your mind. I know you won't. It's that I can't help wishing. Wanting. And I think...I think no matter how much time passes, that'll never change. At least, not as long as I'm here around you. Around *him*."

"What are you saying, Ben?" Her voice is barely a whisper.

I pace away, running my hand through my freshly shorn hair. It's close to the scalp all over, easy to maintain in the long days of driving and no showers I've got ahead of me. I turn back to her, memorize her features, her perfect strawberry blonde hair, her pale skin, her blue eyes, her body. God. I love her so much, and I've never even held her hand.

"I'm saying…I don't know how to be in love with you and be your friend at the same time. I don't know how. I don't think it's possible. So…I'm choosing to show you I love you the only way I have left." I pinch the bridge of my nose, breathe deep, and then look up into her eyes. One last time. "I'm leaving, Kylie."

"Leaving? Where are you going? For how long?"

I shrug, shake my head. "I don't know…and I don't know. Anywhere but here, and possibly forever. For as long as it takes for me to get over you. Find someone else, maybe. I don't know."

She sniffs. "I don't want you to go." Her eyes are wet, but she doesn't wipe them. "You're my best friend, Ben."

I shake my head again. "No, I'm not. I'm your *oldest* friend." I point at the doorway into the studio. "*He's* your best friend."

She nods. "So you're just…running away."

I growl. "Fucking hell, Kylie. Don't make this any harder than it has to be." I want to punch the wall, kick the dumpster, kiss her senseless. I do none of this. I'm used to wanting her and not letting myself act on it. I'm good at it; I've got almost ten years of practice, after all. "I'm not running away. I'm letting you go."

"But I might never see you again."

I nod. "Yeah. I mean, I'll try to come back for Christmas, but…I don't know where I'll end up."

"What about college? You're leaving Vanderbilt too?"

I nod. "I finished the semester. I haven't officially withdrawn yet, but I doubt I'll be back in the fall. I might transfer somewhere else. Or I might try out for the minors or something. I don't know. I don't care. I'm just going. I've got to get away from you, Kylie. You're…you're *in me.* In my head, in my heart, in my life. But you don't want me the way I want you, and this city just isn't big enough. So…so…"

Kylie sighs, and finally wipes her eyes. "I get it." She looks up at me. "When are you leaving?"

"Right now. I've already said goodbye to everyone else."

She moves closer to me, and my heartbeat ratchets up to a hammering crescendo just from the scent of her shampoo. She hesitates, then wraps her arms around my middle. I freeze solid, don't hug her back. Don't dare. I just let her hold on to me and try to remember to breathe. She lets go finally, and looks up at me from far too close.

Without my permission, my hand lifts, touches her cheek. "I wish—" My voice is close to breaking. "I wish I'd at least kissed you. Just once." Her eyes widen, and she stops breathing. Then, before I do anything truly stupid, I step away. "But I didn't. And now…I never will." Another step backward. "Goodbye, Kylie." I turn away, and it takes every ounce of willpower I possess to do so.

"Ben?" Her voice stops me. "Will you be okay?"

I stop, but don't turn around. Slowly, I nod. "Yeah. Eventually."

A long tense silence. She's about to say something else. I can feel it, and I wait for it. But then, with a sad exhalation, all she says is, "'Bye, Ben. I'll miss you."

I want to look back, but I don't. I blink hard against the aching burn in my throat, in my chest, in my eyes. "Yeah. Me, too." It's unclear, even to me, whether I mean I'll miss her, too, or whether I'll miss me.

Both, maybe.

I don't look back. Not at her, and not at Nashville as I drive past the city limits. When I'm far enough away that I don't recognize the landmarks, I turn on the stereo, hunt through the songs I've got loaded onto the flash drive. Find one that speaks to this moment. It's a Kylie song, the kind of thing I listened to for her.

It's "Let Her Go" by Passenger.

I listen to it on repeat until my throat hurts from singing along, and eventually I let the radio take me to other songs, as the road takes me to other places.

I remember what Colt said by the creek that day: Sometimes there is no *where,* there's only *go*.

And I go.

Postscript

Kylie

One Year Later

PERFORMING NEVER GETS OLD. It never loses its patina of wonder for me. Every single time Oz and I get up on stage, I feel alive, like raw energy replaces the very blood in my veins, like life itself is bigger and more colorful and more amazing. We're on tour with Mom and Dad and The Harris Mountain Boys. This tour has been, very literally, the most amazing experience of my entire life. Each and every day, even if we're just rolling across the country on the tour bus, holds new joy and fresh and exciting things to see and feel and hear and do.

Oz and I get better each time we play together. Oz, not surprisingly, has turned out be an intense and tireless lyrics-writing machine. He's got an endless well of emotion and life experience to pull from, and once I persuaded him to give it a try, he found he couldn't stop the words from pouring out. It works for me, because I'd rather write the music.

We're on the last leg of the summer tour, making the arc across the northern border and down through Michigan—where Mom and Dad are both from—and back to Nashville. The last date of the tour is Nashville, and I'm scared to fucking death for that show. It wasn't announced until less than a month ago, and it sold out in under an hour. We sold out the Ryman. In an hour.

Andersen has been instrumental in all this. He's gotten us huge press over the summer, increased our visibility in a way we could never have expected. Mom and Dad put together the tour, but Andersen used his industry connections to get us noticed, to get people talking about us.

Oz and I? God, I love that man. We haven't gotten a lot of time alone together over the tour, seeing as we're sharing a bus with Mom and Dad, and they won't let us bunk together. It's okay, though. We sneak off together after shows, or during lunch breaks while we're traveling. Gareth, Amy, and Buddy, being more our age than Mom and Dad's, are sympathetic to our plight, so they find ways to give us privacy on their bus whenever possible.

Oz is creative, too. He cornered me backstage one time, in Portland, Maine, I think it was, and dragged me outside into the maze of equipment crates. He pressed me up against the wall, hiding us between a pile of sound equipment boxes and an empty crate that held I don't know what. We were all but invisible there, and he took full advantage of it. His hips pinned mine to the wall, and his fingers busied themselves lifting my shin-length skirt up around my hips. I wrapped my legs around his, grinning into his neck as he realized I wasn't wearing any underwear. My giggle at his surprise turned rather quickly into a groan of need, and from there into a barely stifled squeal as he filled me. He silenced me with a kiss, kept his mouth crushed to mine and ate my cries and whimpers, sucked down my breath and gave me his own, holding me aloft with strong hands cupping my ass.

It wasn't long before we were both trembling and gasping together, straightening clothes just in time to see a sound tech rummaging for a cord. He grinned at us, as if he knew exactly what we'd just been doing. Maybe it should've, but it didn't bother me that he'd known.

I'm still going to school. I'm at Belmont now, studying for a degree in music management. I love playing, and I will to the day I die, but I also love the technical end of it, the business side. I love working with Andersen to get exactly the right sound, tweaking and tweaking and tweaking until the song is perfect. Oz is content to perform, I think. He and my dad have gotten close, and they're talking about opening up a classic car restoration business together. Dad used to do that for a living, and Oz has a knack for the kind of details that make a restoration look authentic. That's what Dad says, at least, and I have no idea what that's supposed to mean.

I am wondering about our future together, though. I know we're in love, and I know there will never be anyone else for either of us. But I'm still living with my parents. Oz has his own apartment now, and when we're in Nashville I stay there more nights than not, but it's…it's not the same. Whenever I talk about officially moving in with him, he kind of dismisses the subject, glosses over it and makes it seem like we've got all the time in the world to figure it out. And, I mean, we *do*, I guess, but I want to be with him all the time, and I want that *now*. I don't want to have to always go back to Mom and Dad's for clean clothes. I don't want to be split between their house and Oz's. I belong with Oz now. He's my home.

But he just seems reticent to rush things. That's his big excuse: *I don't want to rush things.* What the hell is that supposed to mean? We knew each other a matter of months before we had sex together, and it was not much longer than that before we both knew we loved each other. Less than a year, and we were totally serious and committed. How much more rushed can you get? I don't need more time. It's not like I'm pressuring him to propose; I don't expect that level of commitment from him yet. Don't get me wrong—I'd say yes before he got the words out if he asked, but I know that's a big deal. It is for me, too, but I think it's just different for guys, especially one who grew up as nomadic as Oz. He could still get the urge to travel, to move on. I don't think he'd just up and leave. He'd want me with him, and he knows I'm committed to finishing my degree.

All this means that despite how happy I am, in general, there's a tiny little nagging bit of impatience inside me. Like a teeny pebble in your shoe, not painful, just…irritating. I want *everything* with Oz, and I want it now.

As our tour gets closer and closer to Nashville, the more antsy I get. I don't know why. Oz has been acting odd, too. Going off with Dad at strange times, whispering together. They're writing a song, I know that much. I know what songwriting looks like, and that's what they're doing. But why the secrecy? They always clam up if I get near them, and it's starting to bug me. Plus, Oz has been on the phone a lot, with I'm not sure whom, or why.

Something's up, and I want to know what.

A day out of Nashville, our second-to-last show, in Detroit. The Fox Theater is sold out. Oz is jittery, distracted. Mom and Dad are almost done with their set, and Oz and I are getting ready to go on for ours. I take Oz's hands in mine, stand chest to chest with him, look up into his gray-brown eyes.

"Oz…I know you're hiding something from me. Just…just tell me if I need to be worried about whatever it is. Tell me if it's something bad. About me, or us." I hate how insecure I sound, but I need some kind of reassurance from him.

Oz nudges my forehead with his, sighing. "You don't need to worry. I know I've been acting weird lately, and I'm sorry. It's nothing bad, I promise. I love you, only you, and I'm not going anywhere."

"Then what is it?"

He grins at me. "Well, I'm planning a surprise for you. That's all I'm gonna say."

I frown. "Can't you at least give me a hint?"

Oz shakes his head. "Nope. No hints."

And then we're on, and there's no time for talking. We go on, and I have to push away my curiosity, my distraction.

The show was fantastic, but all the way from Detroit to Nashville, Oz is jittery and nervous and strange. Dad keeps looking at me, and then at Oz, and then grinning.

It's not that I hate surprises; I don't. I like surprises. I just…this one seems big, for some reason, and I don't know what to expect. I just have to wait, I guess.

Finally, we reach Nashville and get to spend a night at home in our own beds. Friday night we have an end-of-tour celebratory dinner—Mom and Dad and Oz and I, plus Amy, Gareth, Buddy, and a lot of the crew who've been on the road with us since April. They're like family now, and I know Oz especially has gotten close with some of the guitar techs. It's good to see, really. I know Oz doesn't make friends easily, so watching him open up a little to people who are not me or Mom and Dad is cool.

We spend all day Saturday at the Ryman, practicing, putting together our set list, getting everything tuned and dialed in. And then, just when I think I'm going to get a few minutes alone with Oz, he vanishes with Daddy. I turn to Mom, huffing in irritation.

"What the hell is going on with them, Mom?"

Mom just shrugs and shakes her head. "I don't know, sweetie. It's a big secret, though. Dad won't even tell me what's going on. Says it would ruin the surprise." She wraps her arm around me. "Here's a little advice, though, honey. When guys do things like this, on their own, and don't involve us women in it, you know it's something romantic. The only time a man will go to these kinds of lengths to keep something secret is if he's got something huge and sexy and sweet up his sleeve. I really, *really* don't think you need to be worried. Just...be prepared for anything."

I lean into her. "He's never secretive. It's weirding me out."

Mom laughs. "I know, honey. But try not to freak out. Oz loves you, and that's all that really matters, right?"

I nod and try to push away the worry. "Right."

Eventually, Oz and Daddy come back, and we four have dinner together. Oz and Dad act like nothing at all is amiss, so I try not to as well. Later that night, as Oz and I let ourselves into his apartment, I decide to try a little seduction-interrogation.

As soon as the door is locked behind us, I push Oz's back against the wall, take his keys from him, toss them aside, not caring where they land. Oz's eyes are narrowed, as if he knows what I'm planning. He's wearing a plain white button-down, which I make short work of removing, leaving him deliciously sexy in just blue jeans and boots. I pause to strip, peeling my T-shirt, bra, jeans, and panties off in record time. Naked now, I kiss my way from his jaw to his chest, down his ribs to his navel. I slip the end of his belt out of the buckle, unbutton his jeans, tug them down. The act of getting his jeans past his hips has pulled the waistband of his boxers down just far enough to let the tip of his cock show, and I grin up at him.

He licks his lips and sucks in a deep breath. "Kylie, babe. What are you planning on doing down there?"

I slide his boxers off, keeping my eyes on him. "What do you think I'm planning on doing down here?"

"I think you're fishing for information."

I wrap my lips around him and suck hard, tasting his flesh and the essence that begins to seep out of his tip onto my tongue. When he's groaning, I lift my mouth off him. "Is it working?"

"Nope." He tangles his fingers in my hair. "You might have to try again."

I laugh, and then comply. This time, I grip him at the base and slide my fingers around his thickness as I work the head with my lips and tongue. He starts moving in time with my suction, and when I know he's close, I take my mouth away. "How about now? Tell me what's going on, and I'll let you come in my mouth. I know how much you love that, and it's been a while. Since Montana, right? You know you want it."

He groans. "Goddamn, Ky. That's mean. Cruel and unusual punishment."

I laugh and flick his tip with my tongue. "But effective, right?"

He shudders and his hips piston, trying to get closer to my mouth, seeking relief. I don't give it to him. "Fuck, baby. I'm not…not telling. It's a surprise. A good surprise. You want it to be a surprise. Just try to trust me on this, will you?" He growls. "I'm going crazy here, baby."

"Just a hint?" I beg.

He hisses as I pump my fingers up and down his length. "Fuck…*fuck*. If I give you a hint, you'll make me come?"

"So hard, baby. I swear."

He laughs, and then lets his head thump back against the wall. I slow my hands on him, drawing it out. He can't help moving into my touch, and I know I've got him.

But then he moves like a striking snake. There's no warning, no chance of resisting. One second I'm in control, on my knees in front of him with his thick cock in my hands and my lips descending to finish him off, and then the next second I'm on my hands and knees, and he's behind me.

I open my mouth to protest, and but all that comes out is a gasping shriek. He's in me, sliding deep, fast, hard, and I can only whimper.

"Oz…Jesus, Oz. Oh, god." All my demands and plans are ruined. He's in control now, hands gripping my hips, pulling me against him, drawing moans from me.

He leans over me, bites my earlobe. "You want a hint, baby? I'll give you a hint. It's a surprise. A really, really, *big*"—he emphasizes this with a hard thrust that has me rocking forward—"surprise."

I can't help but move back into him, needing what he's giving me now. "Why won't you tell me?"

"Because you have to wait till tomorrow." He breathes into my ear, his breath hot. "Don't you trust me, baby?"

"Yeah, I trust you," I gasp.

"Then let it be a surprise."

I'm on the edge now, a few strokes away from coming hard. "Okay, Oz. Okay. Okay. I trust you."

He pulls out, and I whimper in shock. "NO! Fuck, Oz, put it back in, please, I need it, I was right there!"

He chuckles, and I feel the tip slide in, but it's nowhere near enough. "You trust me, baby?"

I nod and try to rock to get the fullness back. "Yeah, Oz, I trust you."

He flutters his hips, giving me tiny, shallow, insufficient, teasing thrusts. "You wouldn't want to ruin my surprise, would you?"

"No…no." I seek relief, unashamedly begging. "Please…please…"

He's groaning, growling. "You were sneaky, Kylie. That was a very sneaky and devious thing you did."

"I'm sorry…I'm just…I'm dying of curiosity."

He pulls out, and I whimper, but then he rolls me to my back, lifts my heels over his shoulders and drives in, sudden, hard, and perfect. "You're afraid, is what you are."

"Yeah, you've never kept any secrets from me."

"I know. But this is a good secret."

"A good secret?"

He slides out and back in, and I'm whimpering abjectly. "Yeah, sweetness. A very good one. That's all the hints you'll get."

"It almost worked, though, didn't it?" I ask, watching him through the "V" of my legs.

He nods, eyes fluttering and shuttering closed. "Very…very nearly. Why do you think we're doing this on the floor? A few more seconds, and I would've told you."

I groan, partly in frustration and partly in delighted pleasure as he starts to rock into me hard and fast. "Fuck, Oz. I almost had you?"

He groans. "Yeah, baby. That sweet mouth of yours…oh, shit. I'm right there…"

"You'd better not stop, Oz. You'd better not fucking stop…"

"Hell no…"

And then we explode together, my heels wrapped around his neck, and then he's leaning over me and my legs are clenched like vises around his back and we're gasping and trembling and rocking together, breathing together.

A few moments of his weight resting on me, and then Oz stands up, lifts me in his arms, and carries me to his bed. "I can't believe you tried that."

I laugh and curl into his arms. "What, tried to suck the truth out of you?"

"Yeah. Is it that hard to just trust me?"

I feather my fingers over his cock, needing more already. "Yeah. You've been acting really weird, babe."

He huffs a laugh, then moans as he starts to harden in my hand. "God, Kylie. Insatiable, aren't you?"

"Would you have it any other way?"

"Fuck no! I'm the luckiest guy on earth, sweetness, and well I know it. But do you really think I'd ever do anything to hurt you?"

"No," I say, throwing my leg over his hip and straddling him. "I just…I guess I still can't believe how much I love you, how happy you make me, and I don't—I don't want anything to change that."

"Nothing can, Kylie. Nothing in the whole world."

This time, it's slow and tender and gentle, and his eyes never leave mine, and as we implode together, his lips meet mine and our breathing merges and time stops and the heaven itself shatters through us, weaving our souls together.

Sunday, the day of the concert. Pre-show jitters have us all a little on edge. This is the biggest show any of us have ever done, even Mom and Dad.

The Harris Mountain Boys go on first, Mom and Dad second, and Oz and I third. At the end of our regular set, Mom and Dad come out, and the four us play a few songs together, and then Amy, Gareth, and Buddy come out, and we all jam for almost half an hour, and the crowd is going crazy.

Finally, the show is over. We're all saying thank you, bowing, basking in the wild energy of the crowd.

The lights go down, and we all make our way off-stage.

And then the lights go on, and Oz and Daddy are back on the stage, plugging their guitars back in.

"Ya'll don't mind one more little song, do you?" Daddy asks into the mic.

"*NO!*" comes the enthusiastic response.

Mom and I glance at each other. This wasn't part of the planned set; this is the surprise.

"Good, 'cause Oz and I here have a little surprise." He claps Oz on the shoulder.

Oz seems really nervous. I can tell by the set of his shoulders, by the way he scuffs at the stage floor with the toe of his boot. "This surprise is for you guys," Oz says, "'cause ya'll are what make us able to do this, and we love you for it. But it's also a surprise for the girls. For Kylie, especially." He turns and waves me over. "Come on out, baby."

Colt looks at Mom. "You, too, Nelly."

Everyone is confused. Mom and I go back out on stage, and two stagehands bring us stools. We sit three-quarters turned, facing the stage and the guys.

"If anybody out there is old enough to have watched Nell and me play when we were first starting out, ya'll might remember a particularly memorable night in New Orleans." Daddy's looking at Mom with eyes that speak of their love, that speak of the secrets of twenty years of marriage. "I played a song that night. A very special song. One we haven't played live in…oh, hell, ten years? Anybody remember that show? Which song I played?"

Oz is fiddling with the tuning knobs of his acoustic guitar, fixing a capo onto the strings. I watch him, and his eyes meet mine. The nerves are obvious in his eyes, and I smile, trying to reassure him.

The crowd is restless, muttering, and I hear a single voice shout from way in the back, "'Falling Into You'!"

Daddy nods. "That's the one. Ya'll are about to hear a very special version of that song. Oz and I tweaked it a bit for this occasion, so now we're calling it something different. This is 'Falling Under.'"

He taps the flat of his guitar to count out the beat, and then they both start playing. Mom is watching, hand over her mouth, and then she turns to glance at me, and her eyes are already wet. She's twisting her diamond ring on her finger. Oh. *Oh.* Realization hits me as Dad and Oz start in on the first verse.

"All my life it seems
I've been barely keeping
My head above the water
And then I saw you
You saw all the pain
Hiding in my eyes
And you wanted
To take it away

But I had no words for you
'Cause I was falling under

And I am falling, falling under with you
I can't resist you, baby
I'm falling, falling under with you
Your love healed me

Fate has intervened
Conspiring to draw us close together
And tangle our lives
The siren of your song
And the music of your heart is calling
Whispering my name

And now I have the words for you
'Cause I'm falling under with you

Now I'm falling, falling under with you
I can't resist you, baby
I am falling, falling under with you
And I'm falling still
I'm falling still

Now that fate has intervened
And drawn us close together
Past our fears and all the pain
Behind our eyes
Despite the ghosts trailing around us
Like a fog of haunting souls
You're still trying hard to heal me
To take my pain and make it yours

Your beautiful eyes are smiling
Into mine

Now I'm falling, falling under with you
I can't resist you, baby
I am falling, falling under with you
And I'm falling still
I'm falling still
I'm falling still
Falling under with you."

Dad keeps playing, but the sound tech turns the volume down, so the melody is a faint refrain, a soundtrack for what's about to happen. Oz swings his guitar around by the strap to hang from his back, turns toward me, grabbing the mic off the stand.

"Kylie…this is it. Are you ready?" He grins at me, stands in front of me. I can only nod and try to breathe. "Twenty years ago your dad played that song for your mom. I wanted a special way to do this for you, and your dad thought this might be perfect. I actually watched a video of that proposal, and I don't mind admitting to being jealous of your Dad's awesomeness. I'm just grateful he doesn't mind me stealing his idea, and even conspiring to help me make it that much more perfect."

He takes a deep breath, reaches into his hip pocket. "I love you, Kylie. You're it, for me. You saved me, you know. Life had me running. Had me by the throat, and I really was falling under, losing hope. And then I met you, and you gave me a reason to keep my head above water. You taught me to swim. You taught me to live. And instead of giving up, I fell in love. I fell under your spell, Kylie, and every single day since, I've fallen further and further under for you."

I'm crying, unabashedly weeping, and I don't care who sees. I stand up and reach for Oz, but he falls to one knee at my feet, holding up a ring. It's a small ring, simple, a thin white-gold band and princess-cut diamond but, to me, in that moment, it's the most beautiful thing I've ever seen. Except for Oz's face and the love in his eyes.

He looks up at me, clearly struggling with his own emotions. "Kylie Calloway, will you—"

I don't let him finish. I fall to my knees and lunge into him, crash my lips to his. We fall backward to the stage, and the crowd is going crazy, howling, cheering, clapping. Oz kept hold of the ring and the mic so, with me lying on his chest, he lifts the mic to his lips.

"I take it that's a yes?"

I hold up my left hand, and he slides the ring on. I take the mic. "Yes, Oz! Of course yes. With all my heart yes."

We devolve into kissing, heedless of the thousands of people watching.

I hear Daddy talking. "I can't ask you to marry me again, Nelly baby, but I can tell you how perfect the last twenty years have been. I can tell you that I love you now infinitely more than I did then. And I can tell you that I'll spend every moment of the next twenty years loving you that much more."

The crowd can't even handle it. They're completely wild, apoplectic with glee. Finally, Oz and I have to pull away before it gets too heated.

Mom is crying, too, and she grabs the mic from Oz. "You know what's funny is that I didn't let Colt finish his proposal, either. Like mother, like daughter, huh?"

She looks at Oz. "Your last name isn't Calloway, but Oz, you are so much like my husband that it's a little scary sometimes. And I really couldn't think of anyone better to marry my daughter than you."

Her attention goes to Colt. "Baby…you're so perfect it makes me dizzy sometimes. I love you so much I don't even know how to express it, and I really never have. I've spent my life trying to show you how much I love you, and I've never been able to get it right. And I'm just thankful I've got the rest of our lives to keep trying."

I snatch the microphone from Mom. "My turn. Ya'll are so romantic it's almost sick. But I love you.

Oz, all I can say is I'm just as much under your spell, and I'm so glad you didn't let me seduce this secret out of you." Mom and Dad both roll their eyes at this, but I keep going. "Mom and Dad…just thank you. For everything. And to you guys, our fans? Thanks for sitting through all this. For supporting us on this tour, and for demanding this amazing hometown show."

The crowd hasn't stopped cheering all this time, but now they ratchet up the intensity until it's deafening. The four of us stand up and take hands, face the crowd, and bow together, and it takes a full ten minutes before the crowd seems ready to let us go.

We're all giddy and overwhelmed with adrenaline as we make our way off-stage, and as soon as we're out of sight of the audience, I turn and leap into Oz's arms.

"I can't believe you!" I bury my face in his neck. "That was perfect. So perfect."

He just laughs. "I wasn't sure you'd like it. But your dad assured me that you're enough like your mom that you'd appreciate a proposal like that. I just didn't think a proposal over dinner would be as special."

"I loved it."

He grins, and then lets me down. "I have one more surprise for you, actually."

"You do? What?" I can't imagine what else there is to be surprised by.

He reaches into his back pocket and pulls out a set of keys. "You know that little house we saw?"

Before the tour started, Oz and I were taking a drive together. We ended up getting lost in the suburbs, and we came across this adorable little house for sale. I got out and peeked in through the windows, and got all girly about it. I had this fantasy of us buying it, and even tried to convince Oz that we should. He seemed to brush it off, saying we weren't ready for that yet, and I let it go. Mostly. I may or may not have looked at it online every so often over the past few months, stalking it on Zillow to see if it was still for sale.

"Yeah?" I ask, feeling excitement thrill through me.

He puts the keys in my hand. "It's ours."

"*Really?*" My voice is shockingly shrill, and I have to rein it in. "I mean…ahem, really? You bought it?"

He shrugs. "Yeah. I had…help, though."

Daddy comes over. "Happy engagement, baby."

That Oz let my dad help him buy me a house…it's…unbelievable. I don't know who to hug first, so I end up hugging them both. "You two…I love you so much."

"Love you too, babe," Oz and Dad say in perfect sync.

I can only laugh, and try not to cry for the third time in less than twenty minutes. "When do we move in?"

"I've got a truck rented for tomorrow to get my stuff from my apartment and whatever you need from home," Oz says.

Kate appears beside me, pulls me into a hug. "I'm so happy for you two. It'll be lonely in that apartment without Oz."

Oz rolls his eyes and tugs his mom to him. "You know we'll visit, Mom. And you know you're always welcome. Just not…you know, *too* often."

Kate sniffs and pats Oz's chest. "I know, baby."

After that things get crazy, with the crew congratulating us and Andersen trying to shake everyone's hand at once, and the promo manager telling us we've got a massive lineup for autographs waiting. Through it all, I can't stop looking at the ring on my finger, and imaging how amazing it will be to live with Oz all the time.

Pretty amazing, I think.

In the car, finally alone, I stop Oz from putting it into drive. "You've made my life perfect, Oz. I know you said I rescued you, but…you rescued me, too. Now I get to live with you? How can it get any better?"

"I don't think it can," Oz says. He kisses me. "Oh…it can. Let's go home, and I'll show you."

Playlist

"Monolith" by Stone Sour
"We Stitch These Wounds" by Black Veil Brides
"Home Sweet Hole" by Bring Me the Horizon
"Life of Uncertainty" by It Dies Today
"Breaking Out, Breaking Up" by Bullet for My Valentine
"I'm Still a Guy" by Brad Paisley
"Goodbye Town" by Lady Antebellum
"Four on the Floor" by Lee Brice
"Hell on Wheels" by Brantley Gilbert
"The Sadness Will Never End" by Bring Me the Horizon
"In Place of Hope" by Still Remains
"A Beast Am I" by Amon Amarth
"Freedom Hangs Like Heaven" by Iron & Wine
"Come On Get Higher" by Matt Nathanson
"Kiss Me" by Ed Sheeran
"Cannery River" by Green River Ordinance
"Down" by Jason Walker
"Set Fire to the Third Bar" by Snow Patrol (feat. Martha Wainwright)
"She Is Love" by Parachute
"Love Is a Verb" by John Mayer
"Let Her Go" by Passenger

A Note From the Author

This book was somewhat tricky to write, in a sense. It takes place when the children of Nell and Colt and Jason and Becca are grown. Obviously, then, it takes place about eighteen years after the events of *Falling Into You* and *Falling Into Us,* making it the theoretical future. But, in order to follow the pattern of the first two books, I had to include music, which is vital to the core of these stories. I had to use music that would capture the personalities of the characters, capture the heartbeat of the story, match the prose and the rhythm. The songs referenced in this story, then, are from our time, the present. Inventing pop culture and indie songs from "the future" wouldn't have had the same effect. They had to be songs that you could look up on YouTube, iTunes, Grooveshark, Spotify, or wherever. They are meant to feel like current references to songs Oz and Kylie would have been familiar with, however anachronistic this may technically be.

As for Oz's music…it may not be for everyone. It's far from the style of music I typically use in my books, so I know some—if not most—of my readers may not enjoy it, or understand it. It's heavy metal and various subgenres thereof. It's Oz's music, important to him, central to the way he emoted through most of the book. Including it was necessary for me, as the author, to get into Oz's head, into the soul of who he was. I have to extend thanks to my brother-in-law for the band suggestions, even though I know he probably won't ever read this book, or this note. Thanks anyway.

Continue reading for an excerpt from

ALPHA

Coming in April from
Jasinda Wilder

"MISS ST. CLAIRE. COME IN, PLEASE." My boss, Mr. Edwards, waved a hand at the two chairs facing his desk. "Have a seat, Kyrie." He says it wrong, as always, pronouncing it *Kye-ree.*

"My name is *Keer-ee,*" I couldn't help correcting him for what must be the eighteen thousandth time.

Mr. Edwards slid into his modern black leather desk chair, and then unbuttoned his suit coat. "Yes. Of course." He tugged at the cuffs of his pressed white button-down shirt, cleared his throat. "Well, Miss St. Claire, I'll cut right to the chase. We're letting you go, I'm afraid. It's nothing to do with you—it's simply that we're streamlining our workflow, and as the newest, and least experienced, member of our team…well, your services have become somewhat superfluous."

I blinked. Twice. Three times. "I'm…what?"

"Superfluous. It means—"

"I *know* what superfluous means. I just don't understand how this is happening. Just last week Don said I was next in line for a permanent position—"

Mr. Edwards cut me off with a raised hand. "Don was incorrect, and I do apologize for the misunderstanding. You see, Don had a rather unfortunate habit of making promises he had no authority to make, and no wherewithal to keep them. He, too, has been let go." A discreet clearing of his throat indicated the subject was closed. He opened a drawer and withdrew an envelope. "Your final paycheck, Miss St. Claire. It includes a two-week severance allowance. You'll clear out your desk immediately. Should you require a referral, you may submit a request in writing through the appropriate channels."

I shook my head. "No, please—Mr. Edwards, you can't do this. I need this job, you don't even know. I've never been late, never failed to do my job better than anyone else in my pool. Please, give me a chance—"

"Miss St. Claire. Begging will not change the facts. It has been done. You were assigned to us through a temp agency. Temp, meaning *temporary*. As I said, this isn't a punishment. We are not firing you—we are simply letting you go now that your position is no longer necessary. Now, if you don't mind, I have a conference call in a few moments." Mr. Edwards arched an eyebrow at me expectantly.

"Fine." I stood up, smoothing my navy pencil skirt over my hips, turning away. "Prick."

"Excuse me?" Mr. Edwards rose to his feet, a fist clenched at his side. "What did you say?"

I lifted my chin. "I said, *prick*." I used the same condescending tone he so often affected. "It's a derogatory term meaning penis. Meaning, you... are...a...dick." I turned away again, and grabbed the doorknob and twisted it.

I was stopped by a hand on my wrist. "Now, now, Miss St. Claire. You don't want to go name-calling, do you? I can very easily call your temp agency and make sure you never work in their pool again." His fingers tightened on my wrist, and I felt his breath on my neck. "And...you know, there may be *one* way you could keep your job. Possibly even get that permanent position you mentioned."

I felt him press up against me, felt the evidence of what he wanted from me. And, I won't lie, the thought crossed my mind. Once. Very, very briefly. I needed this job. I was already two months behind on rent, three months behind on my electric bill, barely keeping up with my tuition and my brother's, plus the ever-mounting costs of caring for Mama. I could do what this doucheknob wanted, and keep my job. It wouldn't take long. A few unpleasant minutes, if that long. He was old, past sixty, I'd guess. Fit enough for his age, but by no means virile.

But…no matter how desperate I might be, *that* would never happen. Not like this. Not with this guy. If he was hot, and I wanted to, maybe. If it was a kick-ass job that really paid the bills. But it was a temp job. Hourly, and a shitty hourly rate at that. Barely enough to cover *one* bill, much less all the bills I had to pay.

I turned, letting him hold on to my wrist. For the moment. I lifted my eyes to his, putting on my best poker face. "Yeah? Just like that? That easy, huh? Suck you off, and you'll let me keep my job? Let you fuck me over the desk, and I'll get the permanent position, too, I bet."

He missed the dangerous calm in my voice. "Now you're thinking." He licked his lips, lifted a finger to touch the apex of my cleavage, what little of it I had showing in this conservative work outfit. "You're a very attractive young lady, Miss St. Claire. I'm sure we could come to an agreeable arrangement."

God, I hated the arch, faux-formal way he spoke. "An agreeable arrangement." I forced down my revulsion, just for a few more seconds. "What did you have in mind, Mr. Edwards?"

My spine crawled with disgust as his eyes leered and his tongue flicked out over his thin, pale lips. He made short work of his belt, and I heard the telltale *zzzzhhrip* of his zipper going down. I didn't look, didn't want to see what he'd just pulled out.

"Well, let's just see how you do, and we'll go from there." He leaned back against the edge of his desk, a greedy smirk on his face. "And…unbutton the blouse a bit."

I toyed with the button of my shirt, staring into his sludge-brown eyes. "You want a little show, huh, Mr. Edwards?" I freed the top button, which I would've done on the elevator anyway. I felt my breasts loosen a bit, no longer quite so constricted. His eyes devoured the expanse of cleavage. "How's this?"

"Very nice. But…how about a bit more?"

I nodded, as if this was perfectly reasonable, still refusing to look down at his crotch. And then, without warning, I snapped my head forward, felt my forehead connect with his nose, felt cartilage break. I stepped away as crimson blood sluiced from his nose. "How about *fuck you,* Mr. Edwards?" I left him bleeding, sagging against his desk. I shuddered as I caught an accidental glimpse of his wrinkled, veiny, now-flaccid penis hanging over his zipper. "God, I could've gone the rest of my life without seeing that."

I opened his door and walked out, glanced down at my shirt, and cursed as I realized I had a few droplets of blood on my blouse. I stopped in the women's room and dabbed cold water onto the droplets, then retrieved my belongings from my desk. I didn't have much to get, a few granola bars, some spare tampons, and—most importantly—my framed photo of Mom, Dad, my younger brother Cal, and me. It was taken several years ago. *Before*. Before Dad was murdered. Before Mom got sick. Before I went from innocent, naïve, privileged college girl to primary breadwinner for three people, one of whom didn't even recognize me most days. Before life went completely down the drain, putting all my dreams out of reach, leaving me desperate, exhausted, stressed, and frustrated.

I stuffed my things into my purse and walked with as much dignity as I possessed to the elevator, and had to hide my mirth as I saw Mr. Edwards being escorted out by security. His pants were buttoned, but not zipped, and his once-impeccable suit was drenched in blood. Two more security members were going from cubicle to cubicle, looking for me, I supposed.

I took the stairs.

I took the bus to the temp agency, since the temp agency never had any parking spots available.

My contact, Sheila, tapped on her computer for several minutes, then turned to me with a slight frown. "I'm sorry, Kyrie, but we just don't have anything else right now."

I tried to keep breathing. "Can you check again? I'll take anything. Literally anything."

She looked again, then glanced back up at me with a shrug. "Nothing. I'm sorry. Try again in a few weeks."

"I won't have an apartment in a few weeks."

"I'm sorry, honey. Things are tight. What can I tell you?" She laid a manicured hand on mine. "Do you need a few bucks? I can spare you—"

I stood up. "No. Thanks." I did need the money, desperately. I'd skipped lunch today, just to have a bit more to go to rent. But I wouldn't take pity charity. "I'll figure something out."

I walked slowly back to my car, started it, and then remembered that I'd just been fired. I wouldn't get my parking slip validated. Shit. There went another fifteen bucks I couldn't spare. The drive home was long. I'd been working in an office downtown, and I lived over forty-five minutes away in the suburbs outside Detroit. My car was running on fumes by the time I got home, and my stomach was empty, rumbling and growling and gurgling.

I struggled to hold back the tears as I checked the mail. I was fumbling through the envelopes, muttering *"fuck...fuck...fuck"* under my breath at each new bill. There was DTE Energy, Consumers, AT&T cable and Internet, water, gas, Cal's tuition, my tuition, Mom's hospice bill...and a plain white envelope, no return address, just my name—Kyrie St. Claire—handwritten in neat black script in the center, along with my address. I tucked the other bills into my purse and stuck the envelope between my lips as I inserted my key into the lock.

That, of course, was when I saw the white notice taped to my apartment door. *Eviction Notice: pay rent or quit within 3 days.*

I was still a hundred dollars short on rent. Or rather, short of the one month's rent I could scrounge up. I had been hoping to avoid this long enough to be able to catch up on the past due amount. Now I'd just been fired.

Still holding back tears, I opened my door, closed it behind me, and stifled a sob. I let the envelope fall to the floor at my feet and covered my mouth with my fist, tears hot and salty in my eyes. No. No. No tears, no regret, no self-pity. *Figure it the fuck out, Kyrie. Figure it out.*

I pushed away from the door, knelt to retrieve the bizarre envelope, and flicked the light switch.

Nothing.

Of course the power had been turned off.

All I had to eat at home was one package of ramen, some ketchup, two-week-old Chinese carry-out, and a bag of baby carrots. And a single, lonely little cup of black cherry Chobani.

Thank you, Jesus and all the Greeks for Chobani. And thank you for the fact that the yogurt was still cold.

I took my yogurt from the dark, still-cool fridge, opened it, grabbed a spoon from the drawer, and stirred it up. I opened my blouse all the way, unzipped my skirt, and perched on the counter, eating my yogurt, relishing every bite. I had one paycheck for not quite eight hundred dollars for two weeks of temp office work, plus severance.

Finally, I couldn't hold back the sobs any longer. I gave in. Let myself cry for a solid ten minutes. I tore off a piece of paper towel—my last roll—and dabbed at my nose and eyes, making myself stop. I'd figure this out. Somehow.

The envelope caught my eye where I'd set it on top of the microwave. I reached over and grabbed it, slid my index finger under the flap. Inside was…a check?

Yes, a check. A personal check.

For ten thousand dollars.

Made out to me.

I took a deep breath, put the check face down on my lap, and blinked several times. Hard. Okay, look again. Yep. It said *pay to the order of Kyrie St. Claire, in the amount of ten thousand dollars and zero cents.* At the top left of the check was the payer: VRI Inc., and a P.O. box address in Manhattan.

And there, in the bottom left-hand corner, on the single line opposite the illegible signature, was a single word. *YOU.* All caps, all in the same bold, neat script that appeared on the envelope. I examined the signature again, but it was little more than a squiggly black line. I thought there might be a "V," and maybe an "R," but there was no way to be sure. I guess that would make sense, given the fact that the payer was VRI Incorporated. But that didn't tell me much.

No note, nothing in the envelope except the check. For TEN THOUSAND dollars.

What the hell was I supposed to do? Cash it? Ten thousand dollars would pay current rent due, as well as the past due amount, it would get the electricity back on by paying what I owed them…it could pay all my bills and still leave me enough to get the brakes on my car fixed.

Ten thousand dollars.

From whom? Why? I knew no one. No family other than my mom and brother. I mean, yeah, I had Grandma and Grandpa in Florida, but they were living off Social Security, and were about five minutes from moving into a nursing home…that I couldn't pay for. They'd asked me for money last year. And I'd given it to them.

What if I cashed this, and it was…like, the Mob? And they'd come for what I owed them, and they'd break my knees. Okay, that was stupid. But for real, who on earth would send me money at all, much less this much? I had one friend, Layla. And she was almost as desperate as I was.

Nonetheless, I called her. She answered on the fourth ring. "Hey, bitch. What's up?"

"Did you—this is going to sound really dumb, but you didn't mail me a check? Did you? Like, you didn't secretly win the lottery?" I laughed, like it was joke. "I mean, you didn't, right?"

Layla guffawed. "Have you been drinking? Why the hell would I mail you a check? I don't even *have* checks. And if I did, and if I had money to give you, why would I *mail* it to you?"

"Yeah, right. That's—that's what I thought."

Layla caught the tone in my voice. "What's going on, Key?"

I wasn't sure what to say. "I. Um. Can I come over? For…a few days?"

"Your electricity got shut off?"

"I also got evicted."

"No," she breathed.

"And fired."

"*What?*" Layla shrieked. "Didn't you just tell me you were going to get the permanent job?"

"I was sexually propositioned by Mr. Edwards."

"Shut the fuck up."

"He said I could keep my job if I sucked his cock. I mean, he didn't say it in so many words. But he made it clear…by pulling his dick out."

"Key. You've *got* to be kidding me." Layla's voice was flat, disbelieving.

"Wish I was. I'll never get *that* mental image out of my head. Ugh." I didn't fake the shudder of revulsion. "Know what I did?"

"What?"

"I head-butted him. Broke his nose."

"You did *not!*"

I nodded, and then realized I was on the phone. "I did. I totally did."

Layla was silent for a minute. Then, "Damn, Kyrie. That's a hell of a shitty day." I heard the light bulb go off. "What was that about the check?"

"Can I come over? You wouldn't believe me if I told you." I had to force my voice to stay calm.

"Of course. Bring your blankie, bitch. Let's have us a sleepover."

Layla would never let me down. I mean, she couldn't pay my rent for me, but she'd let me stay on her couch until doomsday if I needed to. She lived with her boyfriend, Eric, so we couldn't be roommates anymore, but she'd always welcome me. I changed, packed my bags—which didn't take much—and left my shitty, third-hand furniture where it was. Either I'd be able to come back for it, or I wouldn't. Nothing to do about it now.

At Layla's, I kicked off my shoes and accepted the Bud Light she handed me. Layla was half-black, half-Italian, all attitude and curves. Long black hair, dark brown eyes, flawless mocha skin. We'd been best friends since the first day of college, roommates for two years, until she met Eric and got serious enough to move in with him. Eric was…okay. Smart, good-looking, nice…and a small-time pot dealer. I didn't actively dislike him, but I didn't get what Layla saw in him. He wasn't a bad guy, just not my cup of tea. She knew it, and she didn't care. She liked him, he liked her, and it worked for them. Whatever.

I sat back on her ratty couch, drained half of my beer, and then handed Layla the envelope. Or, as I thought of it, *The* Envelope. With Capital Letters of Importance. "I got this in the mail today. Just like that. Out of the blue. Open it."

Layla frowned at me, then examined the outside. "Nice handwriting."

"I know. But look inside. And…maybe sit down." I took another long pull of my beer.

Layla perched her butt on the arm of the couch beside me and withdrew the check. "Holy *shit!*" She looked at me, her eyes wide. "Key, this is *ten thousand* dollars. You know what you could do with this?"

"Yeah. I do. But…where did it come from? Who sent it? Why? And more importantly…do I dare cash it?"

Layla sighed. "I get your point. I mean, part of me says 'duh, cash that bitch!', but the untrusting part of me says 'hold on now, sister.'"

"Exactly. I'd never be able to pay this back. Not ever." I finished my beer, and got up to get another one, found a box of old pizza in the fridge. "Can I?" I lifted the box.

Layla shrugged. "Go for it. So what are you going to do?"

"I don't know, Layla. I wish I did. I—I'm at the end of my rope. If I didn't have you, I'd be living in my car right now. Daddy's life insurance policy ran out six months ago. I'm short on rent, and all my other bills are past due. Cal's tuition needs paying, and so does mine. Fuck, *everything* is due. And I don't have a job. I looked for *weeks* to find even this temp job. I'll never find another one. And now…right when I need it most, *this*"—I snatch the check from Layla and shake it—"shows up. I don't see how I can *not* cash it. I'll just have to hope I don't end up owing, like, Sal the Slicer, or something."

Layla nodded. "That's a risk. You don't know who this is." She taps the check. "Did you Google this VRI Incorporated?"

"No electricity, remember? I couldn't use my computer. And I'm out of data on my cell phone plan."

"Oh." Layla slumped into the chair in front of her PC, which was almost as old as mine. She brought up Google, typed in the name and address, and scrolled through the result. "Nothing. I mean, there are tons of companies with that name, and the fact that it's a P.O. box means whoever it is doesn't want to found."

"No shit, Sherlock. Short of hiring a fucking PI or something, I don't see how I can find out who this is."

"So you cash it."

"So I cash it."

We spent the evening drinking. I got blitzed on about six beers and passed out on the couch, since I didn't have to be up in the morning. Layla and I both had an afternoon class, so we slept in until almost eleven, which was nice. After breakfast and a shower, Layla and I went together to the bank. I stood in front of the teller, two checks in my hand, which was shaking like a leaf. Eventually, I managed to hand them to the teller, and asked her to deposit them, and give me back a thousand dollars in cash.

When that was done, the teller handed me a receipt, and an envelope full of the cash she'd counted out to me. I put two hundred dollars in twenties into my purse, and left the other eight hundred in the envelope. I stared at the receipt: *$9,658.67*. We left the bank, got into my car, and drove to the university. True to form, Layla made no mention of the money, no hints at how many bills she had due, how much she could use even a couple hundred bucks. Couple hundred? Shit, to girls in our situation, even twenty bucks would be a godsend. She wouldn't ask, not ever, no matter how much money I had. Just like I wouldn't ask her if the situation were reversed. She'd never ask for anything unless she was in dire straits like I was now. Before we got out and went to class, I grabbed Layla's hand. Put the envelope of cash in her hand.

"Here." I folded her fingers over the edge. "I know you need it."

Layla stared at me. "Um. No."

I nodded. "Um, yes. You didn't think I wouldn't share with my best friend, did you?"

"Kyrie. You can't give this to me. You need it."

I smiled at her. "You do, too. I have enough now. You're not just my bestie, Layla. You're…you're like family. So just take it and say thank you."

She sniffled. "You're gonna make me smear my mascara, hookerface." Layla took a deep breath, blinked, and visibly forced away the tears. "Thank you, Kyrie. You know I love you, right?"

That was a big deal for her to say. She'd grown up in a tough household. No abuse, just cold and closed off, not the kind of family that exchanged declarations of love on a regular basis. I knew she loved Eric, but I'd never heard her say it. I was very much the same, growing up in a stable and happy home, but not one given to frequent hugs or I-love-you's. Layla and I had been best friends for more than three years. We'd gone through thick and thin together, faced near-starvation, faced asshole boyfriends and dickhole professors and betraying ex-friends, bar fights and cat fights and apartment break-ins. I'd been there for her when Layla had been sexually assaulted by a jealous ex-boyfriend, and she'd been there for me when Mom had her breakdown, necessitating long-term hospitalization. Yet, for all that, despite the fact that we'd both take a bullet for each other, we didn't tell each other we loved each other.

My turn to blink back tears. "I love you, too."

"Now shut up with the girly bullshit. I've gotta get to class." She leaned over and hugged me, and then left my car, clicking across the parking lot in her three-inch heels.

I sat for a few more minutes. My class was a lecture, so I could easily slip in the back and catch up on what I missed if I needed to. I pulled the bank receipt out of my purse and stared at it, wondering if I'd just made the biggest mistake of my life, taking that money. I mean, I needed it so, so bad. No question about that. I was at the point where I'd have to resort to stripping or hooking pretty soon, and that wasn't much of an exaggeration. And that'd be just to feed myself, let alone keep a roof over my head. This money was literally a life-saver.

But the one lesson in life I'd learned was that *nothing* was ever free. Someday, someone would come looking for what I owed them. I'd just have to accept that, keep it in mind, and try to not be too surprised when my debtor came knocking.

I tucked the receipt away and went off to class. Afterward, I popped into the tuition office to pay my bill, and then stopped by the rental office on the way home and paid up what I owed, plus next month's rent. That was an incredible feeling, knowing I was caught up through the entire next month. I sent out checks and spent the evening on the phone with utility companies, getting caught up. By the time all my bills were paid, my checkbook ledger said I had a little less than two grand left, including my final paycheck. My brakes would cost a few hundred to replace, which would leave me with a tiny little cushion to live on.

Thank you, whoever sent me that money. I pushed the thought out into the ether, wondering, not for the first time, and certainly not for the last, who was behind the mysterious check. And what he, or she, or they would want in payment.

In the middle of the following month, I was collecting the mail on the way home from work. I'd finally, after weeks of filling out applications for hours every day, found a job. As a hostess at Outback. Yuck. But it paid. Not much, but something. I'd stretched the cushion from that big anonymous check as long as possible, but it was gone already. I was caught up on my bills, and didn't have to pay rent for another few weeks, but the panic was still there.

So imagine my shock when, tucked between a utility bill and a coupon circular, was *The* Envelope. Same script, no return address. And inside? Another check for ten grand.

On the notes line, another single word: *belong.*

You belong.

Shit. Not good. Not good. Not good at all. I called Layla, and she agreed that the meaning could be ominous, but she also agreed that since I'd cashed the first one, I might as well cash the second one. I was in deep; I already owed whoever it was more money than I'd ever be able to pay back, so why not dig myself in that much deeper? If they came collecting I'd be just as fucked, so I might as well enjoy it while it lasts, right?

So I cashed it. Paid bills. Fixed the AC on my car, and replaced the long-dead radio. I went behind Layla's back and paid her rent. Attended class, went to work, begged for extra shifts, begged to be trained as a server. I eventually got the server position, which helped a lot. The month passed, and soon it was the middle of the month again. As the days folded one into the other, I tried to ignore the hope that I'd get another Envelope.

I did.

My hands shook, as they always did, when I opened it. This time, there were two words on the notes line: *to me.*

Ohshit. Shitohshitohfuckohshit.

You belong to me.

Layla was justifiably freaked out, as was I.

But still, there was no hint as to whom I belonged.

So, with nothing else to do, I kept on living. Paid my bills, tucked away some extra, helped out Layla.

I got a free day. A canceled class, and I was not scheduled to work. So I visited Mom. I hated visiting Mom. It was my duty as her daughter to visit her every once in a while, but I didn't usually see the point.

I parked outside the nursing home, made my way past the elderly residents as they listlessly watched TV in the rec room, passed open doors with sick, frail lumps in mechanical beds, passed closed doors. I stopped outside Mom's door, which was always closed. I took a deep breath, girded myself with as much strength as I could summon, and pushed in.

Mom was sitting on her bed, knees drawn up to her chest, hair lank against her skull, unwashed and greasy. She hated showers. *They* could get to you through the showerhead, Mom claimed. Getting her clean usually took several orderlies and a sedative.

"Hi, Mama." I took a hesitant step closer, waiting to see how she'd be today before trying to hug her.

Some days, the paranoia made it dangerous to get too close to her.

"They're laughing at me. They're closer today. Closer. Coming in through the windows. CLOSE THE BLINDS!" she shrieked suddenly, lunging off the bed and tearing at the window with her fingernails, scrabbling for the nonexistent cord.

I grabbed her wrists and pulled her away. "I'll close them for you, Mama. It's okay. Ssshhh. It's okay."

She hesitated, peering at me. "Kyrie? Is that you?"

I felt my breath catch. "Yeah—yeah, Mama. It's me."

Her eyes narrowed. "How do I know it's really you? They try to trick me sometimes, you know. They send agents. Lookalikes. Sometimes the nurses in this awful prison you've got me in pretend to be you. They dress up like you, and they talk like you. Tell me something only my daughter would know. *Tell me!*" she hissed, baring her teeth at me.

I tried to stay calm. "I fell off my bike when I was nine, Mama. Remember? I cut my knee open and had to walk four blocks back home. My sock was so full of blood I had to dump my shoe out. You gave me a Popsicle. Grape. Only, I was crying so hard, I dropped the popsicle into the tub. You made me rinse it off and eat it anyway. Remember that?"

"Maybe it is you. What do you want? Here to cut my rations? Take my privileges?"

I felt my heart crack a little. "I'm just here to see you, Mama. You know this isn't a prison. It's a nursing home. They take care of you."

"They *beat me!*" She pulled up her sleeve, showed me fingerprint bruises on her arms.

I'd freaked the fuck out the first time she'd showed me those. She did it to herself, the nurses said. I didn't believe them at first, but then I'd seen Mom gouging her fingers into her own arm, had seen her hitting herself so hard she had to be sedated.

"Mama, I know you did that to yourself. They don't you hurt you here. I promise."

"You would promise, wouldn't you? They make me hurt myself. Mind control. It's in the medicine they give me. Mind control, to make me hurt myself. You'd say anything to get rid of me. You hate me. That's why you've got me in prison. You hate me. You've always hated me." Her lip curled, and her eyes took on a frantic gleam I knew all too well.

I braced myself for the inevitable.

I feel a tear prick my eye. "No, Mama. I love you. You know I love you."

"You love me. My daughter would never say that. You're an impostor! A fake! You're *their* agent! Get out! Get away from me!" Mama rushed me, and I had to back away quickly to avoid her flailing hand.

I jerked open the door and fell backward through it, felt myself caught by a nurse.

"We've got her, sweetie. She'll be okay—she's just having a hard day. She didn't sleep well last night. She hasn't had her meds yet, because we've got to give her a shower today." The nurse patted me on the shoulder. "She knows you love her. She was asking for you the other day, you know. Asked if you'd come to visit her soon."

"She—she did?" I heard my voice break.

"She did."

"Well, if she asks again, tell I love her. Tell her—tell her I'll visit again soon."

Inside the room, another nurse was talking Mom down. I watched for a moment, and then turned away, waving at the nurse.

I cried on the way home, as I always did after visiting Mama. After Daddy's murder, she'd gone from bad to worse, and then from worse to impossible. She'd always had mood swings and bouts of paranoia, but it had been manageable, especially as long as she stayed on her meds. But then Daddy was killed, and the schizophrenia had taken over, and no amount of medication could keep her level. Daddy's life insurance policy had paid the bills for several years, but eventually it ran out, and that left me in a really bad place. I couldn't bring myself to apply for welfare, and my applications for student loans and grants and scholarships were still processing. And all the while, Mom got worse and worse.

My brother Cal had his head in the sand about it all. He went to school in Chicago, never came home, never visited Mama, never called me. He had his life, and as long as I helped him pay for his tuition, he'd be fine. He worked, too, paying for his own room and board, but I'd promised myself I'd take care of him, no matter what. I'd cooked and cleaned for him, gotten him to school, packed his lunches and helped him apply to Columbia College, helped him find an apartment and a job and taught him how to budget. So it wasn't that he wasn't thankful for me and all I did, he just couldn't handle Mom. I didn't blame him.

I sent him some extra money when I got home from visiting Mom, and then dashed off a quick email to him, asking how he was. He'd respond after a day or two, probably.

Meantime, the checks kept coming. One a month, ten grand every time. The notes ended, though, after that short, cryptic, and frightening message. I kept cashing them, kept tucking away as much as I could afford to save. I never stopped wondering who was sending them, but there was never any clue. I tried looking online again, but never made any headway.

Months turned into a year, and I was a semester away from finishing my bachelor's in social work. I needed a master's for what I wanted to do, though, so I still had a lot of school left.

Exactly one year later, I owed my mysterious benefactor $120,000.00.

And then, on the one-year anniversary of the first check arriving in the mail, there was a knock on my apartment door. I'd just gotten out of the shower, so I wrapped a towel around my torso and another around my hair, then slid the security chain in place and cracked open the door.

"Yes? Can I help you?" I asked.

There was a tall, slender man of indeterminate age standing on the other side. He was dressed in a black suit with a white shirt and a black tie. He was holding the kind of hat that limo drivers wore. He also had on a pair of black leather driving gloves, and, if I wasn't mistaken, there was a bulge at his chest that indicated he was carrying a pistol.

His eyes were pale green, hard, cold, and scarily intelligent.

"Kyrie St. Claire." It wasn't a question. His voice was low, smooth, and cold as wind-scoured steel.

"Yes?"

"Get dressed, please. Wear your nicest clothes."

"Excuse me?"

"If you own any lingerie, put it on. An evening dress. The blue one."

I stared at the man through the door. "What? What are you talking about?"

His face remained impassive. "My name is Harris. I'm here to collect you."

"*Collect* me?" I spat the word. "What am I, a piece of jewelry?"

"Did you or did you not cash twelve checks, ten thousand dollars each, for a total amount of one hundred and twenty thousand dollars?"

I swallowed hard. "Yes, I did."

"Do you have the funds available to repay it?"

I shook my head. "I don't. Not all of it."

"Then you will comply. Now. Please, dress. Your finest lingerie, the blue evening dress, jewelry. Style your hair. Apply makeup."

"Why?"

"I am unable to answer any questions." He stepped closer to the door. "May I come in, please?"

"I'm—I'm not dressed."

"I am aware of this. I will pack your belongings while you dress."

"Pack my belongings? Where am I going?"

He lifted an eyebrow. "Away."

I swallowed again. "For how long?"

"Indefinitely. Now, no more questions. Let me in, please." It was phrased as a question, but it wasn't. He could easily break down the door, of that I was certain. And he had a pistol. His eyes pierced mine. "Please, Miss St. Claire. I know this is an unusual situation. But you must understand. I am here not only to collect you, but to protect you. I will not harm you, I swear. I will not attempt to watch you change. I will pack your clothes and other belongings, and I will accompany you on your journey. I cannot answer any more questions."

"I just—I don't understand what's going on."

Harris blinked at me, and then let out a short breath. "I'm sure you remember the message from the first three checks."

I couldn't breathe, couldn't swallow past the lump of fear in my throat. "'You belong to me,'" I whispered.

"Yes. That is what's going on. My employer has sent me to collect what is his."

"Me."

"Precisely."

"What does he want with me? Who is he?"

Harris's eyes narrowed in irritation. "I told you, Miss St. Claire, I cannot and will not answer any further questions. Now let me in. That chain is a nuisance, and my job includes removing nuisances. Do not make this difficult, please."

I closed my eyes, counted to five, and then realized I had no choice. I knew he was armed, and I knew I had no way out of this. He'd promised he wouldn't hurt me, but that was little consolation. He was a scary-as-fuck man, and I was a girl alone, in a not-so-great apartment in a pretty shady neighborhood. No one but Layla would even miss me if I disappeared.

"Can I call my friend to tell her I'm—going away?"

"After we're *en route*."

"What will you do if refuse to cooperate?" I asked.

Harris lifted a corner of his mouth in a smirk that chilled my blood. "That would be…unwise."

I held my ground. "What would you do?"

"I could open the door, overpower you, sedate you, and bring you along regardless."

"What if I called the police?"

Harris sighed. "Miss St. Claire. That is entirely unnecessary. This is not a bad thing that is happening to you. I am not a Mafia enforcer. I'm not going to break your legs. I'm here to bring you to meet my employer, who has so graciously provided for you this past year. He only wishes to arrange…repayment."

"I don't have the money to pay him back. I never will."

"He isn't interested in money."

"He. You said *he*. So he wants…me?"

Harris licked his lips, as if he'd erred. "You will comply willingly. Nothing will be forced on you."

"But I don't want to go with you."

"No?" He lifted an eyebrow. "Surely you must be curious."

"Not enough to go with you. You scare me."

"Good. That's part of my job. But I promise you, I will not harm you, and I will not allow any harm to come to you. You are safe with me. But time is short. If you're going to refuse, I'll be forced to go back to my employer and report your recalcitrance. The next step would likely involve forcible methods of confinement. Just come with me. It will be easier for us all."

I sighed. "Fine." I closed the door, unlatched the chain, and let Harris in.

He eyed my apartment with open amusement. "I must say, I would have expected you to find yourself a nicer place with the money you've received."

"Nothing lasts forever. I had no guarantee the checks would keep coming. I can afford this place on my own. Sort of."

"Wise of you."

Trying to delay things, I asked. "Can I get you anything to drink?"

Harris blinked at me. "No. Thank you. We don't have much time. Get dressed, please."

I went into my bedroom, rifled through my closet until I found the blue dress I'd worn to a fund-raiser gala with my last boyfriend. Harris knew I had a blue dress, and that in itself was terrifying. It wasn't an expensive dress, but it fit me like a glove, showed off my curves and accentuated my skin and hair. I glanced at Harris, who had my two suitcases—Mom and Dad's old luggage—on my bed and was packing all of my jeans, yoga pants, skirts, blazers, dresses, and blouses with military efficiency.

I lifted the dress. "Will this do?"

Harris looked up, examined the dress, then nod-ded once. "Yes."

I dug the one set of lingerie I owned out of a bottom drawer. It wasn't expensive, but again, it was perfect for me. Deep crimson lace, the perfect shade to offset my tanned skin and blonde hair. I stepped into the bathroom, locked the door, and dropped the towel. I examined myself in the mirror.

I was medium height, a touch over five-seven, with naturally tanned skin and thick blonde hair. I was curvy enough, on the heavier side of average for my height and build. I saw myself as being pretty on most days, and sexy if I tried hard enough on a good day. Nothing special, but not ugly.

I put on the lingerie, then set about doing my hair. I did it in loose, spiraling curls, pinning my bangs to one side. I slipped my dress on, zipped it up the back, and then applied my makeup. I didn't wear much, just some foundation, blush, eye shadow, and lip stain. Nothing heavy or overdone. I put on a pair of teardrop diamond earrings and a matching necklace, a high school graduation gift from Daddy. Finally, after about thirty minutes, I was ready. I looked at myself in the mirror again.

Not bad, Kyrie. Not too bad. I nodded at my reflection, summoned my nerves, and stepped out.

Harris had my suitcases packed, and was closing the drawers of my dresser. He looked me over. "You're very beautiful, Miss St. Claire."

I ducked my head, oddly pleased by his compliment. "Thank you, Harris."

He nodded. "Now, if you're ready?"

"Everything is packed?"

"All your clothes and underthings, jewelry, and the phone charger. I assume everything else you need is in your purse." He lifted the suitcases and moved toward the front door.

I followed him, then paused as he opened the door. "What about my apartment?"

He set the suitcases in the hallway, waiting for me to exit so he could close the door behind me. "Everything is taken care of."

"What—what about Cal? And Mom? And—"

"I repeat, Miss St. Claire: Everything is taken care of. All you need to do is follow me." He watched me, his pale green eyes calm, patient.

I let out a shaky breath. "All right, then. Let's go." I shouldered my purse, shut off the lights, and locked the door.

I followed Harris outside into the late evening sunlight. There was a low, sleek black Mercedes-Benz parked away from the other cars, angled to take up two spots. He set the cases by the trunk, withdrew a key fob from his pocket, and the hatch opened, and then he placed the cases inside. He had this done before I had a chance to even put a hand on the door.

Harris opened the back right passenger door, held it for me as I slid in, and then closed it gently. Within seconds, he was in the front seat, and the engine roared to life.

He drove us to a small airport, passing through a security checkpoint, and then he parked on the tarmac beside a huge private jet. I swallowed hard as I stared out the tinted window at the airplane. Was this really happening? Ohgodohgodohgod. I was nothing short of terrified.

"If you wish to make a phone call, now is the time, Miss St. Claire," Harris said.

I dug my phone from my purse and called Layla.

"What's up, Key? Wanna meet for drinks?"

I let out a breath. "I—can't."

"Why not? What's up?"

I blinked hard. "I'm going away."

"Wh-what? What do you mean? Where? Why? For how long?"

"I don't know, Layla. I don't know. The checks? All that money? I'm about to meet the man who sent them."

"Who is it?" Layla demanded.

"I don't know. I don't know anything. A man showed up at my door an hour ago and said he was here to collect me. I've been *collected,* Layla."

"Does he know you're calling me? Are you, like, in danger?"

I forced myself to breathe calmly. "I don't—I don't think so. I don't really have a choice, but I'm not in danger. Like, I don't think anyone is going to kill me. I am scared, though. What's going to happen to me?" I whispered the last part.

"Kyrie…Jesus. This would only happen to you." I heard her breathe, sounding as shaky as I did. "Where are you?"

"Oakland County International Airport. About to board a fucking massive Gulfstream or something like that. A big private jet. Right now I'm sitting in a Mercedes-Benz."

"Ohmigod, Kyrie! So whoever this guy is, he's loaded."

"Yeah."

"And you owe him—what, a hundred and twenty grand?"

"Yeah."

"How are you going to pay him back?" Layla asked

I blink hard, fighting tears of fright. "This guy, Harris, he said my benefactor isn't interested in money."

Layla sucked in a sharp breath. "He's interested in *you,* then. Something tells me you'll have to put out a hell of a lot to pay back that much money, honey."

"Layla!"

"Just sayin', babe. It's true."

"I'm not a whore. I'm not going to use sex to pay him back." My voice shook.

"You may not have a choice."

"I know. That's why I'm so scared. I mean, I'm no prude. You know that. But…what if he's, like, eighty? Or some kind of…sultan? You know? Those girls who end up in slavery in Saudi Arabia?"

"I'm scared for you."

A knock on the window startled me. Harris opened the car door. "It's time, Miss St. Claire."

"I have to go, Layla."

"Be—be careful, okay? Call me as much as you can, so I know you're alive."

"I will."

"So…I'll talk to you later, Key." She tried to sound casual about not saying "goodbye." I loved her fiercely for that.

"Later, babe." I used the fake accent that always made her laugh.

She laughed, and then hung up on me. I sniffed, smiling, feeling somewhat reassured by talking to Layla.

Harris closed the door behind me, and then gestured to the movable stairway leading up to the door of the jet. "Ready?"

I shook my head. "Not even close."

"Understandable. There's champagne and other refreshments on the plane. Shall we?" He touched the small of my back with three fingers, a gentle nudge.

I ascended the steps on jelly-weak knees, and entered the jet. It was…stunning. Like in a movie. Cream leather seats, flat-screen TVs, thick carpeting, a silver bucket of ice sitting on a special tray near one set of seats, with a bottle of what I assumed was hideously expensive champagne. A flight attendant in a navy blue suit was waiting, ready to wait on me.

I glanced at Harris in shock.

"You're entering a whole new world, Miss St. Claire," he said. "One with many privileges. Sit, relax, and try to calm yourself. You will not be harmed, you will not be entering into any kind of slavery. You are merely…changing situations."

I nodded, unable to speak. I sat, buckled, and held on to the arms of the seat as the jet taxied and took off. When we were airborne, the flight attendant poured me a flute of champagne, which I sipped slowly and carefully. I need to take the edge off my nerves, but I needed my wits about me for whatever came next.

The flight was a little over three hours, and then we landed with a small, gentle bump and I had no idea where we were.

I exited the plane and followed Harris to a waiting car, this one a stretch limousine. He held the door for me, closed it, and then slid into the driver's seat.

He said nothing, only waited as someone else loaded my suitcases into the trunk.

I'd half expected to see someone sitting in the shadows of the limousine, but there was no one. Only long expanses of black leather, lights and a radio, and more champagne. I folded my hands on my lap and waited as Harris drove us through what looked to be New York. Over the Brooklyn Bridge and into Manhattan. We wove through thick traffic, heading uptown.

After more than forty minutes of driving, high-rises piercing the night sky all around, Harris pulled the limousine into an underground garage.

My heart was hammering as Harris led me, sans suitcases, to the elevator. The elevator rose quickly, leaving my stomach in my heels. Harris was silent beside me, hands folded behind his back. The elevator stopped, the doors opened, and we stepped out. We were in the foyer outside what I guessed was the penthouse. Thick dark slate-blue carpeting, navy blue walls, a floor-to-ceiling window showing a breathtaking view of New York City. Wide mahogany French doors, a flowering tree in one corner.

Harris stopped by the doors and turned to face me. "This is it. As far as I go." He reached into his suit coat pocket and withdrew a length of white cloth. "If you agree, I will put this blindfold on you. By allowing me to put it on, you are agreeing to willingly follow every instruction given to you without hesitation. If you do not agree, I will take you home, and repayment of the funds will be expected forthwith." He blinked at me, waiting. "Do you so agree?" His voice was formal.

I took a deep breath. "I don't have a choice, do I?"

Harris lifted a shoulder. "There is always a choice."

I searched myself. Could I do this, knowing what would likely be expected of me?

I lifted my chin, summoned my courage. "I agree."

Harris nodded once, and then moved behind me. I felt him place the blindfold over my eyes, the white cloth folded several times so I couldn't see a thing. He tied it gently but firmly behind my head, and then I felt his hand on my back, the same three fingers he'd used to nudge me onto the jet. I heard a handle turn, the faint hush of a door sliding across thick carpet.

A push, and I made my feet carry me forward. Two steps, three, four, five.

"Until the next time, Miss St. Claire," I heard Harris say behind me, and then the *click* of the door closing.

It was a decidedly final sound.

I stood, shaking, trembling, blindfolded, waiting.

A footstep, off to my left. "Hello?" I asked, my voice tremulous, breathy.

"Kyrie. Welcome." The voice was deep, smooth, lyrical, hypnotic, rumbling in my bones and thrumming in my ear.

A finger touched my cheekbone, warm, slightly rough. The fingertip scraped ever so gently across my cheek, up over my ear, brushing a loose tendril of hair away.

"Please, don't be afraid." He was close. I could feel the heat emanating from him. I could smell him—spicy, masculine cologne, soap. His voice, god, his voice. It made me shiver. Confident, almost kind, warm. "I have waited a long time for this moment, Kyrie."

"Who—who are you? Why am I here?"

A pause.

"You don't need my name just yet. As for why you're here?" His voice lowered, became hushed, a growling murmur that made my stomach clench. "You're here because I own you, Kyrie."

Watch for Alpha, coming in April.

About the Author

New York Times and *USA Today* bestselling author Jasinda Wilder is a Michigan native with a penchant for titillating tales about sexy men and strong women. When she's not writing, she's probably shopping, baking, or reading. She loves to travel, and some of her favorite vacations spots are Las Vegas, New York City, and Toledo, Ohio. You can often find Jasinda drinking sweet red wine with frozen berries.

To find out more about Jasinda and her other titles, visit her website: www.JasindaWilder.com.

Made in the USA
Charleston, SC
18 July 2014